Wolf Whistle

By the same author

I, Claudia
Virgin Territory
Man Eater

Marilyn Todd

Wolf Whistle

MACMILLAN

First published 1998 by Macmillan
an imprint of Macmillan Publishers Ltd
25 Eccleston Place, London SW1W 9NF
and Basingstoke

Associated companies throughout the world

ISBN 0 333 74308 3

1 3 5 7 9 8 6 4 2

A CIP catalogue record for this book is available from
the British Library.

Phototypeset by Intype London Ltd
Printed and bound in Great Britain by
Mackays of Chatham plc, Chatham, Kent

To Tara, whose guidance and whose friendship are valued in equal measure

I

Rarely do moneylenders, when faced with non-payment of debt, veer towards benevolence. But this one was in a good mood. In fact, so keen was he, today, to demonstrate his generosity, that he offered Claudia a head start before unleashing his dogs.

'Ratbag!' she yelled over her shoulder. That was the last time she'd do business with him!

At the first turn, she slewed the honey-seller's table across the lane behind her. Dozens of small red pots oozed their sticky sweetness on to the pavement. Although Claudia was running too fast to catch the shopkeeper's exact words, she believed he called her a something-something-little-something, and threatened that if she ever came back he'd something-something her, which seemed none too polite, but then gentlemanly conduct tended to be thin on the ground around here.

'Stop her!' cried one of the dog handlers. 'Stop that woman!' But the crowd had no intention of being deprived of their free entertainment. They cleaved a path.

Croesus, thought Claudia, haring down the street, it was a hardboiled pack that bloodsucker had put on her tail and no mistake. Baying and slavering, you'd think they hadn't eaten for days. She skidded into a charcoal dealer, sending his coals tumbling over the cobbles. Hell, maybe they hadn't, but no way did Claudia Seferius intend to be on their menu tonight! Skirting a pile of slippery fish guts which the fishmonger had jettisoned into the gutter, she paused at the tallow man's.

'I turned left, understood?' She threw the candle-maker sufficient bronze to keep him in food (or more probably drink) for a week.

His appreciative grin showed a row of blackened teeth. 'Left, yer said.'

Good. If duff directions didn't put the dogs off the scent, the stench from his rotting teeth would. Before ducking to the right, Claudia stopped to check her pursuers. The tallow man was pointing directly her way.

She ran and she ran, darting left, hooking right, constantly cursing the strong Judaean perfume which blazed a trail for zealous snouts. What was wrong with that moneylender? For heaven's sake, we're only talking a few hundred gold pieces (all right, a thousand; who's counting?). It's not as though she intended to decamp with his money! It was merely that, at present, the repayment date required a modicum of flexibility . . . surely he could trust her on that? Fine cottons, gold rings and the ivory combs in her curls had been reassurance enough when he was dishing out the loan, and look how his eyes had popped when she'd written down the address! Quite right, too. It was a bloody good address. Up on the Esquiline, where the patricians hang out. A rather modest house, perhaps, by Esquiline standards, with a courtyard of shade and gentle fountains and sweet singing birds. You can't miss it, she'd told the moneylender. It's right opposite the goldbeater's.

Which it was. It just happened not to be Claudia's address.

Jupiter, Juno and Mars! Whichever way she turned, the lanes twisted, narrowed, doubled back and led relentlessly downhill. Damn! The dogs were not giving up, either. One had a distinctive howl – not dissimilar, she mused, to the sound her cat, Drusilla, made this morning when her tail got caught in the door.

Kneading the stitch in her side, Claudia paused and looked around and felt a sudden chill of terror. She could not say when or where it had changed, but twisting wynds had turned into stinking runnels, sedate apartment blocks were now crumbling tenements. A standpipe dripped at the end of the street and a young mother with a child at her hip blew her nose with her fingers. Daylight was beginning to fade, too, exacerbated by the heavy grey clouds which had been building up during the course of the afternoon. Doors were being slammed, latches fastened, shutters drawn. With panic rising in her breast, Claudia knew she was well and truly lost. While the dogs still bayed close by.

'Hello?' Someone help me. Please. But only shadows and vermin roamed the alleys amid the raw sewage, the vegetation rotting on the middens, the bloated corpse of a puppy being picked over by rats. A three-legged truckle-bed sat upended where it had been dumped, broken pots crunched underfoot, and from open windows came the sounds of drunken bullies beating their wives and their children in the name of obedience. Spooked by the rank-ness that defines sheer and utter hopelessness, Claudia went spinning down the lanes. Stumbling. Tripping.

Oblivious to the cess trenches, the dogs and the thugs who ran with them, she had to get out . . .

'Shit!'

Swallowing hard, she blinked back the tears as she again came face to face with the truckle-bed, the rats and the dead puppy dog.

'Shit, shit, shit!'

Perhaps, then, it was time to use brains and not footwear? A raw-boned mongrel, grey around the face, wandered up to the broken bed, cocked its leg then lolloped off. Dear Diana! Impossible to imagine that all roads lead from Rome, reaching even the darkest outpost of our mighty Empire, while these alleys criss-cross like the Minotaur's labyrinth.

'There! There she is!'

Dammit, they'd caught up! Claudia shot down the nearest passageway, then skidded to a halt. The mongrel was examining something dark and sticky on a rusty skillet. The inspection appeared to be in its early stages. Plenty of time for a girl to unclip her blue cotton wrap, rip it with the brooch pin and ram the poor mutt's head through the hole before it even a had chance to snarl its disapproval. Stung in the rump by a shard of pottery, it shot off down the street, flapping oceans of blue cotton in its wake. Blue cotton heavily scented with Judaean perfume, no less!

As she flung open the nearest tenement door, Claudia realized her ploy had failed. The dogs wanted to follow the scent, but the handlers had sharp eyes. The gap was closing. Claudia flew up the dimly lit stairs two at a time. While they searched the lower floors, she could hide. She ran along the corridor, testing door after door until, finally, one surrendered.

'Anyone home?'

A toothless crone sat on a stool supping porridge straight from the crock.

'Can you hide me?' Claudia panted. 'I can pay.' She pulled off a ring set with emeralds.

Watery gruel dribbled down the old woman's chin. Sweet Janus, was she blind?

'Please!' A cupboard. Under the bed. There must be some way out of this mess! 'Will you help me?'

'Oi!' Fists pounded the door. 'Open up!' The hinges were weak, they would not stand much rough treatment.

Rheumy eyes watched disinterestedly as the crone continued to slurp from the bowl. Bugger! Claudia ran to the window and looked down. The front door was bulging more and more with each shove from the moneylender's thug.

'No way out, luv,' he crowed. 'You're trapped!'

Really? Ignoring the dizziness, Claudia climbed on to the sill. What about that balcony over the way? She took a deep breath.

Now eight feet is not very far. Measure it out and you'd be hard pressed to fit in, say, a decent bout of shadow-boxing or half a game of hopscotch, you couldn't even rig up a funeral pyre. So, no, it's not very far . . . on the ground. Heart pounding, mouth dry, Claudia launched herself into space.

Yes! As her hands connected with the balustrade, she felt a rush of such elation that she actually laughed aloud.

Then she heard the crack.

This wasn't a rail. This was woodworm holding hands!

Her knuckles were white as she glanced down. Janus! It must be seventy feet at the least! Waves of nausea washed over her as she struggled to swing her body on to the balcony before the rail gave way.

Too late. With a splintering sound, the balustrade began to bow inexorably downwards. Claudia closed her eyes. And wondered which great Olympian divinity owed her a favour.

It was true, then. At times like this, you do hallucinate. Claudia could have imagined glimpsing flashes of her past as she hung there, limp and helpless, like a festival banner on a wet and windless day. Maybe her mother, drunk as usual. Perhaps her father, despite his being absent most of the time. Or post-childhood scenes; say, that sea of leering faces as she danced, or coins changing hands and not necessarily for dancing. Definitely she'd have expected Gaius Seferius to pop up – he was the man she'd married after all. Ah, yes! Rich, shrewd, fat, old Gaius. Who had not loved her, but who had required a trophy wife. Maybe, even, she'd see the glinting piles of money that he'd left her when he died, Instead, as the wood cracked relentlessly, Claudia heard a voice.

'Oh, oh, oh, oh!'

A voice, it would appear, in the final throes of ecstasy.

'Oh, yes, Venus! O-oh, yes, yes!'

Her wits solidified with common sense. That was no hallucination, so where the devil was it coming from? Pinpointing the sound to the room one down, Claudia noticed that it, too, had a balcony. Could she make it? Did she have a choice?

'Yes! Yes! *Venus, yes!*'

Actually, old chap, she thought, as the rail finally parted company with its mortice and tenons, we might shortly be giving a new dimension to the phrase coitus interruptus.

The wooden floor absorbed her tumbling weight and when Claudia eventually found the courage to unclamp her eyelids, it was to view a tiny apartment with one narrow pallet, one chair, one table laid with one cup, plate and knife. Curiously, its tenant was prostrate on the floor, mother-naked, mumbling what appeared to be abject apologies.

'F-forgive me, blessed lady.'

Heavy footsteps rumbled on the stairs beyond, accompanied by a backdrop of yips and yelps. Damn! The handlers had raced across the road and were already searching this block.

'I am but a worthless wretch.' He was a scrawny individual, whose appearance was not enhanced by jug ears and heavy pock marks, although it was his twisted backbone which explained his solitary tactics for gratification. 'Do not punish me harshly, oh goddess.'

Goddess? Claudia blinked and blinked again. In fact, had there been a competition for blinking, she'd have won the laurel crown. He couldn't—? Nobody in their right mind—? Not seriously—? But he did. Incredibly, the hunchback believed Venus had dropped down from Olympus to punish him!

'I'll n-never take your name in vain again. I swear!'

The footsteps on the stairs were drawing closer. She had just one chance . . .

Claudia stepped forward purposefully. 'Remember Actaeon?'

Already pale, the poor chap blenched. Actaeon the warrior had stumbled across the goddess Diana as she was bathing. His punishment was to be turned into a stag, whereupon he was promptly torn apart by his very own pack of hunting dogs.

'Oh, divine one!' They could probably hear his gulp back in the Forum. 'I s-swear on the life of my mother—' The rap on the door cut short his grovelling and Venus watched him turn green.

'Mortal, here is thy test. Breathe one word of my divine presence, and thou shalt suffer as Actaeon suffered. Answer the door.'

The hunchback's gibbering denials more than convinced the gruff questioner, and Claudia's breath came out in a hiss. Juno be praised, that was close! When she looked up, pleading eyes were upon her.

'You think Venus does not keep her word?' she asked indignantly. 'Leave the room, mortal, and do not return for two hours.' A little harsh, but he wasn't the one scheduled to satisfy some hungry tripehound's appetite!

As he pulled on his tunic and scuttled down the stairs, Claudia pressed her hands to her forehead. So far so good, but I've still got to get out of here! She'd long since realized she was in the notorious district between the Esquiline and the Viminal, but where towering blocks had frustrated navigation, being five storeys up meant she could now see a way out of this maze. Lost she might be, but thanks to the march of the aqueducts and the statues high on temple roofs, trapped she was not!

Once outside, with the sound of disappointed dogs

fading into the distance. Claudia dusted her hands, took a deep breath, and set off up the darkened street. An unseen tomcat howled, but nothing else stirred, and neither did she expect it. Too poor to light candles just for the hell of it, darkness signalled bedtime for the denizens of the slum. Any man abroad after sunset would certainly be up to no good.

Especially a group of burly individuals holding a blazing torch apiece.

Claudia melted into the shadows, surreptitiously slipping her rings and her ear studs into the pleats of her cotton stola. The men waved their brands back and forth as though searching and she realized, with horror, that these were the Midden Hunters. Men who scoured the cess pits and rubbish dumps for babies to raise into slavery.

She shivered in the darkened doorway. Who hadn't heard of these ghouls? Until now she'd imagined them legends, bogeymen born out of rumour. Empty-handed, the four moved level with Claudia's niche and a thousand crawling insects prickled her skin. She dared not breathe as the flickering torchlight distorted their features in a way that, elsewhere, would have been comical – except for the bearded man. The scar on his cheek, vermilion and shaped like a horseshoe, made her flatten her backbone tight to the stonework.

'Well, Captain, you owe me another denarius.' The voice was cultivated, quiet, jocular, even. 'That's three out of three I've been right.'

The man addressed as Captain, the man with the scar, snorted. 'Your luck can't hold, lad. Double or quits.'

'Hear that?' A lushly embroidered sleeve gestured to

the two men bringing up the rear. 'You boys are my witnesses, when this miserly sod tries to dodge out of it!'

When their footsteps and laughter had faded, Claudia released her pent-up breath and set off at a run. In theory, she supposed, Midden Hunters could be seen as men who were saving the lives of the newborn, but Claudia wouldn't give you that (mentally she snapped her fingers) for theory. It was not difficult to see why mothers here abandoned their babies. Where food was scarce, money was scarcer; precious few mouths could survive. The Emperor had stamped out the worst of the poverty by issuing males over ten with the dole, but all too often those wooden tablets changed hands on the black market for wine, leaving the men befuddled and the women half-starved. By exposing their infants on the middens to be seen – or rather heard – attention would be drawn to their plight. For all the unwanted children born in this city, there was an equal number of barren women sobbing through long, lonely nights for a babe of their own. When dawn showed the child to be gone, its mother would weep with relief and pray to Cunina, Goddess of the Cradle, to protect it. Claudia wondered how easily these poor women would sleep if they knew the stories about the Midden Hunters were true.

The relief she felt at leaving the slums and its secrets behind her could not be put into words. Why is it, she asked herself, some folk sail through life with not a hint of trouble, whereas it haunts me like a lovesick ghost? No matter, she thought, turning her aching feet towards the Argiletum, apart from the fact that Gaius' mother and daughter and a squad of his aunts were set to descend for the Festival of Fortune, life was pretty much plain sailing.

She knew why the old trouts were coming, of course. Festival be damned! Money is relative, they say, and how true. Indeed, the more the money, the greater the number of relatives.

Well, if these old cats hoped to disinherit Claudia Seferius, they had another thing coming!

Thank heavens, the Argiletum was deserted. During the daytime, this thoroughfare was thronged with merchants, porters and a veritable army of rich, idle wives flanked by their slaves and retainers as they checked out the latest footwear, fingering the leather and admiring the stamping. The air vibrated with hammering from the lasts, but now it was merely heavy with the tang of their hides. Upmarket booksellers also congregated along this street, their wares ranging from rare volumes to—

Claudia was wrong. The street was not quite deserted. A small boy sat in the gutter, elbows on knees, fists balled into his cheeks. His face was puffy from crying, the tears had left runnels in the grime.

'Hello, soldier.'

Melancholy eyes rolled up to look at her. Words did not come.

Hmm. That was not a head of hair you could ruffle. Not unless you had a stomach for beetly things. But you couldn't just pass on. Not while his little lower lip still trembled.

Claudia plumped herself down and mirrored his pose. 'Want to talk about it?' she asked softly.

Small shoulders shrugged. Bewildered, dejected, he was determined not to give in.

Claudia studied him as closely as she could by what paltry light was cast from an upstairs window. Maybe five years old, his clothes had been stitched and stitched again, and his bare feet were clearly strangers to leather.

'Lost, are you?' Too well she knew what it felt like for a grown-up – the terror and the claustrophobia – what must it be like for a tiddler?

A small chin jutted out defiantly before he nodded. 'I want me ma.'

Will I never get a hot bath?

'I asked that lady to take me home, but she wouldn't help me.' A grimy finger pointed towards a shuttered bookshop. There was, of course, no one there.

'No?' Claudia stood up and shook the folds of her tunic. 'Well, I'm here now. Come along.'

'She's asleep.'

'Who is? Your ma?'

'That lady there.'

Poor kid. 'What's your name, soldier?'

A half-smile flitted across his tear-stained face. 'Jovi.'

'And where do you live, Master Jovi?' Merciful heavens, please don't say back where I've come from!

'Dunno.'

Dumbfounded, Claudia leaned down to look him in the eye. 'Say that again.'

He gripped one thumb in his fist and stared at his little blackened feet. 'I've never bin away before.'

He was making such tremendous efforts not to cry that, in spite of herself, she ruffled his matted hair. 'You'd better fall in line then, soldier, because tonight you're on escort duty.'

Jovi stood up and cocked his head on one side. 'Yeah?'

'Yeah. You can deputize as my bodyguard and walk me home, and as a reward, you shall receive a hot pie and a bowl of honeyed apricots, and after breakfast I will take you home to your ma. How does that sound?'

'Promise?'

'Upon my oath, young man. First thing in the morning, we'll have you washed and scrubbed so clean your mother will think she's got two sons called Jovi.'

'You won't forget you said apricots, will you?'

As a small, dry hand slipped into hers, Claudia had a feeling they were not entirely alone on the Argiletum. It could be the lamps flickering from the upper storeys. It could be the dark, damp, starless sky. But she had the strangest feeling that wretched lovesick ghost was back to haunt her.

The one whose name was Trouble . . .

II

Less than a mile away, in the smart town house of the pepper merchant, Marcus Cornelius Orbilio killed time by admiring the exquisite decor. Sweeping pastoral frescoes, so perfect you could almost hear the goats bleat. Hanging lamps with six or seven wicks lit the room brighter than a midsummer noon. A bronze dog was curled in the corner and rare aromatics filled the air. He glanced at the water clock. It was not like his informer to be late, but these were difficult times. Less than a fortnight before, the Empire had been rocked to its core when Marcus Vipsanius Agrippa – at once the Emperor's closest friend, finest general, son-in-law and Regent – had returned from campaign and promptly died. The shock waves could not have been greater had the earth itself trembled, because if the Fates could cut this man's thread at fifty-two, what chance for Augustus who was the same age?

Orbilio slid open one of the doors to the garden, where torchlight breathed life into the marble statuary and made gems of the whispering fountains. But cloying wallflowers did not understand sophisticated room scents and he closed it again. What chance for Augustus, indeed? There was many a fellow who, in his youth, had been Julius Caesar's man and had been outraged when Augustus ingratiated himself to become the Great Man's heir.

Although more rational men blamed Caesar for setting his catamite above his natural-born son, any waverers had their doubts dispelled after Caesar's murder, when the catamite showed the people precisely why he'd paid such a high price for adoption.

First he dealt with Brutus, then he dealt with Cassius and, finally, he dealt with Mark Anthony. Orbilio had been only six at the time, yet still he remembered the tremendous ripple of excitement which spread through Rome when Augustus promised an end, once and for all, to three generations of civil war. After that, he went from strength to strength – annexing Egypt, Galatia, Spain, all the Alpine territories, Liguria, Illyria and Germany, as far as the Danube. He eliminated piracy, set up a network of trade hitherto unimagined and certainly unparalleled and finally, with his promise fulfilled, he disbanded the army's part-time peasant farmers in exchange for a hard core of professionals, releasing the land for full-time farming. Small wonder his people took an ever swelling pride in their new roads, their sewers, the aqueducts which carried sweet water from the springs in the hills. The Emperor Augustus had given them twenty years of ineffable stability, their bellies and the Treasury were full. The spoils of war had turned their temples into marble masterpieces, bronze heroes galloped across the Forum, public baths, libraries, theatres and gardens were springing up pretty well everywhere.

Who, now, remembers that, to be on the safe side, Augustus had felt obliged to murder Caesar's natural-born son?

Who, now, cares?

No one. But then sedition doesn't always hinge on

history and past grudges. Money is a factor. And let's never forget the lure of power for its own sake. The Empire was poised on the brink of disaster.

The heat from the braziers had reached unbearable proportions, and Orbilio shrugged off that symbol of his birthright, the toga. That was a real perk of being attached to the Security Police, dispensing with the toga! Heavy and unwieldy, it restricted a man's movements, although gentlemanly attire was a necessary evil when mingling with the wealthy and the noble (and naturally he'd worn the black toga throughout the public mourning for Agrippa). However, life must move on, and nine days at standstill takes a heavy toll on commerce and industry, there was much catching up to be done.

'Marcus!' A young woman, pink and immaculate, swept into the room. 'Am I terribly late?'

Who said informers were restricted to the dross of society, or that they should be exclusively male?

'I'm early,' he lied, drinking in Mevia's full breasts and rounded hips as she turned the key in the lock.

'It's this silly market day that causes so much chaos,' she pouted. 'You'd think we hadn't had one for ten weeks, much less ten days!'

'When you hold them every eight days, people become dependent upon the routine.' Disrupt that routine and you disrupt the structure of their lives. Praise be to Jupiter, we're right back on schedule. 'So, Mevia. What have you got for me?'

'Just myself,' she purred, slipping off her sandals. 'But you won't be disappointed.'

Damn right, he thought, watching her girdle slide to the floor. The greatest threat to the Emperor came not from the army, but from wealthy merchants banding together and for that reason, he'd made contact with Mevia. The hem of her tunic rose with tantalizing slowness to reveal first a pair of finely turned ankles, then her shapely calves. Halting half-way up her thighs, Mevia turned slowly round, watching him over her shoulder as she teased the pale pink linen up over her bottom, then her back and then finally drew it over her head. Sometimes she had information about the activities of her pepper-merchant husband and sometimes he drew a blank. Well, it was his duty, in the interests of the Empire, to pursue every angle, was it not?

Mevia, still in the shape of a letter Y, draped herself lengthwise on the couch. Not a hair out of place, not a smudge to her make-up, he noticed.

'I like,' she said, parting her lips to trace the line of her teeth with her tongue, 'watching the muscles of big, tall men ripple in the lamplight.'

'Is that a fact?' he asked, unfastening his loin cloth and tracing his eye over the curve of her breast. There was a time, and not so long ago, when, so long as she was eager, he didn't give a damn whether his bedmate was wealthy or poor, brainy or dim, giggly or ardent. But increasingly these days he was not so much making love as going through the motions. The seduction was mechanical, an assembly line of flattery and platitudes, with an end product which satisfied the customer if not the manufacturer. And it was not that he was lazy, lax or incapable. It was simply that another woman's face would float in front of him, a face with proud, flashing eyes framed by tumbling dark curls, and he would yearn to reach out and touch a waist so slender a man's hands could almost meet around it . . . not that he'd ever tried, you understand! There are certain parts of a chap's anatomy that he prefers to remain attached to him, so one does not take liberties with Claudia Seferius!

Absently his mouth closed over Mevia's nipple, but it was an ache for the girl who threw back her head when she laughed that made Orbilio groan. Whenever they breathed the same air, he and Claudia, it was like a storm before the rain. White lightning crackled between them – electrifying, frightening, exhilarating. A man never knew where the next strike would come, but one thing was for certain. With Mistress Seferius, it was never the same place twice.

As Mevia arched and wriggled beneath him, cooing his name through artificial red lips, a sound, small and insubstantial, cut into his awareness.

'I can't help feeling,' Orbilio rolled off the bed, 'that before long there'll be a return to the old custom of husbands running their wives' lovers through with a sword.'

Mevia surveyed him through half-lowered lids as she propped herself up on her elbows. 'What makes you think that?'

'Because' – to her astonishment, Marcus pulled on his tunic – 'I can hear his horse in the yard!'

'*Darling! I'm home!*'

'Run!' squealed Mevia. 'He'll come in the back way!' She pointed to a door, which was opening even as she spoke.

'What' – the pepper merchant strode into the perfumed boudoir to find a handsome, tousled stranger standing over a bed in which his red-faced wife lay stark naked –

'the bloody hell's going on here?' His hand had drawn his dagger before he'd finished the sentence.

'For gods' sake,' snapped Orbilio. 'Can't you see I'm a doctor?'

'Eh? Oh.' The dagger sank back in its scabbard. 'I thought . . . is it serious?'

'Tick fever,' replied Orbilio, clearing his throat. 'Fatal, I'm afraid, unless we treat it straight away. I . . . I've been bleeding her with leeches.' He hastily pulled up the covers. 'But you could help by fetching a mix of alum and mandrake, three to one. Only for gods' sake, man – hurry!'

Three minutes later and striding in the opposite direction to the apothecary's, Marcus chuckled to himself. He'd had closer shaves in the past (the auctioneer, for instance, who'd caught him licking honey off his young bride's back), but there was nothing like the old physician trick to pull a chap out the mire! Worked every bloody time. Orbilio rubbed his hands together and looked up. The clouds were low but not threatening, and he decided to grab a bite to eat from Galen's tavern before sauntering down to the wharves to see what gems his other, less attractive informants had garnered during the course of the day. He pushed open the door where the steam, the heat, the laughter, the smell of wine and cooking nearly knocked him back into the street. Being market day, he'd expected the place to be busy, but this was ridiculous.

'This way, sir. I'll clear a table,' Galen said, jostling his way through the crowd, but Orbilio put a restraining hand on his shoulder.

'I'll be fine here,' he replied, resting his weight against the wall. 'Just bring me a pie when you're able – venison if you have it, otherwise rabbit.'

He had no desire to see a group of hungry stevedores turfed out simply to make room for the aristocracy, it was not his style, and in any case, standing might strengthen the weakness that the arrival of a jealous husband had brought to his kneebones.

The noise in the tavern almost made the walls bulge out. Tonight men and women from every walk of life were carousing in earnest, pushing to the back of their minds the uncertainty which had gripped Rome following the death of their Regent. The fact was that the Empire was now without an heir because, despite being married to Augustus's only child, Agrippa had died without issue. There was no one with royal blood to claim the line, which meant that should anything happen to Augustus, the field was wide open . . .

Still savouring the rich venison gravy and the ribald jokes of the revellers, Orbilio called for a second cup of wine and a dish of black pudding, because when it came to black pudding, there was no place to match it. Galen added onions and leeks and pine kernels, he seasoned with pepper and garlic and caraway, but there was something else – that indefinable something – which made this sausage so special. Was it the crunchy bite? The fact that they smoked it, but only slightly? Or that they cooked it over scented charcoals, possibly rosemary?

That, thought Marcus Cornelius, is what sets man apart from the beasts. Whereas animals rely on certainties in their daily existence, man thrives on the elusive. The thirst for knowledge, despite what the philosophers argue, is by no means sufficient. The piquancy of life comes from *not* knowing, from *not* fully understanding.

Which is why, perhaps, his thoughts habitually

returned to Claudia Seferius. Orbilio knocked back the last of his wine and combed his hair with his hands. Mother of Tarquin, talk about spirited! The last time they'd crossed swords she'd pushed him in the pool and hurled missiles at him. Oh yes. His mouth twisted into a one sided grin. She was a hazard to health and no mistake!

Not least because she had burned her way into his soul . . .

He had no doubt that their paths would cross again – living as she did on the edge – but in the meantime, with the scent of sedition heavy in the air, it was time to recoup some of the money shelled out to his narks, and if Mevia had not been able to help, the next best place to start was with a lowlife aptly nicknamed Weasel.

Entrusting his toga to Galen for safekeeping, Orbilio observed one of the drinkers from the corner of his eye. A cube of a man, thickset, with a limb on each corner, it was the man's attitude that caught his attention. Head down, eyes averted, it was the stance of one who wishes not to be noticed. Yet here he was, in a thronging tavern. Holding, yet not drinking, his wine. Orbilio thought he vaguely recognized that surly square face, perhaps that accounted for the fellow's shifty appearance, but this was no time to re-open old cases. His priorities lay in protecting his Emperor, because now all that lay between the might of Rome and a downward spiral back into civil war was the life of just one middle-aged man.

There was no time to lose.

After the fierce heat of the tavern, the outside air felt chill and damp as mist rose from the Tiber and swirled between the lofty warehouses. It was up to the praetorian guard to sniff out uprisings in the military (and Remus, there were enough ambitious generals to keep tabs on!), but Orbilio sensed that the cornerstone to any coup would, this time, be money. While few patricians would be prepared to risk an uprising, he knew of many a rich merchant who'd throw their cap in the ring. Hence his visit to the wharves and the warehouses, to see just how many eaves had been dropped Weasel's way. He turned the corner by one of the spice stores, its towering windowless walls exuding pungent aromas despite the sour smells of the river and the encroaching, suffocating damp. The crowds had thinned, congregating in taverns and restaurants and well-lit streets, away from the gloomy, twisting alleys where they were forced to earn their living. There was just himself and two others now. Almost in sight of the Tiber, he turned left towards a nondescript building where the boys inside were soft enough and pretty enough to pass as girls. When two men appeared in the street in front of him, Marcus Cornelius paid scant attention. There were any number of reasons why men visited this particular quarter of the Aventine, and the house ahead was just one of them. Then, with a chill, he recognized the square-faced cube from Galen's tavern.

Turning, he realized he was trapped. The two men behind had blocked the narrow alley.

'Come and get it, motherfucker,' growled the cube.

Orbilio could see bronze glinting from the stocky man's knuckles, he had a suspicion it wasn't his wedding ring.

He had trained in the gymnasium, he had trained on the field, why shouldn't he hope to outfight them? But four against one were bad odds, and in his heart all he could realistically hope for was that (a) they planned only to hurt and not kill him; and (b) he could inflict some serious damage before he went down.

For several minutes, Orbilio managed to hold his own, fending off the punches and the kicks. He heard a rib crack under his fist, a nose crunch, then a well-judged kick in the balls brought the odds down to three. He was leaner, fitter, faster than his assailants, and all it needed was just one other person to walk down the street and the alarm would be raised. But it was that time of night, when anyone who was going anywhere would have got there by now and when it was far too early to go home.

As the blows rained down. Marcus could feel his defences growing weaker. His face was wet with his blood, he could taste it, and now whenever the cube landed a punch with the knuckleduster, he cringed as it connected. When he slipped on the cobbles, a shower of hobnailed boots kept him down, and before long it was all he could do to curl up into a ball and let his ribs take the battering.

When the kicking stopped, his aching lungs released a groan of relief, but the respite was brief. All four thugs fell upon him, each grabbing an arm or a leg and lifted him high off the ground.

'Right, boys?'

Despite one eye blinded by blood, Orbilio realized with surprising calmness what was about to take place. He'd been wrong about their intentions, the beating was no more than a preliminary. These bastards meant murder.

'Say your prayers, arsehole!' sneered the cube.

Powerless to resist and buggered if he'd give them the satisfaction of begging, Marcus Cornelius Orbilio could only watch as they ran him head first towards the solid wooden door that fronted Weasel's whorehouse. Vaguely he wondered what his father would say, when they met up in the Afterworld.

He imagined he'd be cross.

III

The second Claudia set foot through her own front door, she was swamped. Could she enjoy the fragrances of lavender and myrrh wafting from the censers? Could she ease up and relax among the tall, marble columns, the gaily painted friezes, the array of potted ferns? Could she hell!

First Leonides, her beanpole of a steward, thrust his way forward. Then Cypassis, her big-boned maidservant, all but throwing her arms around her mistress with relief. Junius, the head of her bodyguard, his handsome face unaccustomedly drawn, appeared at her elbow, urging Claudia to next time please, please, not leave him stationed two streets back. Finally Drusilla, her blue-eyed, cross-eyed cat, saturated with anxious vibrations, launched herself to cling round her neck, a living fur collar. Claudia's ears buzzed with the babble of voices – male, female, human, feline – until suddenly they all stopped at once.

Drusilla's reaction was to dig her claws deep into flesh. Leonides' was rather more pragmatic. 'What's that?' he asked, wrinkling his nose.

'That,' replied Claudia, carefully extracting the cat, 'is a Jovi. To whom I have promised a hot pie, a hot bath and a dish of honeyed apricots, so Junius? Would you mind?'

'Me?' The young Gaul jumped as though scalded.

'Come, come, the fleas'll wash off! And I did promise our friend here a lesson in martial arts. When he grows up he intends to guard the Emperor personally, don't you, soldier?'

'Yes, ma'am!'

Since Jovi had not yet learned how to jump to attention and salute simultaneously there was an awkward sprawl of limbs, yet in the short time it took for Junius to scoop the wee lad off the floor, the Gaul had been won over. Dangling him backwards over his shoulder, he carried his mucky, chuckling charge away to the kitchens.

Claudia turned to Cypassis. 'Stop snivelling, girl! Rumours about setting dogs on me? Utter rubbish! I was simply making arrangements for Gaius' aunts, you know how fussy they are.'

Personally she'd order funeral biers for the whole damned lot, but she presumed that was out of the question. The Thessalian girl sucked back her tears and wiped her eyes with the back of her hand.

'That's better. Now, fetch my pale lemon tunic, the one with long sleeves, and a fresh set of underwear then meet me in the bath room. Oh, and bring a wrap, will you? My sunflower yellow one.' Heaven knows, I need something cheerful after those gloomy alleyways! 'I'll need a comb and the mirror with the lotus-shaped handle, and my skin feels dry, so that little alabaster pot, the one which smells of camomile when you open the lid, fetch that, too.'

A long soak, a dab of scent, what more could a girl ask for?

'A slab of ham and some sausage would go down well, and there's bound to be a crusty loaf hanging about. I'll need wine, red please, to wash it down, one of the fruity ones for preference, and see whether the cook's managed to get his hands on one of the new season's melons, will you? They should be in from Egypt by now.'

As Cypassis disappeared, repeating the list aloud to herself and omitting an item each time, Claudia looked up at her steward. 'What do you think you're laughing at?'

The Macedonian tried, without success, to straighten his face. 'Nothing, madam. Will that be all?'

'All? Good heavens, man, I've only just started! Once I'm done with my bath, I want to catch up on that huge pile of correspondence—'

'You called it twaddle earlier, said to throw it in—'

'Don't interrupt, Leonides, it's rude. You just bring those scrolls along to the peristyle in an hour's time, there's a good chap.'

As Claudia swept along the atrium towards the steam room, the lanky Macedonian smiled to himself. This was a grand house! Two upper galleries, well designed gardens and a magnificent banqueting hall. When the master was alive, the household ran like clockwork, lunch at this hour, dinner at that, guests were regular, quiet, and impeccably mannered. Much of the routine changed once Master Gaius married Miss Claudia (that bloody cat, for a start!), but since she became mistress in her own right, he could not recall a single dull moment under this roof. For Master Gaius, Leonides would have bent over backwards and done handstands. For the young mistress, he would lay down his life.

In her bath room, Claudia dismissed the attendants with a clap of her hands and sank into the luxurious hot water, where flowerheads of hyacinth and cyclamen and pink-lilac sea stocks bobbed about like ducks, wafting out their fragrance as they passed. Gradually muscles stopped screaming, lungs ceased to burn, and Claudia's thoughts turned to the moneylender. Or rather, to the reason she had needed him in the first place. Where had it gone wrong? For the average woman, of course, dragging themselves out of the gutter and marrying, for his money, a man who obligingly pops his clogs when you're still twenty-four would have been ample. Unfortunately when you're not Miss Average but are addicted to thrills, the path is more often prickled than primrose and when danger is no longer around to seduce you, the buzz has to come from somewhere. Hence the fall of the dice, the pluck of the gladiators, the fluke of the turn for a chariot. All too quickly, though, Claudia discovered Luck was no reliable investment counsellor. Gambling debts mounted, her inheritance dwindled, the dealings with moneylenders increased. She crumpled a marigold in her fist. Worst of all, the wine business Gaius had left her was ailing, purely because men refused to deal with a woman! Somehow she'd rectify that, but until then . . . youth comes but once, so why waste it?

Refreshed and replete, she hooked the door to with her toe, grappling with wraps, jars and mirrors under one arm and a jug of Falernian wine under the other. There were two honey cakes in her right hand and a goblet, half-full, in her left. The tortoiseshell comb she gripped with her teeth. The atrium, thank heavens, was deserted, affording privacy, air, space to breathe, time to appreciate the birds captured in silent song by the artist's brush, to—

What was that?

Claudia tipped her head on one side. There it was

again. Three knocks at the vestibule door. Not hard, not soft, but certainly not tentative. Curious, she decided against calling the porter back from his break and, after a valiant juggling act with her burdens, eased open the door herself.

The comb spat from her mouth.

The man leaning in the doorway would have been taller still, had it not been for the stoop where he was clutching his stomach. His hair was dark, with a tendency to curl, although right now most of it was matted with dark, sticky blood, which trickled down the side of his face to join the growing stain on his once-white tunic. His left eye was red and swollen and closing fast.

'Lovely evening,' he rasped. 'Don't you think?'

With unexpected grace, he slithered slowly down the door jamb into unconsciousness.

Claudia's instinct was to slam the door in his face. By the gods, she didn't need this! She threw down her wrap and the jug and the mirror, but not in order to play nurse. This man (correction, this human ferret) was the only person in Rome who knew the truth about Claudia, the single weak link in an otherwise sturdy chain. And now he turns up here! The honey cakes bounced, but the fall of the alabaster pot was broken by a heap of yellow cotton. Look at him! It wasn't the first time they'd crossed swords, but every time it was akin to tossing water on to acid. Explosive. Tentacles of grey mist coiled up the street, bringing with them a conglomeration of onions, damp donkey fur and the sickly scent of pomegranates fallen from a cart. Lips pursed, Claudia prodded the comatose lump. He'd been worked over by experts, but the damage was purely superficial. Hell, let him bleed on his own wretched doorstep!

From a distance she heard a voice saying, 'As far as I am aware, the gods of this threshold do not actually require a blood sacrifice.'

Incredibly, the voice appeared to be hers.

Marcus Cornelius Orbilio spluttered his way back to the land of the living. 'When I give, I like to give generously,' he said. At least that's what it sounded like. It was hard to tell with his lip so puffy. 'And anyway, you should see the others.'

Dammit, thought Claudia, if I wanted to laugh, I'd go watch a comedian.

'Another of those quiet nights out with the boys?' she asked, pushing him roughly towards the bath room.

'Not exactly.' His smile turned into a grimace of pain as she dabbed at his forehead. 'They were Nerva's men.'

'Really?' The cut was deep, but she did not believe it needed stitching. 'They look pretty damn confident to me.'

'Not nervous.' Orbilio gripped his ribs, because it hurt like hell when he laughed. 'Nerva.'

He smelled of sandalwood and wine, and you could tell his tunic had been aired over rosemary, even through the coarser scents of mud and blood. Claudia pressed harder on the cut. 'The aedile responsible for restoring the Temple of Neptune?'

'The very same. Only instead of dipping into the sea for inspiration, he's been dipping into the State Treasury. That's an exile offence, so he set his thugs on me. Four of them to be precise.'

Claudia shuddered. This was a night for foursomes,

she thought, recalling the Midden Hunters trawling the slums. Funny, but she could have forgiven them, perhaps, had they been dirty and down-at-heel, skulking in the shadows. Instead she remembered the lavish embroidery, the cultured voice, and the bearded man with the horse-shoe-shaped scar.

The wounded warrior was making a brave stab at humour. 'I taught one or two of them a lesson, I think.'

Claudia examined the lump on his head and applied a compress. 'They didn't need extra tuition, Orbilio, they were doing perfectly well on their own. Will you sit still?'

'That hurt!'

'Don't be a baby.' It was only vinegar to flush out the wounds. 'What happens next?'

'Oh, I'll have them in irons by midday, and then they can decide for themselves whether the money they were paid was worth the price of their lives.'

Claudia debated whether to tell him she was reaching for the salt and decided it would only make him fidget even more. 'Actually, I was enquiring, in my usual polite and roundabout way, whether Nerva's heavies had followed you here. Are we, for instance, needing to batten down the hatches and repel boarders?'

'No need, they scarpered once the – *Youch*!'

'You were saying?' she asked sweetly.

Orbilio made a grab for the salt and applied it himself, a tad more gingerly she noticed. Wimp.

'Those bastards meant to kill me. Goddammit, they were using me as a human battering ram! When Weasel's door sprang open, I'm not sure who was the more surprised. Nerva's men, me, or Senator Plautius with some curly-headed rent boy on his arm.'

Irony indeed! Had it not been for a senator who preached the high moral ground by day and stalked catamites by night, Orbilio would be floating half-way to Ostia by now.

The painkilling properties of her opobalsam salve were beginning to work. 'How do you feel?' she asked, as he struggled to his feet.

'I'll live.'

'I was afraid of that. Now tell me what you're doing here.'

'Me? Oh. Just passing.'

'On your hands and knees?'

A muscle twitched at the side of his swollen lip, but before he could respond, a small child had come barrelling into the room.

'Hello, I'm Jovi, who are you? I got lost. Claudia found me on the Argiletum. I asked another lady to help, but she was asleep, so Claudia brought me to her house for the night and she gave me a hot pie and a bath. Have you had a hot pie?'

'Um. No. But I wouldn't mind one.' Orbilio glanced hopefully at Claudia, who made a great show of finding a clean place to dry her hands on the bloodied linen towel.

'I'll fetch you some from the kitchens,' said Jovi. 'They're very good pies, I ate two. *And* some honeyed apricots. There was a cake on the hall floor, I ate that as well, actually there was two, so you can have the other one if you like.'

He pulled Claudia's second honey cake out from his shirt and handed it across. The transformation was astonishing, she thought. Clean, his hair was at least two shades lighter, and his face was quite cute, once the dirt'd been scrubbed off. The lice had probably clogged up the drains.

Marcus studied the hot, misshapen offering and politely declined.

'Why do you wear a long tunic?' Jovi pointed to Orbilio's trademark patrician attire. 'I've never seen a man in a frock before, are you a priest?'

'He has knobbly knees, soldier. People laugh at them, so he keeps them covered up. Shouldn't you be in bed?'

'Pff! I'm far too excited to sleep!' Jovi stuffed the honey cake into his mouth. 'I'll go fetch you them pies,' he said, crumbs spraying everywhere. 'There's lots to choose from, I had quail and then I had duck, but there's all sorts of others, which do you want? Cypassis says beef for brawn, fish for brains—'

'He already has fish for brains, Jovi. You bring back anything that looks nice.'

As his little feet pitter-pattered up the atrium, Marcus sluiced water over his matted hair. 'Why, Claudia Seferius, I do declare you've been unfaithful in my absence.'

Claudia froze in her tracks. That was the trouble with Supersnoop. He disturbed her. He disturbed her and she resented him for it, and when she turned there was ice in her eyes. 'Don't get ideas above your station, Orbilio. Didn't you know this is National Stray Day? I'm merely doing my bit for the Empire.'

He studied her lazily for several seconds. 'How much are you in for?'

'I beg your pardon?'

'The loan sharks. How much are you in for?'

Claudia brushed an imaginary speck off her pale-lemon tunic. 'Nasty crack on the head you sustained. Makes you ramble.'

'My steward informs me' – Orbilio winced as he combed out his tangles – 'that a moneylender called at my house recently. Apparently he required to speak with a lady by the name of – well, I forget what she called herself, it really doesn't matter.'

'If it doesn't matter, why are you telling me?'

'Now my steward is a cautious type of chap. He's Libyan, you know, and they're instinctively suspicious. He wondered whether this might be a ruse, to find out who lived there with a view to burglary, or perhaps casing the goldbeater's opposite. You do know there's a goldbeater's opposite?'

'Opposite where?'

'The point is,' he continued amiably, 'my steward, being Libyan and extremely quick off the mark, realized at once that the description of this mystery woman fitted you down to the ground.'

'Rubbish. He's only seen me once.'

'Once, Claudia, is enough,' said Orbilio. 'So I'll ask you a third time. How much are you in for?'

Claudia's eyes narrowed. 'Mind your own business,' she replied, sweeping out of the bath room.

'That much, eh?'

She pulled up sharp by the family shrine and drew out a handkerchief. 'With my dear, sweet husband,' she sniffed, 'still warm in his grave—'

'Claudia. You married Gaius because he was old and filthy rich, and unless he's interred over a volcano, it's unlikely his ashes have stayed warm for seven whole months.'

There was, she decided, an unseemly twinkle in his eye for a man addressing the recently bereaved.

Claudia let the handkerchief fall. Sometimes it works, sometimes it don't. 'Orbilio, I do not go into debt lightly.' (Hell no, I sail in fully laden!) 'At the moment I admit, I have a short-term cash-flow problem.' (When I die, it's finished with.) 'So while we're in the business of repeating things, I'll say it again. Mind your own damned business.'

The lanterns flickering from their bronze and silver stands brought the painted songbirds to life. Greenfinches. Goldfinches. Goldcrests. An oval fountain splashed and danced, a marble athlete considered his next throw of the discus and in a vase on a podium, two dozen Syrian tulips found their slender stems could not support the weight of their rose-red heads.

'I was offering to help,' he said, scanning the crocodiles and papyrus plants on the great Nile fresco which covered the east wall of the atrium.

Any second now, Leonides, Cypassis or one of a dozen lesser servants could come wandering out of the slave quarters and Claudia did not want eyebrows raised at the lies she would be required to tell. As Orbilio turned his attention to a yawning hippopotamus, she swept the vase of flowers on to the floor.

'I don't need your bloody patronage!'

His shoulders stiffened. 'That's entirely your prerogative,' he said, and though the tone remained mild there was no laughter left in his eyes.

'Damn right,' she snapped. 'Just because I gave some bloodsucking usurer the wrong house number doesn't give you the right to come tramping in and out of my home whenever you've the odd hour to kill!'

'You know, Claudia,' Orbilio sighed and leaned down to collect a single rose-red tulip, 'for once,' he sniffed in vain for a scent, 'you may be right.'

With a farewell salute, he tucked the flower into his bloodstained tunic and stepped over the debris to disappear into the night.

The atrium seemed bigger, suddenly. The ceiling higher, the columns colder, the galleries darker, and the finches and the warblers were no longer three-dimensional. Claudia hurled the libation jug at the Nile fresco and an ibis turned red with the wine. Bugger Egypt. Bugger Rome, come to that. And – she threw a votive cake at a po-faced sphinx – bugger you, too, Marcus Casual Liaisons! I hope you've got concussion!

'Has he gone, then, the man in the frock?'

Jovi's arrival made her jump. Well, so what if he's gone? Who gives a shit?

'Was there a fight in this room, was it the man in the frock?'

A miracle, thought Claudia, no one else heard the crash and came running.

'Did he chase off some burglars, were they trying to kill you?' Jovi held up the pies in his fists. 'What'll I do with these, can I eat them?'

'Maybe one,' she said absently.

'I don't think they'll give me the burps, not like those honey cakes, so can I have both? Ple-ease?'

Claudia peered down at his scrubbed and eager face. 'What are you? A gannet?'

Jovi fell on to his knees. 'No, I'm a bear.' He stuffed the last corner of the pie into his mouth and scampered round the floor. 'A big, brown mountain bear – watch me. Grrr!'

But Claudia wasn't watching. Her eyes remained fixed on the vestibule door, where the image of a man with still-damp tendrils round his forehead remained imprinted on her retina and whose sandalwood ungent lingered persistently. She heard again the gentle drop of the latch as he left, and the street sounds he'd momentarily admitted – the plod of an ox, the rumble of a barrel being unloaded – echoed repeatedly inside her head.

Oh, sod it.

'Call that a bear?' she said, turning to Jovi. 'I'll show you bears.' Looping up her arms, she made claws of her fingers and chased him round the fountain. 'Arrrrr!'

I have a wine business, I have a house, I have a villa and vineyard in Etruria. What more, Claudia asked herself, diving round the pedestals and podiums, could I possibly want?

In a dingy garret boasting ill-fitting shutters and a damp patch on two walls, a stinking tallow burned low. There was no incense to sweeten the air here, no joyful frescoes, and the only window faced a blank wall. Because you had to really crane your neck to see the street below, it was easier to lift your eyes to the roofs all around you. You could see whose tiles were missing, who had sparrows under their eaves, who was superstitious enough to grow houseleeks to ward off Jupiter's thunderbolts.

The man in the garret rarely looked out. The sounds rising upwards didn't touch him – not the rattle of chariot wheels, nor the crank of the building cranes. Hunched in his creaky chair, he dipped the nib of his reed pen into the inkwell and wrote carefully.

He did not wish to blot.

Satisfied with his efforts, he paused and looked round his walls. In pride of place over his bed – where else – he had nailed the original. Every day he dusted it, lightly, with an ostrich feather stolen from the market, and every day he examined it for signs of deterioration. If the paper curled, he would push a small tack in, but already the edges were ragged; brown marks were creeping relentlessly. Not that there was anything wrong with the ink. Top quality, imported from India, it withstood the test of the elements. The words, and he knew them by heart, still stood out clear. But he could not take chances.

He had only received the one letter from Claudia Seferius. He had no intention of losing it to mishap.

Pursing his lips in concentration, he returned to his work and the only sound he heard was the scratching of the nib. He did not smell apples baking in the apartment below, he did not hear the giggles of the newly-weds next door, he did not feel the damp from the Tiber meet the damp from the low clouds and creep its way into his bedding.

Satisfied the copy was perfect, right down to the angle of the serifs, he sat back and admired it for several minutes then picked up his hammer and four nails. Where should he put it, this precious document? Here? Over here? What about – yes, what about over there, just above the door and to the left?

Next door the newly-weds laughed at their neighbour's ritual. They had been married but a month, yet every night at precisely the same hour came the hammering of four solitary nails. Sometimes they listened out for it, a signal to blow out their own lantern and dive under the covers.

Once, she had met her neighbour on the stairs and asked him what it was he stuck on the walls every night, but the look he gave her shrivelled her to the spot and she averted her eyes whenever she saw him after that.

She would have moved house altogether, had she known that his walls were plastered with more than two hundred such reproductions of Claudia's letter.

IV

Darkness in Rome did not signal an end to the working day; for some it was merely a beginning. Come dusk, wheeled traffic, which was not permitted during daylight hours because it clogged the narrow streets, began rumbling along, nose to tail. Low-sided wagons carrying everything from crated hippos to Phoenician cedars clanked along ruts made by centuries of ox-carts before them. There'd be salt brought in from the flat coastal plain, wool from Campania, hemp from the Rhone and Corsican pitch. By the light of a thousand flickering brands, carts would roll through the arches and up at the Collina Gate, the northernmost gap in the city walls. The thirtieth of March was a night like any other.

Now spring had arrived and the seas became navigable, luxury goods from the Adriatic ports travelled the Via Salaria and the guards marvelled at great tusks of ivory, peacocks from Samos and glittering sapphires but, since the road from the Sabine Hills also ended here, mostly it was the common stuff. Venison, boar meat and barrel upon barrel of thick olive oil, because everyone knew Sabine oil was the best, but my word, the price of it! Night after night you'd see them, two dray horses pulling a cart loaded with one large barrel, which sat right behind the driver, plus three smaller ones to even up the weight. The gatemen knew the drivers; the drivers knew the gatemen; the banter was as constant as it was cheerful.

On the far side of the Collina Gate, however, it was a different world. Snubbed by traffickers and guards, tired shanties with walls of mud supporting bowing thatches leaned against the greyish-yellow stonework for support. The folk who eked out their short existence in these rank and squalid hovels did not care that this was where the enemy Hannibal once had made his camp. What use was history? Today's enemy was starvation and fever and snakebite and dysentery and, for all the good it did them, Sabine oil might as well be gold. Oil for lights? For cooking? Do me a favour! When we have to beg for alms, scavenge for our firewood, sell our bodies behind the tombs which line the roads to anyone who'll give us the price of a loaf? The people here had sores, they had roundworm, they had night blindness, they had rickets.

They also had babies.

'Well, Captain, any luck?' A cultured voice called across the plodding stream of wagons.

A thin, wiry individual with a horseshoe scar dodged past a muleteer and shook his head. 'Not a bloody one, Dino. Not even a girl.'

Lately they'd taken to splitting up to search, this was the meeting spot. 'Arbil won't believe this,' said the younger man, with a laugh in his voice. 'He'll think we spent the whole time rabble-rousing.'

'Not with this pong clinging to us, he won't,' the Captain muttered. 'Croesus only knows what caused that,' he rubbed at a stiffening stain on his tunic, 'but it stinks like shit.'

'Probably is shit,' sniggered the henchman Vibio,

joining up from the east. 'In which case, I ain't sitting next to you in the cart home.'

'Fuck off,' said the Captain good-naturedly and turned to his well-groomed companion. 'So then. Is that it for tonight, Dino?'

'We're wasting our time here, that's for sure, and I can see little point in prolonging it.' Dino rolled down his embroidered sleeves. 'What's the tally, Vibio? Just the two?'

'One,' replied Vibio, kicking aside a bundle of muddy rags. Too late he realized there was a small child inside, it whimpered as it scuttled into the night. 'That second bairn was already dead, poor little sod.'

Around them came low moans of pain and the smell of green wood smoking. Somewhere an old woman cackled in mirthless laughter.

'Save your pity, lad,' said the Captain. 'If it grows up here, it'll have a bloody tough life, lucky to make it into its teens, and then it'll probably have ulcerated lungs and a rather nasty sexual disease. Better off dead, if you ask me.'

'Tell that to the boss's face,' the henchman retorted. 'See if Arbil agrees!'

'I blame Agrippa.' Dino cut short any arguments. The tally was low, the job was unpleasant, tempers were short. 'His death, plus those nine days of mourning, have completely buggered up the system.'

They nodded at what they thought Dino meant. That because babies were exposed only on market days – a silent signal for childless couples to search for human treasure – it seemed logical that tonight's poor catch could be attributed to confusion in the minds of the slum girls following a national emergency.

But this was not what Dinocrates meant. Arbil the slave master had recognized in Dino a sharpness and intelligence from a very early age, and instead of being trained for trade or simply sold on unskilled, Arbil had lavished special care on Dino's education. Elevated to a position of trust and authority in the organization, and now third in command, wealth and responsibility had not dimmed his native intuitiveness. What he meant – and what the others would not understand – was that the ripples radiating from Agrippa's sudden and premature death went far beyond commerce and industry. The fragility of life had been rammed home in such a way that Dino believed that for many mothers, parting with their babies would be out of the question. The fight for survival would be stretched just that little bit further . . .

As they waited for the fourth member of the party to join up, Dino reflected on the Emperor's reaction to the tragedy. He'd coped well, he thought, with the death of a man closer to him than a brother and his eulogy had left strong men weeping fountains. He had lit the pyre himself, declared public mourning, read Agrippa's will aloud to the people and when he'd reached the part where his friend bequeathed his aqueduct slaves to Augustus, the Emperor once more proved his worth by turning these twelve score men over to the Senate as public servants. Furthermore, he had promised not only to continue Agrippa's civil engineering programme, by the gods he would extend it, creating the brand new post of Water Commissioner for a start. Afterwards he had personally supervised the interring of the Great Man's ashes in that tall, cylindrical structure faced with travertine down on the Field of Mars, the Emperor's very own mausoleum. What a man!

For Arbil the Babylonian, and to a lesser extent, for Arbil's son, Sargon, the death of Agrippa was purely nuisance value. A disruption of routine, a complete re-scheduling. No grief, no sadness. Dino often wondered what it must be like for them, so far from the motherland and with no loyalties to Rome, which invariably set him questioning his own identity. For an orphan from Chios who'd been raised under Babylonian law, why this strong pull towards Rome and the Romans? Dino was heartily glad when the fourth henchman arrived.

'What sex is it?' he enquired, as they pushed through the oncoming traffic towards the post house where they'd arranged to meet Sargon.

'What?'

'The child we picked up tonight.'

'Male,' confirmed Vibio.

'That's some consolation for Arbil,' said the Captain. 'It's tough these days to offload the girls.'

Vibio's brow furrowed. 'Yeah?'

'Regrettably so.' Pulling his cloak tight round his shoulders, Dino answered for the Captain. 'With the size of country estates on the increase, landowners need more and more muscle to dig over their fields, tread their grapes, pick their olives. There's only so many manicurists required on the open market!'

'I can think of a use for the girlies,' leered Vibio, rounding the corner of the posting station. Horses snickered, wheelwrights hammered out repairs by the light of bright torches.

Dino spun round, grabbed the man by the scruff of

his tunic and pressed him hard against the buckboard of a two-wheeled cart. In the glare from the yard, the lackey could see the young man's features clearly. Darkly handsome, tanned, oiled and athletic, right now his face was twisted with menace.

'Don't you ever, not once, make that filthy suggestion again.' Dinocrates released the tunic, but the flare in his eyes didn't lessen. 'What we do is both legal and honest, we train these children, give them a craft if they're able, ensure they have a roof over their heads and a full belly for life, even if they only end up as labourers.'

'I didn't mean nothing by it, Dino—' The midden hunter rubbed where the wood had dug into his backbone.

'I don't care whether you did or you didn't, the fact is you thought it. Just remember one thing, my friend. These babies might grow up slaves, but they grow up respected. And think, before you open your big mouth again, where *you* came from.'

'I—' He was floundering, and he knew it. Sweat was breaking out on his forehead, because he didn't understand what was happening. Dinocrates never lost his rag over something so trivial. 'Honest, Dino, I didn't mean—'

'He rescued you, he rescued me, he rescued Tryphon here.'

The Captain looked up from where he was checking the infant in its tiny basket and nodded solemnly. It wasn't often Dino referred to him by anything other than his nickname. 'Right,' he growled. 'So remember where your allegiance lies, lad.'

'I do, I swear.' It had been meant as a throwaway quip, the sort of joke men always make when they're together, like it's expected or something.

'Then you show the ladies respect,' pressed Dinocrates. 'Is that clear?'

'Yes, sir.'

'Good. Now let's hope Sargon's early so we can get moving. This bloody damp's right in my bones.'

A man, this side of thirty, stepped from the shadows with a swirl of his long, flowing cloak. 'Did somebody mention my name?'

'By Janus, lad, you gave me a bloody fright!' The Captain had nearly dropped his precious basket. 'What the hell are you doing out in the yard?'

Post houses were primitive, by and large, but there was always a waiting room where a large, open fire would crackle and spit and keep a man of standing safe from the elements, and there was no mistaking Sargon for a beggar. Not with wool that fine, or gems like those in his rings.

The Babylonian grinned. 'It wasn't me they objected to, Tryphon. It was Silverstreak here.'

At the mention of its name, a rangy canine loped to his side, yawned then casually licked its chops. Tawny coloured with a black tip to its long bushy tail, Silverstreak had acquired his name from the broad stripe of white fur which ran down his backbone. It was not that he was bad-tempered which people found so intimidating, it was more the fact that Silverstreak was a fully-grown wolf.

'I trust you had a more successful evening than the rest of us,' grumbled the Captain, although in all the years he'd worked the middens for Arbil, he still didn't know what role Sargon played when they came into Rome and he envied Dinocrates for being privy to such secrets.

'So-so.' Sargon moved across to Dino and spoke so only the two of them could hear. 'Remember the praetor's wife, the one who's right up the duff and her poor old husband stuck in Iberia this past twelvemonth?'

'Indeed.'

'The deal's on. She's due any time and when it's born, we're to relieve her of the brat and she'll hand over the cash.'

It wasn't the first time, and it wouldn't be the last. Wealthy wives paid fortunes to maintain the illusion of virtue, and so long as men and women found one another attractive, it would remain a profitable sideline.

'You've got to hand it to her, Sargon, she's hidden it well.' The number of women who took to their beds with mysterious illnesses while their husbands were absent beggared belief.

The Babylonian laughed. 'So did the censor's wife, Dino, and remember how that one turned out!'

The poor cow had been mortified at finding herself pregnant, and at one stage wondered whether to pass the baby off as her husband's. However, unable to remember who she had slept with, in the end she let prudence take precedence and handed the child over to Sargon.

'No mistaking him for the censor's,' laughed Sargon. 'That kid was as black as Nile mud!'

V

The last day of the month protected by Mars dawned (if that wasn't too strong a description) dull and grey and drizzly. Roof tiles darkened to the colour of blood, hides across windows hung shiny like satin, doors swelled and got stuck. In the homes of the better-off, Spanish oil topped up lanterns lit more for comfort than necessity as a swarm of industrious hands took oiled cloths to metalwork to ward off the rust.

To celebrate the passing of the month, a year-old sow was to be led through the streets to the goddess Luna's shrine up on the Palatine where, to the sound of flutes, she would lay down her life, and may Luna's powers be great from her sacrifice. Claudia checked the level on her water clock. Two more hours before the festivities kicked off. Sailing over the windowsill, Drusilla left daisies of mud on the tessellated stag-hunt before pushing her chiselled features into Claudia's breakfast. She did not take kindly to the feast being interrupted by Leonides, flattening her ears and hissing pointedly before returning the way she came in.

'You clash,' Claudia told her steward, indicating the purple shadows circling red-rimmed eyes. 'Is anything wrong?'

He checked Drusilla's departure was permanent before

venturing further into the room. 'Perhaps a little lack of sleep, that is all.'

Oh-oh! She'd forgotten she'd left him waiting in the peristyle. Time, methinks, to change the subject!

'I presume you've reunited Jovi with the bosom of his family?' Claudia toyed with a pancake, gave up and pushed back the plate.

'N-n-not exactly.' Leonides scrunched up one side of his face. 'Junius carried out your instructions. He posted a Message . . .'

She had to prompt him. 'Yes?'

'No word came back.'

Claudia practically rolled off the dining couch. She'd expected at least a dozen mothers queueing at her door, frantic to claim their misplaced rug-rat. 'What about the military? Has Junius enquired?'

'He has, and they have not received a visit, either.'

'I see.' Claudia tapped the side of her mouth with her forefinger. 'What about Jovi?' Dammit, she'd given him her oath! 'Have you questioned him?'

'The little chap has latched on to Cypassis and although she has tried repeatedly to coax clues out of him, I regret we are no closer to identifying even so much as his district, madam, let alone the address.' He relayed the gist of Cypassis' probing.

Which hill is closest to your home, Jovi? Dunno.
Are you near the river? Dunno.
What about a temple? Dunno.
Are there tall buildings round where you live? Nod.
(To him, all buildings would be tall, they could be tenements, storehouses, just about anything). So

what's the strongest thing you smell from your room? Wine.
(Aha! Could it be that wine warehouse down by the Aventine?) Tell me, Jovi, do you see lots of men coming and going? Yeah! They visit me ma!

Claudia groaned. Warehouses. Whorehouses. What's an 'h' and an 'o' between friends? 'Sooner or later,' she said, 'some silly bitch is going to twig on that she's a child short at dinner.' But until then, guess who's lumbered! She ran her hands through her hair. 'Just keep him out the way when that pack of hyenas arrives!'

She had no intention of explaining to the aunts what she'd been doing, tattered and torn, on the Argiletum – in the dark – without her bodyguard! The old hags had already got wind of her flutter on the horses, any further misdemeanour would be more than sufficient for them to whisk her into court and have her discredited as unfit to manage Gaius' business empire. However, provided she maintained a low profile for the next couple of days, that would not be a scenario she need worry about.

'Tell me, Leonides, is my mother-in-law still coming? No heart attack, perchance, no nasty fall to immobilize the boot-faced old barnacle?'

The Macedonian was too slow for his smile. 'Mistress Larentia is as fit as ever, madam.'

Shit. Jackals at a carcass, thought Claudia, the whole damned bunch. All winter long the jungle drums had been beating and now spring was here, the pack was on the move. Aunts, cousins, sisters, related by blood or marriage, what did it matter so long as they swelled the numbers. Led in the van by that septic old fossil, Larentia!

'With regard to your correspondence—'

Claudia felt a chill wind blow through the dining room. 'Those . . .' She cleared her throat. 'Those letters sealed with the cobra.' The ones she made him intercept. 'Do they still average two a day?'

In the bowels of the house, a pot crashed into smithereens unheard by either of them. The universe had shrunk to the walls of this room. The only sound was their breathing.

The steward stared intently at Drusilla's daisychain of mud. 'The frequency has increased a little lately.'

'How many of these filthy letters does he send me now?'

'Oh.' Leonides scratched his ear. 'Perhaps three.'

A knot tied itself round Claudia's throat. 'You're holding out on me, I can tell.' She was not sure the words came out as flippant as she'd hoped.

The Macedonian would not meet her eyes. 'It's the tone that bothers me. Each of these revolting notes gets more . . .' He searched for the right word then replaced it with, 'Aggressive.'

There was a loud drumming, which Claudia identified as her own blood pounding past her eardrums. These were dirty, dangerous letters at the best of times. And now the creep who wrote them was turning even nastier. 'You burn them, though?' It was the only way to eliminate the feeling of contamination they left behind.

'Every one.' The intensity receded. The icy breeze slithered away, the universe grew and familiar sounds intruded into the room. Whistling. A deliveryman's banter. Amphorae being rolled over stone floors. Plus a clanking, which was not quite so familiar. 'As to the rest of the correspondence—'

He stopped, because a man wearing a quantity of bruises and a long patrician tunic burst into the room. He was flanked by a soldier in uniform, hence the jangling. Claudia buried her head in her hands. One million people live in this city. Five hundred thousand, therefore, are male.

Why this one?

Why me?

She closed her eyes, counted to five then beckoned her steward. 'Throw them out,' she said. 'Lock the door, bar it if necessary, but never, ever, on pain of your life, let *this* man,' she pointed to Marcus, 'into *this* house again.'

'Sorry.' Orbilio grinned like a cat with a quail. 'Official business.'

'Is it?' Claudia addressed the legionary, who smiled wanly and thereby managed to avoid committing himself.

Leonides peered at the taller of the two visitors. 'Are you all right, sir? Those cuts? Can I bring you—'

'Leonides, you couldn't even bring him to his senses, he's so thick. You could, however, fetch Junius, if you will, plus a couple of other big, strong, muscular types. Our guests have stayed long enough.'

The soldier did his utmost to look invisible, which is not easy when you've bright red feathers in your helmet, so he settled for shuffling his feet and fixing his gaze at a set point on the mosaic. Claudia thought that, personally, the front end of that stag would be a more attractive bet. But then she wasn't a soldier.

Orbilio advanced towards Claudia. 'I shall need more time to consider your proposal of marriage—'

'My *what*?' She did not actually recall springing to her feet, but miraculously she was upright.

'Last night,' he continued cheerfully, 'you said – in fact, you were adamant – you didn't want me flitting in and out, so naturally I assumed—' He broke off to pat Claudia on the back and help her through the coughing fit.

'You're insane,' she said hoarsely, gulping down a whole glass of wine in one go. The legionary, she noticed, had perked up considerably.

'Because I didn't accept straight away? Quite possibly, but in the meantime, I have something of a problem on my hands. It's just a little thing—'

'Size is not important, Marcus. Don't feel bad about it.'

This time it was the soldier's turn to choke.

Orbilio had covered his mouth with the back of his hand. 'Is—' It took him a good ten seconds to compose himself. 'Is Jovi still here?'

Claudia's head was spinning so fast, she thought it was in danger of flying right off. She hadn't realized for a moment that Leonides had answered.

'He is indeed, sir.' Claudia glowered at him to keep his stupid mouth shut, but the signal missed its mark. 'I'll take you to him.'

'Not so fast.' She held up a restraining hand. 'What's so important about the ragamuffin that it brings the Security Police clodhopping round here during breakfast?'

The legionary's eyes were darting from Orbilio to Claudia and back again, his mouth had all but fallen open.

'You!' she barked. 'Out!'

The soldier glanced at his superior officer, who nodded

assent and instructed him to wait outside the door. Claudia thought the feathers in his helmet drooped a little as he left.

'A woman's body has been discovered on the Argiletum,' explained Marcus. 'I'd like Jovi to take a look and see whether he can identify her.'

'Orbilio, you insensitive clod, you can't just show him a corpse and say "tell us, old chap, is that your mummy?" '

'Too subtle, you think?' Orbilio's expression grew serious. 'Claudia, the Market Day Murderer has struck again. I presume you know about the previous two?'

Who didn't? It was the talk of all Rome! At first, the gruesome find was believed to be a revenge killing, because the girl in question, a slave, had been in with a bad crowd. Mess with gangsters like that, and you're left as a lesson to others. When, eight days later, another girl was found slashed to pieces, people began to ask: was it the same man, or a copycat killing? Little doubt now. Three successive market days. Three successive victims.

'As I say, she was found on the Argiletum – and if you recall, Jovi told us he'd seen a woman "sleeping" there yesterday evening.'

And he'd have said if it was his mother!

'Of course,' breezed Marcus, slicing off a hunk of cheese, 'I'll need you to come along as well, to show me exactly where you found the lad. After all, it's a long road and this could be coincidence.'

Leonides coughed quietly. 'The time, madam. The ladies—'

'Ladies?' Orbilio spoke through the cheese.

Claudia's mouth twisted down at the corners. 'Gaius'

relatives, female branch. Like salmon gathering at the river to spawn, they're on the move and heading this way.'

'Very shortly,' stressed the beanpole.

'For the Festival of Fortune,' she explained. 'Which, as you well know, is tomorrow. So I'll describe exactly where I found our Jovi, and you can be about your business.'

Two male voices competed for air time.

'Madam, you don't understand. Fortune's tomorrow, but the ladies are due—'

'For gods' sake, Claudia, this is murder—'

Claudia scooped up a handful of raisins and popped them in her mouth. 'Are you still here?' she asked Marcus, fluttering her eyelashes.

He threw up his hands in despair. 'Goddammit, woman, this is an official enquiry!'

'I doubt that,' she replied, reaching for the shrimps. 'You're the Security Police and the Empire is in crisis. Unless someone rich and powerful got topped – which of course she isn't, or you wouldn't need young Jovi to identify the victim – this looks like another of those cases you have taken to investigate in your own time. Am I right?'

He shrugged. 'The law is inadequate,' he replied, 'you know that.'

Technically, the death of a slave is the responsibility of their owner. The rules change when there's a serial killer at work, but even then it comes way behind treason.

'Please, Claudia. I need all the help I can get.'

Claudia considered the aunts. Then a vision of the murder victim flashed through her mind, the girl's mutilated corpse lying stiff and unclaimed in some filthy back alley . . .

'No.' I cannot, I dare not, get involved.

The twitching of his cheek was the sole sign of irritation, but Orbilio was by no means defeated. 'There's a butcher on the loose—'

'No.' Too much is at risk. My house, my security, for gods' sake, my whole future!

'He's killing them slowly, Claudia.'

'Excuse me, madam.' Claudia's big-boned maidservant popped her head round the door. 'There's a dozen ladies in the atrium. Should I show them in here?'

The steward's bony shoulders slumped. 'That's what I was trying to tell you,' he said. 'They were due here today.'

Claudia heard teeth grinding and had a horrid feeling they were hers. 'Cypassis, whatever else you do, keep them in the hall. Take their cloaks, wipe their feet, offer them refreshment, just keep fussing till I get there.'

Goddammit, that stupid policeman actually seemed to find this amusing! Well I can't have him around, for a start. If they recognize Orbilio from my previous run-ins with the law, I am doomed – especially when the investigator in question is black and blue from fighting! Quickly she ushered him through the far door and, with a finger to her lips, cautioned Leonides to silence. Now for the checklist.

Gaius' marble bust? Out of the attic and dusted.

Business accounts? Doctored.

Jovi? Out of sight and out of earshot.

Moneylender? Knocking at some other mug's door.

Snooping detectives? Banished to gardens.

Murder? None of my business.

That's right. It's none of my damned business.

Satisifed there was not the slightest whiff of scandal for the battleaxes to pick up, Claudia patted her curls, smoothed her gown, adjusted her ear studs and glued a very large grin into place.

Serenely she opened the door to the atrium. And walked straight into the smirking legionary whom she'd stationed there.

VI

The Argiletum, Claudia discovered, turning into it from the Forum, was doing its customary roaring trade. As though pushed into some kind of civilian uniform, rich merchants drew their togas over their heads to protect themselves from the rain, but the majority of men – the slaves and street porters – had no such umbrella. Ankles splattered with mud and slurry, they clutched the necks of their tunics to minimize the drips which would trickle inside and more than one bemoaned the cheap fabrics which shrank, cold, to their flesh. Beneath an awning carried by slaves, a thickset widow considered how best to spend her inheritance, and this did not include cloaks for her staff. Claudia pulled her own wrap lower over her brow and became as anonymous as everyone else tramping about in the drizzle.

Over on the Palatine Hill, where the aunts sheltered in the dry of a marble colonnade, the Priest of Luna would be double-checking the placement of his sacred paraphernalia, for if even the slightest thing was adrift, the ceremony would at best start all over, at worse be abandoned.

Let no one forget that the taking of a life was of supreme sanctity.

Let no one trivialize the event.

Swamped by the smell of wet wool on this street of bookshops and cobblers, Claudia smiled to herself. Confronted by a dozen hostile women and a soldier in her house, she did what any girl would have done.

'Cypassis,' she chided. 'If I've told you once, I've told you a hundred times, the instant our dear relatives arrive, we are off to the Palatine!'

Most of the old trouts looked suitably confused, but it was the ringleader you needed to watch. 'Luna?' Larentia queried. 'You've got us seats for the Festival?'

Provided Junius rode like the clappers, there should be ample time to persuade a dozen decent citizens to give up their place, and idly Claudia wondered how many would require silver assistance. 'We'll need to leave now, though,' she said. 'It's quite a long walk.' Which, with luck, would do for the old bitch.

'Walk?' quailed at least nine of the women. '*Walk?*'

'Best form of exercise,' she insisted, flapping her hands behind her back as a signal for Cypassis to dismiss her litter.

Larentia jabbed a bony finger at the legionary. 'What's he doing here?'

'Him? Ah. The soldier is . . . an official escort!' She turned a full set of teeth upon the leering legionary and spoke through them. 'You squire us, I visit murder scene,' she hissed. 'Tell Orbilio.'

Less than a minute later, a baritone laugh rang out from the peristyle (which Claudia took to be confirmation that the deal was on) and then the only obstacle was to absent herself from the ceremony. No problem. As the women were grouping themselves in front of the white marble shrine, Junius ran up to inform his mistress that her best friend was suffering a miscarriage, please come quickly, it was an emergency and so utterly convincing was he in his role that Claudia very nearly called for a doctor herself.

A chair turned into the Argiletum, bouncing so badly as the bearers dodged the glistening puddles it was a wonder its occupant wasn't seasick. And suddenly Claudia remembered why she was here. She stepped aside for a woman with a pot of forced lilies under one arm and a bawling infant under the other, who was collecting her husband's boots from the menders, then listened as a Sarmatian bartered in bad Latin with a Parthian whose vocabulary was worse. She lingered at a stall specializing in foreign books, helping the wizened shopkeeper secrete his treasured scrolls beneath a yellow cloth to keep the damp at bay, she passed the time of day with an inkseller extolling the virtues of soot and pitch and octopus juice and she allowed the slipper-maker to ramble on about the guild he belonged to, but my, my, where were his manners, would the lady feel the softness of his leather?

Then finally . . . no more shops. No more diversions.

No more excuses.

Claudia positioned herself at the back of the small crowd which had gathered, anonymous under her cloak. She could still turn away. Cypassis sat on a three-legged stool outside the vellum maker's, she had Jovi on her knee and was recounting how the raven had been turned from silver into black for telling tales. Jovi, unaware, chuckled merrily.

'More, Passi. Tell me more!'

The crowd had been denied a view of the grisly crime in the alley, yet they chewed on every lurid detail.

'Who raised the alarm, was it Zosi?'

'That's right, the speech seller. He said finding that corpse made him sick to his stomach.'

'Slashed to ribbons, so they say.'

'Just like the others!'

Speculation, embellishment and innuendo rippled round the swelling horde and when Claudia shivered it was not from the cold. Try as she might, she couldn't escape the bitter comparisons between the horror on the Argiletum and the dignified ritual on the Palatine. There, the Priest of Luna would be inspecting the sacrificial sow for blemishes, assuring the worshippers who had gathered at the shrine that the beast was as close to perfection as was possible, a worthy sacrifice for the goddess. He would then wash his hands, for he too had to be pure.

Whether or not he had yet called for silence, it was not too late for Claudia to join in, because here, on the Argiletum, a solemn-faced Orbilio was busy wiping dark stains from his hands. He had not seen her. Sorry, Marcus. Another time, huh?

One eyebrow twitched slightly as Claudia threw back her hood and stepped forward. 'Is this the place where you found Jovi?' There was nothing in his voice to suggest he'd ever doubted she would not honour the bargain. 'The boy doesn't remember.'

The investigator's voice did not carry as far as the gawpers and they shuffled their feet in noticeable disappointment.

Claudia cleared her throat. 'Yes.' Even in daylight you could barely make out the narrow cul-de-sac between the bookseller's and the satchel shop, much less by night. 'Is that where . . .?'

As her voice trailed off, she considered the worshippers and the temple attendants, duly hushed, heads bowed low. With street sounds drowned by the sacred flutes, the Priest of Luna would sprinkle holy salt on the pig's head to purify the sacrifice. There would be no smells of turnip stalks and piss up there; no buzzing flies or scuttlebugs. From the hurly-burly of the street, Claudia's ears picked out only Cypassis relating the bitter-sweet story of Echo and Narcissus and how poor, pining Echo was reduced to hiding in caves. And darkened alleyways, Claudia added silently! With heavy feet and a heavier heart, she approached the pitch-black tunnel. From a million miles away, a man's voice was urging her for gods' sake, don't go down there, but Claudia heard only her maidservant's crooning, growing fainter as it became muffled by the high walls of the passageway.

The priest would be finishing his solemn intonation. One of his attendants would purify the sacred hammer and he would ask, is this the right moment to strike, my lord?

Someone had snatched a torch from its bracket on the bookshop wall and was running after her. He was calling out her name and shouting, come back, but Claudia was mesmerized by the figure in the alley. White? Dark? No, it was parti-coloured. Part light. Part dark. That was the effect of the blood.

The pig would now be stunned with the sacred hammer. A second attendant would then turn to the priest, who would gravely nod his assent.

The figure was seated. Back to the wall. Facing forward.

The second attendant would turn the dazed animal's

head to the heavens and the Priest of Luna would speak words of reverence.

The figure was naked. Her hair had been hacked off and laid in her lap. Dark, limp, it resembled a cheap and shaggy blanket.

Luna's second attendant would turn the pig's head towards the hallowed earth and the Priest would utter prayers.

The figure's wrists had been bound behind her back. Her legs had been bound at the ankles.

Lest the sacrificial beast recover from the blow which had stunned it, the Priest of Luna would draw the consecrated blade clean across its throat.

At least it was quick.

Which was more than you could say for this poor cow in the alleyway.

VII

Rome isn't Babylon. No swaying date palms, no native willow, no light Euphrates poplar. No great wide streets to face the winds and blow the smells away, no glistening whitewashed houses. No scorching sun, no private bathtubs, no jugs fetched home on heads. No ale. No lard. No harems.

Here, on his lands below the Sabine Hills, Arbil was surrounded by all manner of dismal trees, home to all manner of verminous creatures, and he mourned the vast unbroken flatness that was Babylonia. Except Babylon was dying. The great metropolis sat back while other cities sniped at its trade and found the price for complacency was slow obliteration. Soon it would be nothing but a ghost town, a shadow of its mighty past, and a man with sons must change or shrivel with it. Arbil was not a surrenderer. That gutless peacock, the self-styled Augustus, now there's a defeatist, he thought, and he might fool Romans with his tales of his glory, but by Marduk he did not fool Arbil. He called it an empire, yet would not fight wars. What a prick! He fobbed his people off with temples paid for by other mens' campaigns and sold it back to them as a 'Golden Age of Peace'. He was nothing but a conman.

Which was all to Arbil's good. As a result of those

pacifist policies, the first thing to dry up was a hitherto steady stream of prisoners of war, the traditional source of slave labour upon which the Roman economy depended. When Arbil heard about the practice of leaving babies on midden heaps, he knew at once he had a goldmine on his hands, a perpetual source of income, and he'd hardly have to work at it! He'd chosen a site not too close to Rome, yet private enough, from which to operate, and naturally this was subject to Babylonian law and none of that namby-pamby stuff the Romans professed to enforce. If a wife kills her husband, she is impaled. If a son strikes his father, his hand is cut off. If a couple commit adultery, they are tied up and thrown in the river. Simple, but effective. There was never any trouble on Arbil's property.

Even from a distance, a stranger approaching would see that this was not the standard design of four wings round a central courtyard. A short-toed eagle, cruising for snakes and frogs and lizards, would have a better view, and he would see a shape not dissimilar to his own silhouette. A stubby head, the remains of the original building, with a garden as its eye, and beyond, a broad stocky body, the earliest of the many extensions. Splayed from the middle, he would see eight long blocks, huge 'wings' of wings either side and, finally, a splayed tail block at the end. However, there would be too many people milling around, quite literally hundreds, for the short-toed eagle's comfort and he would move on, skimming the ridge of the hill in his search for juicy reptiles.

Arbil would not have been among the buzz of humanity caught in the scan of the eagle. The weather was invariably foul and he spent all of the winter and much of the spring closeted indoors, swaddled in a long woollen mantle over numerous ankle-length robes. There were times when he would have swapped half his fortune for a Babylonian drought, even the odd swarm of locusts would have been more comforting than this bloody damp. Why go out in it? He had men for that. Overseers. Physicians. Managers for the various wings. Eunuchs to look after the girls once they reached puberty. Arbil had enough to do without supervising the supervisors. In fact, his whole organization was structured round routine, and that included his personal life.

First he would summon his wife and make love to her (twice, if he could manage it). Next he would bow to the rising sun. Then he would pray to Marduk. So powerful was this patron god of Babylonia that Arbil's bedroom was devoted entirely to his holy symbol, the dragon, and it was from the dragon Arbil drew his strength. He patted his ample girth and smiled. His stamina, now! That came from the the goddess Ishtar, whose eight-pointed star he'd had inlaid with ivory over his bedhead and it was to Ishtar that he turned every morning. (Twice, if he could manage it.)

After breakfast, he would bathe, for without his body perfumed and massaged, without his rebellious straight hair crimped in the traditional style and his beard snipped and curled as he liked it, he was in no fit state to reel in one of the many tentacles of his organization and absorb the latest news from the city. After all these years away from the motherland, he still baulked at mingling with men who wallowed like hippos in communal bathwaters and who worshipped gutless pagan gods.

He must have been daydreaming, maybe he'd even

fallen asleep, because the next thing he knew was his wife saying 'Arbil, Arbil! Are you all right?'

'What?' His vision was fuzzy, his mouth was dry. 'Of course, I'm all right.' He looked round. How did he come to be in his office? Wasn't he in his bedroom just now? He never came into this, his favourite room, painted blue like the night sky to show up the gold in the lamplight, before his ablutions were complete.

'I brought you flowers for your desk. Marigolds.'

Arbil looked up. Apart from a mist around the margin of his vision, he could see her doe-like eyes, her blue-black hair swishing when she walked. How old was she now? Twenty-seven? Twenty-eight? After twelve years in the marriage bed, no blemish had yet marred her olive skin, no wrinkle, not so much as a droop to those delicious breasts. Yet today wasn't the first time he'd not been able to get it up . . . Shit.

'Yes, Angel, very nice,' he said, shooing her out of the room with the back of his hand then tipping the pathetic little bunch in the bin when she'd gone. He mightn't remember coming into this office, but by Marduk, he didn't intend to start work without his hair being crimped.

'*Fuck me!*'

His hair *was* crimped! Arbil peered into the mirror. And his beard. Curled in at the tip. He sniffed his forearm. It glistened with oil and smelled of pine and spice. His favourite unguent. What the fuck happened this time? Dazed and trembling, surrounded by the bulls of Adad, artefacts of gold, horses of stone, Arbil realized that the time he had lost must have been close to an hour. Sargon would be waiting . . .

Hell, he'd have to wait a moment longer. He daren't let his son see him like this.

His antiques orientated his befuddled mind, especially the free-standing zodiac tiled in lilypad green, which was his favourite. Money box excepted, of course! Above the locked chest and nailed to the dark blue plaster hung the calendar which, being Roman, told him that today was the Festival of Luna. Despite his aversion to the people who had, like the Assyrians and the Macedonians before them, defiled his native city, it was in his interests to understand their hollow cults. Arbil knew about Luna. Crescent moons framed Luna's face like horns, but Arbil would have no knee bent here to poor imitations. For his army of child slaves, it was Zin who governed their moons. Adad sent their thunderbolts. Ishtar was the true goddess of love. He sighed. Maybe it was not she who'd let him down this morning, maybe it was something he ate? He'd have to check his diet, call his physician. Normally he went like a stallion . . .

Fuck these lapses!

'Come in, boys, come in!' he called out in his thick, gutteral brogue.

They made a good team, did Sargon and Dino. Both had shown an aptitude for business, Arbil trusted them implicitly. Sargon was his son, his firstborn, but not always do sons turn out as you'd hope (by Marduk, they do not!) and Dinocrates, the orphan he'd picked up on Chios and whose potential he had spotted, was – well, if not a son, damn close.

'Shut the door, there's a terrible damp in the air.' He indicated chairs. 'Now sit down, take the weight off.'

The two young men exchanged glances of amusement.

Every morning between November and May they lingered in the doorway as a means of admitting fresh air into a room which boasted many heavy unguents but not a single open window.

His vision might have cleared, his mouth no longer felt dry, but until the shock of losing that hour had passed, Arbil was content to shuffle through his table deep in scrolls and tablets pretending to search for something.

Sargon waited patiently. Unlike his father, worship played no part in his life, neither the old gods of home nor the newer gods of Rome. His devotions were of a more personal nature, and any spiritual fulfilment he might require he sought at the tailor's, the dice table, the drinking den among men of his own ilk. To his father's dismay, he also embraced modern art and Roman ways, wearing the toga and attending whichever ceremonies amused him – and, radically for a Babylonian, he shaved his face. It was vanity, as opposed to ancestry though, which kept his hair halfway down his back, because the combination of mane, wolf and wealth made him a magnet to ladies in every stratum of society. If he hadn't made a living out of slavery, Sargon could have made a fortune as a gigolo.

Arbil finally tapped the scroll he'd pretended to look for. 'I have an approach here for thirty unskilled workers for a brickworks on the Via Tiburtina.'

Dino's breath came out in a whistle. 'That's over 10 per cent of our annual output,' he said. 'You'll need a new money box for that lot, Arbil.'

His employer nodded slowly several times, but his eyes remained fixed on his son.

Sargon folded his arms and pulled at his lower lip. 'I'd

offer him ten at 2,000 sesterces,' he said at length. 'Then tell him that if he wants the other twenty, he'll have to pay skilled rate.'

Arbil's eyes glittered.

'But, Sargon,' Dino protested. 'We've got sixty unskilled boys for sale.'

Sargon smiled knowingly. 'If this brickmaker has approached us, not the other way round, you can bet your fancy fringed boots he knows about our training policy.'

'But—' A flick of Arbil's wrist cut the Chian short.

'My guess,' Sargon continued thoughtfully, 'is that once he's handed over his silver, he plans to sell them on himself as trade apprentices, pick up his brickmakers at public auction and then, when he tallies up his accounts, he'll expect to see a healthy profit.'

Dino's face creased into a slow smile. 'You sly bastard! You're planning to screw that old brickmaker?'

'A matter of justice,' put in Arbil. 'Teach him not to go into business on his own.' It was impossible to keep the smugness out of his voice. This was the first real test he'd been able to give Sargon, the boy came out with colours flying. Proof, if it was needed, that the business was in safe hands should anything happen to him.

'Word will spread,' added Sargon, 'that you don't mess with the Babylonians!'

No, thought Arbil, you do not. He thought back to the merchant from Pisae who'd refused to pay for his order, saying they were females, for gods' sake; he wanted proper workers. For a while Arbil had been reasonable. The merchant wanted slaves to weave his linen, he gave him slaves to weave his linen. Cheerful, nimble-fingered girls who'd be quick to learn. Give them a chance, he had said. Then other customers started complaining, hoping to lower the price, squeeze a refund. So Arbil taught the linen merchant a lesson, and once people saw his ears pinned to the wall, they'd stopped quibbling.

Arbil leaned back in his chair, the signal that the meeting was over. Sargon and Dino stood up.

'I received a report from Rome,' the slave master said casually, 'saying another girl was killed last night.'

Two Adam's apples tensed. 'Rough districts, some of them,' said Sargon.

'Real no-go areas,' added Dino.

'Mmmm.' Arbil's eyes fixed themselves on the green-tiled zodiac scorpion. 'I'm told this girl died of twenty-seven cuts with a knife.'

Dino glanced up sharply. 'Twenty-seven?'

Arbil's eyes moved to the lion, symbol of courage. 'That makes three girls who have been killed from *exactly* twenty-seven wounds. Odd, don't you think?'

No one answered. Drips from the eaves splashed into puddles of mud beneath the window. Arbil's spicy unguents seemed to cloy, especially the cade which clashed with the cedarwood scent from his hair oil.

'The authorites are too busy wetting their pants over his Imperial Majesty's health,' he said, pulling his long woollen mantle more snugly over his ankles, 'to be concerned about slaves.'

Sargon and Dino stared straight ahead, and pretended they didn't notice the heat in this dark blue room of antiquities.

'But I am,' the slave master said quietly. 'Especially when they could be traced here. Do either of you have information on these killings?'

The word 'No' came in unison.

'Then that'll be all for this morning.' Arbil's hirsute cheeks bunched into a smile as he chafed his hands together. 'The shipment that's due out – those three boys for the bakery – I'd like to check it over personally, could you see it's brought to the house, Dino?'

Two jaws relaxed visibly.

Arbil waited until the two men had reached the door. 'Oh, and boys.'

'Father?'

'I can take it as read, can I not, that the five of you in no way disbanded last night?'

Neither Sargon nor Dino so much as blinked, but it was Dino who first found his voice. 'Absolutely not, sir.'

'Good. Good. Then I'll see you later.' Arbil stood up and admired the rings on his short, stubby finger joints. 'Dino.'

'Sir?'

'You'll be going to Rome?' He buffed up a band set with chalcedony.

'With the shipment, yes. I'm also looking for buyers for those copyists, now the deal with old Nerva fell through.'

'Quite.' Who'd have thought Nerva would fiddle the books? 'Well, while you're in town, see if you can find out the name of the dead girl.' He spat on the precious white stone. 'And Dino?'

'Sir?'

'Let's make sure this stays within the three of us. Eh?'

When he was alone once more with his Mesopotamian treasures, Arbil walked round his table and picked up the thin-bladed knife which he used for breaking the seals of his letters and studied it carefully for several seconds.

'Neat.' A young man in a long grey cloak stepped out from behind the green-tiled zodiac and smiled a lazy, lopsided smile. 'Very neat.'

Arbil let out a soft snort that was part irritation, part amusement but, it had to be said, principally admiration. He didn't bother to enquire what it might be that this visitor was complimenting. 'How long have you been standing there?' he asked.

The cloak was what he'd have expected the man to wear on a day when the clouds were so low you were part of them, a colour to render its wearer invisible.

'Long enough to prove a point.'

'Which is?' Even as he asked the question, Arbil knew the answer.

'To remind you that your investment in my training wasn't wasted.' He plucked the knife from Arbil's manicured fingers and, with an exaggerated wink, dropped it down the top of his boot.

Arbil sighed resignedly. 'I suppose you heard?'

'The acoustics in this room are really quite remarkable,' the visitor replied, running his fingertips over the relief of Adad's sacred bulls. 'You know, Arbil, you and your son have much in common.'

'I am very proud of Sargon,' the Babylonian said stiffly. Not once had his eyes left his visitor's face.

With an extravagant flourish, the man in grey shook Arbil's paper knife down the sleeve of his cloak and sent it twanging into the maplewood desk. 'Oh, but I was referring to your other son,' he said slowly. 'Shannu.'

'Shan—?' The colour drained from Arbil's face to leave two bright spots of rouge above the beard line. 'Shannu?'

Before he could recover his powers of speech, the

visitor had unhooked the shutter and had his long leg halfway over the sill. 'Magic!' he laughed, twirling his cloak.

Within seconds, his camouflage was complete and, as Arbil poured a glass of strong, fermented date liquor with a hand which trembled badly, he was left wondering whether he had imagined the entire episode. The same way he couldn't get it up and hours blanked out, his mind, also, played tricks.

Then Arbil saw the knife, quivering upright in the wood.

When he shivered, he was not sure whether it was from the cold coming in through the open window or from the spectre of his youngest son. Shannu.

Wringing his hands, Arbil fell on his knees and thanked Marduk for his daily round of schedules.

Only his schedules kept him sane.

VIII

By the time Claudia had brought up her breakfast, her supper and possibly even yesterday's lunch, the crowd of ghouls on the Argiletum had all but dispersed. Not out of shame, or because every fibre of their clothing was waterlogged, or even because they had better things to do, it was simply that now the undertakers had left, there was nothing more to gawp at. One or two among them sneered, the way people do when they think they've been short-changed, but the majority trickled quietly away as Orbilio began to question the neighbours. Each time he drew a blank. Even from Zosi, the speech seller who discovered the body. Zosi was a disenchanted, middle-aged bachelor with a penchant for the grape and he was adamant. Yes, his room was directly overhead. No, he didn't hear a thing. Well, possibly a scuffle, but he keeps himself to himself, don't he, and all right, maybe he did hear a small boy calling for his ma, but it ain't none of his business what goes on, same as that bloke whistling his dog.

'What dog?' Orbilio's ears pricked up. 'When was that?'

But Zosi couldn't say, and in the end all Orbilio had for certain was that Zosi had heard a whistle, three short notes in succession, and that it was some time after midnight. As he said, just a bloke calling his dog. Whit-whit-whit.

Wiping her mouth with her handkerchief, Claudia straightened from her groggy knees. What kind of mind can slash a girl unrecognizable? Could stand there, perhaps laughing at the pain he was inflicting, but far more likely aroused by his own sadism? She looked round for Junius, couldn't see him, and stumbled into a bookshop to wait. The instant he returned, she'd be off, and that wasn't a reaction to the crime down in the alley, more to the man who was investigating it. This was the first time she'd seen him on home turf, his face grey and pinched with anger at the atrocities committed, mastering his fury and masking his revulsion in his ordered questioning, his note taking, his painstaking attention to detail as he searched the scene of the crime, demonstrating both his professionalism and, at the same time, his vulnerability. It struck a chord Claudia did not wish to hear. Picking up a wax tablet from deep inside the bookseller's, she flipped open the hinge.

'Claudia?'

This was not a voice tinged with a Gaulish accent and so she lifted the book to cover her face.

'I do believe,' the baritone continued, taking the tablet from her hands, 'that to truly appreciate the poetry of Virgil, it helps to hold it the right way up.'

'Clog off.'

'Clogs,' replied Marcus, sucking in his cheeks, 'are two shops down, on the left. Come. I'll walk you home.'

'You will not.' Claudia flounced out of the shop. 'I kept my side of the bargain, now we're even.'

'There's something I want to talk over.' Orbilio let her

scan the dripping shopfronts for a whole minute before informing her that he had taken the liberty of dismissing her bodyguard.

'And he went?' She'd have that young Gaul's giblets! 'Just like that?'

'Junius and I have an understanding.'

'Then I hope you'll both be very happy,' Claudia replied, sweeping down the street, her skirts swishing with the speed of her stride.

Orbilio's laughter made the vellum-maker scratch his calfskin. 'You can come to the wedding,' he said, catching her by the elbow and spinning her round. 'Providing you live long enough.'

He pushed her into the shelter of a shopfront. Dammit, it was the slipper-maker whose sales pitch she'd pretended to listen to earlier!

'For gods' sake, you need protection,' Orbilio was saying.

'From what? Fleas? Mice? Measles? You!' Claudia turned to the slipper-maker. 'If you don't shut up about your goddammed guild, I'll make you eat your bloody leatherwork, and no, for the umpteenth time, the lady does not want to feel the softness!'

'Which roughly translated,' Marcus told the shopkeeper evenly, 'means the lady has no feelings. Ouch!' He half-limped, half-hopped up the street after her. 'Claudia, this is serious.'

'I only stepped on your toes.'

He forced himself to be solemn. 'I'm talking about this.'

From his soggy linen tunic, he pulled out an equally bedraggled document. Once it had been a crisp, clean oblong of paper. Then someone had written on it. Then it had been rolled and sealed. Finally, it had been crumpled and pushed into a charcoal oven. Claudia felt a chill descend in the air. She did not need to see the seal to know it was a cobra. Legend had it, the Orbilio clan traced itself back to Apollo. Claudia wouldn't mind betting that somewhere along the line, bloodhounds had been bred into it.

'Where did you get hold of that?' It's not easy to talk when your teeth are gnashing together like quern-stones, but she managed.

This time it was a bookshop he'd shoved her into, and the owner was happy for the customers to browse.

'You realize the man who writes these letters is clinically insane, don't you? He's obsessed to the point of delusion, talking about, what was it –' Orbilio's finger traced the lines '– *our destiny together.* And, look, this bit here, *united for all eternity.* These are death threats, Claudia!'

'He thinks they're love letters.'

'Love letters?' Orbilio almost choked. 'Threats and pornography?' The things this joker wanted to do were not only disgusting, degrading and debauched, they were downright illegal.

Claudia found she was shaking. She usually did when she read one of these letters. 'He's sick,' she admitted, 'but I don't think he's dangerous. Had he meant harm, he'd have tried it by now.'

Orbilio's eyes narrowed. 'How long has this sicko been writing to you?'

She tried to make light of it. 'I'm young, I'm rich and

I'm single. Cranks write all the time. Mostly I send a polite, but firm reply, it does the trick.'

'So you've written to him?'

'Possibly.' She heard him swear under his breath. Across the room, the shopkeeper was growing curious. 'He'll take this,' she said, picking up the nearest book and indicating Marcus.

Outside, Orbilio shook his head in disbelief. '*Weapons Drill Vol. IV*?'

'It was a snip, I thought, at three sesterces.'

'You missed the nought at the end.' He forced himself back to the matter in hand. 'This tide of filth.' He paused, looking at the charred edge where the bottom had burned away. 'I presume it's anonymous.'

After what had transpired in the alleyway, Claudia was too weary to lie. 'Sort of,' she said. 'He signs them "Magic".'

'Well, I'll arrange for a legionary to stand shifts,' Orbilio said swiftly – but not swiftly enough.

'Oh no, you won't!'

They were entering the Forum now, where advocates argued over law, customers argued over prices and philosophers argued over a load of abstract rubbish. Barbers set chairs upon the pavement in the hope the weather might improve, tavern keepers brought theirs indoors, because it wasn't going to. Furriers were busy, goldsmiths were not, florists had packed up and gone home. Under an awning attached to the gem cutter's, infant voices parrot-called the twenty-four letters that comprised the Latin alphabet, and further up the Via Sacra, a snake charmer played his flute to an audience of nil.

'Claudia, your life is in danger! An armed guard outside the door will scare this maniac away.'

Or turn his attentions elsewhere. In front rose the Rostra, the public speaking platform which stood twice as high as herself and was overlooked by bronze knights on snow-white marble columns. 'I don't want protection.' Her voice was as cold as the metal prows from the captured warships which studded the front of the Rostra.

'Why not?' Orbilio stepped forward to block her path. 'For gods' sake, woman! Tell me why not.'

Claudia considered him. He meant well, this patrician turning from red to purple as the bruises took their course. He was ambitious, and he took his job seriously. But . . . Pulling out her drawstring purse and keeping her eye fixed on a topknotted Sygambian in flowing scarlet robes, she fumbled around until her finger found the phial it was seeking. Then Claudia Seferius smiled a smile displaying her entire stock of ingenuity.

'Very well, Marcus Cornelius. All shall be revealed, but first you buy me lunch.'

Caught offguard, naked suspicion danced across his face, but being first and foremost a gentleman, he led the way past the prison where Nerva's thugs bemoaned their fate in chains and up the hill towards a tavern favoured by the gentry. Ordinarily it would be thronging to the rafters, but since the senate was in recess, it was quiet.

'If you must know, it's the aunts,' she explained, when they had settled at the table and given their orders. 'The old crabs plan to disinherit me.'

'Your husband's will was perfectly legal.' Orbilio knew, because he'd once had to try and disprove it. 'What's the problem?'

Claudia pulled a face. 'They believe they can prove me unfit, as a woman, to manage the inheritance. They want me to marry Porsenna.'

Orbilio buried a laugh in his handkerchief. They had more chance of building a snowman in summertime. 'Who,' he asked, keeping his kerchief close to hand, 'is Porsenna?' Outside, two small boys chased a piglet up the street.

'Their puppet,' she explained, sinking her teeth into a piping hot scallop dripping with garlic. 'The mouse man.'

A squid ring fell off Orbilio's knife. 'The what?'

'Porsenna breeds dormice for the banquets of the rich and famous.' Young, dull, pliable – what more could Larentia ask? Rumour had it, he spent most of his waking hours writing recipes for cooking his precious fattened profitmakers. 'So what I don't need,' she said, crunching on a stick of celery, 'is a soldier clumping about in armour to draw attention to myself.'

Orbilio laid down his chicken bone. 'Come on! Even your mother-in-law couldn't blame you for wanting protection against a madman.'

Claudia sipped at her wine. It was good. Better than Seferius wine, in fact. 'The problem with Magic is that somewhere along the line, he's started to believe it's reciprocal.' She speared a mushroom and waved it at Marcus. 'That's right. This creep actually thinks we're in a two-way relationship.'

'Larentia wouldn't believe that!'

Claudia leaned over and broke off a chunk of hot, steaming chestnut bread. 'Of course she wouldn't. But will that stop her convincing a judge I encouraged him?' The slightest excuse, no matter how tenuous. Think of the money at stake! 'So we're agreed, then. No legionaries?'

He tilted his chair back against the wall and folded his hands behind his head. 'No legionaries,' he agreed. 'Until after the old trouts have left.'

Claudia waited.

'But until then,' he continued eventually, 'I shall have to take other precautions to safeguard your life.'

Claudia set her drawstring bag upon the table and patted it. 'Such as?'

He even made out he was considering other options. 'You leave me no choice,' he said gravely. 'I shall have to protect you myself.'

Now why is it I had a feeling you'd say that? 'And just how do you plan to do that?'

'By moving in, you can pass me off as a relative, a servant, even your agent. We'll think of something.'

We certainly will. 'Oops.'

Bending down to retrieve Claudia's bracelet which had fallen on to the tiles. Orbilio thought he detected a flash of movement from the corner of his eye, but when he straightened up, she was helping them both to a rich gamey stew of venison and hare.

'I have a plan,' she said. There was no sign of the little blue bag on the table. 'It's one I've used before and I call it my Runaway Success.'

'Foolproof?' He was so suspicious, he almost checked under his plate.

'Foolproof.' But it takes half an hour. 'I'll explain, but in the meantime, tell me this. Do you think Jovi is in any danger?'

'Because he saw the "sleeping" lady, and possibly the

killer, who thinks he might identify him?' Orbilio mopped his stew with his bread. 'No,' he said decisively. 'My guess is that yes, Jovi saw the victim in the alley. It was dark, he was lost and frightened and alone, and he wanted help, but that's when the killer got lucky. I think the victim had already been knocked out – the other two had bruises on their skulls, that's how he ties them up and strips them without a struggle. So when Jovi came bumbling along, the killer simply melted into the shadows until the boy gave up.'

Around the tavern, smells of meat juices dripping from the spit mingled with guffaws of raucous male laughter from the corner. Logs from the fire crackled as the flames licked round their splintered edges.

'Then that's one cold-blooded bastard you are looking for.'

'Isn't he, now!' Marcus combed his hair with his hands. The torn flesh on his knuckles was healing over, she noticed. 'We know the girl was unharmed at that stage, and Jovi would certainly have said if she'd been naked, so having secured himself both victim and secluded killing ground, our man simply toughed it out.'

Roaring fire or not, it seemed cold all of a sudden.

'He? You think the killer's a man?'

'Do women do things like that to each other?'

Claudia shivered. 'Was he . . . slicing her up while Jovi and I were there?'

Orbilio pushed back his plate in distaste. 'That girl died in the early hours of the morning,' he said in reply, 'and she took one hell of a long time to do it. But to answer the question you are too damned proud to ask: no, Mistress Seferius, you could not have saved her life.'

His face had gone white and his lips were pursed to nothingness. 'Instead, I'd have had three bodies lying in the mortuary, instead of one.'

She waited for the lump in her throat to subside. 'And the only clue is a man whistling his dog?'

'That's one more than the previous two murders,' he said ruefully. 'Jupiter alone knows how many men whistle their dogs along the Argiletum at night, but I've got a man going back after dark to find out – and hopefully one of the witnesses can give us a pointer.'

Claudia swallowed a mouthful of wine, as much to get rid of the taste of that alley. 'What do you make of the market day connection?'

Orbilio ran his hands over his face. 'It suggests the killer, rather than his victims, comes from out of town, but what I don't understand are the knife wounds. Why twenty-seven?'

An elm log rolled off the fire and sat glowing against the brightly bronzed dog. The landlord returned it to the fire and, by way of thanks, it spat red-hot darts in his face.

'In addition,' Marcus continued, 'each victim had a distinctive tattoo on her shoulder. A blue dragon. Unfortunately, tracking down its significance takes time and resources.' He rubbed at his eyes. 'Both of which are denied me at present.'

For several long moments they stared into space, their thoughts converging on a young girl bleeding to her death in a stinking, dirty runnel and pondering the significance of chopping off her hair. Whatever the gesture symbolized for the killer and his victim, laying it in her lap after death meant the bastard had stayed around long enough to watch her die.

'Anything for afters?' The serving girl who came to clear away the tray was refreshingly cheerful. 'Cook does lovely buns, full of candied fruit and nuts they are.'

'Maybe later,' Orbilio said, and then, turning to Claudia, asked jauntily, 'So tell me, madam, what constitutes a Runaway Success?'

She smiled. 'Mostly a large dose of carob beans mixed with figs, dates and a dash of castor oil –'

He looked puzzled.

'– which for obvious reasons is best disguised by a very strong taste. A rich gamey sauce, for instance –'

He looked worried.

'– and it takes a half hour to work.'

He looked at the water clock.

'Runaway success?' he asked, feeling the first faint gripes in his stomach.

'Foolproof,' she smiled. 'And the latrines, I believe, are thatta way.'

IX

In a smoke-filled kitchen on the Caelian, a small boy clung to the broad hips of the girl from Thessaly and sobbed convulsively. Servants milled around him, and it wasn't that they were indifferent to his plight – they slipped him pomegranates and dates, and Hylas the carpenter even carved him a small wooden horse – but right now they were in a rush to provide for the deluge of womenfolk who, having returned from the ceremony on the Palatine, were looking forward to a good hot lunch, having changed their clothes, unpacked their belongings and then swapped sleeping accommodation, because no way would Julia share with Aemelia, which meant Fortunata had to sleep with Eppia, but what about Fannia, because everyone knows she snores.

Larentia, scrawny and shrewd, revelled in these wranglings – what better cover for a good poke round? Only her son's bedroom appeared locked and that, the steward informed her, had been so since the day Master Gaius had died and the mistress had retained the key. Slightly unsettled but not quite sure why, the old woman moved on to inspect the gold and silver plate using an inventory she'd drawn up from memory, because she'd never actually lived under this roof. Gaius had bought the property during the early days of his prosperity, and because his eldest son, her grandson, had been too young to take over the Etruscan estate, Larentia had acted as chatelaine, a position she enjoyed even after the boy had taken a wife. But there was nothing wrong with her memory!

'Buggery, sodomy and fuck!' She banged down the lid of the chest. Not only were the pieces on her mental list present and correct, it would appear the bitch was adding to them! Three silver platters as wide as a man's reach, and a gold fluted bowl with swing handles! 'Damnation!'

' . . . so I said to the mercer, either they all have red piping or none of them do . . .'

The shrill voice of Larentia's sister penetrated the walls, and that was another reason she chose to live in Etruria. Foolish women! She had no time for idleness, all her life she'd worked for what she got – her husband had been a builder of roads, for gods' sake – and yet these stupid cattle twitter on about jewellery, clothes and the hairdresser. Ach! Dragging her daughter, Julia, away from her unpacking, Larentia led the way to Claudia's office. Occasionally, and today was one of those times, she fell prone to pondering how she'd produced such a dull, plain duckling and why, later, the child did not do what others had so often obligingly done and turned into a swan. Julia had grown up a goose.

'Read the ledgers,' she instructed curtly, for her illiteracy remained a constant thorn in her side, even among her own family.

Julia was at once grateful, delighted and flattered and thumbed through the tablets and scrolls, calling out the figures for her mother to digest, her hooded eyes fair closed with excitement at the prospect of bringing down her sister-in-law. She had not forgotten the night, in this very house, when her own husband had made his advances. True, he'd come back from the encounter with a squashed and bleeding nose, but the insult had still stung. Her husband lusted after the bitch.

Literate Julia might be, numerate she was not. 'Well, Mother, what's the verdict?'

'It would appear,' said Larentia slowly, 'that the accounts are not only in apple-pie order, Gaius' business is thriving.'

'Shit.'

'Precisely.'

'Have you checked out her debts with the bankers and moneylenders?'

Larentia kicked the tripod brazier which was counteracting the dampness in the room and her mouth soured. 'What debts?'

'Shit!'

'Precisely!'

They took a long, lingering look at the intricate ivories on the shelf, especially that exquisite figure with a fawn round his shoulders and a peacock by his side, before moving into the dining room, where the life-size bronze of Venus served only to depress them further. The table was piled high with swordfish and salmon, peafowl and venison and at least five types of cheese – and was surrounded by a gaggle of excitable hens.

'... she gave me a beautiful little cameo for my birthday, I'll show it to you later ...'

'... my dear, I have it on the highest authority, this year's colour will definitely be coral ...'

'Fannia, have you just eaten that whole tray of quails eggs?'

The servers, to-ing and fro-ing with yet more silver platters, were truthfully able to report to Verres the cook that the gourmet dishes he'd prepared were much appreciated, especially the fricassee of antelope, although his peppered flamingo tongues were going down a treat.

And Jovi continued to hack. 'Why don't she come, Passi?'

Cypassis, having no answer, stroked his wracked shoulders and cooed into his hair. Even a five-year-old knew that by now there wasn't one square inch of Rome that had not been covered in an attempt to reunite him with his mother. Messages had been posted, criers were calling, and in the warrens where Jovi lived, word travels fast. Tight-lipped, Cypassis unhooked the balled fists from her tunic and led him away to the corner where the oil jars were stored. Two dark ovals stood stark on her sky-blue cotton tunic, their wetness cold through her undershift.

'Passi, have I been so very naughty?'

She fell down and hugged his hiccupping shoulders. 'Oh, Jovi! Of course you haven't!' She could feel him gulping against the lushness of her hair and her bones dissolved with pity. 'You're a good boy!'

Verres the cook, passing, rumpled the little lad's mop and offered to show him how you bone a hare then stuff it with truffles and oysters, if he liked? The head embedded itself deeper into Cypassis' neck.

Steam spiralled from bubbling saucepans. The cauldron which hung over the fire gurgled contentedly, and fat from the goat on the spit hissed as it dripped on the charcoal. A kitchen maid strained carrots in a giant iron ladle, then dipped bream into white wine and parsley, wrapped them in cabbage leaves and laid them on the hearth. A shanty started up, and before long the whole kitchen was alive to the rhythm, voices joining in whether they knew the words or not. Cypassis patted his convulsions to the beat as almonds were ground in a mortar and smoked sausages were cut down and fried. And she thought what a contented, happy scene it was, were it not for Jovi.

As another tune took over, she considered his mother's options. Too ill to claim her child, would she not send someone in her place? Cypassis could not understand abandoning a five-year-old to strangers and confusion. Who'd do such a thing? Tears streamed down her cheeks and filled her dimples right until the moment Verres the cook caught his finger on the gridiron and swore, with great fluency, in at least seven different languages.

Even Jovi laughed.

Up in his attic, the man who called himself Magic had his head bent low over the page. The light from his smoky tallow picked out patchwork walls blistering in the damp, cobwebs trailing from the ceiling and the remnants of a meal which had long since congealed. Six storeys below a dispute over a right of way was turning acrimonious, but for him, such things were trivia. A weight had been lifted from his heart, there was no time to lose. He smoothed out a clean sheet of parchment and flipped open the inkwell.

'*my beloved soon shall we be free—*'

He'd been so stupid! It was as clear as the waters from an Umbrian spring what had been happening. Other

People were keeping Claudia from her beloved Magic. His fingers curled into claws. It was his fault! He should have realized sooner! All those letters he had sent without a solitary word by return – it was obvious! Her letters had been intercepted. The knuckles on his hand grew white. Now he knew Other People were between them, it was easy. He wrote and told her so.

'*true love will always conquer*,' he wrote, and the candle guttered when he laughed. Theirs was a love which would last for all eternity. Other People could not keep them apart. He wrote that down as well.

'*other people can not keep us apart*.'

Magic laughed again, and had there been fresh eggs in the room they would have curdled. He could not be sure, of course, that Claudia now received his letters, not when Other People interfered. He'd have to send her something else. What? He chewed his bottom lip for inspiration. What would scream his feelings for her, let her know she had not been abandoned.

'*i have not abandoned you*.' Write that down as well. Cobs of sweat broke out on Magic's forehead. Somewhere, hundreds of letters, written in her own sweet hand, lay mouldering in a box. '*i will find them*,' oh, yes he would, and then he could take down all those poor, unhappy copies from his wall and nail up the genuine love-filled articles. All of them.

Well, now he knew his letters were being read by Other People, they ought to know who they were dealing with. Yessir, they ought.

'*when you my darling love slave press your rosy nipples to my lips and plead with me to whip and beat you—*'

He felt a jolting in his loins, and the nib flew across the page as he envisaged all that he would do. He described the taste of blood, the pain, the pure, exquisite torture . . . He had nearly filled the page before he remembered his mission.

'*and when we fly to heaven sated and complete then other people will not need to die.*'

Would they understand, he wondered? Yes, of course they would. They were clever people, these stealers of letters. Almost as clever as Magic was himself.

X

The door at which Claudia rapped was about as impersonal as a door can be. Hinges iron, studs without rust, timber durable, common, and because holm-oak rots down slowly, there were no clues as to the age of the door – a criterion which applied equally to the servant who opened it. Stolid and dough-faced with a nose like an anchor stone, the woman could have been any age from fifty-five to seventy. Her hands, puffed and red from scrubbing, offered no hint, her hair was dyed black and she wore a yellow scarf which concealed the lines around her neck. Claudia felt herself on shifting sands. Doorkeepers, *without exception*, were male.

'I'm here to see Kaeso,' she said breezily. 'Is he in?'

'Nnnn.'

Claudia thought irreverently of Cypassis telling Jovi about poor little Echo, spurned by Narcissus and reduced to repeating other people's endings. However, this was no cave and this, certainly, was no nymph. Not now. Not ever! Doughface was examining the visitor like a fisherman inspects a mackerel and Claudia felt her blood start to bubble.

'If it's too difficult, I'll rephrase the question. *Is he in*?'

'Nnnn.'

Just as Claudia was about to yank on the scarf round

this awful creature's neck, Echo stepped aside and wagged one swollen finger to indicate that the visitor should remain in the atrium. Had she been a dog, Claudia suspected she would have been expected to sit.

The hall, like the entrance, was miserably neutral. A bleak geometric mosaic, black, white and brown, hardly a challenge for the designer, and the walls had been painted yellow and green, the colours of spring, but the lack of ornamentation and the dogged repetition of colour blocks denied more imaginative connotations. There was, of course, the obligatory pool in the centre but again, this was a passive rectangle of water, not a sparkling, chattering fountain.

She could leave, of course. Walk out now. Hire another tracker, heaven knows there were plenty to choose from – men who traced runaway slaves, errant wives, missing children. But Kaeso had a reputation which went way beyond mere pursuit . . .

Time passed. Claudia's ears strained for sounds, and picked up none, and that was the worrying part. The street itself sat tucked away on the flat of the Quirinal, comprising mostly of tenements for the moderately well-off artisans, craftsmen, self-sufficient freedmen. A quiet, respectable suburb, where no dogs barked, no hawkers touted, no children kicked inflated pigs' bladders through your windows every half hour. But indoors? In a house this size, you'd expect to hear servants scurrying about, floors being swept, pans clattering in the kitchens. Here there was only silence. And where were the smells that make a home? The camphor scent of rinsed linen? Or yellow cones of juniper burning day and night to keep the snakes at bay?

Invisible eyes seemed to follow her every movement and gooseflesh crept up her arms. This was turning into an Assyrian horror story, one of those gruesome tales the desert nomads seemed so fond of as they sat around their camp fires, while jackals howled in the hills. *Let me tell the true tale of the House of Silence, where the door was held fast by invisible demons, imprisoning for eternity all who passed through its portals . . .*

Never had Claudia found stumping steps more reassuring, and she had to physically refrain from grabbing those red, chapped hands and showering them with kisses. This time, Echo eschewed vocal communication in favour of a jerk of the head and set a cracking pace up the atrium. The peristyle at the end offered shelter from the drizzle, although precious little comfort in the summer. No busts, no statues, no fountains, no shrines, just the one marble seat covered with birdlime. Even the garden was depressing, devoid of any plant that could not be classified as functional. At the far end of the peristyle, the door-keeper stopped short, flung wide a cypress door and all but pushed Claudia inside.

From the cold detachment of its spartan surroundings, the contrast here was dramatic. A log fire crackled majestically, filling the room with a haze of applewood smoke, and had the bear still been inside its skin on the hearth, no doubt this was the place it would have chosen to lie. The walls were painted a rich dark red, like old mellow wine, embellished with gold and with green, and from a lampstand dangled four bronze lights illuminating a vast assemblage of busts and curios. So busy was Claudia, digesting this warm, inviting treasure trove, that she failed to realize she had company.

'I trust my collection amuses you.'

She spun round. He was standing in the corner, in the shadow, perched against a chest. She would not show what he'd intended her to. 'Are you Kaeso, or simply another lackey?'

It was hard to tell, him being shaded, but she thought she caught a change of expression, which might have been amusement. Or then again, might not.

'I'm whoever you want me to be.' Was that a yes or a no?

'Then you're not the man I'm after,' she said. 'The man I seek is quick and decisive, and I've been waiting half an hour—'

'I am Kaeso.' He shifted his weight, that was all. 'And I very much regret the delay. You see, this is just a room I rent, Tucca had to fetch me.'

Tucca, not Echo. And this was not Narcissus, fallen in love with himself, there was not a mirror in the room. The voice remained in shadows.

'She might have explained.' Let him make small talk. Sooner or later he'd have to come out.

A flash of teeth showed in the corner. 'There is a slight problem with that,' replied Kaeso. 'Someone cut out her tongue. She's a mute.'

Claudia wanted to whistle, to say, 'No shit!' but held back.

'She lives here alone,' he was saying. 'Tends the whole house herself, apart from the groceries, and her daughter does that.'

'I'm surprised any man bedded her once, never mind enough times to give her a child.'

Claudia hadn't realized she'd spoken aloud until she

heard Kaeso chuckle. 'Oh, Tucca was married. In fact it was her husband who cut out her tongue.'

Bastard. 'Where is he now?' Despite herself, she was curious.

'Officially? Lost in a shipwreck. In practice? Planted in the lawn, between the bay tree and the yew. You passed him.'

Claudia tipped her head on one side. 'Are you a keen fan of Assyrian horror stories, by any chance?' she asked.

'No. Is it relevant?'

'How about Tucca?' she persisted. 'I suppose it's too much to hope she comes from a long line of desert nomads?'

This time his laughter was rich and unrestrained. 'You don't run with the pack, do you?'

Prising himself off his perch, Kaeso stepped forward and Claudia was glad she had steeled her senses earlier. Imagining some terrible deformity which had made him wary, she was unprepared for raw perfection.

'No, sir, I do not.'

Claudia watched him cross the room to stoke the fire. As to his age, she put him at thirty, but admitted she might be out five years either way. Not exceptionally tall, he was strong, she could see rounded biceps strain the sleeves of his tunic, saw powerful calves below the muscular knees of the athlete. On a man who trains hard in the gymnasium, it was unusual to see collar-length hair. In the darkened recess, it looked dark and yet now, under the light, it seemed almost fair. Tawny.

'Please. Take a seat.' He poured white wine into pale-green slender glasses, but instead of taking the second chair, sat on the bearskin rug at Claudia's feet, staring into the crackling flames. His profile was pointed, rugged even, with a jaw that was sharp rather than square. His musky scent mingled with the applewood burning in the hearth, and now his hair seemed golden. Sleek.

Oh, yes. The war machine was sleek.

As the logs glowed red, Claudia waited.

'Claudia Seferius,' he said lazily, his grey eyes watching soot motes dance up the chimney.

She felt a jolt down the length of her spine. She had not given Tucca her name.

Kaeso rose to his feet and began to pace the room. 'Let me think. Your husband died last September, no, I'm wrong . . . last August. He bequeathed the entire estate to his young widow and nothing whatsoever to his family.' He turned his sharp, lean face towards her. 'Contrary to expectations, though, the widow did not liquidate the assets, she tried to make a go of it.'

Claudia stared into her glass and hoped her cheeks were not as red as she feared. The reflection in the glass showed no break in the fluidity of his tread.

'But there are problems for a woman going solo in commerce. The men, they are against her. They will not accept her in the Wine Merchants Guild, and thus they hope to ruin her.'

Now when Claudia's face burned, it was from fury. Bastards! Once close friends of Gaius, the minute he died they were like vultures, circling his business and hoping to pick it clean without cost to either coin or conscience.

'They won't,' was all she replied. She would beat these sons of bitches, so help her, yes she would. She would bring them crawling on their knees. 'But that's not why I'm here.'

The powerhouse faltered in his pacing. 'Is it not?' He padded back and coiled himself in the empty chair. 'Then what does bring you to Kaeso?'

'I heard you are very good at finding people.'

He bridged his fingers and considered her. 'Not always do they wish to be found,' he replied.

'But you find them, nonetheless,' she countered, and he smiled.

'Are you hungry?' he asked, drawing a tray of steaming chestnuts from the fire.

Watching as he squatted on the bearskin, one knee raised, prising open shells, Claudia saw now the reason for the apparent change in hair colour. It was not one shade, but a blend of several making up the whole. As one of the nuts proved stubborn, he dropped it, sucking at the finger it had scorched, and the long mane bounced. Yes, mane. In fact, now she came to think of it, there was much of the animal in Kaeso. The pointed features, the strong grey eyes, the trained physique, the lope. For a moment, she could not place the animal. Then suddenly it came. The wolf. The ultimate tracking beast.

When he'd finished digging out the chestnuts, he passed half across, dribbling them slowly into Claudia's cupped palms. Between them, logs crackled and spat and glowed orange, and the apple-scented smoke spiralled upwards, blue and hazy. Finally, Kaeso sat back in his chair, put his feet on the table and said, 'Who is it you want found and why?'

Claudia nibbled the succulent nuts. 'Why is not your concern.'

'I beg to differ. Have another glass of wine.'

She studied the collection of artworks. Busts, ivories,

a faience vase showing leaping billygoats, a marble cat with jewelled eyes which must be at least five centuries old.

'I want you to locate a man who calls himself Magic,' she said. 'He signs his letters with the seal of the cobra.'

Kaeso unfurled himself from the chair and threw a log on to a fire which did not need additional fuel. 'Is that all you have to go on?'

He meant, is that all you intend to give me.

'Those are the only tangible facts I have,' she replied slowly. 'But if, during the course of your enquiries, you come across a woman who has mislaid a small son answering to Jovi—'

'And what,' interrupted Kaeso, 'shall I tell this Magic when I find him?'

'Tell him?' Claudia set down her glass and leaned forward. 'My dear Kaeso, I think you are under something of a misapprehension. I don't want you to *tell* this Magic anything.' She shot him a dazzling smile. 'I want you to kill him.'

XI

Marcus Cornelius Orbilio emerged from the tavern, gingerly rubbing his belly and deliberating which direction to take next. Should he turn right and head for the Field of Mars, because if there was loose talk to be overheard, it was there at the baths and along the porticoes, amongst the running, wrestling and fencing? Or ought he to cut up to the Palatine, give his report to his boss and catch an update on policy and matters of state? He sighed. It was all very well, wanting to clap the Market Day Murderer in irons, but when the security of the Empire was at stake, a man had to be clear about his priorities. Nevertheless, there was a Scythian tattooist on the Vicus Tuscus, was there not, who might shed light on blue dragons . . .?

Having made his decision and with his thoughts firmly centred on a wild adventuress who made his heart turn somersaults, Orbilio went out of Silversmith's Rise. Say what you like about the weather, it never affected life in the Forum. From the winter winds which blew straight off the marshes to sticky summers riddled with insects, the hucksters continued to go with the flow. On the wet, slippery steps of Concord's temple, cloth merchants spread gaily coloured bales to tempt the ladies, while over by the basilica, fortune-tellers promised riches and happiness for the price of a meal, and four men carried a strong box to a depository.

'Marcus!' Every man within a half-mile radius must have halted, not just him.

Waving from a seat sheltered by the sacred lotus tree of Vulcan was his Great Aunt Daphne. Orbilio groaned inwardly. Rumour had it, his grandfather's sister slept in a bath full of ice and thrived on a diet of cobbles and vinegar. Now she was bearing down like a trireme in battle.

'Long time no see! Still playing Greeks and Spartans, are we?'

'If you mean, am I still attached to the Security Police, the answer is yes,' he smiled. Greeks and Spartans, indeed!

Behind her, four liveried slaves struggled with baskets and packages wrapped in oiled cloth. Rain could not and would not deter Daphne from her purpose. Knowing her, it moved out of her path.

'I'm all for a boy sowing his oats while he's single but now it's time you got yourself a proper job, my lad. Your cousins have magisterial seats, and you've a lot of catching up to do, if you plan to take a seat in there.'

She pointed over his shoulder to the Senate House, with the famous letters SPQR engraved on its pediment. Smallest Problem Quick Retreat, he mused irreverently, or Superior Profile Questionable Reasons?

'My career isn't a game, Daphne—'

'Your father never forgave you for turning your back on a good career in law. He'd spin in his tomb to think you were spurning the family tradition!'

A troop of soldiers marching at the double scattered street vendors and pedestrians alike, their armour jangling, their hobnail boots clanking in eerie unison. In the confusion, a porter's pole caught the edge of a perfumer's tray and fragrances of citrus oils and lilac, hyacinth and oakmoss exploded as his phials hit the flagstones.

'There are alternative routes to the Senate,' Orbilio explained patiently.

'Come to dinner tonight, Marcus. It so happens your uncle will be entertaining a praetor as well as a retired consul and it will do you no harm to become acquainted with the men who have influence in this city.'

'Tonight? Sorry—'

'The praetor's daughter is ripe for marriage and you've been single too long. You need a wife and a family. Marcus – these things count at election time.'

'I've been married once,' he reminded her. 'She ran off to Lusitania with a sea captain, remember?'

'Tch! I told your uncle at the time there was too much inbreeding in that girl's lineage, but you're divorced now, nothing to stop—'

'Excuse me,' a small voice piped up alongside. 'Are you Mistress Lovernius?'

Marcus looked down. A sprite, no taller than his shoulder, her fair hair caught loosely in a bright cerise ribbon, smiled up at his great-aunt. Salvation came in the most unexpected packages, he thought cheerfully.

'Who wants to know?' she barked.

The sprite held her ground. 'Mistress *Daphne* Lovernius?' Clean clothes on a personable frame clearly passed muster with the older woman, because she nodded curtly. 'Then I wonder, might I have a brief word?' The scrubbed face turned speedwell blue eyes upon Marcus. 'In private?'

Daphne pulled a face which suggested she supposed

so and with a great sense of release, Orbilio turned towards the Vicus Tuscus where the tattooist plied his trade.

'I'd be much obliged if you'd wait for me, Marcus!'

Bugger. So this is what a thrush feels, caught in the hunter's net. You could *see* a way through, but finding it was a different matter entirely . . .

'But of course, Daphne.' His professional smile encompassed the elfin creature as well, and although his great-aunt was clearly baffled by the young girl's approach, Orbilio could hazard a strong guess. She was perfect for the job. Older than she looked, with her long fair hair and sing-song voice, that wholesome appearance would be her stock-in-trade.

He was damned if he'd loiter in the rain, so he took himself up the steps to shelter inside the soaring temple of Juno's handsome father, god of agriculture and holder of the state reserves. Poor old Saturn! No sooner had his temple been restored after decades of neglect than it promptly burned down, but Augustus invested the proceeds from a Syrian campaign to create a majestic new building, with columns six times the height of a man and marble and gold in eye-watering abundance. The Great Laws of Rome, inscribed on bronze tablets and illuminated by torchlight, hung on the back wall for everyone to read, but below the shrine, secret and well guarded, sat the treasury. Many a thief had wandered round, paying his respects at the wooden feet of Saturn, working out how to get his hands upon those ingots. None had so far succeeded.

'Diabolical child!' Daphne thundered, marching down the aisle to join her nephew. 'Of all the bloody cheek!'

'Begging?' he suggested amiably, his eyes fixed on a sickle the height of a cartwheel in Saturn's right hand. A hard-luck story from a well-dressed character often proved remunerative.

His great aunt shot him a glance. 'I suppose I'd better tell you,' she said sourly. 'In your line of business, you'd probably find out soon enough, now that little bitch has aired it.' She paused, looking up at the giant statue for a full thirty seconds before saying, 'Walk me home.'

'I—' He thought of the coups and the murders and the crises rocking the Empire, and then looked at this proud, old woman, dwarfed by the temple. 'I'd be delighted.'

As she slipped her arm into his, he realized that Daphne had been considerably rattled by the encounter. All her energies had been expended in bluster, and he was not surprised that she did not speak until they reached the Esquiline, that pocket of aristocracy known as Nob Hill, and even then it was not to him, but to dismiss her servants. Continuing past her own front door, she led him to the public gardens which, unsurprisingly on a day like this, were deserted. Why this urgent need for privacy, he wondered, passing the nodding purple heads of fritillaries and spikes of larkspur pushing up through feathery leaves. The air was heavy with the resinous scent of terebinth trees and with the sound of songbirds calling out their territories.

'There.' Daphne pointed past the elegant portico which, on a summer's day, would cast shade on the rippling watercourses, then tersely addressed the gardener clipping the laurels. 'Leave us.'

His protestations were cut short at the appearance of silver, and Marcus was steered towards an evergreen grotto of box, bay and myrtle, where even the marble seat was dry. Across the pond, a blackbird trilled from a birch.

'I don't suppose you remember Penelope?' she said with a deep exhalation of breath.

And suddenly the reason for secrecy became clear. Marcus Cornelius felt his stomach flip over. For eighteen years that name had been taboo in his family.

'Actually, I do.' It was an effort to make his voice neutral, but he knew he'd succeeded. Penelope, the youngest of Daphne's five daughters, had committed suicide when Marcus had been too young to understand the meaning of the word scandal. But he cherished vivid memories. Her long, fair lashes making 'butterfly kisses' on his cheek. Teaching him to climb trees. Playing tag in the garden. And she bought him a kitten, he recalled, which ran away two days later. 'She was very beautiful.'

Daphne gave a bitter smile. 'Perhaps if she'd looked like a carthorse,' she said 'life would have run smoother for us all.'

A maelstrom of emotion surged up to engulf him. Feelings which, by necessity, he'd kept hidden for most of his life swam now before him. Penelope had meant more to him than his own mother; she'd been brother, sister, friend and conspirator rolled into one, a girl who never walked when she could run and whose laughter and lullabies brightened days like summer heather. For a boy of seven, her death – sudden and without explanation – was like the very sun had set for ever. Who would he chase butterflies with now? Or ride piggyback? The day Penelope died, his childish world became a darker, quieter, rather sombre place and just to speak her name could earn him a thrashing.

For years afterwards he had wondered: was it his fault she was dead? Had he, somehow, failed her?

Secretly, painfully, on each anniversary of her death, Marcus Cornelius Orbilio would consign a garland of poppies, Penelope's favourite flower, into the Tiber where she'd thrown her weighted body.

He swallowed hard. 'She'd be thirty-eight by now.'

'What? Oh. Oh, yes.' Daphne did not wish to be reminded of her own advancing years. 'Anyway, the point is, that . . . that *creature* back there—'

'Yes?' he prompted, inhaling the soothing, aromatic mix of evergreens as a goldfinch searched the germanders.

His aunt gave an imperious sniff. 'Penelope was touched from birth, singing like a common slave, and was there ever a girl for giggling! No decorum, that child. You won't remember, of course—'

He saw no gain in contradiction.

'—but we found her an excellent husband, son of a tribune from Crete. Or was it Mauritania? I don't recall his name offhand, but he died somewhere in Gaul a year before Penelope . . .' She cleared her throat. 'What I'm saying, Marcus, is that it wasn't as though she had nothing to *show* for herself.'

Orbilio felt his world spin. Was this a dream? A nightmare? After eighteen years of the strictest silence, was he really sitting in a sheltered grotto listening to his great-aunt talk about Penelope as though she was the butcher's wife and not her own flesh and blood? Did suicide bring such shame that Daphne could not recall things that even he, young as he had been, could remember in such detail? Or had she never cared how Penelope doted on her *Cypriot* husband? The devastation she'd felt at his death not in Gaul but Pannonia? And, tragically, how the news brought on a miscarriage?

'I don't know what got into my daughter,' muttered Daphne. 'As soon as we heard he was dead, I fixed her up with a merchant from Alexandria, and how did she repay me? Marcus, as much as I tried to beat common sense into that girl, she flat out refused to marry him and suddenly it was men, men, men. Couldn't get enough of them, the dirty little slut. I said to your uncle at the time, she's no child of mine . . .'

Her indignation droned on, but Marcus failed to hear the diatribe and his heart cried back through time. He saw a vibrant young woman laid prostrate with grief, seeking love and affection wherever she could find it and whose frantic succession of lovers was her own way of mourning the loss of her soulmate; a means to forget. How hard was Daphne's heart? Croesus, the girl was twenty, for gods' sake! Had her parents no pity?

'What has that to do with the girl in the Forum?' he asked bluntly.

'Her!' Daphne snorted. 'Crawls out of the woodwork this . . . this . . . Annia she calls herself. Tells me she's Penelope's daughter—'

'*What*?'

'Expected me to take her in, you know. Eighteen years on, I ask you! Have you ever heard anything so ridiculous? I told her straight, you're lucky to be alive, I said; if I'd had my way, you'd have been strangled at birth. Conniving little cow's after money, that's my guess.'

His thoughts were tumbling. He couldn't take it in.

'Is . . . is it true?' Was that fair-haired sprite really his beloved Penelope's child?

'Probably,' replied Daphne, without a shred of remorse. 'She showed me the ring we'd tied round her neck when we handed her over. Not an heirloom, of course, just a cheap band.'

Annia. Her name was Annia. 'She's very pretty,' he said carefully. Dammit, he wished he'd paid more attention to the girl! 'Who's her father?'

Daphne's lips pursed. 'Who indeed? Marcus, that baggage slept with half the men in this city, she could be anyone's from a senator's to a peddlar's, and I can't think why Penelope made such a fuss when we took the brat away!'

'Wait!' Wait a minute. 'You're saying she wanted to keep her?'

'By the gods, Marcus, you should have heard the fuss she made. "My baby, my baby",' mimicked Daphne. 'Anyone would think she'd planned the bloody thing right from the outset.'

Mother of Tarquin! It was worse than he thought! Distraught after the death of her husband, Penelope had sought to replace him with the love of a child. The same child who was snatched from its birth bed and handed to—

'Who fostered the child?' he asked.

'Fostered?' Daphne stared at her nephew as though he was covered in lime green spots. 'Good grief, boy, you don't foster creatures like that. I handed it over to some Babylonian slave dealer, forget his name now. He raises them like cattle, of course, but they have a decent placement at the end and you've only got to look at madam there to see we did the right thing.'

Did the right thing? Wrenching a longed-for baby from

its pleading mother's arms? Handing it over to be raised 'like cattle'? Blind to the realization that life without husband or child was too much for a bereaved girl to bear . . .

Did the right thing?

By the time the whirling eddy in his head had subsided, Marcus Cornelius Orbilio was alone in the park. The goldfinch had gone, the blackbird had gone, but the scent of the myrtle had grown sickly and overpowering. He felt sick. Very sick. Putting his head between his knees until the nausea passed, he wondered whether he'd ever be able to speak civilly to Daphne again.

He could not say how many times he walked round the garden, past the swathes of blue Gaulish crocuses and the gurgling fountains. He did not hear the croak of the frogs in the water margins, or the piercing cry of the peacock in the aviary. He saw only a wood sprite, a fair-haired nymph with wide, blue eyes and slender white hands and felt a twist in his gut that he should have mistaken Penelope's child for a con-artist. How closely Annia resembled her mother he had no idea. Eighteen repressed years had passed, precise features were no longer available to his memory, only vague images which involved sunshine and laughter. But Penelope, too, had had fine golden tresses, he would comb them while they sat on the river bank and she made flower chains and read aloud the poetry she composed for her husband fighting in the Balkans.

Was the shame of bearing a bastard worth the price of one life and the condemnation to slavery of another? The Egyptians had it right, Marcus thought, weighing a person's heart against a feather for their place in the afterlife. Would Daphne bully her way through that trial as well?

'Shit!' Orbilio punched his fist into the palm of his hand.

It was his musing on foreign mythology that made the connection. From Egypt, his mind travelled to Babylon. From Babylon to its patron god, Marduk. And from Marduk to the dragon! The blue dragon tattoo! It could not be coincidence. Those girls who had died slashed to ribbons had been raised by the Babylonian, it was his brand that they bore.

And Annia would be branded the same way! Marcus Cornelius buried his head in his hands and prayed.

'Help me, Penelope. Help me find your daughter.'

Before the Market Day Murderer does.

XII

As dusk spread her cloak across the seven hills of Rome, Claudia slipped in unseen through the garden entrance. The drizzle had stopped. Or had it? It was the sort of day when you could barely tell the difference. Transparent beads of moisture had collected on the junipers and cypress, and fairy pools of water had formed in the crucibles of the peonies; well, water was fine in its place, but what Claudia needed to unwind with was wine, and strong enough to sink a horseshoe, if you please. So then. A glass (make it a jug) of Falernian. A quiet hour reading Virgil, a lavender massage, supper sent to her room. Definitely no sucking up to the old boilers, who'd only want to gossip about the Market Day Murders.

'Claudia.' Fannia was waiting indoors in ambush. 'My bolster – I'm sure it isn't swansdown, and you know how delicate I am. Could you get it changed, or I'll never sleep a wink?'

This, after seeing a girl hacked to mincemeat and just minutes after she had hired a professional assassin to dispose of the maniac who threatened to torture the life out of her! Nevertheless, Claudia was sure she had a winsome smile somewhere.

'My dear Fannia, for your pillow I bought soft *cygnet*

down.' Chickens, swans, they're all birds, aren't they? 'Trust me, you'll sleep well tonight.'

As will the rest of the old trouts. I'm lacing your drinks.

But no sooner had Fannia clucked off, than Claudia's escape route was blocked by a skinny creature with watery eyes and prominent cheekbones who came flying down the staircase. She appeared to be clutching a hairless brown rat under her arm.

'Cousin Claudia! Oh, Cousin Claudia, what are you going to do about Hercules?'

In the Forum, in the colonnades, in the public libraries you will hear philosophers argue daily the finer points of rhetoric. Should one, for instance, go ahead with a birthday celebration, even though the augur has cautioned against it? If the man you find in bed with your wife is your boss, do you still go ahead and castrate him? But never do you hear it mooted what one should do about Hercules.

Claudia stalled for time. 'It's Cousin Fortunata, is it not? I don't believe we've met I'm—'

'It's affected his appetite, you know. Put him right off his din-dins, hasn't it, Herky?'

Claudia goggled. Hercules? That sawn-off runt's named after the hero who undertook feats no other mortal dared? Herky let out a high-pitched yelp, and Claudia realized it wasn't vermin but some sort of dog Fortunata had in an armlock, and thought wistfully that if only the moneylender in the Subura had had a pack of Herkies, it would have been a different story yesterday!

'Terrified, weren't you, baby? Yes, you were. Some spiteful boss-eyed cat chased Mummy's Herky-perky under the bed and Mummy had to throw a glass of water over the nasty beastie. He's very highly strung, you know.'

Not strung up high enough, in my opinion. 'Shall I take care of Herkykins? Come on, darling, come to Cousin Claudie.' She whipped the lapdog out of Fortunata's arms, marched into the kitchens and thrust it at the nearest kitchen maid.

'I can't cook that,' the woman squealed. 'It's still alive!'

Pity. It would have gone down well with a pepper sauce and parsley. 'Find a cellar, lock it in,' she ordered. I'll not have him teasing Drusilla like that! 'What is it, Verres?'

'I was wondering,' said the cook, 'which wines you'd like serving with dinner.'

'Try giving them saucers of milk.' Claudia turned to Leonides, warming his backside by the bread oven. A row of pastry piglets cooled on the rack, and a batch of olive dough was proving in an earthenware bowl covered with linen. 'You miserable traitor!' She picked up a broad-bladed flesh knife and when she pressed it to the tip of the Macedonian's nose, the squeak that came from his throat was not too dissimilar to the one which Herky gave when he bounced off the cellar step. 'Right now I have but one household steward, but I am quite prepared to convert you into a dozen, thinner versions unless you answer truthfully. Did you or did you not show Marcus Cornelius Orbilio my crank mail?'

Someone must have put more charcoals in the bread oven, because sweat began pouring down his face. 'Well . . .'

'Well is not a condition you'll be in for long. Answer me!'

'It was for your own good, madam—'

For your own good. Can any words strike terror into a soul the way those four can? 'I shall be the judge of what's good for me, Leonides, and if I ever catch you with my welfare at heart again, I'll turn you into a human torch and you can light my house for a week, understood?'

A toad-like croak escaped from his mouth and, satisfied this was as close as he was physically able to manage by way of a grovelling apology, Claudia impaled a couple of hot pastry piglets on her knife and flounced off into the atrium.

'Jovi!' Horror of horrors, he was buck-naked in the fountain playing with what had, until recently, been a very elegant potted fern. 'Out!' she hissed. 'Right now!'

'I've given old Passi the slip,' he said, rubbing soil into his hair. 'She thinks I'm in the bog with the guts-ache.'

'And so you will be when I'm finished with you. Out of there, this instant!'

Would anyone notice the colour of the water if she scattered petals on the top? From the upper galleries floated down the sounds of womenfolk preparing for an evening, the scrape of clothes chests, barked instructions, the sickly mix of unguents, creams and perfumes. Sweet Juno, please let the old crabs be perfectionists! Please don't let them come down yet! As Claudia lunged for the boy, he darted out of the way, crashing the flat of his hands on the water. To some extent she sympathized. Previously, when he'd encountered the stuff, it had always come in a pail. After five attempts, however, Claudia was ready to negotiate.

'If you come out of the pool, I'll let you play there all

day tomorrow and we'll even heat the water for you, how does that sound?'

'Can I keep the plant?'

Call that a plant? 'Yours for ever, Jovi. Only come here, please.'

'Do I get a hug, too?'

Anything, anything, just name your price! I'll give you the sun, the moon and the stars, only please, please climb out of the pool before those wretched aunts find out!

'Ah, Larentia. Julia. How nice.'

It was too late now for explanations, anything she said would seem like a cover-up. Imagine it from Larentia's viewpoint. She walks in to be confronted by her son's widow and a small boy in his birthday suit, cuddled up so tight they're both dripping wet and covered with mud. Could one paint a cosier picture of domesticity? Jovi jumped down and began to prattle about everything and nothing to his new audience, and Claudia decided her only recourse was to silence. Even when Jovi told them proudly he had no idea who his father was and Larentia snapped 'I'll bet you don't, boy!', Claudia merely clamped her teeth tighter together. When that dessicated old bag learned the truth, there would not be a plate large enough on which to serve her humble pie! In the meantime, it was reward enough watching her frosty-faced sister-in-law turn puce when Jovi, quite without guile, took it upon himself to show Julia his willie.

After a mortified Cypassis had rounded up the runaway, Larentia crossed one hand over the other on her stomach and turned to face her daughter-in-law. 'I think,' she said, spitting out one word at a time, 'this might be as good a time as any to discuss finance, so let us begin with my granddaughter's dowry.'

Well done, Larentia! Just when I thought we were only ever going to eat the bloody thing, you finally start talking turkey!

The dowry, of course, was a sensitive issue. Legally the girl was Claudia's stepdaughter, but from birth, Gaius had foisted his unwanted daughter on to his frigid, childless sister. If for nothing else, Claudia had loved him for that, because in the five years that Claudia had known her, the girl had proved awkward and sulky and dull, traits which in children can be overlooked, forgiven even, but not when she was entering womanhood and a competitive marriage market. Even in an arranged marriage, a man needs to feel some attraction for his wife. Claudia's stepdaughter had all the sex appeal of a plucked goose.

'Or would you,' snapped Larentia, 'prefer we start with Julia's endowment?'

Claudia carefully examined her nails. The lyre player she had hired for the evening began to warm up in the banqueting hall. 'Since when, pray, did Julia have an endowment?' she asked quietly. Gaius had left Claudia the lot.

The old woman's eyes narrowed. Clearly she had been expecting blackmail to be an easier path. 'Morally—' she began.

'Morally?' Claudia evicted soil from under her thumbnail. 'A strange word to use, when you and I both know, Larentia, any money I bestow on Julia would be swallowed up by her wastrel of a husband—'

'What?' squawked Julia. 'How dare you call my—'

'—who has already "borrowed" his foster child's generous annuity.'

As Julia fought to grasp the issues, it occurred to her that both women were talking as though she wasn't here. She'd expect that gold-digging whore to cold-shoulder her, but Mother?

'It's quite beyond belief,' continued Claudia, raising her voice to override Julia's shrill protests, 'how an architect can run short of money when the Emperor is undertaking the restoration of over eighty public buildings and temples, not to mention flood defences, bridges, aqueducts and parks.'

Larentia waved that aside. 'Everyone knows my son-in-law's a prat—' She broke off and turned to Julia. 'For gods' sakes, woman, if you have nothing sensible to say, go away. Go on! Shoo!'

For several seconds, Julia's mouth opened and closed like a river pike before she finally withdrew, eyes brimming. But beneath the tears, Claudia observed something the old woman had not – Julia's burning hatred for Larentia. Julia was thirty-five. It was not an age to suffer humiliation lightly, especially in the face of the enemy.

Larentia waited until her daughter left the hall. 'My point, you money-grubbing bitch, is that whatever my son-in-law's faults, it's not fair Julia should suffer.'

'So invite her to live with you in Etruria. I'll increase your allowance to cover the pair of you.'

'I'm not sharing a roof with that self-righteous cow and you know it. I have a good life up at the villa, I've got friends—'

'Do you all fly out of the same cave at nightfall?'

A bony claw jabbed into Claudia's breastbone. 'Think

twice about mocking me, you degenerate hussy. You can't parade your bastard brat under *my* nose and get away with it.'

Bored with her cuticles, Claudia settled herself on the edge of the pool and threw one long leg over the other. 'Maybe I'll get married again,' she said lightly.

The changes which skipped over Larentia's face were pure entertainment. Surprise. Disbelief. Amusement. Puzzlement. Fear.

Claudia trailed one of the severed fern fronds in the water and didn't wait for Larentia to stop spluttering. 'As a widow, I'm a free agent.' She flashed the old witch a keen glance. 'And if the man I choose happens to be a butcher's boy, then a butcher's boy I shall marry.'

'You'll do no such thing!' snapped Larentia. 'Ours is not a family of alley cats! Respectable families don't cross-breed and you'll do well to bear that in mind!'

Her husband had been a humble road builder. It had been Gaius, her son, who had slogged night and day to build up a business and establish a reputation for his fine wines. Gaius who had raised the family from freeborn to high-ranking equestrian status. Gaius who had married his silly sister to an up-and-coming architect. *Gaius who died and left all his money to some high-handed bitch instead of his own blood relatives!*

Larentia looked as though a rotting rodent had been wedged up her nostril. 'Tch! We're getting nowhere!' she snapped. 'But just you remember, you can't wriggle out of your obligations, my girl.'

'Why, Larentia!' Claudia's eyelashes fluttered like butterflies round a hyssop bush. 'Let me show you the accounts some time, dear.' Another delectable flash of suspicion crossed the old woman's face. 'The business is booming, I have extended wine sales right across the country and am hoping to expand into Gaul in the summer. If I chose, the dowry could be double what Gaius had promised.'

Greed lit the old cat's rheumy eyes like candles at Saturnalia, but she still had the last word.

'Frankly, daughter-in-law, your business acumen surprises me, but make no mistake. When I find the father of that brat and prove you cheated on my son. I'll have you disinherited as an adulteress and thrown on the street with barely a rag to your name.'

She stormed off to her room, leaving Claudia fanning the warmth which had rushed to her cheeks. On the whole, though, Claudia felt she had argued her case rather well, considering the business was foundering and she was deeply in debt; and, whilst Jovi might not be her child, if Larentia actually dug deep enough, she'd have cause to throw Claudia Seferius out on the street at least two dozen times.

In a house of a very different shape, in a room of very different furnishings, a weapon lay swaddled in cotton. The cotton was maroon, to match the cornelians in the knife's handle, for this was no common kitchen knife, no carpenter's companion, no genteel dining implement. Once it had been an illustrious heirloom, handed down from father to son upon each boy's coming of age, but that had been during the time of the Republic. Since then, civil wars had ravaged three generations, taking its toll just as heavily on the nobility as on the plebeians and the knife had suffered a similarly chequered career.

Stolen by a trusted secretary upon the death of its owner and sold for a mere fraction of its value, it first passed to a legate, who bequeathed it to his grandson, who in turn was captured by buccaneers off Gaul and held for ransom. For a while the knife did sterling service, changing hands in a series of fierce piratical raids until it was requisitioned in the name of the Empire by the captain of a warship who bequeathed it to his only child, a daughter. She, having no use for such an artefact, bejewelled or otherwise, sold it for enough to buy a small house in Frascati to keep her handsome Cretan lover safe from the prying eyes of her fat and ageing husband. Then again, it could have been because she had learned that, way back in its bloody history, the weapon had been given a name.

Nemesis.

But whatever her reasons for selling, the knife was back where it belonged. With a fond and loving owner, one who would cherish its sinister beauty and keep the blade sharper than any barber's razor.

Had the weapon ears, it would have heard, as the Day of Luna faded, the flurry of activity which accompanies any household as it settles for the night. The splash of washbasins being emptied with iron ladles. The clatter of shutters opening and closing, as hopeful eyes once more wondered if the weather wasn't changing for the better. Instead, the sumptuous weapon was left to reminisce, inside its wine-dark cotton shroud, on its fortunes and adventures; how its worth had varied from owner to owner, and how its owners, too, had varied – male to female, noble to criminal, light of touch to downright light-fingered. And yet, with the exception of the naval captain's daughter, every owner from the date of its first and splendid forging had used the weapon to kill and to maim. Sometimes in anger, maybe in defence, all too often in war, that same thin blade had slipped between ribs or sliced through a windpipe, leaving behind scars and widows in its wake.

The household slid into a silence broken only by the occasional coo of a pigeon in the roofspace or the creak of a mattress as its occupant turned. When the air began to chill, the knife was removed from its hiding place and laid upon a bed, the cotton drawn back, fold by tender fold, until the cornelians glinted in the single flickering flame of a candle and the blade shone blue in the shadows.

'Tomorrow the sun moves into Aries,' a voice whispered as a finger traced the line of the blade. 'Tomorrow, the temple of the goddess they call Fortune will be purified, and you know who worships Fortune, don't you? Women!'

A cloth began to buff the blood-red gems.

'Not rich bitches – that lot pray to Venus. We're talking slaves and whores, Nemesis, which means. . .'

Warm breath misted the steel, prior to the blade being burnished.

'We don't have to wait until market day for our special girlies to be out.'

XIII

Fortune's Day, and about time, too. I thought the night would never end! Tumbling out of bed, Claudia flung wide the shutters, to be greeted by another damp and misty morn, which barely dispelled the grisly images which had torn at her dreams, jolting her awake over and over again to lie, trembling in the darkness, as she re-lived the terror of twenty-seven savage cuts. What hatred, she wondered, peeling off her nightshift and trickling water from the jar into the washbasin, inspired a man not only to inflict immense pain upon a fellow human being, but deprive them of their dignity in the process? The mind that could abandon them, bound and naked, in a lake of congealed blood amid rotting turnips and spokeless wheels as though they, too, were the detritus of society, transcended comprehension.

Claudia drew deep breaths and waited for her stomach to stop churning. Thank Jupiter, her involvement in this wretched murder was finished! Slowly she reached for the pumice. She'd done her bit by helping to pinpoint the timing and by encouraging Supersleuth to air his worries in the tavern and, since he'd posted a soldier in the Argiletum, no doubt there'd be a clutch of reliable witnesses lined up already. One might even be able to identify the killer.

She blotted her face with a towel. No, that chapter in her life (and the tall dark patrician that went with it) was well and truly closed. The Runaway Success saw to that. Right now, she was more concerned about Kaeso!

From the moment she knocked on Tucca's door, he'd been playing with her. Why? Because she needed him more than he needed her? Who knows? But one thing was sure, the meeting in that mellow room of curios had ended in a stand-off. For a fraction of a second, as she rubbed the moisturing sap of aloes into her cheeks, Claudia thought she saw reflected in the washbasin the outline of the wolf man. The sharp grey eyes. The tawny mane. The loping tread. Thrusting a fist into the water, Kaeso disappeared in a thousand angry ripples.

Dammit, she'd asked him to kill the maniac who stalked her and his sole reaction was to arch one eyebrow slowly. Without so much as a word, he'd stacked more wood on the fire before coiling himself in the chair directly opposite. Throwing an arm casually over the back, he'd tipped his head to one side and said, 'That's a very unusual request.'

The fire leapt as the flames caught at the logs, billowing out waves of scented applewood, yet all she had smelled was Kaeso's clove-like unguent.

'But then,' he had added, 'you're a very unusual woman.'

It was the roaring fire, surely, which turned her cheeks crimson. 'But you will kill Magic?' she asked.

Kaeso had an object, which he was rippling back and forth between his fingers. Not a coin, it was too well rounded, more like . . . Claudia's hand flew to her earlobe. How the hell . . .?

'*That's* magic,' he laughed, tossing back her missing stud.

Claudia snatched it out of the air and fixed it back in place. The man was starting to annoy her with his piercing gaze and lazy, powerful frame. She wondered when he'd slipped her earring off. She didn't remember him leaning so close, and yet – he was dangerous, this Kaeso. And danger is intoxicating . . . Well, she would not ask again. Let him make a move. She knew he would. And until then she'd called his bluff by studying his strange collection of animals and athletes, frozen by the carver whether in ivory or marble, pottery or bronze.

'When I am asked to extinguish a light,' Kaeso said eventually, rising to his feet. 'I deem that light of sufficient importance to make my decision with care. Call back tomorrow, and I'll give you my answer.' There had been no time to protest as Kaeso hurriedly covered the width of the room. 'Tomorrow,' he stressed, over his shoulder, and by the time Claudia had reached the polished cypress door, the garden and peristyle were deserted. She ran towards the gate and tugged it open, but Kaeso was nowhere in sight and when she looked back to the house, Tucca was standing by the yew tree with her fat hands on her hips, grinning horribly.

But that was yesterday. Today, a new beginning!

Claudia stepped out on to her red-painted balcony, and peered down on the street below. Reassuringly noisy, a small boy dangled a duck by its twisted, broken neck and made his sister cry. Sellers of mushrooms and willow, acorns and rueberries funnelled out of the mist towards the Forum. A match-man with his packs of yellow sulphur jostled asses bent beneath herbs and hides and harnesses, and a basket seller balanced his wares on his head with professional ease. Unfortunately for Claudia, the price for wanting Magic off her back was to return to that awful House of Silence, but in the meantime, there was much to cram in! Below, professional mourners beat ash-covered breasts at the head of a funeral procession, probably that of the old Persian tin merchant; he'd been looking grim for ages. In the whole of Rome, she thought, that poor old sod must be the only citizen unaffected by what was arguably the busiest day of the year.

With so many events converging, Claudia had been hard pressed to decide which to choose for the aunts. Resting her elbows on the rail as funereal drumbeats filled the air, she watched the procession pass down the street. Country dwellers mostly, the old boilers were well aware that disease could strike sprouting crops any time and they'd appreciate rites where peasants and landowners, wholesalers and farmers were eager, if not desperate, to placate Venus, the goddess who presided over the month. Then again, Claudia could take them to the Forum, where the Vestal Virgins were out and about on active duty, or to the Capitol, to rituals sacred to Juno, whose holy day this was.

Claudia leaned down and inspected her pot plants. The irises were doing nicely, the blue Attic variety looked terrific beside the yellow Damascans. Of course, being Fortune's Day she could take the Aunts down to the cattle market, that was always good for a laugh. On this one day of the year, middle-aged matrons were suddenly beset by an urge to see for themselves the stockmen beside their beasts and haymen selling their bales – then, my, my, what a coincidence, I'm right outside the Temple of Fortune!

You know, I never realized it was here! Such a tiny temple, must have missed it in the past, and what a lot of girls with yellow hair. *Working* girls? You mean it's true? Fortune really does protect the harlots? What's that? Every woman's sex life? Ha, ha, ha, how quaint. And having scoffed at all the rituals – the washing of the statue, the strewing of the petals – off they'd trot, these women, railing against the scourge of prostitution and the scandal that painted trollops were allowed to roam around in daylight, yet each would wander off a trinket short. Which would have miraculously made its way to Fortune's tiny altar!

In the end, though, Claudia opted for the Blemish Rites. They'd have seen nothing like it, and would go away soaked with its memory. She moved on along her tubs and planters. The narcissi were looking good, almost as though they thrived in this wretched mist and drizzle, their scent remained quite unaffected! She picked eight snow white and four bright yellow, then added a couple of irises.

'Drusilla!' She crooked a finger. 'Drusilla, come here, please!'

The cat unfurled herself from the foot of Claudia's couch and trotted over, her tail in the shape of a question mark.

'I've told you before, you little toad, not to use these pots as a litter tray!'

'Mrrrow.' Small wonder my white rock rose isn't flowering! 'Don't you dare rub round my ankles while I'm talking. Sit!'

'Prrr.' Drusilla leapt up on to the balcony rail, then completed her journey to her mistress's shoulder. 'Prrrrr.'

'Yes. Well.' Claudia patted the vibrating pelt. 'Let that be a lesson to you. Oh, there you are, Cypassis! Where on earth have you been? The morning's half over!'

'It's little Jovi, madam.' The Thessalian girl laid out a fine robe of apricot linen. 'He's so clingy.'

'Not for much longer.' Claudia sank back in her chair and let her maid make sense of her curls. 'In fact, I wouldn't be at all surprised if his mother doesn't claim him this morning.'

'Because prostitutes worship Fortune?' Cypassis asked. 'You think she'll take time off to collect him?'

'Good grief, no! This woman's holding out for a reward!' If that's what was needed, so be it. Claudia had offered a hefty sum to lure Jovi's mother out – although if the greedy bitch expected to collect, she had another think coming! Trying to make capital out of a five-year-old's misfortune indeed!

'Now then, Cypassis, is everything on schedule for today? I mean, the musicians and acrobats do know it's tonight? I don't want them saying they thought they were playing tomorrow or Monday, and you'll remember to put food out for Drusilla?'

The tortoiseshell comb cut the air like a conductor's baton. 'Yes, yes, I hope so, and . . .' She bit her lip and frowned. 'Was there another question?'

After the Blemish Rites it's on to the Field of Mars for the Bull Dance then a concert, and back here this evening for a farewell banquet. With emphasis on the FAREWELL.

'I'll need flowers strewn right across the floor, plus garlands for each of the old . . . of my dear husband's relatives.' What better display of wealth and extravagance? But there's a snag. Flowers on that scale are prohibitively expensive. 'You'll have to send some of the slaves out, I'm afraid, to pick from the wild.'

'Wonderful, madam! They love a day in the country.'

Was she serious? Knee deep in bugs and weeds? Surrounded by nothingness? What about the cowpats and the pongs? 'I want corn cockles and honesty, periwinkles, speedwells, fritillaries.' Claudia counted them off on her fingers. 'Crown daisies, alkanet and violets. Have you got that?'

'Most of it,' Cypassis said doubtfully.

'Good.' Claudia checked her curls in the mirror then ferreted around in her jewel casket until she found a silver brooch in the shape of an owl. Can you imagine a more perfect offering for my very own protectress? Claudia kissed the pin. For you, Fortune. May you continue to smile upon me!

'There's been a bit of a stir among the master's relatives this morning.'

Claudia threaded a purple ribbon in her hair and selected a matching wrap from her chest. 'Hmm?' Apricot and purple. Very elegant.

'Mistress Fannia couldn't sleep last night.'

Probably that chicken-feather bolster. Claudia fastened the owl to her gown and stood back.

'Neither could Fortunata or Miss Eppia.'

Silver wasn't right. It needed gold. Ah, that little filigree dolphin! Just the ticket. 'One more night' – hoo-bloody-ray – 'and they'll be back in their own beds.'

'But they said . . .' Cypassis gulped. 'It was *ghosts* walking Master Gaius's bedroom.'

Oh, dear. 'Cypassis, you organize the wild flower raid, let me deal with the spirit world, all right?' Gaius checking out his aunts and cousins? I don't think so. More likely Larentia seeking arteries to sink her fangs into!

Downstairs, all the old hens were gathered in the atrium, a convoy of litters was lined up outside. However, for the sake of impact, Claudia had protracted the departure. Being the Kalends, the hearth was garlanded with marigolds, the calendulas from which the day took its name, and Claudia felt sure some prayers and a couple of rituals would go far to impress the old bats. She held out her arms, palms upwards and with every appearance of solemnity, intoned: 'Mighty Juno, on this, your holy . . .'

She got no further. A fair-haired young man clad in a snowy white toga breezed in. 'I'm so sorry, am I interrupting?'

'Porsenna!'

Credit where it's due, thought Claudia, Larentia had the decency to feign surprise.

As the other women fluttered their greetings, Claudia turned her own attention to the stranger in her hall. Why the shock? What had she imagined the mouse man to look like? Why should he not have a face like a pancake?

'Aunt Larentia, you're looking absolutely wonderful!'

Young. Handsome. Well dressed. Can't expect his eyesight to be perfect as well.

'And you must be Claudia. Larentia, you naughty girl. You omitted to tell me how stunning the young widow was!'

The prospective bridegroom picked up Claudia's hand and kissed it, and perhaps that was just as well.

Otherwise she'd have balled it into a fist and slammed it straight into Larentia's teeth.

*

High up on the Capitol, in the shadow of the mighty temples of Jupiter and Juno and behind the portico that links them, you will see, on the left, two wooden gates. This is the entrance to the deceptively spacious home of the aedile in charge of the forthcoming games. Long and narrow, it abuts the libraries, school and assembly hall that are an integral part of the temple complex and on most days the chant of monies, weights and measures from the classrooms and all the comings and goings that these establishments entailed tended to override the gentle hum of industry from within the aedile's house. But not today! The Megalesian Games kicked off in less than three days and the run-up was proving a nightmare.

The aedile, had he hair left to pull out, would literally have had his hands full. 'What do you mean, the sponsors won't stretch to another two grand?' he shrieked to his cowering minions. 'How can five charioteers all go down with the fever at once? Where are my lions? By the gods, man, I ordered tubas, not cymbals!'

His reaction to the news that only half the scenery had been painted drowned even the honking from Juno's sacred geese, so if you were a slave in this household and you had a quadran's worth of sense, you'd steer clear of the master for a while. Zygia planned to do just that.

'You're still in bed!' Severina shrieked, returning to the box of a room that they shared. 'Zigs, he'll go spare!'

Instead of throwing the covers aside, Zygia stretched lazily. 'He won't notice with that lot going on. It'll be like three days holiday for us.'

'For you, you mean!' Severina wagged a long slim finger. 'One of these times, you'll push it too far, and don't say you weren't warned.'

Propped up on one elbow, the swarthy slave girl watched Severina run a comb through her hair. Such long, fair hair. When it caught the light, it was like a waterfall of molten gold cascading down her back. And such beautiful blue eyes, shining with life, and a complexion translucent with health. Zygia sighed. She sure was a stunner, was Sevvi.

The smell of baking filtered through from the kitchens below. Freshly baked rolls, pancakes and spicy, plump sausages. Pans clanked on the gridirons, there was stirring and scraping and chopping. She glanced round the tiny room. No artists, they'd made the most of it by sneaking in paint and covering the plaster in blues and purples and lavender and splashing out on a portrait or two. It was as close to home as either of them would ever get.

'Relax, Sevvi, and come back to bed.' Zygia snuggled lower under the covers.

Severina giggled then laid down her comb. 'Are you sure we won't get into trouble? He has a spiteful temper.'

'All bark and no bite. You leave the master to me.'

'Well, bunking off we might be, but . . .' When Severina smiled, it was like the sun bursting through the rainclouds. 'You've still got to get up, you lazy piglet!'

As she lunged for the counterpane, Zygia's hand clamped over her wrist. 'Excuse me. Did you say *piglet*?'

The blonde girl whipped away the sheets with her free hand. 'Lazy *fat* piglet, if you prefer!'

'Sevvi, that does it!' Zygia jumped out of bed. 'I'll get you for that!'

She dived towards Severina, who squealed in delight. 'Piglet, Ziglet, can't catch me!'

Round and round the tiny room they darted and

chased, over the bed, under it, screeching at the tops of their voices until finally Zygia brought down her quarry on the couch.

'Gotcha!'

Severina lay on her back, panting. 'Told you you were lazy,' she puffed. 'I thought you'd never catch me.'

Zygia's mouth closed over the blonde's. 'Liar,' she whispered hoarsely, unhooking the drawstring on Severina's tunic and exposing a pretty, pert breast. 'Beautiful, sexy, wonderful liar.' She blew lightly on the skin and watched it flutter. 'Have I told you lately.' Her nightgown slid to the floor. 'Just how much I love you?'

Severina gasped as Zygia's tongue flicked over her nipple. 'I love you, too. So much, sometimes it hurts.' Zygia felt her stiffen, and when she looked up, Severina's eyes were filled with tears. 'You won't leave me, will you, Zigs? Not . . . not without telling me first?'

The older girl jerked back sharply. 'What on earth made you say that?'

Severina sniffed back her tears. 'The way you've been behaving lately. Secretive. Biting my head off. Little things which . . . add up.'

'Oh.' Zygia sat back, tucked one foot under her thigh and spiked her fingers through her short dark curls.

Severina gulped nervously. 'Is there someone else?' The look of horror on her lover's face answered for her. 'So, what then?' She leaned forward impatiently. 'Zigs, if you're in trouble . . .' The blood drained from her beautiful face. 'Sweet Janus! It's this, isn't it?'

She ran her finger round the outline of the dragon tattooed on Zygia's arm and felt a chill of pure terror when the dark girl nodded.

'Yes.' Zygia's hand closed over Severina's. 'I've thought long and hard about this, love, but provided I stay indoors next Friday' – she could not bring herself to say 'market day' ' – and we say I've got the fever,' she kissed Severina's palm, 'there's no problem.'

Although even under the aedile's roof it was impossible to be a hundred per cent certain. Too many entrances, exits, visitors bringing retinues of their own as preparations for the forthcoming games were stepped up. Which is why she'd taken to sleeping with a small stabbing knife slipped between the mattress and the webbing. Although she saw no need to worry Sevvi with the knowledge.

Severina chewed her lower lip. 'Are you holding out on me?'

Zygia shrugged and avoided all eye contact.

Sevvi yanked her hand away. 'All right, if you won't tell me, I'll work it out for myself.' A heather broom began to scrape along the corridor outside their room. The sweeper was humming. 'Let's think. You shared a dormitory with those other girls, didn't you?'

She looked at Zygia, chewing the edge of the sheet. So much they had shared, her and Zigs. Suddenly Severina felt a millstone collide with her stomach. So much they had gone through, concealment of feelings was out of the question.

'Oh, no.' Sevvi sank down on the bed, the colour leached from her face. 'Holy shit, you know who the killer is, don't you?'

Her friend's tortured face needed no answer.

'Mars almighty, you can't keep this to yourself, your life'll be worth zero! You must go to the authorities—'

Zygia ruffled the blonde girl's hair. 'The Empire's in crisis, Sevvi, everything else is shelved—'

'Even a butcher on the loose?'

She gave a short laugh. 'Since when did the deaths of a few common slaves compare with the life of a middle-aged philanderer? It's who you are that counts, Sevvi, not what you are. Remember that.'

'Then share your secret with me!'

'And put your life on the line?' Zygia held Severina's face between her hands. 'No way.' She kissed her lightly on the lips. 'Anyway, I may be jumping to conclusions.'

Severina snorted. 'Twelve of you billeted in that wing and three sliced to bits? You must take me for a right bloody fool!' She jumped off the couch and began folding clothes furiously.

The other girl buried her head in her hands. 'I didn't mean to insult you,' she said thickly. 'It's just that . . .' Her voice trembled. 'Sevvi, I am so damned scared.'

Severina ran across and cradled her. 'So am I, Zigs, so am I! But we can't go on hiding away. If the army won't help, can't *we* do something?'

'For instance?' For the first time in days, hope surged in Zygia's breast.

'Suppose,' Severina said thoughtfully, 'we band together with the other eight girls and kill him before he gets another one of you?'

Zygia pressed the heels of her hands into her eyes. 'I don't know where the others live,' she said wearily. 'It was hardly in Arbil's interests for us to keep in touch, in fact the only girls I've seen since I left have been Didia and Annia – and Didia they found in the Argiletum yesterday!'

Severina stroked her thick, dark curls. 'Lord, you're

tense. Roll over and I'll massage your shoulders.' She paused in her kneading. 'What about Arbil?' she asked. 'He raised you, why can't he sort this mess out?'

'Arbil would only step in,' Zygia said, 'if it was proving detrimental to his business.'

'I felt you tense up.' Severina poked Zygia's shoulder blade. 'You always tense up when you lie.'

'All right, so I'm worried about a cover-up,' Zygia confessed. 'And who gets her mouth shut permanently for blabbing? You know how ruthless they are, these Babylonians.' She flipped over on to her back and stared at the lavender-painted ceiling. 'On the other hand, I suppose it wouldn't hurt to pay a brief call on Annia.' Her mouth turned down at the corners. 'Providing I can drum up the courage.'

'Oh?' Severina rubbed almond oil over her lover's breasts in a gentle, circular motion. 'I thought you lot got on well in the dorm?'

'Most of us, but there's no love lost between Annia and me.' Zygia wrinkled her nose. 'The trouble was, she thought herself a cut above the rest. All that crap about blue blood in her veins! I – we – rather put her in her place.'

'Gave her all the dirty jobs, you mean? I'll bet you jibed her rotten, too.'

'She deserved it, sanctimonious little cow. Talk about airs and graces! I'm not proud of my behaviour, Sevvi, but we were young and that's how it was in that place. You either mixed or . . . paid the price. Oh, but she was a pretty one, that Annia. You two could pass as twins from the back, *and* the same colour eyes.'

Severina shivered. 'Suppose the killer mistakes me for her?'

A lump formed in Zygia's throat. 'Don't be daft,' she said, forcing a smile. 'Nothing, Severina, will happen to you and that's a promise.' She pulled her into her arms and hugged her till the choking had subsided. 'And I shall never, ever leave you, do you understand?' How could she survive without Sevvi? She kissed the cascade of blonde hair and slid off the couch. 'So maybe I'll nip off to Annia's. Get it over with.'

'*Now?*'

'Yes, now.' Outside, in the yard, the aedile was screaming for his secretaries. 'When I won't be missed!'

'Please be careful.'

'Severina, my love, you worry too much!' She pulled on a fresh tunic scented with bayberries. 'Today's the Festival of Fortune, not market day.' She tied a single blue ribbon round her short, dark hair and splashed a dab of scent behind her ears. 'So one thing we can be sure of. In broad daylight, with all those crowds buzzing around, I couldn't be safer had I an armed escort alongside!'

XIV

Despite Porsenna's limp and limpet charm, Claudia was in a buoyant mood. The Blemish Rites had proved a rip-roaring success, the idea being that in exchange for a gift of frankincense and myrtle, Fortune renders invisible a woman's sags and wrinkles. Believe that and you'll believe anything! But the number of women who just happened to be passing with a fragrant white wreath in their hair beggared belief! The aunts had thrown themselves into the ceremonies with relish, and providing the old sourpusses were happy Claudia was happy. One more night, just one more night, and her life would be hers again.

As morning moved to afternoon, the litters loaded up and yet again Claudia allowed herself to be engineered into sharing the mouse man's carriage, with its comfy cushions and turquoise screens which screamed of intimacy and privacy. And yet again, Porsenna failed to deliver. Claudia smiled to herself. Poor old Larentia! Finds the perfect foil for her takeover of Gaius' business, only he's too weak even to understand what it's about. When Larentia told him to be charming, he must have dashed out to buy a book of platitudes and, bless him, he'd used them all. However, so long as Claudia smiled in all the right places and nodded appreciatively, Larentia would remain unaware of her puppet's shortcomings – and that was sweeter still!

From time to time, as the litter wallowed its way towards the Field of Mars, Porsenna's voice drifted in and out of her awareness. '... roll the mice first in honey, then in poppyseeds ... keep them caged and keep them fat ... the skins alone can fetch a price ...'

And from time to time, she interjected a 'really' or a 'no!' and sometimes a 'tell me more', but her mind was elsewhere. Part of it was with the astrologers who'd been hanging round the baths, because on the morning when the sun slid out of Pisces and sneaked into Aries, the time was ripe for mapping out futures, and if this involved vain women parting with silver, who's to complain? Another part of her mind was with the water organ (star of the concert), and another part was with the Thessalian horse riders who'd be taking on the bulls this afternoon. It had filed Kaeso to one side, blocked out the Market Day Murder and thus it was purely nuisance value when the litter was halted, its path blocked because a cart had caught its offside wheel on the curb and overturned. All around, citizens were cursing.

'This bleeding building programme! Fine for Augustus to say tear this down, put this up, restore that other one, what of us what lives here?'

'Scaffolds over half the city, brick dust in yer hair! Do they have to lug great wagonloads of tufa through in the middle of the day? Everyone else makes do with night deliveries, why can't they?'

Yet one voice stood clear from the sea of shouts, the thrashing of the oxen on their sides, the hundred different dialects. A distinctive canine howl! Claudia felt her blood run chill. It was that shaggy black dog which chased her off the map two days ago! So close, she could even hear him sniffing.

'I know a diversion!' she hissed to Porsenna.

'Then I'd better tell Larentia,' he replied. 'Won't be a tick!'

Too late. Claudia thought. You already are one. Close by, the dog yelped. She fingered her filigree dolphin and wished now she'd left it for Fortune . . .

'Listen to me, slimeball!'

Oh no! That was the moneylender! A trickle of sweat snaked its way down her backbone as shaking fingers parted the turquoise cotton drapes. Dammit, his stall was set up not fifteen paces away, she could see his balances and moneybox. Heedless of the weather, the hounds were straining on their leashes. The loanshark grabbed his whey-faced client by the cloth around his neck and pulled the man's face close to his. Claudia recognized the man he was snarling at, it was a baker from the Caelian.

'If you don't settle up, in full, in six days from today, I shall personally tear your ovens down, smash your millstone and hang your kneecaps round your neck.'

'B-b-but—'

'Six' – the moneylender released the baker's collar – 'days.'

Claudia felt her blood congeal. The same fate would befall her, unless she coughed up. Did his thugs receive job lots for kneecaps?

When Porsenna returned, she was buried deep behind a treatise on mouse food.

'Just a splintered wheel and a few scattered building blocks, we'll be on our way shortly,' he said, climbing back in and wiping a splatter of mud from his shoe. 'I say. You . . . you can keep that book, if you like.' He leaned forward earnestly. 'The most important thing to remember is, last thing at night, leave them fresh water . . .'

Claudia bared her teeth and hoped he read it as a smile.

Once, the Field of Mars had been a patch of marshy ground in the elbow of the Tiber fit only for frogs, snakes and mosquitoes. Later it had found a use in horseracing, a place for inspecting the troops, but now. Talk about a facelift! Tombs and temples, halls and colonnades glistening with travertine and marble. Grass, watered to keep it green the whole year round, upon which every outdoor activity under the sun took place. Wrestling, fighting with staves, fencing, you name it, they did it! Agrippa built his baths here as well as his Pantheon and he added a variety of porticoes. There were parks and gardens, groves and sacred fountains, lakes and pools, libraries and obelisks. Whatever the weather, it was packed.

The civil servant who had sponsored the Bull Dance couldn't run to too much splendour, he'd hired the little wooden amphitheatre just behind the Pantheon and jollied it up with awnings of gold and green and indigo which, on a normal first of April, would be shimmering with filtered sunlight.

Within seconds, the old cats had started.

'No, no, dear, if you sit there, I can sit beside Eppia, and Fortunata can sit with her mother. Julia, could you move up three spaces . . .?'

Shuffle, shuffle, wriggle, wriggle. Then it was Fortunata's turn. 'Could we have another cushion, here? Mummy can't see. Might I borrow yours? Yours too, Eppia, please. Still too low? Fannia, pass your pad over.'

By the time she'd stopped fussing, Fortunata's mother was propped precariously, half the aunts were cushionless, but, by some strange quirk of fate, Cousin Fortunata remained square upon her original padded pillow.

'Ooh, mulled wine,' cried Fortunata, as Porsenna dug deep into his purse, but by this time Fannia felt in need of some limelight.

'This is too bitter! Can you add honey? Now they've made it too sweet! Porsenna, would you mind? Get them to top it up with spiced wine? Not too peppery. Ugh, now it's cold. Could . . .'

'I'll go!' Claudia snatched Fannia's goblet from her hand, determined to fill the bloody thing with cabbage water and see what she said about that!

Air. Give me air.

The street outside was thronged with queues at every entrance. Claudia pushed her way to the corner, bought an almond bun off the street vendor and took it away to a quiet grove of olives. The seat was set upon an artificial mound. It was a good vantage point from which to watch virile young men, oiled and naked, at work in the exercise yard. She began to nibble the bun. Stuffed with almonds and red, candied cherries, it was still slightly warm from the oven. She had munched less than a quarter when, from the back of the yard, a familiar figure strode into view.

Later she told herself that her eyes had been drawn by the fact that he alone was clothed among the gymnasts, but that was not strictly true. All men going in and out of the baths passed that way. A large majority of whom also wore the long, patrician tunic.

His brow puckered, his face brooding, Marcus Cornelius Orbilio passed the vaulters and weightlifters, his hand stroking an imaginary beard as he turned out of the exercise yard in the direction of the theatre. As Claudia rose, shook the crumbs from her skirts and composed some witty remark to spring upon him, she was aware of a woman walking towards him in the street. Tall, nearly as tall as Supersnoop himself, younger than him, though. And devastatingly beautiful.

To this day, Claudia could not explain what made her draw back into the purple shadows of the olives.

Draped in linens the price of a gelding and dripping with gold and with sapphires, the dark-eyed beauty called out his name. Orbilio looked up, then the expression on his face changed completely. Indeed, Bacchus couldn't have looked happier the day Jupiter announced he was to be god of wine.

Miss Syrian Linens called his name again as she held out her arms and Claudia watched him run into them. Literally run. Then hug her tighter than a drumskin. They examined each other at arm's length, and they laughed. Her bangled arm pointed to the theatre. He shrugged an objection. She pouted. He gave in.

Surprise, surprise.

Claudia's narrowed eyes followed them up the road, arms about each other's waists, laughing. Happy. With her wrap tight about her shoulders, she watched them out of sight.

Her instinct about Loverboy had been spot on, she thought bitterly. Whether it's cold commercial negotiations or hot limbs writhing in a bed, sure they'll dally with the merchant classes, fool with the freeborn, lavish trinkets on girls from the slums. But when push comes to shove, patricians don't sign a contract outside their own caste.

She threw the almond bun on the floor and ground it under her heel. Oh yes. Blue blood always runs thicker than a merchant woman's scent . . .

XV

Since there is nothing like a Bull Dance to fire the blood, the atmosphere was electric. Surrounded by the rainbow awnings, trumpet fanfares, cymbals, horns and rattles, a troupe of bare-breasted dancers with painted nipples snaked up and down the aisles, tapping tambourines and clacking castanets. Dwarves in masks and clowns in silly hats scampered over the sand, mimicking the audience and telling bawdy jokes while buffoons in motley dress ran loose among the crowds, lifting skirts and tunics, blowing down the backs of necks. Ten thousand feet stamped on wooden boards, vibrating the benches and echoing round the elliptical timber structure. Voices roared and, captured by the cambric roof, the temperature catapulted upwards.

'My word, this is not what we're used to,' observed Cousin Fortunata, casting sly wistful glances towards the buffoons. 'Most uninhibited.'

Claudia ignored her. Theirs were good seats, but they were not the *best* seats. The best seats were reserved for the aristocracy, and there they were, in the very front row, applauding the antics of the clowns. Supersnoop appeared to have his arm fused to Miss Lovely's shapely shoulders and they threw their heads back together when they laughed. Claudia's nail snapped where she chewed through it.

Shuffling closer to Porsenna, she rested her arm against his. If Loverboy looked over, he'd see her practically sitting in his lap.

If!

Not that she gave a damn, anyway.

As the dancers, clowns and motley melted away, a hush fell over the auditorium. The temperature climbed further, heating the marjoram and mint strewn on the steep wooden terraces. Wraps slipped off shoulders, sleeves were rolled up, and the exposure of flesh added to the earthiness inside the amphitheatre. It was perhaps solely down to the silence that Claudia noticed the meeting of two long-haired dandies, red-faced from recent exertion, each apologizing for their own lateness, but this was not what drew her attention. That was the wolf with a streak of silver down its back! A rumble of drums interrupted both the hush and Claudia's astonishment. With a blast on the trumpets, the curtain at each tip of the oval drew back and horsemen in bright scarlet loincloths galloped into the ring. Gasps rose up. The skill of these Thessalian plainsmen had not been witnessed in Rome before now. They rode bareback, they did handstands, they rode balanced between two foam-flecked horses, cutting across one another with breathtaking precision. As far as Claudia was concerned, the wolf was history as horsemen turned somersaults or rode clinging to their black stallions' bellies. And this was merely a taster. The Bull Dance had yet to come!

Still Marcus Cornelius did not turn his head.

Claudia coiled herself round a smug looking Porsenna and regretted not doubling the dose of her Runaway Success.

Larentia smiled. But then, so do crocodiles.

To tumultuous applause and earsplitting whistles, the panting horsemen collected their wreaths and their accolades and retired. Musicians and tumblers came on in the interlude, and it was only when Orbilio moved to stretch his long, patrician legs that he noticed the stunning creature in the apricot gown six rows behind him. One curl, as usual, had come adrift from its mooring.

'That blond rider was particularly handsome,' Fortunata was saying. 'Don't you agree, Cousin Claudia?'

'Not a patch on Porsenna,' she simpered, linking her hand into his and pretending not to notice the tall aristocrat turning in the seat below as she whispered 'It's so hot in here' to Porsenna. Let Hotshot make of that what he will! From the corner of her eye, she saw him ease his way up the steps.

'That'll be the crowd,' replied the mouse man.

Give me strength! Nevertheless, Claudia set free a silvery laugh. 'Oh, but Porsenna, I feel we've been alone from the moment we first met!' She glanced up at the man hovering in the aisle. 'Orbilio. What a surprise.'

He seemed amused. His eyes were twinkling. Did he think she hadn't noticed his hands all over Miss Syrian Linens down below? But of course he did! This slick, handsome bastard was playing on the fact . . .

He indicated the food and drink vendors. 'Can I get you anything?'

'No thanks.' Her eyes swivelled to the handsome mouse farmer, who was dispensing his charm to Larentia. 'I have everything *I* need right here.'

Emotion flashed across his eyes, she thought it might have been hostility. Or something worse.

He was on the point of speaking when a legionary appeared at his elbow. 'There you are, sir!' When he tried to salute, his arm was compressed in the crush. 'There's been an incident on the Palatine—'

'Holy Jupiter! The Emperor?'

'No, sir. Sorry, sir. Didn't mean to alarm you. It's another murder, sir.'

Claudia stood up and smoothed the folds of her gown as though the conversation meant nothing to her. Her eyes followed the convoluted movements of the acrobat. But her ears . . .

'Well, I can't come now, I'm—' Even Supersleuth didn't gave the gall to say he was busy. Not when he'd been run to ground in a theatre. He glanced at the dark-eyed beauty in the front row clapping time to the lute player. Claudia bent down to check the clasp on her anklet, and refrained from sinking her teeth into his leg.

'I think you ought to, sir. It looks like another Market Day Murder.'

'Come, come, man, the market's six days off.'

The legionary struggled to hang on to his helmet in the jostling throng. 'I know, sir, but—'

'Will you kindly stop sirring me, and relay the facts. And only the facts, please.'

'Over in the Wolf Grotto, si— They found another body. Butchered, like the rest.'

Claudia watched the patrician age ten years in as many seconds. 'What colour hair?' he demanded.

The soldier looked confused. 'Um—'

'For gods' sake, man, was she blonde? Yes or no?' Orbilio shook the boy roughly by both shoulders.

'N-no, sir. I believe she had dark hair.'

The years dropped away again. Claudia heard him exhale. 'Then let's go.'

From a discreet observation post beneath the royal box, a young woman in an apricot tunic watched a wavy-haired aristocrat bend over the bench and gesticulate towards the entrance. The dark-eyed beauty's face dropped and as he twirled his toga out from underneath his seat, it half-concealed the kiss he'd leaned across to plant, and then he was gone, striding through the actors' doorway as though he owned the place. Claudia moved across and sat beside her.

'It's Lucina, isn't it?'

Miss Fancypants smiled tentatively. 'Camilla, actually.'

'That's what I said. Marcus has told me so much about you. Never stops!'

Camilla's exquisite features puckered. 'You know Marcus?'

'Intimately,' she purred. 'I'm his wife.'

Beautiful eyes widened in surprise. 'But . . . I thought you were divorced. Weren't you living in Lusitania? With a—' Decorum stopped her.

'Sea captain?' Decorum never held Claudia back. 'That's what he likes to tell people. I think he's ashamed of me, on account of the stink I kicked up at the time.'

'Of the divorce?' Camilla moved up so Claudia could get comfortable.

'At the time of the scandal – Did you say *divorce*? Oh dear, I suppose the fiction makes him feel more comfortable about his, er – Well, best not to speak of it.'

Lights danced off Miss Lovely's multitude of gold. 'I'm sorry, I . . . I don't understand.' Her voice softened. 'Please tell me,' she pleaded. 'It is . . . very important to me.'

Claudia laid a sympathetic hand upon her arm. 'It's not a pretty story,' she sighed. 'In fact, I'm willing to bet he didn't arrange to meet you here, that this was some chance meeting in the street.'

'Why, yes. As a matter of fact, it was.'

Claudia tutted. 'And was he coming out of the gym? He *was*? You know, I really hoped he'd change,' she said sadly. 'Was he alone, Camilla? Or was there a pretty boy holding his hand?'

'*Boy?*'

'Please. Camilla. Don't distress yourself, it's just the way Marcus is. For years,' she dabbed at her eye, 'I've resigned myself to being –' she considered 'celibate' and said '– childless.'

Camilla looked aghast. 'You're not making this up, are you?'

Claudia's eyes widened convincingly. 'Next time you see him, ask him where he got those bruises. Or better still, ask that chap over there.' She pointed to the gallery, to a kohl-eyed transvestite surrounded by a dozen powdered youths. 'It was in his whorehouse, dear. And that's the truth!'

Some distance from the Field of Mars, in a house untouched by the thunderous echo of hooves or the clouds of sand kicked up from the ring, more mundane pursuits were in progress. Silver was buffed up, torn seams mended, skillets scoured, chickens plucked. Outside, shops which had closed for siesta were starting to re-open with the inevitable clangs, drowning the background oaths of builders trying to lay the foundations of yet another splendid public building.

Nemesis, tucked beneath a couch and wrapped in a cloth stained with red, was aware of none of it.

When the street herald trumpeted the hour, the door to the bedroom creaked open and the weapon's owner padded into the room. A deep, fulfilled sigh rippled the air.

'This is good,' the voice whispered. 'Very good.'

Discarded clothes, rank with freshly clotted blood, were bundled into a sack, along with the piece of cloth in which Nemesis lay wrapped, then the knife was plunged into a bowl of warm water, where, to a gentle whistle, it was agitated until the water turned red. It was shaken, examined, then, with great reverence, Nemesis was raised high and twisted slowly to the left, then slowly to the right, so that all its deadly contours could be inspected and each wicked gem admired.

'You are mine, Nemesis.'

Twisted to the left. To the right. A tunic slid to the floor. To the left. To the right.

'And I am yours.'

Cold steel rippled upon hot flesh. To the left. To the right. Between the legs.

'Oh, yes!'

Panting, sweating, sated, two hands clutched the hilt and held the knife aloft.

'Good boy,' the voice whispered. 'Good boy!'

With a final hiss, Nemesis was sliced through the air before the maroon cotton shroud concealed it from view. Until the next time it would be needed.

*

If the Forum is the heart of Rome, then the Palatine is the brain. It was from here the arch-strategist Augustus stamped out banditry, opened new trade routes, tightened up the law and consolidated the might of the Empire, and it was from here that he would have to unravel the mess left by the premature death of his close friend and Regent, Marcus Vispanius Agrippa. All around, imposing architecture reflected the Palatine's supremacy – the Imperial Palace; the semi-circular basilica where Augustus heard petitions; the temples honouring Victory, Apollo – in fact honouring anyone you could put a name to, really. There were marbles from Alexandria, limestones from Sicily, creamy *corallina* from beside the Sea of Marmora. A far cry from the days when the hill looked down upon the river and wide open spaces of its marshlands and the villagers huddled inside huts!

But the origins remained for all to see.

The shrine of the shepherd goddess who gave the hill its name might now be encased in gold and Numidian marble, but the Festival of Pales still smacked of country ritual. One single hut, with a thatch and walls of woven osiers, had been preserved as a national monument, a reminder of Rome's humble past. And finally, facing the setting sun, was the Lupercal. Once a dank, slimy cavern famous only for being where the she-wolf suckled Romulus and Remus, Augustus had turned the site into a magnificent indoor grotto complete with bubbling spring, painted statues and a fig tree. Although the vast oak grove which once sheltered it lay beneath the Circus Maximus, gilded goat horns and acorns fashioned from gold studded the ceiling, goatskins and pan pipes hung on the walls as mementoes of its rural roots.

It was behind the bronze she-wolf, between the statues of Faunus and of Pan, that the body lay in its lonely pool of blood.

'Move along, now,' the soldier addressed the gawping crowd. 'There's nothing here to look at – oh, it's you, sir. Beg pardon, only I didn't expect to see you at the crime scene.'

The legionary, a wily old footslogger called Ancus, hurriedly crossed the marbled floor to where the patrician Orbilio lingered at the entrance, his unfocused gaze taking in the misty hills across the river, and saluted.

'Why's that?' he was asked.

'This is quite straightforward, sir. Throat cut, no signs of sexual interference.' Ancus stared down at folk hunched under their hoods and cloaks, hugging the walls of the great racecourse for shelter. 'Probably find the boyfriend round the corner, his eyes cried out of their sockets, saying how he never meant to harm her, but when he realized she was dead, he tried to cover his tracks by making it look like the others.'

'The young soldier – what was his name, Probus? – seemed convinced we're dealing with another ritual murder.'

Ancus made a dismissive gesture. 'As you say, sir, the boy's young.' From the escarpment, he could glimpse the murky flow of the Tiber, her ferries quiet, since the public parks on the opposite bank held very little attraction. Indeed, only a fool (or a soldier under orders) would be out of doors on a day like today. 'You know what they're like at that age, everything's sensationalism. He sees a body bathed in blood and – Sir?' The aristocrat was no longer at the cave entrance. Squinting, Ancus could see him hunched over the body.

'Who found her?'

'Don't rightly know, sir.' He had to raise his voice to carry beyond the gushing springwaters. 'Me and Probus were on patrol when we heard people yelling, and by the time we'd got here, quite a crowd had formed.'

'Was she like this when you arrived?'

Ancus scratched his head. 'Dead, you mean?'

'I mean,' Orbilio said patiently. 'Was she lying on her back?'

'Oh. Er, no, she was propped against the podium of the she-wolf; look.' He held up the torch to reveal a puddle of blood at the base. 'I pulled her away to look for the hair.'

'What hair?'

'Well, that was it.' The old footslogger smiled pityingly. 'There wasn't no hair, not even lying underneath the body. As I said, Probus jumped the gun.'

Orbilio lifted the torn flaps of the girl's sleeve. 'The blue dragon.'

'Yes, but as you can see, sir, the throat's been cut, and those other wounds were made after she had died.'

Same thing happens every time, thought Ancus. No sooner do we get a batch of ritual killings, than some other warped bastard comes along and tries to imitate them.

The tall patrician straightened up, brushing his hands. 'Possibly,' he acknowledged. 'But ask around, Ancus. See whether anyone heard a whistle, only don't say why.' So far, the whistle was something only the military knew about. 'Find out her name, start asking questions about her background, who she was friends with—?'

Ancus scratched his armpit. 'We know her name, sir, it's Zygia. Don't look surprised,' he chuckled. 'She's well known for running errands for the aedile who organizes the Games. Lives up there on the Capitol.' He smiled knowingly. 'Take it from me, sir, this'll be the work of a boyfriend.'

'What makes you so certain?' Orbilio leaned his weight against Pan's cloven hoof.

'Well, her clothes have been ripped off, but her hands and feet weren't tied and there's no hair in the lap, but most of all,' Ancus tapped the side of his nose, 'this place, sir. The Wolf Grotto. I'd say she gave him the old heave-ho and he turned nasty. Perhaps it was a married man she was meeting here in secret – folk do that, you know.' He laughed outright. 'They think this cave's romantic!'

The young investigator smiled non-commitally back.

'No, don't you waste your energy worrying about this girl's killer, me and Probus will have the boyfriend in the nick in no time. You concentrate on protecting the life of the Emperor, sir. Here, did you know they've already uncovered one plot . . .'

Few things in this life can be classed certainties, but one thing you *can* bank on. The older the soldier, the more gossip he'll have to impart. Ancus didn't stop talking for a full ten minutes.

XVI

With thoughts of the latest murder banished to a cold, dark place in her mind as she made her way to Kaeso's house on the Quirinal, Claudia was singing the Bull Dancers' anthem.

> 'From beyond the Pindus Moun-tains,
> To the Paga-saean Gulf.
> Da-di-da di something some-thing
> And a da-di da-di dum.'

Was there anything to match those Thessalian daredevils! As a side-effect of peace, of course, people need more and more excitement in their diet, hence pedigree horsemen on shiny black stallions thundering after the bulls. The silver bells on their bridles offset the snorting fury, and gold streamers in their manes shone through the clouds of sand. Over they jumped, the riders, on to the backs of the bulls, gripping their horns and twisting their necks so they 'danced'. How no one got gored was a miracle!

> 'From beyond the Pindus Moun-tains,
> To the wide Thessaly plain.
> Da-di da-di – What, ho, Tu-ucca,
> Nice to see your face again.'

Still singing, she pushed her way past the mute and waved an imaginary baton to the rhythm as she made her way through the echoing house. In the dismal peristyle, a brindle dog lay dozing, as Claudia danced up to the polished cypress door that separated the outside world from Kaeso and she breezed inside. Damn! This time she took care to check the shadows, but no. She really was alone. Applewood logs still crackled on the fire in this wine-dark, mellow studio, bringing the leaping curios to life.

'It's a fine collection, isn't it?'

Where the hell did he spring from? Her eyes had swept the rooms as she passed through, the garden – Suddenly she looked at him with different eyes. The shoulder-length hair mane. The grey eyes. The powerful build. She thought of the brindle dog. Oh, for gods' sake! No one believes in Shape Shifters . . .

She tossed back her head. 'Have you made your decision?'

Kaeso clicked the door behind him and his musky scent engulfed the applewood. Swirling his cloak from his shoulders, he leaned his forearms on the back of a chair and bridged his fingers. 'You'll have to tell me why,' he said, staring at the pictures in the flames.

Claudia studied the chiselled profile. Kaeso wouldn't keep two women dangling. Kaeso wouldn't ally himself to a woman whose blood was the same hue and still flirt with a rich merchant's widow . . .

'You don't give up, do you?' she asked.

'Never.' He turned his craggy smile on her. 'It's a fault.'

It was too warm in here for a fire, she thought. 'Then read these.' Opening a secret pouch in her cloak, she drew out a sample of Magic's ramblings.

Kaeso read them through several times. 'These,' he said at length, 'are deeply unpleasant.'

There was an even longer wait as his fingers evaluated the parchment and its blob of golden wax. 'He won't be an easy man to track down.' He squinted hard at the seal. 'Third grade pith, the most common, and cobra rings are enormously popular.'

'But you can find him?'

'I can find him.'

'And you'll kill him?'

'He won't trouble you again.'

'That's not what I asked.'

Kaeso's head turned sharply. 'I'll get rid of him. For a price.'

Naturally. Claudia's finger trailed over the faience vases, the ivory cats, the marble stags, the figurines. These were no cheap market knick-knacks. Quality on this scale had to be paid for. 'How much?'

'Nothing you cannot afford.' He was leaning against the wall, with his arms across his chest, staring at his feet.

'Kaeso, you don't strike me as a man of imprecision. Can you be a little more specific?'

She waited for him to answer, struck by the spooky silence of the house around her. All you could hear was the spitting of the logs. Orange flashes leaped out of the flames to land as dead, black ash. Blue smoke spiralled up the chimney. The scents of musk and applewood swamped the tiny room.

'I am aware of your financial position,' he said at length, fixing his gaze on an ivory kingfisher. 'I was hoping to negotiate a fee of a rather different kind.'

Claudia's eyebrow lifted. Oh, were you.

'Not,' Kaeso held up his hand, 'what you're thinking. A favour in return, shall we say? When the time is right?'

She lifted the vase of leaping billygoats and held it to the light. Faience. Exquisite. Golds and reds and greens with a silvery sheen to the glaze. 'That smacks of blackmail,' she said, turning the vase in her hands. 'Oops.' It crashed to the floor, a thousand shimmering smithereens.

She heard his jaws snap. Or was that a crackle from the logs upon the fire?

'Magic is not some husband I want to get rid of, or a lover who's proving tiresome.' Her eyes flashed every bit as brightly as the flames. 'This man poses a very real threat, with his pornographic fantasies and—'

'I understand what he is, Claudia.' Kaeso ran his tongue round his lips and then pursed them. 'And there was never any question of blackmail.' Sad eyes surveyed the broken billygoats. 'So which is it to be? Silver, or payment in kind?'

'I've always said, one good turn deserves another.'

'Then that's settled,' he said. 'You go home.' He tossed a glistening object through the air. 'And leave the Magic to me!'

With a swirl of his cloak, he was gone. Claudia examined the gold and emerald bracelet in her hands. He must have relieved her of it when she handed him the letters, but all the same . . .

Outside, the mute's garden was deserted. Apart from a brindle dog, snoozing beneath the yew!

Arbil groaned. It was happening again! His vision was fuzzy. He felt sick. When he went to wipe his face, his hands were shaking, and moreover his fingertips were wrinkled, like prunes. The image of Enki, the water god, rose up before him then vanished into the mist of his vision.

'What . . .?' His tongue was too heavy to string words together and he thought the frogs round his fishpond croaked better.

Enki solidified, and Arbil realized he was sitting in his bathtub. The water felt tepid. No wonder he was shivery! He hauled himself out and blotted his face with a towel.

'Shit!'

Thick streaks of black dye stained the linen, and pulling on his beard he could see immersion had straightened the crimping. He swore and kicked at the bathtub till water sloshed over the sides. How did he get here? How long had he blanked out this time?

Think, Arbil, think. Be logical about this. What's the last thing you remember?

I remember lunch.

And?

It was with Dino and Sargon, and Dino was pouring out the ale and teasing me, asking when I planned to abandon the Babylonian practice of eating upright in favour of reclining on couches and I pretended to cuff him round the ear. I remember that quite clearly. We ate stuffed turbot and sucking pig, and Sargon was slipping titbits to Silverstreak under the table, and don't think your father hasn't noticed, I joked.

Then what?

Then – Arbil scratched his head. Yes, then I took a pee.

After that?

I went into the office, like I always do. Poured myself a date liqueur, picked up the ledgers and sent for Tryphon, now what was it I had to speak to him about? No, no, no. I've got it the wrong way round. Tryphon came to see me. That's right, there was an outbreak of fever in the seventh block, the Captain said, nothing to worry about, though.

Can you remember your reply?

Absolutely. Keep them quarantined for a week, I told him, we don't want any more going down – or you either, come to that. Tryphon's been looking decidedly peaky of late, so I said, take the rest of the day off, man. Go to Rome. Have some fun!

Did he?

Have fun? Tryphon? No idea. But he thanked me and said in that case, he'd tag along with Dino and Sargon.

Then what? What did you do after the Captain left you?

Nausea swamped Arbil again. He didn't know. That was the problem. He didn't fucking know!

Naked, Arbil waddled into his bedroom, where Marduk's golden image with its bejewelled crown and feathers gave his servant strength. He could feel it seep through his skin and into his muscles until it reached his very bone marrow. His reflection stared back from a sheet of polished copper on the wall. Plump, he decided. Not fat. Definitely not fat. And still able to go like a stallion. Arbil pumped up his biceps. Perhaps the problem was not him, but Angel. Maybe she was boring him? He rummaged around in his chest and brought out a batch of drawings sent from a man in North Africa who specialized in the refinements of love-making. Yes, yes. He looked at the drawings, one after the other, but his loins didn't stir. He closed his eyes and imagined Angel doing that to him. And still his lingham didn't move.

'Angel!' He bawled. 'Angel, come here!'

Briefly he wondered whether he ought to make her coax it into life, but his vision was still funny round the edges and his head was swimming, and let's face it, even stallions have their off days. He glanced at the eight-point star across his bedhead. Ishtar wouldn't let him down. She'd see him right.

But soon, he prayed. Please, Ishtar. Make it soon, eh?

The fabulous creature with the blue-black hair and doe-like eyes called Angel came running. 'What is it, Arbil? What's the matter?'

His answer died in his throat. She was dressed as he insisted a wife of his should dress for dinner. A tight gown of pure white linen to show off her perfect, nutbrown skin, with bangles round her wrists and round her ankles. Her small tight breasts thrust forward, and they were not false nipples that she wore. Her lips and cheeks were carmined. Kohl smudges lined her eyes. He had forgotten quite how beautiful she was!

'What the hell are you all tarted up for?' he snapped.

'Dinner's almost ready,' she replied.

Arbil felt himself reel. 'Dinner?' It can't be. It bloody can't be. Not already. He stumbled to the window and pulled open the shutter. It was dark. Panic rose in his throat. Not an hour this time. Not even two. He'd lost a whole fucking afternoon . . .

'W-where's my orange robe?' he asked. It was his favourite, and he couldn't find it anywhere.

'I don't know. Where did you put it?'

Arbil slapped her with the back of his hand. 'If I knew that, you stupid cow, I wouldn't have to ask.'

Angel rubbed her throbbing cheek. 'Maybe you left it in Rome this afternoon.'

'Rome!' His sarcasm cut through the air.

'Well, you went there, didn't you?'

This time it was the flat of his hand which connected with her face, sending Angel reeling to the floor. 'Don't get fresh with me, you uppity bitch. You know damn well, I never go to Rome! Now find that robe, you lazy slag.'

Angel staggered to her feet. 'You did too go—' She never finished her statement of defiance. Arbil's fist saw to that.

Tears welled up in her eyes. 'If you don't believe me,' she blubbered through the blood, 'ask Lugal. He drives you every week!'

'Liar,' he said, although there was less conviction in his voice than he'd intended. 'Dirty, lying bitch.' A strand of hair had blown across her face and was sticking to the blood. 'Clean yourself up, you're a mess.' Her blood was on his knuckles, too. 'Go on. Get out of my sight.'

For several minutes Arbil stood staring at the blue dragons which writhed over his walls. Marduk gave him strength, but it was to Shamash, the sun god that he should turn now. Shamash, seeker of truth. Shamash, dispenser of justice. Because if that long-legged bitch was winding him up, he'd give her a scar to match Tryphon's! She could whine and wail and plead all she liked, by the time he'd finished with her, no man would want her. As Sargon had said only recently, you don't mess with us Babylonians.

Arbil dressed with care, although his hands were shaking badly as he rubbed the cedarwood oil into his hair and beard to make them shine. She was making it up. Of course she was making it up. He hated the city, and the pigs who lived in it. Why would he go there? What did she mean, every week? The bitch was winding him up, that was all.

'Lugal.'

'Sir?' A young groom looked up from where he was straddled across an ass's hind leg, gouging a stone from its hoof. The stables smelled of acid manure and damp mule hair, of clover feed and polished leather.

'Come here, boy.'

What did Arbil know of Lugal? Not much, except that like Dino and the Captain and a score of others he could name, the boy had shown promise in his field. Which meant Lugal was trustworthy.

'Is something wrong, sir?' He patted the donkey's flank and walked to where Arbil was standing.

'No. No, of course not.' The slave master studied the boy's face carefully. 'I was looking for an old orange robe of mine. Have you seen it?'

Lugal shrugged. 'No, sir. Do you want me to check the gig?'

In what he hoped would be interpreted as a casual gesture, Arbil leaned against the stable door as the strength drained from his knees. 'Gig?'

'I've not had time to clean up, yet. Nubu there,' he indicated the donkey he'd been attending, 'he's been limping, so I thought I'd see to him first.'

He disappeared round the stable door, and after a count of ten, Arbil followed him. There was mud caked on the spokes, and splatters all over the buckboard.

'Is this what you're after, sir?' Lugal was pulling his favourite orange robe from under the passenger seat.

Arbil cleared his throat. 'Yes. You can . . . you can keep it, if you like, Lugal. It's just an old thing.' He'd never wear it again, that was sure! 'Tell me, when we went into Rome this afternoon . . .' He waited to be contradicted.

'Yes?'

Shit. 'When we went to Rome, what did I do there?'

Lugal shrugged and look blank. 'I don't rightly know, sir. I dropped you off at the usual place—'

'The what?'

'The Collina Gate, sir. Where I always drop you before I call you a litter and return to the post house to wait. Have . . . have I done something wrong?'

Arbil took a deep, deep breath. 'No. No, Lugal, you've done nothing wrong. I'm . . . I'm just checking you get all your facts straight, lad. You need that, if you're to stay long-term with me.' There was another awkward silence, then he said. 'How often do I go into Rome?'

No need to question Lugal further to see he had his facts at his fingertips. 'Always on a market day,' he said proudly, 'and lately sometimes in between. Can I go now, sir? Nabu's in a bit of pain.'

XVII

What a sight to behold in Claudia's banqueting hall! The pickle merchant's gold plate shining for all it was worth (and it was worth plenty!) The ex-consul's ivories. The senator's bronze Venus. Tomorrow they'd have to go back, of course, but for tonight the room looked magnificent. A private flower meadow carpeted the floor, lush garlands hung on the walls and the porphry merchant's lampstands lit the place like midsummer sunshine. But it was the sight of three hefty trunks sitting in the vestibule which made Claudia practically cartwheel into the room.

'Claudia! We were just saying, weren't we, Fannia, what a wonderful concert this afternoon! Such a pity you missed the finale!'

'And the Bull Dance was breathtaking, such mastery of horseflesh!'

'So generous of you, Cousin, to lay on not only a banquet for us later, but to treat us to apperitifs of rose wine now, before we get changed.'

The Dragon From Hell sidled up. 'I must say, daughter-in-law, you have done us proud.'

That was the plan. 'Thank you, Larentia.'

'I speak for us all, when I say we've enjoyed every minute.'

Oh, me too. 'I'm so pleased.'

'You've spared no expense –'

Tell me about it!

'– and I want you to know we appreciate the effort you've put in on our behalf, don't we, ladies?'

Was there no end to deafening choruses?

'Also.' She tapped one claw against her jewelled goblet. 'I fear I owe you an apology.'

Damn right. 'Water under the Milvian Bridge, Larentia.'

'No, no, credit where it's due,' the old woman said, and Claudia winced. That was the trouble. By noon tomorrow, credit would not be where it was due, and the moneylender seemed very preoccupied with kneecaps of late!

'I refer, of course, to the urchin.'

'Jovi?' Claudia passed round a plate of raisin bread.

'I was talking to him –' Interrogating, more like. '– and I may have jumped to conclusions.' Old Leatherchops began to pick plump yellow raisins from her chunk of bread. 'What I mistook for a speech impediment appears to be the nasal twang of the slums.'

I know. Claudia nibbled at the sticky, warm dough. Mine took years to eradicate.

'He told me what happened, and how you brought him back here –' Oh, Jovi. Please don't mention the man in the frock! '– fed him honeyed apricots and pies, and I understand you've posted a reward for his mother to come forward.'

None too successfully, either. Two women had turned up, neither of them the little chap's ma. Claudia had doubled the reward to lure the money-grabbing bitch out of her hole. 'Charity is my middle name.'

Since her bread now resembled a colander, Larentia began to plug the gaps with the raisins on her plate. 'Moreover, you have managed my son's business most admirably . . . from what you tell me, of course!' At least the old fossil had the grace to blush. 'I mean, it's obvious the firm's prospering.' A crabbed hand swept through the air towards the bronze goddess in the corner and encompassed the lavish spread which the servants were still laying out.

It worked! The old harpy was finally won over! Claudia resisted the urge to shout 'Yahoo', and reached for the scented wine instead.

Larentia had replaced all the raisins in the bread, except for one, which appeared not to fit anywhere.

Claudia raised her glass to her lips.

'So.' Larentia popped the spare raisin in her mouth. 'As you're doing so well for yourself, we've all decided to stay on.'

Wine sprayed all over Claudia's gown.

'Madam, please!' Cypassis trotted behind her mistress as she marched up and down the bedroom floor. 'That's the third curl to break loose.'

Claudia threw her arms in the air. 'You are out, do you hear me, o-u-t, out.'

'But—' The big-boned peasant girl lunged with the curling tongs and missed.

'Thanks to your stupidity, my house has been turned into a trout farm and all you can say is stand-still-madam-there's-three-ringlets-on-the-prowl—'

'Four, actually.'

'—when you should be prostrate on your knees, begging me not to sell you at auction. Why didn't you tell me those trunks were coming in, not going out?' She grabbed the handmirror. 'What do you mean, four?'

'Five, now,' Cypassis puffed. 'If you'd only keep still a second—'

'How am I supposed to feed them?' Moneylenders are not the only people who get the hump when you forget to settle up. The fowler was turning pretty nasty. 'Not that you care. Or whether I end up with a bathsponge for a brain from endless bloody small talk.' Small talk! Any smaller and it'll be downright invisible. 'Now, are you going to fix my hair or run up and down this room all night long? I can't see a thing for curls in my eyes!'

Claudia plumped down in the chair. Why? Why, when right across the city you'll hear nursemaids crooning lullabies and schoolboys stammering over homework, can I hear nothing but teeth grinding like pine nuts in a pestle? The mirror crashed against the wall and left a gouge in the plaster. What am I supposed to do about that bloody gold and silver plate?

'Tomorrow you stay by the back door, and if anyone calls who looks like a debt collector, you're to say,' she put on a squeaky voice, 'are you the doctor, come about the typhus? Practise.'

'Are-you-the-doctor-come-about-the-typhus.'

'Good. Now what about the wine stain, do you think it'll come out? I'm very fond of that apricot tunic and – ye gods, what's that?'

Screaming had broken out from the kitchens. Pans and plates clattered off the tiles, there were shouts, shrieks and curses, then a table overturned. Claudia rushed out of her room and leaned over the gallery.

'Correct me if I'm wrong, Cypassis, but that –' she pointed to a small creature with a long tail and a round black face, '– looks like a monkey shinning up the atrium drapes.'

'Ah,' the broad-cheeked Thessalian scratched at her ear, 'Jovi's pet must have slipped its leash.'

'Which auction block would you prefer to be sold at, Cypassis? The one in the Forum by the Arch of Augustus, or would you prefer to watch dead goats float down the Tiber as you stand by the Sublician Bridge?'

'I thought it was one of your jokes, madam, honest I did. It came in a little brown sack with a note saying "With love from the man in the frock".'

Wait till I get my hands on his windpipe!

'Perhaps that's what kept Miss Fortunata awake, the monkey?'

'Fortunata is a silly, neurotic cow, that's what kept her awake, Cypassis. Now show that simian the door.'

'But Jovi loves it!'

'NOW!'

Drusilla arrived to check out the kerfuffle, but Claudia scooped her up and shut the bedroom door, amid howling protests. 'You've done enough damage, thank you, chasing Herky-Perky round the cellar.' Her fingernails raked the cat's upturned chin. 'I say, it wasn't you chasing mice in the night, giving the old ducks the idea that we're haunted?'

'Prrrrr.'

'Ghoulies and ghosties, indeed!' She set down the cat. 'Wait a sec!'

'Mrrr?'

'Doesn't Fannia sleep on the right of Gaius' bedroom?'

'Mrrow.' Drusilla reared up to be cuddled.

'And Fortunata on the left?'

'Brrip, brrip.'

'Sorry, poppet.' She unhooked the cat's claws from her lilac linen robe, and noticed six small snags remained as souvenirs. 'It's probably nothing more complicated than a hiccup in our chemistry experiments – some of the knockout drops stronger than others.'

Playing up their, shall we say, hallucinogenic properties? Claudia deposited a carmine outline of her lips between the cat's crossed eyes and, checking the hall was clear of aunts and monkeys, ran lightly down the stairs. I know you, Gaius Seferius. You'll have far better ways of spending your afterlife than clumping around scaring your cousins! But all the same. It was no coincidence that the occupants of both rooms either side had heard noises. Best check it out!

'Package for you, ma'am,' called a bald Sarmatian slave, and handed across a small hide pouch sticky with mildew. 'Left inside the vestibule.'

'Inside?'

'Yes, ma'am.' He pointed to a mosaic fish. 'Right there.'

Tentatively. Claudia opened the bag. Inside was a strip of peach-coloured linen, and a letter folded in four. Her stomach lurched at the familiar cramped writing . . .

'*so you will know i've not abandoned you i send this blindfold and when we fuck i'll—*' The parchment trembled in her hands. By the gods, this man is sick! Where does he get these vicious, warped fantasies? She forced herself to read on, and the last line jarred her to the marrow, '*and know i am watching you*'.

Hugging her body, she scanned the busy street. Pack mules weighed down with panniers. Itinerant salt vendors. A young blade in his chariot. Early carousers heading for taverns. Nothing sinister. No one lurking in doorways. No suspicious characters loitering on corners. For the first time, Claudia wondered why he called himself Magic . . .

She ran up the stairs fishing Gaius' key from the folds of her gown. Stupid, bloody thing. Wouldn't stay still. Get in that lock, dammit! Now turn. Turn, I said! There was sweat on her forehead when she closed the door and leaned her weight against it.

The room had not changed since her husband had died here. Garish walls, loud textiles. Friezes where there ought to be frescoes, too much silver, too much marble, a leopardskin rug. To Gaius, these things spelled success, confirmation of his rise to equestrian status, but for now, the room was strangely comforting.

She gripped the bedrail for support. Her heart seemed to be playing kettledrums with her rib bones, and someone had stolen her lower limbs and filled the gap with aspic.

Why did he do this? Why did he write these reams of filth? What was he hoping to achieve? If it was a power trip this Magic character was on, he was out of luck. Any signs that he terrified her Claudia kept to herself, and if they were 'genuine' protestations of love, why didn't he reveal himself? She did not have the answers, but one thing was certain. Magic was creeping closer and closer . . .

Claudia released the bedrail and wiped the dust off her hands down the pastel lilac linen. Her husband was nothing if not orderly, everything sat in its place. His desk, his inkwells, his basketweave chair. Even his symbol of rank, the equestrian sword, still hung in his sheath on the wall. A lump rose in her throat. Last August. She had walked in and found him slumped upon that very weapon. For a moment, she could still hear the flies and smell the blood . . .

'Gaius, you silly daft sod!'

Picking up his clothes-brush, she ran the ox's tail several times through her loosely clenched fist. That, too, he'd had dyed a typical vivid scarlet, because nothing Gaius ever did was subtle. She smiled. Including haunting, if that's what he put his mind to! He wouldn't have settled for a half-hearted clump across the timbers. Gaius Seferius would have done it in style, wailing like a banshee. They'd have heard him as far as the Capitol!

After the funeral, Claudia had insisted this room remain locked, on the pretext of preserving his memory. (Where else could she conceal the true company accounts?) Only Claudia had a key, and since she gave up housework once she heard it gave you warts, thick cobwebs had congregated on the gilt-encrusted rafters and you could have carted out dust by the bucketload.

So, no, it was not Gaius' ghost who'd walked this room overnight. The hairs on the back of her neck curled and prickled.

Phantoms do not leave their footprints in the dust.

Phantoms do not leave their imprint on the bed.

XVIII

When you think about it, there are only two ways to deal with fear. Let it in, or kick it out. And since Claudia was not the type of woman to allow a canker-worm to eat away her character, she left her fear licking its wounds in a dark recess of her consciousness.

'Why, Claudia, what on earth are you doing with that hammer?'

Trust Julia to be wandering round, when she ought to be in her room preparing for the banquet!

'Um.' High female laughter floated down into the atrium. 'Fannia asked me to fetch one.' She gave a silvery laugh herself. 'You know how eccentric she is.'

Julia's hooded eyes narrowed. 'She was always odd, that woman. Told me once, she not only shared a bed with her husband, she actually enjoyed what he . . . you know. Did to her.' Her mouth turned down at the corners. 'Frankly, that hammer doesn't surprise me.'

Stifling a laugh, Claudia returned to her room. 'What's the matter, poppet? Still hankering after the monkey?'

Watching Drusilla disappear into the night, Claudia wished she could follow. We'll stay on until after the Megalesian Games, Larentia had said. Claudia pressed the heels of her hands against her eyeballs. Hell, that's another ten days! I'll be dead before then! She rubbed the back of her neck and looked out. Poor old Rome! Never allowed to settle down for the evening with a good book and its feet up, already it'll be cracking its knuckles, primed for the work which lies ahead. Musclemen cranking open the huge city gates to let wheeled traffic through, dressmakers squinting through lamplight they cannot afford because the client's changed her mind – and pity the poor fisherman, who cannot rely on tides coinciding with daylight!

Claudia slammed the shutters and wished that had been her mother-in-law's face.

It would be hard, the next ten days, but provided no cracks appeared in her facade, Larentia shouldn't catch so much as the faintest rattle of a closeted skeleton, no matter how keen her goddammed hearing! It was called keeping up appearances, and Claudia was an expert.

For Gaius, marriage had merely meant another gaudy trophy, a wife to be wheeled out at social occasions and as such their paths had rarely crossed. With Larentia stuck in Etruria, his daughter fostered on Julia (who in any case had few dealings with her brother), deception had been easy to orchestrate.

Until that desiccated old fossil took it upon herself to test Claudia to the limits!

She inhaled from braziers redolent with the scent of dried herbs – balm and borage, lavender and mint – and thought, you want hospitality? I'll give you hospitality. So much so, you'll be gagging on it, begging to go home to the country! And tonight's off to a good start. I hadn't envisaged this, you wizened old crow, but we've got acrobats and jugglers, fire eaters and dancers, flautists and tumblers. And just to show you how bloody rich I am, guess whose robe matches the *exact* colours of the banqueting hall? Claudia twirled round in her feast gown. Searching examination would quickly reveal an ancient nightshift coloured with cheap vegetable dyes, but the old bats were short-sighted and a range of glittery accessories, coupled with oodles of perfume and some second-hand flounces would—

What was that?

Claudia laid down her gold torque and listened. There it was again, a soft scuffle from the balcony. Then she saw it. A tongue of metal, so thin it could fit between closed shutters, which could only be the blade of a knife . . .

Bloody burglars! There'd been a real upsurge of these bastards since Agrippa died, taking advantage of people's grief and confusion and growing fat on their thieving. She blew out the lantern. I'll give you bloody burglary, mate!

The blade had found the latch and she could hear the tinny scratch of metal upon metal. Picking up a red upholstered footstool by its leg, she weighted it in her hands. Just the job. The latch was lifting as she skipped to the side of the window. Climb up my balcony, would you, chum? The first leaf of the shutter opened to admit a blast of damp air. Claudia could see an inky outline in the gloom.

Taking a deep breath, she counted out his footsteps in the dark.

One . . .

Two . . .

Clonk!

With a thud, the intruder fell flat on the floor, his long thin knife skidding out of his hand and across the polished wooden timbers to land at Claudia's feet. As the burglar began to groan, she covered the blade with one foot and kicked him in the ribs with the other.

'How much are you carrying?'

'Uh?'

'Money, jewellery, come on. What's your trawl so far this evening?'

You might not rob me, sunshine, but by the gods, I'll take every copper quadran you have on you. Trust me. I have no compunction about paying the fowler with your pretty baubles!

'Aaargh.'

'Spare us the histrionics, chum. Just hand 'em over.'

XIX

The intruder dragged himself on to all fours and shook his head like a dog. 'For a foggy night,' he said miserably, 'I'm seeing one heck of a lot of bright stars.'

'*Orbilio?*' Claudia stepped over his back and set light to a couple of wicks. 'Good grief, man, don't you know better than to go around breaking other people's foot-stools!' She jabbed the gaping upholstery. 'The horsehair's coming out in tufts!'

'Listen, if anyone's hair's falling out it should be mine. From stress.'

'There's a leg loose, as well.'

'Mine, probably.'

Claudia sat down on the battered footstool and studied her burglar at close quarters. 'I thought you were a thief,' she explained, resting her chin in her hands. 'Or I wouldn't have hit you so hard.'

'But you'd still have hit me?' Marcus Cornelius leaned back on his knees. 'That's reassuring.'

'What do you expect, creeping around like a common burglar! Didn't you think to try the front door?'

'Would you have let me in?'

'No.'

'Well then.' Gingerly he tested the bump on his head. 'Anyway, the other way was barred.' He smoothed his dishevelled mop, then squinted. 'Is that frock real, or am I hallucinating?'

'Oh no,' she said smugly. 'This is the genuine article, guaranteed to knock the old trouts' eyeballs right out of their sockets.'

'Should you find mine while you're about it, send them home, will you?' He hauled himself to his feet and massaged the back of his neck.

'It's not that bad,' she chided, shaking out her sleeves. 'Scarlet, blue, with a spot of green here and there. What do you mean, the other way was barred?'

'You missed out the yellow, orange, pinks and purples.'

'I asked you a question.'

'I'd have knocked at the shutters, only I heard music downstairs and assumed you were there with the others.'

Claudia rose to her feet. 'That wasn't the question.'

He was right about the music. The best way to defend is by attack and a robust pace demanded robust entertainment, bring on the horns and the cymbals.

'Would you prefer me,' she asked, 'to scream "thief" at the top of my voice? "Arrested for housebreaking" might add a certain cachet to your CV.'

'As I recall, *you* tried to rob *me*.' Orbilio poured himself a glass of wine from the jug on the table. It had not reached his lips before the goblet was snatched from his hand and was flouncing out into the cool night air.

'All right, all right,' he called, as her mouth formed a wide O. 'If you must know,' he stepped on to the balcony to join her, 'I spent last night in Gaius' bed.'

'*You?*'

For a moment, he was non-plussed. 'Mother of Tarquin!' He ran his hand over his face. 'You thought it was Magic, didn't you? That's why you nailed up the shutters!'

'There was a draught,' she said, tilting her chin at where the moon would be, had it not been hidden by so many clouds. 'So I'll thank you kindly to keep your size tens out of that room from now on.'

'You want me to sleep there?' he asked mildly, swivelling his eyes towards the bed.

'I'd sooner take my chance with a sex-starved gorilla!'

'I could wear a fur cloak,' he grinned, 'and pretend?'

She wished now she'd brained him harder.

Fog had risen from the Tiber just like last night and the three nights before that. Along the street, only the occasional hazy slab of light from another window brightened up the gloom, and below, in the street, a man with a Phrygian accent appeared to be suffering pangs of regret at not having bought a new pair of boots, these ones had effing holes in. A few blocks away, the snarl of a lion told of its anger at being caged up for three weeks then paraded through the city after dark, and from the smoke-house across the way came the distinctive smell of sausage, hams and cheeses drying over blackened chips of oak.

'He's a dangerous man, Claudia.' Orbilio picked up the glass she'd perched on the balcony rail and threw half the contents down his throat. 'Unhinged and unpredictable. All joking aside, you cannot afford to take chances.'

'You think that creep bothers me?' she countered with a nonchalent toss of her curls, and Cypassis would have been mortified at how many worked loose this time.

'Then why do you have bodyguards patrolling the streets? Why nail up the shutters? Think that'll deter him?'

He gave a short laugh. 'Magic might not be educated, but he's as cunning as a fox, and until he's locked in the dungeons, I'm staying put whether you like it or not.'

'Not.'

Downstairs she could hear applause for the juggler who had taken over from the rumbustious musicians. No doubt the neighbours would be mighty relieved at the change. Two streets away, the lion roared again.

'Then I give you a choice. He leaned the small of his back against the rim of the balustrade. 'Me or the military.'

'Aren't you supposed to be rounding up conspirators and hunting down killers?'

There was an unseemly twinkle in his eyes as he said, 'So it's the army, then?'

Shit.

Traffic was beginning to clog the crossroads, exacerbated by the perpetual mist and resultant bad tempers. The night air mixed animal ordure with the smells of ripe melons, charcoal and fleeces and pitch. Torch bearers touted for pedestrians to guide home, a cat, not Drusilla, yowled from the rooftops and a woman in tears pleaded with her man to come home. For Claudia, it might be happening a million miles away. She felt her senses dissolve as she braced herself to ask the question she'd been wanting to ask all along.

'Why are you really here, Marcus?'

Time stopped. The rumpus faded into silence, banished by the pounding of her heart. She saw his eyes close, his jaw tense.

'You know why,' he said thickly.

'Tell me.'

'Because—' She could hear the rasp of his breath,

ragged in his throat. Saw a pulse beat in his neck. 'God-dammit, because I—'

'Yes?' The slightest breeze would have carried such an insubstantial sound away.

She heard him mutter. It sounded like 'oh, shit' as he spun away, resting his arms on the balustrade, his head hung heavy. Several seconds and a couple of loaded wagons passed as he fought for words. Claudia held her breath and thought her lungs would burst.

Clearing his throat, Marcus Cornelius straightened up and did not turn to face her. 'It's my duty to ensure the safety of every Roman citizen.' He seemed to be addressing the roof opposite. 'Therefore, until the threat of your stalker has passed – what was that?'

'My pot of white narcissus meeting a cartload of crockery.' Silly cow, what did you expect him to say? 'Wave to the nice waggoner, Marcus, he's waving at you.'

'He's waving his fist.'

'Nah, he's just trying to calm his mules down, the splinters made them skittish.' Claudia rubbed at her toe. It bloody hurt, kicking that pot, but worth every broken bone in her foot. Stupid bitch.

His gaze still fixed on a gutterspout, Orbilio upended the contents of the glass in one swallow. 'So until this maniac's in chains, I shall continue to camp in Gaius' room, and you can be assured of my absolute discretion.'

'Discretion?' She didn't dare look at him. 'The entire plumed cavalry corps racing into battle would have been quieter than your clodhopping!'

'I've had a lot to contend with,' he said stiffly. 'Pacing helps.' A long silence followed, and the next time he spoke, his voice carried its normal inflection. 'When do the aunts leave?'

With an effort, so did hers. 'When do barnacles drop off?'

Now he turned his face to hers. 'They're staying? What changed their minds?'

Her mouth soured. 'Have you ever heard the expression, generosity killed the cat?'

'You mean curiosity.'

You kill cats your way. I'll kill them mine. 'I tell you, Larentia will die at sea to stop me dancing on her grave,' she said. 'And in the meantime, I'm suffocating in a nightmare of domestic trivia.' Turning on her heel, Claudia returned to the gentle warmth of the braziers and slammed the shutters on the acidic night air.

'That,' he gasped, diving through the gap, 'was nearly as athletic as the Bull Dancers.'

Somehow I just knew, Marcus Randypants Orbilio, you'd get around to flaunting your conquests sooner rather than later. Claudia picked up her handmirror. 'I'm afraid,' she said, licking her finger and running it over her finely arched brow, 'that I was far too entranced by Porsenna to notice.'

'So that's the dormouse farmer?'

'I can't imagine what you find so amusing. He's handsome, romantic, chivalrous – and waiting for me downstairs,' she added pointedly. 'He said my face is pure poetry—'

'Did he say which lines he liked best? Ouch! That caught me right in the solar plexus.'

'Pity. I was aiming at your head.'

Marcus picked up the mirror and with a polite bow

tossed it back. 'My head's in enough trouble,' he grinned, lifting up the offending footstool and stuffing its horsehair back into the gaping upholstery. 'Although my backside, I confess, is in worse.'

'You mean your boss found out you'd diverted troops from protecting the Emperor to question passers-by on the Argiletum?'

'Exactly.' He set down the stool and rested one foot on it. 'And a fat lot of use that turned out to be! It's hardly the Esquiline where cohorts of slaves take Milady's lapdogs for walkies last thing at night. Few booksellers want perfumed poodles at their feet.'

'Cobblers,' she said prettily. 'The street's packed with them, too, don't forget.'

He shot her a sharp amused glanced. 'As it happens, shoemakers aren't much at pet-keeping, either. Two fighting tomcats, a pack of feral dogs, one scavenging fox and a ferret.' His mouth twisted down at one side. 'The sum total of a whole night's work! No witnesses, no whistles – and no gold stars for Marcus. Aren't you keeping the mouse man waiting?'

'Patience is but one of Porsenna's endless virtues.'

'Is that a fact.' Orbilio shifted his weight on to the other foot. 'It's not that I don't sympathize with the Emperor's predicament, it's just—' Passion flooded his vocal chords. 'Claudia, I can't stand idle while some butcher slices up Ann—' He broke off suddenly.

'Ann?' she probed, perching against the edge of her maplewood clothes chest.

'Ann-other young slave girl,' he improvised quickly.

'I see.' Down below, a round of applause ended the lyre player's first session, which meant the acrobats were due on. Claudia wondered why she made no move to join in the fun. 'So the killing in the Wolf Grotto this afternoon *was* the work of the Market Day Murderer?'

Orbilio topped up the glass from the wine jug and waited until half the dark red liquid had warmed him inside. 'The official line is, no,' he said slowly. 'True, they argue, the victim had a blue tattoo, but she was killed by a single cut to the throat, in broad daylight, and not on a market day.' He threw back the rest of the wine. 'Her limbs were not bound, nor had her hair been cut off.'

Lavender from the linen in the chest filtered upwards to mingle with the dried herbs in the air. Leonides would be serving absinthe with the omelettes and oysters very shortly, and Claudia realized with a start that she was hungry. Why *didn't* she leave?

'But?' she asked.

Marcus Cornelius stretched himself lengthwise on her bed, tossing aside her bolster and folding his hands beneath his head. His eyes traced the painted flowers on the ceiling, and the lines of the rafters.

'But.' Orbilio propped himself up on one elbow and turned to face her. 'It was raining; there were few people abroad, even fewer taking time off to go exploring the Lupercal.' He flopped back down on the bed and chewed his lower lip. 'Those folk who *were* around, however, reported hearing a man whistle his dog. Three short, sharp consecutive notes.' He put his lips together. 'Whit-whit-whit.'

'Like Zosi the speech seller described?'

'Identical.' He closed his eyes. 'Which begs the question, why would Zygia's killer replicate the one detail we'd kept secret, moreover one which might not even be noticed, yet disregard the more bizarre aspects?'

The smell of roast meat squeezed through the floorboards – wild boar and venison, hazel hens and goose. They would be served up with pastries moulded like artichokes and coarse brown bread to mop up the juices. Then, while the meat course settled, a group of fire-eaters would come in, and there would be blond-haired, blue-eyed Porsenna on call to pay her court and compliments. Claudia picked up a gold bangle and turned it slowly, like a wheel, between her two outstretched index fingers.

'Yesterday you talked about this being, what was the phrase – ritual murder? Bodies arranged in certain positions, the symbolism of the hair in the lap—'

Orbilio stroked his hand along Claudia's damasked sheet. 'Call it a hunch, call it instinct, call it pig-headed stubbornness,' he said. 'But this is the work of the same man, I can smell it.'

Claudia studied the investigator as he lay on the counterpane, eyes closed and his wavy hair tousled. In stark contrast to the gales of laughter rising from below, his voice sounded drained to the marrow and she noticed the first smudge of stubble on his jaw and dark circles beneath his long lashes.

'I've missed something,' he added wearily. 'Somewhere along the line, I've missed a clue, but for the life of me, I can't think where.'

Claudia felt a pounding in her ribcage, a tightness in her throat. He had no right to be here! No right to be lying white with fatigue on her bed, scenting her room with his sandalwood!

'Then perhaps you should not spread yourself so

thinly,' she replied tartly, clipping on ear studs fashioned like seahorses. It was definitely time to join Porsenna and the aunts! 'Decide which case needs priority and concentrate on solving one of them properly instead of three not at all.' She shook out the flounces on her brightly coloured gown. 'Orbilio, are you listening to me?'

Soft snores rising from the bed answered for him.

XX

Can you see it? There, in the shadows of the great striding aqueduct which ferries water from the Anio, that low brick building which looks like a cattle shed? Inside it reeks of cheap wine, stale sweat and the blood of thousands of fighting cocks who have laid down their lives in that deep central pit, yet despite the lateness of the hour, its walls are still threatening to burst. Coins change hands swifter than lightning, tempers flare faster and should proof be needed that Rome is a melting pot, look around. Dark-skinned Numidians, hook-nosed Parthians, moustachioed Celts, the blond men of Belgica. One night you'll see Teutonic tribesmen with horns sticking out of their helmets; another, Lycians snuggled deep inside fur-collared coats. There'll be masons, paviors, magistrates and tax collectors, Cypriots, Indians, Jews.

Dinocrates pushed his way to the front, where Sargon seemed to be having difficulty getting his point across.

'The black fucker, you moron,' he shouted, then turned to his friend. 'I gave that arsehole fifty sesterces, and with only two birds to bet on, he still put our money on the wrong bloody one.'

The bookie in question, a squat Cappadocian with four chins but precious little Latin, was shrugging and pointing to the larger of the two cockerels, which had pheasant-type plumage and a much thinner neck.

'I know that's the favourite,' Sargon mouthed. 'Just back the black bugger, will you!'

'*Our* money?' queried Dino, retrieving his embroidered cuff from the gesticulating fingers of a Spaniard beside him.

'The praetor's wife finally dropped her calf,' his friend grinned. 'So while the Captain plays nursemaid, I set about doubling our remuneration.'

'Call me short-sighted, but your purse seems a trifle unfurnished.'

'My accumulator went down in that last fight, but we still have fifty sesterces.'

'Which rides on that scrawny bag of feathers over there?'

Sargon laughed. 'Your face won't be so sour when we pick up our winnings, Dino, we'll need a handcart to carry them home in. Look at that spur, sharp as a dagger. How come you're so late?'

'Things,' he shrugged. 'Nothing special.'

The young Babylonian pushed his rich, red cloak back from his shoulders as the black cock was shown its opponent at close quarters. A vicious beak lashed out, but the trainer pulled the bird back, a ritual which would be repeated several more times, to wind the cockerels into a frenzy. 'Everything's all right, isn't it?' he asked slowly. 'I mean, you'd say if it wasn't?'

Dinocrates bridled. 'Everything's fine. Why shouldn't it be?'

'No reason.' Sargon's eyes remained fixed on the fighting cocks as they lunged at one other in their owners' strong grip. 'Only you absent yourself rather a lot when we come into Rome these days.'

The two angry birds were released into the pit. The roar from the punters was deafening.

'Can you blame me,' Dino said at length. 'Seeing your ugly mug all the time – and anyway, you're a fine one to talk! Where do you sneak off to, may I ask?'

'That,' Sargon pulled one eyelid down with his finger, 'would be telling. Oh, is my black cockerel a winner or not? *Come on, boy! Get him!*'

Whistles and stamping and roars of encouragement nearly shook the gutterspouts loose from the roof as the birds attacked in murderous frenzy. Arcs of blood spurted as they dived, pecking and gouging and spearing with deadly sharpened spurs. Flaps of comb and wattle spat across the pit as they screamed and tore and stabbed, the men around them hoarse from bawling. For several minutes the contest remained equal, then slowly the squall of feathers subsided as the weaker of the two moved on to a defence that was merely a question of time.

'I tell you him de best, Sargon. I tell you, not de black one!' The Cappadocian's downturned mouth disappeared into copious rolls of flesh. 'I pick you bird for next bout, yes?'

'Fucking loser!' Sargon kicked the pit rail, where, below, the carcass of the black cockerel had been removed and fresh sand thrown over the carnage.

'You or the chicken?' laughed Dino.

'Ha, ha, very funny.' The long-haired Babylonian aimed a mock punch.

'Never mind,' Dino gave him a consolatory pat on the back. 'I reckon we can still run to a wineskin between us!'

Outside, Sargon let out three short whistles and Silverstreak trotted over, nuzzling the palm of his master's hand. A long pink tongue rasped against the skin and the three of them set off down the hill, where ghostly figures loomed in and out of the mist, reeling, stumbling, skulking in doorways. The air here was sour from the tanner's yard, and an owl hooted from an arch in the aqueduct. As they passed, a chink of light revealed a soot-blackened tavern, mine host's customers slumped over their goblets as a one-eyed mongrel lapped at the dregs of spilled liquor. Silverstreak sniffed twice and loped on.

'Know what I think?' Sargon clapped his arm round Dinocrates' shoulder. 'I think we ought to rear our own bloody fighting cocks! Breed ourselves tough little bastards who could make us a fortune.'

'We're hardly on the skids,' Dino said drily. 'Tonight excepting, my friend, these upper-class by-blows thread gold through our tunics, set precious stones in our cloak-pins—'

'Lesson one, Dino. A man can never have too much hair or too much money!' Still grinning, Sargon rapped at a lion's head knocker, where they were swallowed up by a throng of music and dancing, lamplight and laughter. Scantily clad girls came to pat Silverstreak, who rolled on to his back in delight.

'I'm trying to picture Arbil's face,' said Dino, yanking off his fringed boots, 'when he hears you propose to farm chickens.'

A Nubian slave, naked and shaved, washed their feet in scented water while another thrust goblets of wine into their hands. The wolf followed his nose to the kitchens, knowing he'd be slipped titbits of goose and mutton before stretching out in front of an open log fire on which a whole pig would be roasting.

'By Marduk,' said Sargon, wiping his mouth with the back of his hand. 'This is an improvement on my father's gnat's pee.'

Dino spluttered, laughing, into his glass. 'Arbil will have you strung up by your balls, insulting his ale! But I have to confess, I'm with you on this, my friend. I much prefer the Roman ways.' He smiled into the middle distance. 'Much prefer,' he repeated softly.

The crooking of one Babylonian finger brought two lissom young girls running over. One had gold dust painted on her naked nipples, the other wore a transparent tunic and only perfume underneath.

'The attractions are more readily available, that's for sure.' A blind balladeer began to strum a haunting lovesong as Sargon ran his hand absently up and down a shapely oiled thigh. 'Tell me, Dino.' He paused. 'Seeing as how you and I are so attached to the city, how do you feel about transferring here permanently?'

The Greek's head came up sharply. 'Are you serious?'

'Perfectly.' Sargon moved the girl on to his knee, where she proceeded to run expert hands through his long, jet-black hair.

'What about Arbil? He'll—'

'Uh-uh. I'm talking about you and me, Dino. We set our headquarters in Rome and run the whole shooting match from here. What do you say?'

'Go behind Arbil's back?' hissed Dinocrates. 'Croesus, man, we'll end up staked out as jackal meat, the crows pecking our eyes and our liver!'

Sargon slipped his hand under the whore's flimsy tunic.

'I'm not talking about going into opposition, I'm talking about when I take over.' He leaned closer towards Dino. 'You've seen him these past few weeks. Can't remember his own fucking name half the time, babbles to himself, I tell you, the old man's falling apart. Angel says he can't even get it up any more!'

A youth on the pan pipes took over from the blind balladeer, more wine was brought round, and on a nod from the management, the second girl rippled her fingers over Dinocrates' chest. Without thinking, he pushed her away and a flutter of gold dust danced through the air.

'Yes, piss off, you two.' Sargon unceremoniously dumped his girl on to the floor, where she promptly demanded her money. The Babylonian ignored her. 'Whichever way you look at it,' he said to Dino, 'my father is not a well man.' He grabbed the whingeing whore by her arm and thrust his face into hers. 'You've earned nowt, you'll get nowt,' he snarled. 'So shut the fuck up.'

'I let you have a feel, didn't I?'

Exasperated, Sargon fished into his purse. 'Yes, madam, you did. Here's what it was worth.' He spun a copper quadran, the lowest denomination, into her lap. 'Now sod off and leave us alone.'

Humiliated and outraged, she flounced away to complain to the management. The management laughed.

'We'd better go,' Dino said, pointing out that it was time to link up with Tryphon. 'It's already past midnight.'

Neither he nor Sargon had enquired what the Captain planned to do with his day off, he was quite an enigma, was Tryphon, he'd only have growled that it was none of their business. Which was true. So long as he was back in time to collect the child of the praetor's wife (which he had been), what he did in his own time was his affair, yet it was strange, thought Dinocrates, that he never mentioned the one subject which had set the city alight this afternoon. The girl they'd found up in the Lupercal. They weaved their way through the convoluted maze of lanes towards the Collina Gate. Maybe he and Sargon ought to have a word with the Captain? Make sure they got their stories straight before reporting to Arbil? Yes, indeed, a quiet word would do no harm. He was always reliable, was Tryphon.

'That's another thing,' Sargon said, stepping aside to let a wagon piled with bales and fleeces lumber past. Silverstreak, grumpy at leaving the fire, bared his fangs at the mules. 'When I'm in charge, we'll send some other bugger to go searching the middens. It's no job for you and me!'

'We're the only ones your father trusts to do it properly, you know that, but we're slipping from the point, are we not? Granted your father's had a bad run of late, but he's hardly dying, Sargon. There's nothing wrong with his . . . his physical health.'

'Ah, Dino, we grew up together, remember? Shannu might be my baby brother, but,' Sargon grimaced, 'no amount of dancing round the subject can alter the fact.' His voice took on a harsh note. 'Shannu is insane.'

The Greek sighed. No beating about the bush, then. 'You fear Arbil's treading the same path?'

Calling for a torch bearer, Sargon shrugged. 'He's deteriorating fast, you've seen it yourself.'

'Are you not worried for him?'

'I'm more worried for me!' he said sharply. 'That it's hereditary, and who knows when it might strike! That's why I live life for today, Dino. You never know what lurks around the next corner.' They ducked to avoid a cartload of cedars. 'So what do you say? You and me, running the business side by side? Your expertise on the sales side combined with my—'

'Expertise on backing chickens?'

'Ability to increase our income,' he corrected. 'Oh, that makes your eyes light up! Well, Arbil thinks he knows the slave trade, my friend, but I've discovered a way of doubling our turnover. No extra work. No risks. Just this.' He tapped his head. 'Brainwork.'

The Collina Gate loomed out of the swirling mist. The cries of the alms-seekers grew closer, the shouts from the toll booth, the stink of the hovels beyond. Over to the west, the sky danced orange from a tenement which had caught fire, but the screams did not carry this far, there was no indication of the devastation and bereavement it would leave in its wake. Instead, the smell of salt fish mingled with freshly sawn timber, and with dung and hot pies and hemp.

'Are you in, Dino?' Sargon persisted. 'We've grown up like brothers, trust each other, know one another inside out—'

'Apart from the fact you sneak off now and again,' Dino said amiably. 'Are we talking a fifty-fifty split?'

'Sixty-forty, you greedy bastard. But I need to know. Are you with me on this?'

'This', Dino concluded, meant the silent takeover of Arbil's empire. Evidently Sargon was planning to have his father restrained as insane sooner rather than later and he was being asked to join the connivance. He thought of Rome, and what impelled him to come with such regularity, and that thought stirred his loins as well as his young blood. Rescued from Chios, all he'd known was the slave farm up in the hills.

Until recently.

What he'd found here went beyond his wildest fantasies, and the funny thing was, for all the wealth that had been showered upon him, the pleasure he'd discovered in the city came for free . . .

He weighed up the risks of plotting against the powerful Babylonian versus what he'd discovered in Rome. Risk he enjoyed, though. He ran his hand over the stubble which was forming on his chin. No doubt there was a flaw in Sargon's arguments, one which could ultimately prove fatal, but for the life of him, Dino couldn't think of what that flaw might be.

'You know bloody well I am, Sargon.' He wagged a playful finger. 'Provided you let me pick the cockerels in future.'

As nightwatchmen patrolled the warehouses and wharves and scavengers cruised the riverbanks for carrion, the light in Magic's head grew stronger. Like a bright, white ball of lightning, it hurtled relentlessly towards his brain. He could see it, he could feel it, he could even fucking hear it. It was a loud light, screaming, flashing, bursting his skull open.

He tried hiding. Under the table. Under the bedcover. Inside the cupboard. But the light followed, screeching inside his head.

This time it would not go away.

This time there was no voice to comfort him.

•

Tears coursed down his cheeks, he tasted their salt on his tongue and, far beyond the boundaries of the light, he heard keening.

Time passed.

Manure carts and the shovellers who followed clattered on the cobbles far below. Downstairs, an old man snored loud enough to shake the lichens from the rooftiles, but Magic couldn't hear for the serrated ball of flame inside his skull. He could feel it attacking his flesh from within. White hot. Burning. And this time there were no gentle whispers, no soft, sweet songs to stop the light from pressing on his eyeballs.

'Bitch!' he screamed. 'Filthy, treacherous bitch!'

His fingers fumbled for the woollen doll. He'd stolen it this morning, from a child in the Cattle Market, and she'd cried when he snatched it from her hands.

'Bitch!'

With a sharp peeling knife, he hacked and hacked at the doll.

'Take that! And that! And that!'

As the first tinge of dawn reddened the sky above the Esquiline Hill, the baying inside Magic's head began to subside and the hideous light slithered away. He watched a piece of his paper patchwork peel from the wall, touched the globs of fat where his tallow had guttered. Crawling out from under his bed, he stared at the doll in his hands.

At Claudia.

Her shredded tunic hung by a thread on one shoulder. Magic ripped it off and began to keen again, rocking back and forth upon his heels as he pressed the frock over his eyes.

'No one could care for you the way I could,' he wailed. 'No one!'

He picked up the doll and examined the deep gouges on its back and its thighs and its breasts. Not its. *Hers*. Her back, and her thighs, and her breasts. Claudia's breasts. Shaking fingers probed the rip marks in the wool. Claudia's proud, generous breasts which she offered him every night, here in his room, when she came to him alone and in secret. Magic's breathing became ragged. Last night, though, she hadn't come. She had sent the light instead, and the light was evil. She had tricked him. The treacherous bitch had betrayed him.

He shook the doll. 'I'll teach you.' His voice rose. 'This is Magic you're dealing with. Magic, you hear!'

Lighting the wick of another stinking tallow, he picked up his reed, sharpened the point and dipped it in ink.

'*don't think you can deceive me you bitch*', Magic paused and looked up at the welter of copies round his bedroom walls, '*your mine understand you are mine and the next time we meet it shall be for eternity*'.

XXI

The sun was heartily sick of captivity. For a week he'd been bullied by a gang of grey clouds, but now, on the first day of the Megalesian Games, it was time to fight back. What he didn't know, however, because he was behind with the news, was that the bald aedile responsible for organizing the Games had succumbed to the same fever which had laid low his five charioteers, so the sun's first sight of Rome was hardly encouraging. Without expert guidance, the inaugural procession was late setting off, the lictors and statue-bearers hoping to catch up as they quick-marched double-time past the crowds lining the slopes of the Capitol without so much as a thought to the poor aedile wallowing in sweat and delirium. Less would they care about Severina, curled into a ball and howling like an animal for the girl whose throat had been cut in the Wolf Cave . . .

Instead the sun's second punch found a weakness in the cloud cover over what, at first glance, appeared to be nothing more interesting than the office of a moneyed merchant. The window faced on to the peristyle, and so it was across the fountains and the birdbaths, the fan-trained peaches and the herbaries that his rays picked out a desk encrusted with ivory behind a high-backed chair complete with padded armrests and cushions. There were seats for two visitors, upholstered in azure-blue wool, plus chests of satinwood and maple and other grained woods. Fragrant elecampane burned in wall braziers, there were frescoes of flowers, ripe fruits and another of a leopard tamed and entranced by Orpheus' lyre.

All this, of course, our flaming voyeur could find in any rich man's office anywhere across the Empire.

What he wouldn't expect to see, however, were great seas of ink spilling over tessellated peacocks or a flying scatter of scrolls as a blue-eyed, cross-eyed cat twisted from chest to upholstery to fine, damasked drapes in a desperate bid to catch the small creature with a black face and long tail which stubbornly remained one pace ahead, while at the same time a young woman made concerted but unfortunately ineffective snatches in the air, resulting in pens, tablets and styluses rolling under furniture and rugs.

Resting his elbows on the cloudbank, the sun ticked off the laps as monkey, cat and Claudia darted round the room, giving marks out of ten for their balletic leaps and plunges. Then the monkey opened up the game by shinning out the window. Drusilla followed hot on its heels, but Claudia could not. She merely leaned forward, hands on her knees, and prayed her lungs had not sustained permanent damage. In fact, she was still gasping when Marcus Cornelius breezed in.

'The end of another party?' he asked cheerfully, examining the slashes in the damask and claw marks gouged deep in the finely grained woodwork. 'No, I see it's still in full swing.' He stepped over a huge puddle of ink to watch a garden being systematically laid to waste.

'Did it not occur to you,' Claudia wheezed, 'to buy the boy a spinning top?'

Orbilio returned a marble bust to its podium and straightened the two overturned chairs. 'Drusilla was putting on weight and needed the exercise, so say thank you.'

'Bog off.'

'That's gratitude! I entertain your foundling, streamline your cat, redecorate your office and all you can say is bog off. Did you know you have ink spots on your hem?'

The look she gave him sent the sun scuttling back behind the cloudbank, but the investigator was made of sterner stuff. 'Guess what day it is today.'

'The day you walk out of my life?' she rasped.

'Sorry, it's *my* lucky day, not yours – you see, this morning I thwarted the Market Day Murderer!'

Claudia straightened up. 'You have?' In spite of herself, she was impressed. 'You've actually caught him?'

Orbilio picked up some scrolls and laid them on the table beside a bronze stylus jar. 'Thwarted,' he corrected. 'Not caughted. There's a difference. Let me start at the beginning. You remember Zygia, the girl who was killed in the Lupercal? She had a lover, Severina, who told me Zygia knew who the Market Day Murderer was, only she wouldn't tell Severina in case it endangered her life. Are you with me so far?'

'Marcus, you have my undivided apathy.'

'Anyway, Zygia was on her way to warn – what?' Frowning, he looked at the large cedarwood chest whose lid Claudia was now holding open with one hand, while her other seemed to be gesticulating at its contents.

'It's empty,' he said, craning his neck.

'Not for long, Hotshot.'

He glanced towards the garden, to where Larentia and her daughter were bearing down. 'Claudia, you're not serious . . .?'

She gave him a smile as innocent as a freshly laid egg. Then pushed him hard in the stomach.

'Mmmmf!'

'Quiet,' she hissed. 'Ah, Larentia. Julia. The others said to tell you they couldn't wait until you got back from shopping, they've gone on ahead to the Circus.'

Larentia's wrinkles puckered deeper. 'I thought I saw someone in here,' she snapped. 'A man.'

Claudia plumped herself down on the chest. 'Trick of the light,' she replied, indicating the sun's efforts to break through the clouds.

The old woman sniffed suspiciously. 'What the devil happened here?'

'The monkey,' Claudia replied, and indeed no more was needed on the subject, since it had been the bane of everybody's life since it got loose last night. All attempts to catch it had ended in disaster – Leonides sustained an ankle injury, two others knocked themselves out colliding heads and the net used to snare it was shredded from the inside within seconds. Better by far to turn Drusilla on it and trust she gives it a heart attack.

'Fortunata took to her bed,' put in Julia. 'Herky was so affected by the horrid beast, he won't come out of the cellar and she's sure he's having a nervous breakdown in there.'

'Mmmmf!'

'What's that?' asked Larentia.

'What's what?'

'That knocking sound.'

Claudia rested her weight even more firmly on the lid. 'Problems with the underfloor heating,' she said. 'There's a blockage in the hypocaust, that'll be the man inspecting it. Aren't you leaving it late for the parade? I hear they've got elephants, camels, not to mention a lion that jumps through hoops.' Her voice ended on a tantalizing note, and the two women swallowed the bait.

'Are you sure you can't come?' asked Julia, helping her mother on with her wrap.

'If only,' Claudia sighed, kicking the chest in rhythm with the knocks. 'But Gaius' closest friend – you remember Statius? No? Well, he's dying, poor fellow, and I could never –' sniff '– forgive myself for not calling on him before he –' sniff '– passes over.'

'Quite, quite.' They shuffled to the door and she waved them off the premises.

Back in the office, Marcus Cornelius was leaning over the chest, red-faced and gasping for air. 'I thought at one point you were trying to suffocate me,' he said.

'At one point,' she replied prettily, 'you were right.'

'Statius?' he grinned.

'P. Leno Statius. It's the name of the oculist down on the corner, the first name that entered my head.'

'I wonder what the P stands for.'

'Is is pertinent?' she asked.

'More likely Paulus, but that's beside the point. You lied to me, Claudia Seferius. You're not drowning in domestic trivia, you're right in your element!'

'Suffocating, Marcus. I said I was suffocating. As a policeman, you should pay more attention to the cause of my imminent demise.'

'Imminent demise my foot,' he laughed. 'Young lady, you positively thrive on danger – hang on! What did you say?' He slammed one fist into the palm of his other hand. 'Of course!' In three quick strides he was across the debris, hooking one leg over the windowsill. 'Claudia, you're a genius!'

'I know,' she yelled. 'But what about the mess in my office. Didn't your mother teach you to tidy your toys?'

'Later!' he promised, racing down a path strewn with leaves and blossoms, and vaulting over the statuary toppled by Drusilla and the monkey. Cause of death. Pay more attention to the cause of my death, she had said. 'I need to see Zygia's body before they cremate it.' At the gate, though, he paused. 'Do give me the name of your gardener,' he grinned, and deftly ducked the inkwell which came whizzing past his ear.

Claudia surveyed the war zone that had once been an office, then aimed a kick at the trunk which she'd used to hide Supersnoop. Cedarwood, and therefore expensive, it normally took pride of place in the dining room, but something had to make way for that lifesize bronze Venus and where better than here to house the stack of silver plate she'd hired from the banker? Unfortunately the wretched banker turned up at the front door, not the back, where there was no Cypassis to mention the dreaded typhus. As a result, the chest now lay empty. Claudia slammed the lid open against the wall. Painfully empty, in fact, and the big question was: how to stop Larentia finding out? Once the old cat got wind of one borrowed hoard, she'd be off on the scent like a truffle hound!

Claudia was still slumped over the trunk when Leonides hobbled in, his left foot resembling a swaddled infant, and said, 'There's a young lady in the atrium, asking for –' he coughed gently ' – Marcus.'

'What?' Claudia jerked up so hard, she bumped her head on the lid of the chest. 'I don't suppose she happens to be rather well turned out?'

Leonides' stick tapped a tattoo as he advanced across the ink-stained peacocks. 'Indeed she is, madam, and jolly attractive with it, if I might say so.'

'You might not!' Claudia rubbed at the lump which was forming. 'Just show Miss Fancypants Camilla off the premises – better still, I'll do it myself.' And should I leave a footprint on her pretty little bustle, so much the better. She swept past the debris, then paused. 'What's the matter with you?'

'Eh? Oh, nothing, madam. Nothing at all.'

Claudia peered up at her lanky steward. 'You have two choices, Leonides. Either I take this paper knife and cut off your earlobe, or you come clean.'

He smiled thinly. 'My ankle's troubling me, that's all.'

Claudia picked up the knife. 'Another earlobe for my collection, then.'

He gulped, but persisted with the ankle story. Perhaps it's personal, she thought. None of her business. Then she saw the parchment protruding from a fold in his tunic.

'Madam, no!'

'Too late, Leonides!'

The scroll was wrapped round a ball of stranded wool. Strange. Why should this make him . . . not a ball. It had shape. A head, and arms and legs. Claudia felt her skin crimple. Once upon a time, this had been a little girl's dolly, knitted perhaps by her mother, with eyes and nose and a mouth sewn on. It would have had a tunic and some ribbons in its dark woollen hair. She would have taken it to bed with her, kissed it goodnight, it would have been the first thing the child saw in the morning. She would have talked to the dolly, whispered her secrets, fed it from toy cups and plates. Then someone had taken the dolly. Hacked at it with a knife, shredding the body and stabbing the face until only a vague shape remained . . .

The parchment crackled between Claudia's trembling fingers. '*your mine understand you are mine*'. She looked into Leonides' tortured eyes. '*the next time we meet it shall be for eternity*'.

As though both were contaminated, she dropped the doll and letter. 'Can you, um –' She waved an unsteady hand around the room. 'Can you see to the mess, Leonides? I – I'll sort our visitor out.'

'Madam, I'm so sorry! You weren't supposed to—'

Claudia forced her mouth to turn up at the corners. 'Don't be silly, they're merely the ramblings of a madman. We shouldn't take him seriously. Just . . .' Her voice lost its power. 'Just see to this. Please?'

How she wasn't sick, she'd never know. But it took several minutes before the nausea passed, and by the time her fear had translated into anger, she was in just the mood for sorting out Miss Sweet Syrian Linens. In the hall, however, Claudia stopped short. Straight-backed as the visitor stood, this wasn't Camilla. Not unless she'd shrunk overnight, dyed her hair blonde and tied it back with a neat cerise ribbon. More significantly, where Camilla wore jewellery, this girl wore none – indeed, the pleats of her snow-white robe had no embellishment other than a girdle of the same hue as her hairband.

Perhaps catching a reflection, the girl spun round. She had a bright, shiny face and wide eyes. They were blue. Brilliant blue. And the hair was the colour of wheat in the sunshine, her waist slender, her smile all-encompassing. Claudia's dislike intensified by the second.

'Oh!' the girl piped. 'I thought you were Marcus.'

'He tends to be taller and shaves rather more often. What do you want?'

The blonde creature patted one of the columns supporting the upper storey. 'These are good marbles,' she remarked. 'Very good. But personally I feel he should replace them with Parian. It's the finest marble money can buy, and he ought to have the best, don't you think? I'm Annia, by the way, and I'll be moving in.' She glanced from one gallery to the other. 'I wonder which of those is my room?'

Claudia thought of the parade which would be underway in the Circus Maximus, of the rope dancers and jousters and bears. 'None of them,' she smiled, throwing her wrap round her shoulders. 'You see, this is my house and I say who moves in and who doesn't. You doesn't.'

'But Marcus . . .? I followed him here.'

Claudia made the most of the ensuing silence by adding to it, using the time to evaluate the girl. Neat nails. Clean, shining hair. Not a snag or a smirch on her tunic. On balance, Claudia thought she preferred his dallying with Camilla, and idly wondered how many women he kept in his harem.

'Perhaps I should explain,' Annia said, hopping after Claudia as she set off down the hill.

'No need, I'll give you his address, you can catch up with him there.'

'Marcus doesn't live there? But he let himself in with a key . . .?'

Outside the potter's, Claudia spun round and Annia almost cannoned into her. Behind them hummed the rhythmic spin of the wheel, and the acid-sweet smell of the clay filled their nostrils. Three men in short workmen's tunics decorated the bowls with paints of orange, blue and green and an apprentice loaded the kiln. Claudia felt its heat on her back.

'For your information, Marcus Cornelius Orbilio is using my address for his undercover work—'

'Then you must let me stay with you.'

'Must?' This little madam was getting on her nerves.

'Please, Claudia!' The scrubbed face crumpled. 'Please don't let the Market Day Murderer get me, I'm so scared, really I am.'

Claudia set a brisk pace down the Caelian. Cheap little con-artist! 'Whatever your hard luck story, Annia, the answer is no.'

At the foot of the hill, she turned sharp left towards the Circus Maximus. Damn. The sun's come out again, I knew I should have left my wrap at home. She swerved round a donkey which had a black and white goat riding in its pannier.

'Marcus will protect me,' Annia said with no small degree of petulance. 'Even if you won't! And it won't matter whose roof he's under, he'll take care of me, because we're cousins.'

'Are you really.' Claudia resisted the impulse to push her into the fountain they were passing.

'His great-aunt Daphne is my grandmother, that's Daphne Lovernius, you know, she's very well connected. Of course, all we Orbilios are superbly connected, we have a history going back to – oops! Nearly lost you.'

Claudia heard teeth gnashing together. Clearly that loop round the block didn't work, because Annia was still wittering.

' . . . Marcus was following a lead about the girl they found up there.' She pointed up the escarpment of the Palatine whose contours they were following. 'Her name was Zygia, you know. She was killed on her way to warn me, and that's how Marcus found me after all these years, and it gets even more exciting, because he thinks I might hold a clue to the killer's identity, so we're going to work together and—'

'Forgive my interrupting, Annia.' Claudia stared up at the statue of the Divine Julius standing atop the tower by the Circus he'd re-built and wondered what he'd make of his city thirty years on. 'But you see, I possess an entrance ticket and you, I regret, do not. Cheerio, it's been so nice knowing you.'

Amazement washed over Annia's features. 'You don't believe me!'

'Not a word,' Claudia admitted, picking up a honeyed pastry from a street vendor. Cinnamon, almonds and warm, plump raisins danced upon her taste buds when she bit into it. The rumour was true, then! There were elephants in the parade! She could hear them trumpeting.

'I'm next on the hit list, you know.'

Oh lord. In her fantasy world, not only has this creature convinced herself Orbilio's her cousin and she can play a key role in solving the murders, she believes she's the murderer's next victim! How sad. Not unlike Magic in a way. Except Annia's not dangerous!

Claudia wiped her sticky hands and fished out two copper quadrans for the snake dancer who was entertaining a crowd with two fat reptiles draped around her shoulders. An old man played the pan pipes as serpents and dancer writhed in sensuous unity, the snakes' red tongues flicking in and out to smell the crowd. When Claudia turned round, she expected Annia to be gone. Instead, what she saw, she couldn't quite believe.

Another writhing creature. Another tongue flicking in and out. Only this one was blue, and the colour matched Annia's eyes to a tee. But this was no snake. This was a mythical dragon staring back.

'Now do you believe me,' Annia was saying, rolling down her immaculate white sleeve. 'Now can you see I'm telling the truth?'

Claudia shivered and wondered why, when there was so much sunshine about, she should be cold. It was only a tattoo, for gods' sake.

Only a miserable tattoo.

XXII

On the question of necklaces, Claudia much preferred pearl ropes to millstones, and since Annia very definitely fell into the latter category, Claudia saw no reason why said stone should not hang round the neck where it belonged. The girl was a slave, let her master protect her.

'Mistress, actually,' she'd trilled. 'For the past two years I've been dressing the hair of the temple warden's wife, she pays very good bonuses, you know. That's the Temple of Apollo. Oh, magnificent building, have you been inside? Probably not, they don't allow commoners past the portico, but it's solid Numidian marble, and you'll have seen the yellow marble colonnades and all those wonderful sculptures on the outside. Greek, mostly, and though they haven't finished painting all the friezes, they are *so* atmospheric.'

And so it went on. Prattle, prattle, prattle. But beneath it all, Annia was resolute. Wild horses would not drag her back. Point out that fifty, sixty people are employed in the temple, she'd be far safer there, but would she listen? Would she hell!

'The Temple of Apollo is right next door to the Wolf Cave, Claudia, I don't want anything to do with it. I'm sticking to Marcus, he's my cousin and he has an obligation.' Without drawing breath, she'd moved on. 'It's a downright disgrace what they did to me, handing me over to be raised as a slave, my life could have been so different, it could have changed everything. Everything. But I'm only eighteen, it's not too late to start over. Once I receive my Cap of Freedom, I shall take my true place in society and wear diadems and fine slippers and ride in a litter, but of course that's not until October, so in the meantime, I shall move in with Marcus.'

'But—'

'I shall be no inconvenience, you won't know I'm around. But really, Claudia, you ought to let me do something with your hair, you need more than just a few pins and combs to keep it in place. What I suggest . . .'

Belatedly Claudia realized she'd capitulated, simply because Annia wore her down! That the story was true, she had little doubt. Had Orbilio not confessed his desperation to save 'ann-other' slave girl? To save Annia? But the girl's sickly wholesomeness, her innate snobbery and her morbid curiosity about the Market Day Murderer wore Claudia's nerves threadbare. You drop something, guess who pounces to pick it up? You sneeze, guess who's there with a hanky? No, no, you should never match silver with gold, it looks crass, tell me again how those poor creatures died, oh, this plate's worth a fortune, just look at the moulding! In truth, Claudia suspected the temple warden's wife wouldn't have Annia back for all the gold in Dacia.

Meanwhile, the Megalesian Games were ticking by, a festival of gladiators, theatre and athletic events, alongside feasts, conjurors and puppet shows and she was buggered if she'd give that a miss! Stuffing her cushion into the small of her back, Claudia noticed that the Circus Maximus was filling up rapidly. The place hadn't seen a chariot raced round its circuit since Agrippa succumbed, so the excitement and tension was growing minute by minute. She was glad, now, she'd dumped the aunts down the easternmost end and left Annia in Junius' care.

Down at track level, a flurry of activity broke out in the royal box. Five out of six Vestal Virgins surrounded Augustus and his only daughter, heavy with Agrippa's unborn child, but the buzz centred on the arrival of two sombre, white-robed priests. A collective groan rippled round the Circus. The augurs had studied the cloud patterns and declared the omens for the first race unfavourable!

Irritable drivers untied themselves from their chariots, the man from the Blue faction shoving the man from the Red in the back. He retaliated with a high-flying kick, and when the man from the White faction moved in to break up the fight, blood spurted from his nose at Blue's wild punch and he in turn laid into the man from the Green, who had merely been patting his stallion. The crowd loved it, cheering, whooping, baying, booing, because if the priests intended to spend the next half hour playing with their silver censers and pouring new libations to the gods, they needed some form of entertainment! Bookmakers started taking bets on the charioteers instead of the chariots.

Claudia couldn't concentrate on the fisticuffs. How could she? She crossed, then uncrossed, then re-crossed her legs. How could anyone concentrate knowing a crazed killer might call at their house any day?

Down on the racetrack, the priests had finished wafting incense and chanting entreaties to the gods in order to make the omens for the first race favourable. The bookmakers stiffened. The crowd craned forward. The race marshals shuffled. In the ensuing silence, the augur stepped forward, his head covered, and held wide his arms. For three minutes he spoke on the pattern of cloud cover, the shadows cast on the great obelisk of Ramses which sat on the central spine of the Circus. *Yes, yes, but is the race on?* Then he turned to face West and solemnly intoned the significance of each of the twelve starting gates representing a sign of the zodiac. *We know all that. Will the race go ahead?* In his opinion, the augur droned, the Circus Maximus is representative of the entire universe, being symbolic of—

'*Boooo!*'

His words were drowned by the crowd, who wanted an answer. Were they wasting their time here or not?

'Leonides said I'd find you beside the statue of Victory.' A young patrician plumped down on the seat next to Claudia, even though it was taken. The affronted occupant moved huffily up. 'Who's your money on for the first race?'

'The augur,' Claudia replied. 'If he hangs in there long enough, there won't be time for one horse race, let alone twelve and he seems very taken with that number, does our augur.'

'Lip-reading,' Orbilio said, squinting, 'he appears to be down to the number seven and its connection between the drivers' seven laps of the circuit, the seven planets and the seven days of the week. How's Jovi?'

'Confused. In his mind, his mother doesn't love him, whereas complete strangers do.'

'And the monkey?'

'*Boooooo!*'

'Still decimating my house.'

'Actually, I was referring to Porsenna.'

Claudia turned so fast in her seat, her cushion spun off. 'Porsenna makes an excellent companion,' she said stiffly. 'Attentive. Generous. Informed.'

You won't believe what I've learned about dormice this week.

'What can you possibly hold against him?'

'Other than the fact he's a complete and utter jerk?'

A hush settled over the Circus. Apparently the race could go ahead, providing the chariots moved to different stalls, the augur said. The crowd harrumphed, and supposed that would do.

Claudia picked up her cushion and punched it back into shape. 'Porsenna's a damn sight more fun than that horse-faced trollop you unwrapped from the tomb to take to the Bull Dance. Down the baths they call her the Hostess-With-The-Mostest-And-Most-Of-It-Contagious.'

'Camilla?'

'That's her. Camilla the Bedfiller, that's how she's known in the Forum. Knows every stuccoed ceiling in the city.'

His eyebrows quivered a bit, but they never actually lifted off their launchpads. 'You must be confusing my sister with somebody else.'

Did he say sis- His *sister?* Why is it, that at the time you most need a change of subject matter, not a word can squeeze past your tonsils? The awkwardness hangs there, like a badly roped suspension bridge, and there's not a damned thing you can do about it, because your brain's been turned into frogspawn. Claudia bit deep into her bottom lip, and failed to observe the back of Orbilio's hand covering his mouth or that his shoulders appeared to be shaking.

Down in the sand, four bruised and battered charioteers piloted their horses into their newly allotted stalls. The inside mares on Red's chariot snorted and tossed their heads impatiently, and one of Green's stallions started to kick. The dust made the race marshals cough. A rope was stretched across the front of the starting boxes and the trumpeter lifted his instrument in readiness.

'Since we seem to keep missing each other,' Orbilio said, as the magistrate dropped his handkerchief to signal the start of the race, 'after my dashing off to examine Zygia's body, I thought I'd treat you to an update.'

The horses burst free of their boxes. The Red faction, out of the Capricorn stall, lost his advantage in the confusion caused by the trumpeter's delay. And Claudia's feather fan seemed hopelessly inefficient.

'There were rope burns round her neck, proving she'd been lassooed like the others. That's how he does it, you see. Noose around the neck, knocks them out cold while they're struggling, then he ties, strips and . . . well, anyway, that's what happened to Zygia. Dragged backwards, there were scuff marks on the floor of the Lupercal.'

As all four chariots approached the first bend neck and neck, the thundering of hoofs multiplied a millionfold by the stamping of feet on the boards and the seats. Green faction came out ahead, but Blue was hot on his wheels.

'But the hair?' Claudia's larynx croaked. 'If it's so crucial to the ritual, why wasn't Zygia's hair cut off and laid in her lap?'

'That's what I'd missed,' he said. 'When I originally

questioned Severina, I was concerned more with Zygia's movements that day and details of her background. Only later did it sink in that there was nothing for the killer to chop off.' He shrugged. 'Zygia kept her curly hair cropped, like a man's. No, it's the method of killing that troubles me.'

Blue overtook on the inside down the straight, and having forced Green out to give way, made room for White to move up.

'He may simply have bottled it? Perhaps he heard footsteps outside and panicked? Then, when they'd retreated, he realized he still had time to make his pretty patterns.' An opportunity too good to miss.

'Hmm.' Orbilio's gaze fixed on the obelisk. 'Zygia left Severina in the morning, her body wasn't found until the afternoon, what happened during those unaccounted hours? Suppose that, instead of going straight to Annia, Zygia calls on the murderer? According to Severina, Zygia had her suspicions.'

'He lives in Rome, then?'

'Or a short ride away,' he said slowly. 'Imagine: Zygia wants out, she says; safe passage for Severina and herself, or she goes to the authorities. He agrees, or pretends to, but what he actually does is follow her and before she can warn Annia, because Zygia's not the type to let an innocent girl be butchered' – Orbilio clicked his fingers – 'hey presto, he drags her into the Wolf Cave. No more blackmail, but sweeter still for him, she's led him straight to another victim!'

'Who, despite her sugary veneer and unquenchable confidence in you, my dear Marcus, is a very frightened young woman.'

'So she should be,' he said quietly. 'Although once this business is over, I've no idea what the future entails for her.'

'Marriage to you, I shouldn't wonder.'

Orbilio laughed, and it was a rich baritone sound. 'She's a proper snob, isn't she? That, more than the signet ring, convinces me she's Daphne's granddaughter!' Sobering, he leaned towards Claudia. 'But uppermost, she's Penelope's,' he said softly.

For three and a half laps, Claudia listened spellbound as he talked about the girl with the laugh in her voice, the girl who took him scrumping, taught him how to play Twelve Lines, to leapfrog, to harden conkers with vinegar and hot coals. She heard about the husband who volunteered for the army and then died for it, and the desperation with which the young widow mourned. She heard how Daphne Lovernius wrenched young Annia from her grieving mother's arms. And finally how bubbly, blonde Penelope consigned her weighted body and weightier soul to Old Man Tiber himself.

Swallowing the lump in her throat, Claudia knew there was no way now she could turn Annia out of her house. Not the girl who'd been conceived amid such turgid desperation and then simply thrown to the wolves – and who might yet be prey to another, far deadlier predator . . .

Happily, though, there's no law which says you have to like the person whose life it is you're protecting!

'Sometime,' he said – it was down to a two-chariot race, with White and Green still at the turning post while the other factions galloped full-pelt down the straight – 'I'll have to confront her with the realities of patrician life, that you can't just join like a club—'

'She'll argue she was born into the aristocracy.'

Orbilio's sigh could be heard over the roar of a hundred thousand voices cheering on their favourite colour. *Come on, Red! Blue! Blue!* 'Her mother was patrician,' he admitted. 'But as she had no legal father and since Daphne failed to claim her back before the time limit expired, Annia, like it or not, remains the property of the temple warden. The most she can hope for is freedom.' He paused. 'Provided she lives long enough for me to buy it for her.'

Blue was leaning horizontally across his horses to cut down wind resistance. The tyres of Red's chariot began smoking, and the faction mechanic would probably lose an earlobe for being so careless, although the way the crowd was baying when Red finally bowed out of the race, he'd probably consider himself lucky to escape with his life. To tumultuous applause, Blue took his victorious chariot on a lap of honour and as he trotted down the length of the long central spine, he stopped at the lap markers and solemnly saluted. Once, lap counts had been tallied by huge wooden eggs, but that great man Agrippa had gifted the Circus with life-size bronze dolphins which need not be removed, simply reversed, and, when not required as lap markers, water gushed from their mouths into brilliant blue basins. Since this was the first time since Agrippa had died that they'd been put to use, by the time Blue saluted the seventh and final dolphin, there was not a dry eye in the house. Even the Emperor was sobbing.

'That's where I hoped you might come in,' Marcus said quietly.

Let me think. Claudia counted the points off on her fingers. There's a maniac sending vicious death threats. A mother-in-law who is actively seeking ways to disinherit me and who has turned my home into a trout farm. A business which is failing. I'm broke. The ragamuffin I took pity on remains pathetically unclaimed, and the only ray of sunshine in his little unloved life is a monkey intent on demolishing my house. Claudia moved to count the fingers on her other hand. On top of that, we have the man who uncovered my past sleeping in my late husband's bed, while his illegitimate cousin has not only talked me into harbouring a runaway slave, she's wearing a death sentence which might well entice a sadistic murderer to visit my house. Have I missed anything? I don't think so.

'Why should you think I'd want to help?'

'Because life here is too dull?' he suggested.

In spite of herself, Claudia chuckled. 'Just what is it you want from me, Marcus Cornelius?'

Orbilio's unseeing gaze looked down at the racetrack. Oh, Claudia, how can I answer you that? Dozens of labourers were now raking the sand, a man up a ladder reversed the gleaming dolphins and another stoked the sacred flame of Mars before adding sweet-smelling resins, which, as they burned, sent up clouds of pungent black smoke. What I want from you, Claudia, is for you to tell me Porsenna means nothing, that he's no more than a diversion to keep Larentia happy. What I want is to hold you in my arms and as the moon rises high in the heavens, whisper our secrets, our dreams, our hopes, our ambitions. Oh, what I want, Claudia, are your kisses, for my fingers to tangle in your wild, dancing curls, to hear the rich cadences of your laugh in my bed. And, Mother of Tarquin, more than anything, I want the courage to tell you—

'I—' He cleared his throat and turned to face her. His eyes were dark with emotion, she saw, his face strained, and she felt an invisible vice tighten inside her. He was so close she could smell the rosewater in which his clothes had been rinsed, his sandalwood unguent, the sweet warm scent of his breath on her cheek. 'Claudia, this might not be the right place, but I have to tell you how I feel—*Janus!*'

Grabbing her roughly, he jerked her upright and pushed her towards the aisle. Around her, the crowds had risen to their feet.

'Quick! To the exit!'

Claudia tried to shake off his arm, but he was shoving her with the full strength of his weight. 'Will you stop this?' she protested, knowing how a carved wooden soldier feels being shoved along the board. The noise inside the Circus was deafening.

'For gods' sake,' he hissed. 'Can't you see what's happening down there?'

'Only if I had eyes in my hairclips,' she snapped. It might not have occurred to him, but she was going in the wrong direction to look at the race track. 'Orbilio, will you let go of me, people will think I'm under arrest!'

His sole response was to shove harder, and she tripped up the stairs. People were surging towards them, then her feet were more flying than walking. He did not relax either pace or grip until they were outside.

Claudia pulled away and rubbed at the bruise on her arm. 'What was all that in aid of?'

Orbilio fell against the high stone wall and wiped his brow with the back of his hand. 'That –' As he waited to get his breath back, two bands of legionaries converged on the entrance, swords drawn. '– stupid, bloody augur! Didn't you hear him? From the flight of a flock of pigeons passing overhead, he concluded all further races should be cancelled.'

'What?'

After the death of their hero just a fortnight before, devastating the entire populace of Rome, these Games were just the tonic they needed. And since there were only ever seventeen days of the year on which races could be held, they'd really worked up a head of steam for today. For some silly bugger to cancel the Games on account of a few birds was utter madness.

That Orbilio had sensed the start of the riot and steered her so quickly to safety was a credit to him. But it would only make him big-headed to mention the fact . . .

Behind the high walls, shouts and screams mingled with the smashing of wood and the clashing of swords upon stone, which, like young bucks locking horns, was more for effect than anything else. However, the fact that there were soldiers outside said much for the flashpoint at which the Empire stood at the moment. The din of the rioting attracted crowds, Claudia and Marcus had to push their way down to the river, where marketplaces and wharves stood deserted apart from a handful of porters left guarding the goods. Sacks and crates, amphorae and bales sprawled in eerie confusion. An oar slipped out of its rowlock and disappeared quietly under the water, and a bemused mule brayed to its harnessed companion.

'I want you to leave Rome,' Marcus said, leading the way across the Fabrician Bridge. 'It's not safe.'

'Rubbish. There's a fray every month in this city, people need to let off steam now and then—'

'I'm talking about the danger from Magic,' he said firmly. 'You can see what state the Empire's in, how precariously it's balanced.'

Standing beside the Healing Temple in the middle of the Tiber, watching its turbulent currents slam against the honey-coloured piers of the bridge and hearing its yellow, muddy waters slap against the strong retaining wall around the island, Claudia understood perfectly. Augustus would have no trouble calming down the riot, he was probably already showering the crowds with lottery tickets, she thought, and some will win a sticky bun, some a jug of wine and one jammy devil will walk home the owner of a brand new house and villa. Then the augur will backtrack, the races will continue – but the unrest? The unrest will still be there, and the veil of anarchy was growing thinner by the day. Until the crisis was past, and for however long that took, Marcus Cornelius Orbilio would be on call and on duty twenty-four hours a day. By necessity, his interests in stalkers, serial killers and indeed anything else, must come second.

'Rome needs heroes,' she said, plucking a blossom from the tree. 'Go and do your duty, Marcus. I can look after myself.'

Always have, always will.

'My solution,' he said, idly examining the donations left by grateful patients, the wooden cups, the garlands, the cakes, 'is for you and Annia to visit Arbil's ranch—'

'Who's Arbil? And why on earth should I visit a farm? I despise the countryside—'

She didn't think he'd heard her protests. 'It's a very short ride,' he was saying, resting his elbows on the wall. 'If you set off at first light—'

'Orbilio, are you completely off your chump?' Claudia flung up her arms in exasperation. 'Leave the trout farm just like that?' The man's barmy. A solid gold fruitcake.

He lifted his head and there seemed to be a sparkle in his eyes. Unless it was reflection off the water. 'Yes,' he said simply. '*Just* like that, and your old trouts won't suspect a thing, and you know why?'

She didn't dare ask!

'I, too, have a foolproof plan,' he continued, and the maddening twinkle did not abate. 'Which, funnily enough, also takes a little while to work.'

XXIII

Not always does the obvious attract the seasoned gambler. True, he will not turn up his nose at a healthy game of knucklebones, nor thumb the same appendage should a pair of gladiators be slogging it out on the sand. But he'll remain on the lookout for more exciting methods to satisfy his craving. Thus, for Claudia Seferius, the chance to cock a snook at her greedy, snobby in-laws, knowing that if just one of the old dragons found her out, there'd be sufficient grounds for Larentia to drag her into court – well, the temptation was simply too great to resist! As the water swirled round Tiber Island and more and more soldiers rushed from their practice grounds on the Field of Mars towards the great Circus Maximus, Claudia felt the fire burn in her belly.

'I'm listening,' she said casually.

A thin, young woman holding a limp baby in her arms, her face blotched and swollen with tears, negotiated the piles of clay body parts which littered the steps of the Healing Temple to advertise its potency. Because while it was round the interior columns that pilgrims left terracotta organs, limbs, or what have you, then prayed to the god Aesculapius to heal the afflicted part, it was outside, when they'd been cured, that they removed their models to decorate the steps as encouragement for others. In the cool shade of the porch, the priest eased the child from its careworn mother's arms and led them gently inside.

'Then watch this,' Marcus said, and cast around amongst the vast array of donations for cosmetic jars, watched by a suspicious temple warden whose job it was to prevent thieving.

A flotilla of ducks trod the furious waters of the Tiber. Claudia picked up a small yellow cake and crumbled it for the hungry birds, and when the warden came running over, silenced his protests with a look that would have raised blisters on steel.

'Ready?' Orbilio asked.

She nodded.

Chalk and ash are a must on any woman's make-up shelf, and whilst Claudia used cosmetics only rarely (perhaps a little antimony round the eye, a touch of ochre for the lips) she always kept a decent stock to hand. Watching Marcus Cornelius take a dab of ash and a flurry of chalk mixed with water from the river and rub it into his eye socket was quite a revelation. He looked as sick as any of the poor unfortunates clustered round the shrine . . .

'Another Runaway Success for your scrap book,' he grinned. 'With you faking illness on this scale, the old trouts won't even ask questions.' He rinsed away the paste and was walking down the path towards the Temple of Vediovis before he added, 'He's the lowest form of pondlife.'

'Is that the title of your autobiography?'

A muscle twitched in his cheek. 'Arbil,' he said.

'This is the man you want me to visit? Consider me flattered.'

Unlike Aesculapius, hooded and cloaked, Vediovis had

no qualms about nudity. Apart from a cloak slung over one shoulder, he stood tall and proud in his nakedness, his head thrown back, his pelvis thrust forward as he invited admiration. Claudia duly obliged.

'The trouble is,' Orbilio said, leaning against the dark, fissured bark of an alder and sombrely folding his arms, 'there's no law against what he does.'

Claudia pulled faces at a group of children waving from the river bank. 'And what does he do on his farm, this Babylonian?'

'He's a flesh peddlar!' he snarled. 'On a huge scale, taking babies from middens and rearing them for re-sale.'

Claudia's hand froze in mid-waggle, to the great delight of the children who thought it was part of the game. But already she'd forgotten them, seeing instead four sinister figures picking over the middens by torchlight. 'You mean he grows those poor kids like cabbages?'

Orbilio made a kind of snorting sound. 'And Penelope's baby was one of them,' he rasped. Several emotions cantered over his face before he lashed them under his control. 'So will you do it?' he asked quietly. 'Will you help me on this, Claudia?'

She reached up and ran her fingers through the unfurling leaves of a chestnut tree. 'I might,' she answered back, her eyes fixed firmly on the puffs of clouds scudding high above the branches. 'But remember, Marcus Cornelius. The earth's axis turns on trade.'

Just as Orbilio had predicted, the old boilers fell for the fake illness hook, line and sinker. Which is not to say there wasn't a hitch!

'Arbil?' Annia gasped, when Claudia confided the scheme. 'I'm not going back there!'

Claudia had been prepared for this, because Orbilio had explained the link between the murder victims and the slave trader – although that was all he'd been able to establish, he admitted wearily. Granted his cousin knew the victims and was able to put names (if not addresses) to the girls who'd shared the dormitory, but Annia, too, was baffled why they – and indeed she – had been targeted. Now, watching Annia smooth her fine, white pleats into place, Claudia suspected that, although Orbilio had not said as much, he was banking on their visit establishing some form of connection. Without it, he was merely winking in the dark and Claudia knew that, like a Molossan hunting hound, the Boy Wonder was not one to give up on a scent. If the motive lay with Arbil and his vile baby farm, the sudden appearance of Annia could not fail to unsettle the killer – and you didn't need a Greek philosopher's brains to know he'd be hamstrung in so public a place and dared not strike in the open.

'I know you're scared,' Claudia said – the danger lay not at Arbil's, but once Annia returned to the city, by which time Supersleuth would be around to protect her – but before she could begin to explain, the girl's antecedents burst free.

'Excuse me, Claudia! We Orbilios are not intimidated by anyone!' They were standing in Claudia's bedroom, and Annia had her nose in the jewel casket. 'Especially greasy foreigners. Do you mind if I try this on?' She held a filigree torque to her neck.

Claudia phrased her next question carefully. 'Don't you want to help your room-mates, then?'

'Why should I?' Speedwell blue eyes goggled in genuine amazement. 'I never liked them, they never liked me, there's no point in pretending otherwise – whoops!' The ring she'd been examining rolled under the stubby legs of the maplewood chest. Dropping to her knees, she fumbled around in the dust. 'They were beastly to me, but that,' a spider scuttled out, but no ring, 'I suppose, comes from lack of breeding.' She stood up and brushed her hands. 'Naturally, I rose above it.'

Naturally.

Annia leaned over and began to tug on the heavy wooden chest. 'No, no, I can manage,' she puffed, slipping the retrieved band on to her finger. 'And before you ask, Claudia.' With a hefty shove, the chest scraped back into its place against the wall. 'As far as I'm concerned, it's their own fault those girls died. They knew full well there's a maniac after us, they should have taken more care.'

Little Miss Popular!

'Isn't that taking responsibility a tad far?' Claudia ventured.

'Not at all.' On went a bracelet. 'I am in danger, ergo I take precautions. Between Marcus and your Gaulish bodyguard, I'm as safe as the state treasury and it's up to them to do the same, don't you agree?'

'If you feel so secure, why don't you help flush out the killer?'

'For one thing' – Annia slipped a tiara over her long, golden hair, and they both shone in the lamplight – 'I'd just as soon stay here with Marcus, and for another' – she fished out a gold hare inlaid with enamel and clipped the brooch to her spotless white tunic – 'when I do see Arbil again, it'll be wearing sapphires and pearls and to buy slaves of my own. I think sapphires will suit me, don't you?' she asked, preening herself in the mirror.

Claudia wondered whether to post a placard outside, 'Murderers Please Note: Blue Dragons Found Here'. Tempting. Very, very tempting.

'There'll be another market day in two days time,' she reminded her acidly.

'Oh, I know that!' Annia chirruped. 'But don't worry yourself, Claudia. Marcus will look after me. Yes, yes, he's up at the Imperial Palace, you told me – but you see,' blue eyes widened as though addressing a small child, 'Marcus is my cousin.' The voice matched the condescending expression. 'He'd never let anything happen to me.'

And dammit, she was right. As long as Annia was in Rome, Hotshot would be there, emperor or no emperor, coup or no coup, behind her all the way, and she would not give a damn that he was jeopardizing a golden career for an obligation born from eighteen years of bitterly repressed grief. She'd believe it was her birthright.

'You know, my mother's side all have Greek names,' she continued, clipping on a silver ear stud, then swapping it for gold. 'So I'm thinking of changing mine. How do you like Iris? Or does Helen sound more regal?'

Around that time of the night when drunkards awake, lick dry lips and muddle their way home, a candle burned in a corner and Nemesis' cornelians twinkled like stars on a frosty night each time the flame swayed in the darkness.

'Agrippa's death was a sign from the gods,' a voice whispered, buffing the maroon cloth over the hilt. 'A sign that our mission is blessed.'

A finger tested the blue steel edge of the blade.

'The gods took Agrippa in sacrifice to keep the army busy, because while they run around pampering the Great Catamite, we are free to fulfil our destiny.'

A puff on the candle extinguished the light.

'By the time Augustus wrests back control, we shall have finished our work and no one shall be the wiser, and think of the power it bestows. Power over life, power over fools, power over all of fucking Rome!'

A contented sigh rang round the room. In just two days, it would be market day again. Farmers setting out their stalls, spreading out their cheeses and their cabbages, their fleeces and their eggs.

'So many people think they're clever, when they're not.' One hand made a clutching motion, the other slashed the knife through imaginary golden tresses. 'But I know where she lives. And, Nemesis, my faithful friend, I know just how to lure that fair-haired bitch away!'

XXIV

On the morning of the sixth day of April and exactly one week since she was chased round the slums by the moneylender's dogs, Claudia prepared to board her litter in the pre-dawn chill with a completely clear conscience about leaving Annia behind.

'Madam!'

Claudia looked up to see Cypassis, her nightshift flapping as she ran, her enormous bosoms bouncing like ripe pumpkins in a sack.

'Madam, please! You can't go alone!'

'Junius,' she said, pushing aside the fine linen drapes, 'is meeting me at the post house beyond the Collina Gate. Go indoors, it's cold.'

'Who'll pin your hair?' The single plait bounced in agitation. 'Who'll fix your ribbons and fastenings? Who'll brush your clothes?'

'Who'll cuddle Jovi, mop his tears and clear up after his pet if you're tagging along?' Bloody monkey! It spits, raids the kitchens, poops on the beds, yet will it surrender? The Sahara would flood first!

'I suppose so,' Cypassis said doubtfully, but inside she knew her mistress was right. Jovi was clingier than ever. He rarely let her out of his sight. She sighed as she helped Claudia into the litter. 'I think I must look like his mother.'

Claudia settled herself among the soft linen cushions. 'There could be any number of reasons, Cypassis, why he sticks to you. Your scent, your voice, your mannerisms, maybe they do remind him of his mum.' She drew the curtains of the litter together and smiled. 'Then again,' she said, 'it could just be because the wee lad loves you. Move on!'

A glance between the drapes revealed a dark-haired, broad-hipped girl dabbing at her eyes, and Claudia knew it would be every bit a wrench for Cypassis as it would be for Jovi when it came to parting company. She hoped and prayed that hard-hearted bitch of a mother would call before another sunset fell.

Because if Claudia got hold of the woman, she'd thrash her to a pulp and make a necklace of her teeth!

With a surge of exiting delivery carts clogging up the roads, progress was painful. 'Are we in a slug race?' she asked the head bearer. 'I know sloths who move faster than this.'

'Sorry, marm,' he yelled back in his lilting Cappadocian accent. 'There's always a jam near the gates. Too many roads converging, y'see.'

She popped her head out. Wagons were gridlocked, drivers were cursing and ragamuffins scampered in and out of the spokes for a game. 'Set me down,' she ordered.

'Bless my sidewhiskers, marm, I can't just dump you here,' the bearer protested, disengaging himself from the pole and leaving the others to redistribute the weight. 'Junius said the post station, and that's the far side of the Collina—'

'I know where it is, you oaf. I just don't have a week

to get there! Now will you set me down, or do I have to jump?'

The bearer wrung his hands. 'It's still dark, marm—'

'Suppose I say "please"?'

'The traffic won't take long to clear – *Aw!*'

Claudia tightened her grip on his nose and pulled him closer. 'Suppose I say "pretty please"?'

This was not an area of Rome she knew well, but you didn't need a lifetime of navigational experience to realize that all the wagons were facing the same way. Buying a light from a torch bearer, Claudia pushed her way through the braying and the cussing, squeezing through gaps and edging past mules and asses and oxen made skittish by her flame. Three streets from the Gate, her way was finally blocked by a wagon whose wheel had come off. Shit.

Backtracking down the narrow, serpentine alleys to circumnavigate the accident, niggling doubts began to creep in. Traffic had not only thinned, it had downright disappeared, then the reason became clear. She had wandered into the grainstore district, no wonder it looked like a ghost town. Their winter stocks depleted, the towering warehouses stood empty, echoing and lonely, for at this time of year Rome relied solely on daily deliveries. Soon, of course, favourable winds would send the massive grainships whipping back and forth to Africa on an almost weekly basis. These granaries would quickly fill up. But for now there was no need for armed guards to patrol, there was nothing to steal. The whole area was derelict. No bakers' carts, no creaky pulleys, no split sacks causing chaos. No rats, no cats and even the mills were silent. Maybe, she thought, it had not been such a good idea to dismiss the litter. Maybe she should have arranged for Junius to accompany her, rather than meet up at dawn . . .?

Get a grip! It's that damned riot. Made you jumpy! And Supersnoop, saying Rome isn't safe. Hell, it's the countryside's that not safe. All those bears in the forests, the wild boar, the wolves. Not to mention the cowpats.

'There you are!' A stumpy individual with wonky gnashers ran to catch up. 'I thought I'd lost you!'

She could smell the stale sweat from five paces. 'Wrong lady, I'm afraid.'

'A couple of streets back, when the military pushed past –'

'Is this the right way to the Collina Gate?' Dear Diana, did this man need a bath! No wonder the street was deserted. Hell, he'd probably clear Rome when he pulled off his boots!

'– that's when I lost sight of you.'

'Look.' It could happen to anyone, but she wished he'd take his hand off her arm. Heaven knows what sort of a stain it would leave! 'For the last time –'

'Now we can live out our dreams.'

'– I don't know who it is you're chasing, but,' Claudia held the torch up to light her face, 'I am Claudia Seferius.'

There was a manic grin on his face, and his eyes glittered. 'Yes. And now we're free to live out our dreams.'

He was drunk, of course, but it made little difference. 'Let go of me, you clod!' She tried to shake his hand free, but the grip was a vice.

'Where would you like?' Fingers bit into her flesh and she yelped. 'Here looks nice.'

Goddammit, he was dragging her towards one of the

warehouse entrances. Merciful Mars, please let it be locked!

'Help!'

The door gave under a push of the man's filthy shoulder.

'HELP!'

But the only voice which came back was her echo . . .

Claudia thrust the burning bitumen towards her attacker, but as though it was a cake she was offering, he twisted the torch from her grasp and tossed it into the gutter, where the flames fizzled out in the rivulets of the drain. There was no point yelling. Save your strength for the fight! In the murky dawn light, Claudia could make out skid marks left by her heels. She saw sweat stains on his tunic, and clots of stale food.

'Let go of me, you bastard!' Her nails dug into the wood of the door jamb.

His breath reeked, and his lice-ridden hair stank of fish. Almost as though he was oblivious to her frantic struggle, her attacker continued to talk. 'They tried,' he said, his arm locking fast round her waist from behind. 'But I knew they couldn't succeed.'

A filthy black hand began to prise her fingers away, one by one. Squirming, kicking, writhing, Claudia was dragged along the pitch-painted wall. Whatever he was on – magic mushrooms, hemp seed, Sumerian poppy dope – she prayed the effects would quickly wear off. This man not only believed himself Adonis, he had the *strength* of a god!

'Such soft skin,' he said, sliding a calloused hand inside her tunic. 'Such firm tits. Just like you told me.'

He pinched her nipple and when she screamed, she

could feel his sharp intake of breath. 'Look! Flour sacks,' he breathed, wrestling his frenzied victim across the cleanly swept flags. 'Over there, Claudia. Do you see? Soft, white sacks for our bedding.'

The hairs on her neck bristled. The way he said 'Claudia'. As though he knew her . . .

'I don't know how they thought they could keep us apart,' he was saying, and she doubted whether he'd noticed her heel hammering against his shinbone. 'True love will always conquer.'

'Get your filthy hands off me!' she spat, gouging her fingernails deep in his flesh.

True love will always conquer. Where had she heard that before?

'You're on fire for it!' He thrust his tongue inside her ear.

She sank her teeth deep in his forearm. Tasted blood.

'Oh, how you long for it.'

She bit harder.

'Feel me, Claudia. Feel me against you.' He tore off her cloak in one wrench. 'Say you want it. Say how you want me.'

Her heart was pounding. She felt faint. Sick. About to pass out.

'Go to hell!' Was that mouse squeak really hers?

The hand in her tunic squeezed hard on her breast. 'Don't lie to me, Claudia. Never lie to me. Not to me, understand?'

'Please,' she begged, tears clouding her eyes both from pain and from fear. 'Please let me go.'

'Don't be shy.' The hand round her waist slid past her stomach. 'Let me feel you. Oh, yes. Oh, that's nice.'

'Please! You're hurting me—'

Her flailing arms could find no target, and tears coursed down her cheeks. Tears of shame, tears of fear, tears of guilt. How stupid could she be, sending Junius ahead? Talk about arrogance! Even if he had set off now to look, he'd never find her! *Please*, she prayed. *Someone help me!*

'That's really nice, Claudia.' His breath was fast and ragged.

Her frantic kicks and her struggles only spurred him on, she realized. 'Bitch on heat,' he rasped. 'You're a fucking bitch on heat.' The obscenities increased. Vulgar. Repetitive. An ugly, unstoppable chant. Just like Magic wrote in his tirades of filth.

Oh no! Sweet Jupiter, no! Claudia's blood turned to ice and her head swam. Please, no. Not that unstable lunatic! Not here!

'Magic?' she squeaked.

Now she could see the ink blots on his clothing, his hands stained black from it. It was all that he did, writing. It was obvious. He ate only to stop himself starving. Cared nothing for personal hygiene. But now it was no longer a question of rape. This man was a monster, his fantasies warped . . .

'I knew you'd replied to my letters,' he drooled, wrenching her skirts up. 'Only someone was stealing them, did you know that? I'll find him, this thief. I'll bring you his balls as a present. Or maybe his heart? Would you like that? You could eat it.'

As his hand slithered across her naked thigh, his stinking breath threw out another tirade of cruelty. Claudia clawed at thin air. He was strong. Demented. She couldn't break free, she couldn't fight back. Or now could she?

Silly bitch, why didn't you think of it before! If only she could reach that knife she'd strapped to her ankle . . .

Magic threw her headlong into the sacking and lifted his tunic to expose himself fully. 'Want it?' he breathed.

Claudia screwed up her courage. 'Yes,' she croaked.

As he launched himself upon her, she spun sideways. Felt the blade in her hand.

'Whore!' he yelled, then total surprise washed over his face. 'But . . . But . . .'

As Claudia struggled free of the slippery sacks, he knelt staring at the knife in his side. 'Why?' he asked. 'Claudia, why?' His eyes were those of a whipped puppydog, a portrait of utter betrayal.

'Why did you kill me?' he asked. 'Magic loves you! Magic'd never hurt you. Not ever.'

Claudia stood riveted on the cold, stone floor. Physical disease she could deal with. Jaundice, dropsy, pneumonia, no problem. But confronted with mental illness, she froze. She watched, mesmerized, as Magic staggered to his feet. Magic swayed. Magic pulled out the knife. Magic roared. Not with pain, but with anger, and any compassion Claudia felt, any confusion, vanished on the spot. Blood spurted from the wound in his side, gushing on to the flagstones, and suddenly he was lumbering towards her, stabbing with the knife. Her knife!

Terrified, Claudia ran into the street as Magic, hands red with blood, stumbled after her.

'Bitch! You treacherous bitch! Come back here!'

Even in the next alley, she could hear him.

'I'll kill you, you fucking treacherous bitch! Do you hear me? I'll fucking KILL YOU!'

Swamped by nausea, every limb shaking and her teeth clashing like castanets, Claudia fell against a wall for support. Where was everybody? Janus, she'd been dragged off the streets, almost raped *and these people were still sleeping*? Lumbering steps echoed in the grey dawn light. Holy shit, run!

And run she did. Past the mills which, at any other season, were beehives full of millers and sackmen, porters and donkeymen, the dry air alive with clipped orders, where flour would tickle your nose, make you cough. It would never echo like it did now. Claudia could hear her own light footsteps, and a heavier, dragging tread from behind . . . Rounding a corner, she collided with a solid mass of horseflesh.

'Move aside, you're blocking the road!'

The boy who sat perched upon the animal looked down his snooty, freckled nose. 'My father hired this horse for me to try out. It's my birthday.'

'Out the way!'

'He's magnificent, isn't he? I might ask Father to buy him.'

Perhaps the horse might pay more attention. 'Shift,' Claudia told it, 'or prepare for the gluepot!'

Any second now Magic will come stumbling round the corner . . .

The boy was stroking the animal's mane. 'He's called Comet, he's so fast.'

'Is he?' Claudia licked her lips. 'Then it's about time he showed us.' She yanked the kid off and jumped into the saddle.

'Hey!'

It was one hell of a way up. And having never sat astride a monster like this, bloody uncomfortable, too. 'Gee up.' That's what they say, isn't it. 'Gee up'?

'That's stealing.' The boy scrambled to his feet.

'Damn right.' Comet? It hadn't budged a hoof!

The boy was frantic. 'Gerroff, you!'

Claudia leaned into the animal's ear. 'Sssssss.'

'He's mine, give him back!' The boy cried, pulling at Claudia's ankle.

She tried again. 'Sssssss.'

Then there was no question of how Comet came by his name. Houses, shops and streets flew past in a blur as Claudia clung to his shiny black neck. People screamed, cursed and yelled as the horse cut right through them, his hooves clattering and slithering over the cobbles. In the Circus Maximus, they do seven laps then they're whacked. Kid's stuff to this beast.

'Whooa, boy. Whooa!' But the horse wasn't stupid. It knew a cobra when it heard one, and concentrated on putting more distance between them. Claudia began to feel dizzy. Then seasick. Finally, when vital organs started to shake hands with each other, she screwed up her eyes and just clung like a barnacle. She thought of her mission to Arbil's. Dammit, Marcus Cornelius, you'll have to find another mug to play sodding detective. I'm paralysed.

Mercifully, gallop slowed to canter, canter to stop. Claudia prised her eyelids apart. Where the hell was she? Comet seemed happy, clip-clopping his way across this stable yard to bury his big, black nose in the manger. His breath steamed white on the cool morning air. As did Claudia's.

An elderly groom came limping over. 'Comet, old boy! What are you doing back so soon? I thought you'd been hired for the day?'

He seemed not to notice the rider, who landed in a boneless heap on the flagstones. Never mind asteroids, she thought. More like haemorrhoids. The horse snickered with pleasure and chomped noisily on the sweet-smelling hay.

'Madam?' A familiar face thrust itself in front of Claudia's.

'Junius?' The horse has thrown me, I'm concussed. 'What the hell are you doing here?' Doing *where*? What was this? Was she dead? Were Claudia and Comet about to meet Gaius in the afterlife?

'Just after dawn, you said.' The young Gaul helped his mistress to her feet. 'First post house beyond the Collina Gate?'

'You mean—' Claudia looked round in amazement. Of all the ironies . . .!

And yet was it so surprising? She knew she'd been close to the Gate, of course a horse would head home. It's his nature, you clumping daft tart!

Clouds of brown dust billowed from her skirts when she shook them. Dammit, she needed the baths to wash away the smell – the feel – the *taste* – of that slimeball who called himself Magic. Her hands, she saw, were still shaking. From the ride, she told herself. What else?

Come on, it was self-defence, that stabbing. What option was there?

She wiped her hair from her eyes. After a long, slow massage with aromatic oils, you'll be fine. Muscle fatigue fades, so do bruises. You can throw yourself into the

Games, there's five full days left, and today there's a play on by Terence. Later, there's a reading by torchlight. Ovid. Or was it Virgil? Afterwards there'll be dancing and drinking and music, we'll all wear garlands, and incense will burn on every street corner. I must have been mad to think of leaving the city!

'Junius,' she said, spitting out another large chunk of Comet's mane. 'Make sure it's *mares* who pull the car to Arbil's ranch.'

I've no wish to fly Pegasus again!

XXV

The landscape opened up, there were shrines at crossroad junctions, picnickers by the roadside and musicians on the move, making it easy not to think of Magic. Soon the hillsides would be swathed in drifts of blossoms from the blackthorn and the pear. Isn't that this year's first swallowtail, fluttering drunkenly across the clearing? Watch the baby bunnies scatter at the clip-clop of the wheels.

Forget the gush of blood upon the flagstones of the granary.

Forget the rancid stench of his clothing and his breath.

Forget his slithering pursuit. His filthy, ugly hands upon your flesh.

Let the warble of the skylark mask the screeching of his threats. Pray the sight of bounding deer smothers the obscene intimacy of his touch . . .

'I think that's it, there.'

Claudia was jolted out of her nightmare when Junius tapped the driver on the shoulder and pointed to a narrow turning on the right. The rich brown soil had became thinner, she noticed, and less fertile, being mostly olive groves; and the incline had grown markedly sharper. About half a mile along they passed a sign.

THESE LANDS BELONG TO ARBIL.
THEY ARE SUBJECT TO BABYLONIAN LAW.

A few minutes later they caught up with a cart, its axle low from charcoal and logs, fresh rushes and grass. Cabbages and parsnips bulged out of sacks, there were red beets and white, rhubarb and carrots. Coneys, pheasant and teal hung from rings around their broken necks and joggled with the bumps of the wheels. Then the wagon turned into a shed where a gang of youths dispensed pulses, dried fruit and grain. Each had a blue tattoo on his arm, and Claudia shivered. These then, were the Children of Arbil. The enormity of the complex was breathtaking. And the noise! Even prepared for Arbil raising kids as cash crops, Claudia hadn't quite grasped the immensity of his task. The profusion of workers tilling, hoeing, irrigating and manuring the light, dry soil, called to one another as they worked. Oxen bent to the plough lowed mournfully. Chickens clucked, donkeys brayed, pigs, sheep and goats put in their own oars. Babies bawled, children squealed, there was singing, chanting, hammering and sawing from a constant throb of people. Hundreds of children live here, she thought, her eyes brimming with tears. Hundreds of children, for whom this was their only home, Arbil their only parent. Hundreds of them. Unwanted – and unloved.

Her car rumbled through an imposing marble gateway into a courtyard ringed with fountains and shaded with plane trees and shrubs. Statues of strange gods bearing even stranger symbols stood guard. Her eye caught an eight-point star beside one, bulls by another. And there was no mistaking that dragon! Waiting in the cool of a colonnade scented with pots of hothouse lilies, Claudia noticed movement behind the terracotta grid which bisected the garden and on the pretext of sniffing the oleanders which grew against the screen, put her eye to the diamond aperture. Three men huddled round the wicket gate, talking in tones too low to make out. One, she could see clearly. Dressed foppishly, with hair half-way down his shoulders, he bore the hook nose that betrayed his ancestry. That would be Sargon, the son, she thought, but there was something about him that seemed vaguely familiar. Where the devil had she seen him before? And what made her think of music? Of trumpets and drums?

The second of the trio was visible to her only in profile, but his distinctive Greekness stood out. Handsome, strong, he, too, had a sharp taste in dress – look at those fancy fringed boots. But . . . wasn't he also familiar? For a moment she couldn't place him, then, with a shudder, Claudia recognized the lush embroidery on his cuffs. Jupiter, Juno and Mars, this was one of the the Midden Hunters who had passed her the night she found Jovi. The cultured one who'd been taking the bet!

Pushing the bush aside for a better view of the third man, Claudia's heart skipped a beat. He wore a simple belted tunic and high riding boots, but unlike his companions, there were no rings on his fingers, no gold torque hung round his neck. He was nodding, this third man. Making his mane of hair unmistakable.

Now what, Claudia frowned, brings Kaeso out here?

'Yes?' The hostility of the voice could have cracked ice.

Claudia plucked a pink oleander and buried her nose in its perfume before answering. The questioner's raven black hair was knotted loosely at the back, bracelets jangled from ankles and wrists and a turquoise robe set off her Indus beauty to perfection. Only two things marred the girl's loveliness. The cold, narrowed eyes and a bruise on the side of her face.

In explaining the reason for her visit, Claudia expected to encounter resistance, disbelief even. A woman in business? With a proposition for Arbil? Instead the stiffness in the girl's shoulders lessened. 'Come inside.' The lips were no longer pursed.

Surreptitiously Claudia wiped the milky juice which oozed from the plant's leathery leaves down the back of her gown. 'If you don't mind, I'd prefer to wait here. In the cool.'

Instantly the rancour was back. 'As you wish.' Malevolent eyes swivelled to the terracotta grid and back to Claudia. 'But beware!' she hissed. 'The man's a degenerate.'

Curious, Claudia watched her stomp away, the bangles jarring with every angry stride, then she pulled the oleander bush aside and put her eye to the grid. The gate was closed now. Sargon leaned with his hand on the hasp and laughed as the good looking Greek cracked a joke. Of Kaeso there wasn't a sign.

Except, in the spot where he'd stood, a wolf with a streak of silver down its back lay panting in the sunshine.

And then she remembered. That's where the trumpets and drums fitted in! The two dandies, arriving separately – and late – at the Bull Dance.

The same afternoon Zygia died . . .

*

Claudia – let's be clear about this – did not believe in Shape Shifters. Like demons and vampires, these were creatures of legend – and that's where they belonged. Not in modern day Rome! In broad daylight! Kaeso's a natural hunter, she reminded herself. He wears camouflage colours, his movements by definition are lithe and athletic. But if Kaeso wasn't a werewolf, she knew from experience that he was a highly theatrical animal. The magic tricks, the silent house, his standing in shadows, even Tucca the mute were all carefully choreographed. Props to disorientate. A means to control . . .

That he saw her arrive went without question.

That he crept up on her in the courtyard ought not have surprised her.

'I did not expect to find you visiting Arbil,' he remarked. Loosely tethered to a hook on the entrance arch stood a beautifully groomed horse, its chestnut hide glistening under the mid-morning sun.

'I could say the same for you.' Claudia decided her own voice failed to match Kaeso's for casualness.

'Me?' Muscular shoulders lifted and fell. 'I was raised here, grew up with Sargon and Dino.' He nodded to where the dandy patted his wolf's black-tipped shoulderblades and where the Greek stood, hands on hips, gazing up at the clouds. 'I like to keep in touch.'

The hell you do! 'Is that often?'

'When I'm passing.'

'Then I wished you'd been passing the Collina Gate around dawn,' she flashed back. 'Magic dropped in for iced wine and cakes.'

His expression hardened. 'Tell me,' he said.

And she did, adding, 'It was all pretty straightforward. He tried to rape me, so I stabbed him.' The usual.

There was a swift intake of breath. 'Dead?'

'Alas, it was only a flesh wound.'

'Magic,' Kaeso swung into the saddle and kicked his horse into a canter, 'has performed his very last trick, I assure you.'

Now there, Kaeso, I am inclined to believe you. But I'm still interested to know what brings you out here the day before Market Day. Claudia recalled the ritual murders. They, too, were all about control . . .

Shit! This is madness, she thought irritably. I don't know what I'm doing in this Babylonian wilderness. What the hell did Supersnoop think I could achieve from one short visit? She was on the point of leaving when a thick, gutteral brogue apologized for keeping her waiting and, not for the first time, Claudia's curiosity got the upper hand. So this was Arbil? She took in the crimped hair and curled beard (both suspiciously black), and the ankle-length robes which strained over his stomach as he led her to a seat beneath a plane tree.

'So what can I do for you, my dear?'

For a man in his fifties, she'd expected the slave trader to have weathered well under his immense cushion of wealth, but he hadn't. Those pouchy eyes, the skin hanging in flaps from his cheeks, the discoloured whites of his eyes screamed a legacy of drink and debauchery. Had he not been so podgy, she'd have described him as raddled and it was with the Indian's words ringing in her ears that Claudia invented a business proposal which was vague but sufficiently plausible to engage Arbil's interest. Or so she hoped. All the time she'd been presenting her case, he'd been nodding intently. Had it worked? Had he swallowed the bait?

'Come indoors, my dear, come indoors.'

Beware, those bitter lips had said. Beware. But what choice did Claudia have, other than to follow? The atrium resembled no atrium she had ever seen before, it took her breath away. Winged cherubs set with precious gems guarded the doorways and clusters of statues, part-men and part-beasts, huddled in groups, but where were the friendly centaurs, the silly, daft satyrs? The faces of these creatures were twisted in leers, some had three toes and thick horns, others were more reptilian in appearance and one had the body of a scorpion. Claudia shivered. Strange paintings covered the walls, dragons and vipers and whirlwinds, their colours dark and menacing, but dwarfing it all stood a giant bronze female, nude and aggressively provocative.

'Ishtar,' explained Arbil. 'Queen of all heaven, mother of life, goddess of love and of war. Ishtar is both morning and evening star, she protects us one and all. Come.' He took her elbow and introduced her to some of the other barbarian divinities. Shamash, deliverer of justice. Gira the fire god. Adad the storm god, Nabu the scribal god and Nergal, king of the underworld.

'Also there's Ea,' he said thickly. 'One never sees Ea, one only feels him.' He blew softly down Claudia's neck. 'Ea's the South wind. Ouch!'

'Just blocking up the draught,' she said sweetly, as Arbil rubbed his cheek where her hand had slapped it. 'Now are you interested in my prospectus, or shall I take it elsewhere?'

'Of course I'm interested,' Arbil replied, his face

colouring from a rush of blood which far exceeded the area Claudia slapped. 'I—' He frowned, as though his thoughts were elsewhere. He blinked twice, then he forced a smile. 'I shall have to think it over rather more carefully, you understand, but—' Again his mind wandered, and she didn't think it was because he'd been rebuffed or offended. 'But the, er, fundamentals seem sound. How much did you say you'd be prepared to invest?'

'Twenty thousand sesterces,' she replied. 'Possibly more, if conditions are favourable, and to ascertain that I would need to inspect the premises.'

'Naturally,' he said, and his mind seemed to have focused. 'Feel free to ask questions, my dear, I'll get Sargon to show you around.'

He left her studying the bronze tablets inscribed with the fundamentals of Babylonian law which hung between the paintings and shone like a hundred suns in the brilliant lamplight. There were two sets, one in Latin and one comprising squiggles she'd never seen before, and the rules were both harsh and bizarre. Take the penalty for adultery, for instance. The guilty couple to be tied face to face and thrown in the river to drown. Charming! What about this one? Should a son strike his father, let the offending hand be chopped off. Perfect way to mend the family rift! Oh, my goodness. If a wife kills her husband, she must be impaled—

'Hello, I'm Sargon.' The dandy swept into the room, flanked by two men, who he proceeded to introduce. Dinocrates she recognized as his Greek companion in the garden. 'And Tryphon, who we all call the Captain.'

Thin, wiry, Claudia doubted whether she'd have recognized him had it not been for the horseshoe-shaped scar on his face . . . Her nails bit deep into the flesh of her clenched fists.

'Finally, we have Silverstreak.' He looked round, but there were just the four of them alone in the atrium. 'Silverstreak!' he called. 'Here, boy!'

Nothing. Then he whistled. Three short notes in succession. 'Silverstreak!'

The wolf came loping into the room, tail wagging, and Sargon patted his head. He seemed to be telling Claudia there was nothing to worry about, the wolf was a proper softie underneath, but her blood had run cold and she could no longer hear him. That whistle. Whit-whit-whit. That was what Zosi the speech seller described hearing in the Argiletum last week. And then when Zygia died, people reported a man calling his dog. His wolf? My god, Zygia was killed in the Wolf Grotto . . .

'Quick!'

All three rushed forward as Claudia's knees buckled – Dino to catch her, Sargon to fetch a chair, Tryphon to thrust a glass in her hand.

'Ugh!' Claudia jerked back to consciousness. 'What on earth's this?'

Tryphon grinned, and the scar bunched out one cheek. 'Date liqueur, which is not to everyone's palate.'

'Does the average palate survive?' she asked, checking the roof of her mouth hadn't dissolved. 'This stuff's lethal!'

Claudia's tour was as exhaustive as it was comprehensive. She was shown dormitories, workshops, training rooms and classrooms, nurseries and playgrounds and kitchens, her guides veering between professional detachment and personal pride in the smooth running of this huge complex. There was no corner, no cupboard which they did not show, each taking turns to expand upon the management. Babies raised in this wing, toddlers in that. Many boys are apprenticed here, there's the mosaic-laying class in session now, that's the music room over there, and the weaving shed's just across the yard.

Claudia listened, made mental notes, and all the while, Silverstreak trotted behind them . . .

'This is the carpentry block.' The Captain had to shout above the whirr of hand drills and the scrape of metal-faced planes. 'The lads turn out everything from yokes to flutes to plough staffs.'

'And the girls?' Claudia asked, pretending to sneeze from the sawdust in order to cover the flush of excitement which had risen to her cheeks. 'What happens to girls who reach puberty?'

'Strict segregation.' Dino pointed to the southernmost wing of the complex, wider at its base end than the part which abutted the house. 'Women and eunuchs only.'

'Yourselves excepting, of course?'

'Us?' sneered Sargon. 'Here, my lovely, a rule is a rule and there is never an exception.'

He exchanged a sharp glance with the Captain, who said grimly: 'Arbil does not tolerate laxity in any form.'

'Which is why the organization runs so smoothly,' added Sargon.

Admittedly he oiled his hair just a little too much, wore one ring too many, perfumed his body rather too heavily, but Claudia's overall impression of Sargon was that of a tireless workaholic loyal to his father's cause who was backed by a trusted, solid team.

Bugger.

'Is there anywhere else you'd like to see?' Dino asked,

but he knew, and she knew, that she'd seen everything – and yet nothing. Now here they were, back in the atrium, under the watchful eye of Ishtar and her brood of gilded cherubs. Dammit, it was market day tomorrow and Claudia wasn't one single step closer to preventing another grisly death! Instead, what had she proved? That Arbil brands his slaves with blue dragons, a fact they knew already? That Sargon whistled his wolf the way any man whistles his dog?

Admit it, you've failed. If only, perhaps, I had more time, a chance to get to know these people, find out how their minds work. The killings have to be linked with this place, they have to be . . .

'My dear, my dear, won't you please stay for dinner?' Of all people, it was the barbarian, the peddlar of young flesh, who came to her rescue – the very man she had come to investigate!

'Arbil, I should be delighted.' Truly that was no lie. But first I'd like to snoop around your private quarters. 'But first I'd like to freshen up.'

'Be my guest, be my guest,' he beamed back. 'First left, second door down on the right is a bath room.'

Claudia followed his directions and put her head round the door to take note of the decor. Right. Now for the rest of the rooms!

The first was patently Arbil's office, although how he could work in a room painted dark blue beat Claudia, and that ugly green zodiac, yeuk! But the gold she admired, and one thing was sure. Arbil was not stingy with the glittery stuff, it was plastered on the rafters, on the walls, over statues as though Midas himself had passed through. She leafed through Arbil's documents, but they were recorded in incomprehensible squiggles and there was a lock upon his moneybox.

Next door was decorated with dragons and an eight-point star which had been inlaid over a sinister contraption that seemed to pass as a bed. What strange habits these Babylonians have! She looked around. More gold, more statues, and on the wall were two portraits, one of Sargon, the other younger and with features similar enough to pass as a brother. But if this was the second son, Shannu, that Marcus had told her about, why had no one here mentioned him? Claudia continued her search. Arbil's chests and trunks were made of terracotta as opposed to wood (an eccentricity which pervaded the entire complex), and revealed a strange taste in clothing and a clutch of pornographic pamphlets, but nothing, unfortunately, which suggested a propensity for slicing young women to ribbons.

Sargon's room was light and bright and airy, and although there was the odd nod to Babylon, Sargon was not stuck in the past. Claudia whistled. He liked nice things, did Sargon. His jewel casket was the largest she'd ever seen, gold thread ran through his clothing, there was fine leather tooling on his sandals. He had scent bottles of onyx and fine alabaster, pillows stuffed with rose petals, and he owned more cloaks and tunics than you could buy in the Forum on market day! Right at the bottom of a trunk full of togas lay a soft leather satchel and Claudia unbuckled the straps. Scanning the documents it contained, she quickly selected two – one contract, one invoice – and tucked them deep in the folds of her robe.

Oops! The next room was occupied.

'So sorry,' she breezed. 'Thought this led back to the atrium.'

The girl from the courtyard had been changing her gown. Her long hair hung unbound to her waist. Now most women, when a door opens on their ablutions, jump, though usually they'll relax at the sight of another female. Again, these eyes blazed hatred. And instead of reaching for a sheet, the raven-haired beauty thrust her hands behind her back, as though it was more important to conceal what was in them than to cover her nudity. Even more intriguing was that, before the hostility kicked in, Claudia witnessed something else in those eyes. Fear! That was one hell of a bruise on her face. Was it her attacker she hated and feared? And what had the girl tried to hide? White flower trumpets? Why whisk them out of sight? But nothing about this creature made sense. Claudia didn't even know who she was.

Dino's room was her next port of call, a mix of Rome and Babylon and strangely homely. Another man who liked his home comforts, it appeared, but not a man who overdosed the way his employers appeared to – Sargon especially. Claudia searched the hidden corners of the room and found nothing, but all men have their secrets, she thought. Where's yours, Dinocrates? Where is yours? She stepped back and surveyed the room. I wonder. I just wonder . . . It wasn't the first time correspondence had been inserted in the empty tube of a moulded bronze lampstand. She read, then re-read the letters before slowly replacing them.

This is proving to be one heck of an interesting household!

Right, then. One room left, the one at the end. Unlike

the others, though, this did not open at a gentle tug on the latch. Claudia put her shoulder to the door, but it still didn't budge. Then she noticed the bolt at the top. Reaching up, she gasped when a man's hand covered hers.

'Looking for something?' The voice could not have been colder had it blown straight from the Arctic.

She turned to find Sargon standing over her, and a shiver ran down her spine. Gone was the veneer of urbanity. Like the gargoyles in the atrium, his face was twisted, his eyes hard, and Claudia knew she was staring into indiluted hatred.

The hand over hers strengthened its grip.

XXVI

Surprise is the one emotion which cannot be wholly suppressed. He'd have heard her sharp intake of breath, felt the reflexive jump of her body, there was nothing Claudia could do about that. However, the very act of surprise, being so natural, in itself gives a person time to plan their next move. That the timespan might be a mere split-second didn't matter. Claudia was a past master at disguising her emotions.

'Second right, didn't you hear what my father said?' Sargon growled, and she could smell his resinous unguent, felt the heat of his body close to hers.

Claudia tipped up her chin and looked him straight in the eye. 'The only thing in that room, my friend, is some sawn-off barrel and a solid glob of fat.'

His own eyes held their ground for what seemed an eternity, then his lips stretched back and a bellow of a laugh rang round the corridor.

'That's good,' he chortled. 'That's really good.'

Claudia was confused. Sargon was convulsing, clutching his stomach, tears squeezing out of his eyes, and still she did not see the joke.

'Listen to this,' he wheezed, repeating Claudia's words in the atrium, and Arbil grinned, too. 'That's how we wash, we Babylonians. In bathtubs, with soap.'

Claudia's nose wrinkled. Sit in a bowl of your own dirty water frothing fat over your skin? I don't think so! But then the whole place was imbued with barbarism, as she found out when Arbil led her through to the dining hall. No reclining three to a couch here! One perched upright at table on chairs made of rushes like a common workman, and even the food was inedible. Flat crispy discs, call that bread? And the meat, guess what it's cooked in? More lumps of fat! Lard, Arbil called it, how disgusting, and no wine, either, only beer which swirls round your tummy and never stops gurgling.

For all she pushed her food around her plate, dinner was not dull. She'd seen enough of Sargon's mood swings – quiet conspirator, detached professional, sinister threatener, teller of jokes – to understand that inside lay a deep and complex character, and the documents she'd found in his room told her this was a man without conscience. But the objective of trekking into the countryside was to find a link between four butchered women, not to pass judgement, so until she learned more about Silverstreak, far simpler to go with the flow.

'What's good in bed and winks?' Sargon asked across the table.

'I've no idea,' she confessed.

To which he just winked, and even Claudia couldn't help laughing along with the others.

Dinocrates she found herself liking. Intelligent, personable, dedicated and loyal, she remembered the letters hidden in his lampstand and wondered how far the Greek orphan would go to protect his secret . . .?

Tryphon, on the other hand, seemed to have no obvious personality. He was Dino's lieutenant, gruff, capable and eminently trustworthy, but admirable though these characteristics might be, he appeared to lack the ability to think for himself. Say 'Tryphon, do this' and it'll be done to perfection. Ask 'Tryphon, what do you think about so-and-so?' and his eyes will glaze over. With his firm and authoritative manner and ability to respond calmly in a crisis, it was easy to see how he came to be called Captain – yet, surely captains are expected to use their initiative? Moreover, she had not been able to establish where he acquired that livid red scar. Pity his quarters were in the staff block, beyond the scope of her search.

Arbil, squat and smug as he presided over his table, was unquestionably proud of his achievements. 'Without men like me,' he said, 'unscrupulous brigands would snatch children from farms or from villages. I give life to babies left to perish on the middens. If you like, I am their deliverer.'

For that, Claudia understood, Arbil expected both gratitude and obedience, and strangely enough he was rarely disappointed.

The sixth member of the dinner party was the Indian girl who, Claudia was astonished to learn, was Arbil's wife. Throughout the meal, Angel never spoke a word, merely nibbled at her food or fidgeted with the bangles at her wrist and kept her cold eyes cast downwards. Claudia's mind ran over the dirty pictures in Arbil's terracotta trunk. Is that what makes Angel so sour, the prospect of her husband's demands? Possibly, but there was a hardness about the woman, a calculating awareness, that suggested Claudia needed to see more of husband and wife together before jumping to conclusions about this seemingly ill-matched pair.

Dinner was a protracted affair, with music and dancing between courses and if nothing else, Arbil proved a generous and hospitable host.

'Stay the night,' he suggested, and Claudia thought, why the hell not? 'Now perhaps you will excuse us? This lovely lady and I have business to discuss. Come, my dear, come with me.'

As he took her arm, Claudia became aware of a flicker from Angel, and the warning in her eyes was unmistakable. Claudia's brows furrowed in thought as Arbil led the way to his office.

Declining a glass of the thick brown sludge he called date liqueur, she settled herself in a high-backed chair and listened to the mechanics of subdividing the slaves, the methods of identifying those most suitable for training and then the process of deciding which trades they'd be most suited to. She couldn't say at what stage she noticed, but after a while, a strange light burned in the Babylonian's eyes. His fingers began to tap his armrest, his words rambled. Then suddenly he lunged over the desk, his fat hands gripping Claudia's shoulders.

'By Marduk, you're beautiful,' he was saying, his accent slurring heavily as his lips tried to find hers.

She felt his bristly, too-black beard scraping her cheek.

'You're so bloody desirable, Claudia, d'you know that?'

Reaching for the nearest thing to hand, Claudia upended the contents of the liqueur jug over his head.

'Wha—?' Arbil spluttered. The dye from his hair streaked his cheeks, the curls from his beard had dropped out and his jowls were shaking in utter perplexity. 'Claudia, I'm sorry,' he said, wringing his hands. 'Holy

Marduk, forgive me, I . . . I don't know what came over me.'

'About a pint.'

Surprisingly, Arbil didn't even smile. His hands were trembling as he buried his head in them, and he began to babble about memory lapses and blackouts and strange behaviour patterns.

He didn't even notice when she slipped away.

The complex lapsed into silence, broken only by the occasional cry from a baby or the distant bark of a fox, and a velvet sky twinkled with the lights of a million silver stars. From woods high up the hillside, two owls exchanged hoots and the cloying scent of night stocks wafted through the open shutters of Claudia's guest room. It was well after midnight, but she was reluctant to lie on some creaky contraption which threatened to launch her over the treetops at the first threat of a sneeze. The night was warm, and in any case she was far from sleepy. Leaning her elbows on the windowsill, Claudia watched the silent white shape of a barn owl cut through the air and listened to the high-pitched squeaks of the bats while her mind bounced like a stone on a trampoline. Something about Arbil disturbed her, and it was not that ham-fisted charge in his office. Incidents like that she brushed off – no, it was something deeper which niggled away at her composure.

The Babylonian had gone overboard in showing a perfect stranger round his premises. His top management were co-opted as guides, his hospitality had been unstinting and yet it didn't add up. Claudia appealed to the waning moon for inspiration. What was wrong here? She closed her eyes and tried to get inside the slave trader's mind. Oh-oh. Her lashes sprang apart in the darkness. Oh-oh! She had thought – and indeed Marcus Cornelius had thought – they'd been clever by sending her here, but Arbil had rumbled Claudia from the very beginning. The shrewd old sod knew that, sooner or later, a connection would be made between the murders in Rome and his own establishment and that someone would be along to investigate. Her whole visit had been run like a stage play, dammit, she was merely a puppet, they must be laughing in their spring-loaded beds!

A horse snickered softly from the stables. Well, it proves one thing, at least, Claudia thought. Underneath it all, Arbil is nervous, otherwise he'd simply have dismissed the accusation with a wave of his hand. Oh yes, she thought, licking her lips. We are definitely on the right track here!

She was just at the point of asking herself where the word 'we' fitted in, when a movement caught her eye. There was no disguising that waddle and in the bright three-quarters moon she could see he was cradling an object in his arms. Swinging her legs over the windowsill, Claudia hurried after him. Whatever he carried, not only was it large and stiff and heavy, Arbil felt it necessary to conceal his burden under a blanket. It stank of death and putrefaction, and the smell made her retch.

Sticking to the shadows, Claudia followed silently. So still was the night she could hear Arbil puffing with the weight, saw his knees buckle with the strain. They passed rows of cultivated fields, skirted the edge of his olive grove and now the path was leading uphill into deep and denser woodland. For all the night was warm, she wished she'd brought a wrap, she had started to shiver. He stopped in a clearing, and the gibbous moon lit the scene brighter than torchlight. Retreating to a cushion of pine needles, Claudia crouched. And waited.

Arbil looked around, a hideous furtive gesture. Carefully he laid down his stinking burden and Claudia clamped her hand over her mouth as he untied the blanket. So sure was she that the Babylonian had been carrying a corpse that she nearly cried aloud when just three logs and some strange idol tumbled out. She puffed out her cheeks with relief. The idol had a lion's head, and it was that which stank like a charnel house. Arbil had started a fire, but not using his own logs. The fire let off the smell of gum juniper, and small flames licked upwards from a bowl on the ground. Claudia sucked in her breath.

'Shamash!' Arbil's distinctive brogue echoed round the woods. 'Great god who brings us light, great judge of heaven, hear my plea!'

With an earsplitting boom, he beat his kettle drum and Claudia's breath shot from her lungs.

'Take the demon from my accursed body.' Boom! 'Take the demon who has siezed my soul.' Boom!

Seven times that bloodcurdling drum echoed through the trees. Seven times Claudia could not contain her gasps.

'O Shamash, giver of life, cast forth the demon in my body and imprison him in the image I have made according to your wish. See, I have taken dust from a neglected grave and mixed it with the blood of bulls –'

Well, that explained its colour and obnoxious pong, but why the lion's head?

'– to make a likeness of the evil demon Lamashtu' –

(thank you) – 'and I have threaded precious gems round its neck as you insist.'

Arbil made a tripod of the logs around the stinking icon then sprinkled what appeared to be flour in a circle all around it.

'Shamash, I beseech you, take the demon –' before completing the circle, he paused, '– NOW.' A final throw of powder sealed the ring.

'It is done,' he sighed, wiping a hand across his sweating face. 'It is done.'

Placing the bowl of burning juniper close to the white line, Arbil laid himself prostrate on the ground, an intimate communion between himself and his god, Shamash, and when he finally spoke again, it was the lion he addressed.

'I know you hear me, Lamashtu, imprisoned within the magic circle.' His voice was thick with satisfaction. 'Know now that in three days your evil powers shall be gone, for on the third day after sunset I will take you from this place and bury you deep in a spot known only to me, where – for all eternity – you shall remain, alive but stripped of power, a living death.'

He stepped back and nodded solemnly.

'So be it, according to the law of Shamash.'

Claudia waited until he was well clear of the woods before approaching the pagan structure. Lamashtu's snarling face was set with sapphires for eyes and around his neck hung a leather bag containing Arbil's sacrifice of precious gems. What lies so heavily on your conscience, she asked, that you imagine yourself possessed by demons which need exorcising in the middle of the night? What torments you, Arbil?

Back in the complex, Claudia noticed a light still burned in the slave master's bedroom and through a crack in the shutters she could see him, the palms of his hands flat against the wall. Correction, flat against a portrait on the wall. That of the younger son. Arbil was crooning, she could just about make out his words.

'Shannu. Oh my son, my son, what have I done?'

His forehead rested against the handsome painted brow, his shoulders heaved, and from her vantage point outside his window, Claudia watched fat tears roll silently down Arbil's bearded cheeks.

XXVII

By the time Claudia prised her eyelids apart, Apollo had already driven his blazing chariot quite a height above the eastern horizon. She stretched lazily and yawned. The eerie events of last night coupled with this strange, criss-cross mattress combined to give the impression of having spent the night floating on water, and the fact that the bed stood considerably higher off the ground than traditional Roman couches merely added to the drifting effect.

Perhaps Arbil's ritual had been part of that illusion? Now, with the floor bathed in morning sunshine, such behaviour seemed highly improbable. Arbil was a hard-boiled businessman, ruthless in his dealings, a lecher and a hedonist. All too often these traits went hand in hand, he'd be no exception – but superstitious one minute, full of maudlin pity the next? Put it down to the beer, Claudia. It went to your head and made you hallucinate – Hang on! She sat up. Did I say hallucinate? Her brain fermenting, Claudia jumped out of bed. Holy shit! Why didn't I see it before . . .?

The complex was already in full swing as she made a beeline for the segregation wing. Yesterday, Arbil had had his staff primed. Let's see how they react when caught on the hop!

'I can never keep track – look!' The head eunuch

indicated the spacious dormitory with its rows of ratproof terracotta chests, its bright red rugs, the neatly made beds and skylight windows. 'There are a dozen girls in here at any one time, and the turnover's so fast . . .'

It might be different, he suggested, if he slept in there with them, but his job wasn't to police the girls, now was it? It was to prevent the boys sneaking in.

'And do they?' Claudia softened the question with a generous tinkle of silver.

The ageing eunuch declined the coins. 'Arbil sells virgins,' he said. 'What they do when they leave here's up to them, but until then they stay pure.' He grinned. 'That's an order, and you don't need me to tell you how Arbil feels about orders!'

Well, the guards might be conscientious, but when hormones are hot, teenagers become mighty inventive . . .

So Claudia visited the hospital wing, the classrooms, the workshops, she looped past the lake where a score of youngsters thrashed around in the water, but each tutor and nursemaid said the same thing.

'Master Sargon in the girls' wing? Never!'

'Boys and girls mixing? Oh, the shame of it!'

'Silverstreak? No dear, we never let the children play with him, can't be too careful with a wolf . . .'

She gazed around the complex. Childish squeals accompanied piggybacks and hopscotch, one girl tied ribbons to a donkey's tail, a boy mooned at a group of shrieking infants, another hopped on one leg as he tied an errant shoelace. She had not expected them to be happy!

However, it was with a heavy sense of anticlimax that Claudia bumped into Angel picking oleanders in the courtyard.

'I like fresh flowers round the house,' the girl said accusingly, and that was the thing about Angel. She could control her voice, but her body language took longer to catch up. The petals trembled in her hand, and there was a strange look in her eyes.

Claudia remembered their encounter yesterday. Claudia had been standing by those same oleanders peeping through the terracotta screen and Angel had perceived her as an enemy . . .

'They were very pretty flowers I saw in your bedroom,' Claudia said mildly. 'Thorn apple, weren't they?'

Instantly the colour drained from Angel's face, forcing the livid purple bruise into stark relief. Claudia bit her lip. Better by far Angel took the hint from a stranger, than for Arbil to find out.

In the atrium, Claudia glanced at the law plates of bronze and shivered. Oh yes. Far better!

Dino, Claudia decided, was the weak link. About time they had a cosy one-to-one chat!

She knocked on his bedroom door, and a plump housemaid answered. 'Master Dinocrates? Him and Master Sargon'll be in Rome by now, it's market day, see.'

Croesus, she'd forgotten!

'What about the Captain? Does he go with them?' Shit! And Arbil had disappeared, too. Shut himself away, no one knew where, but this often happened of late. Shit, shit, shit!

'Well, there's so much business to conduct on a market day, ain't there?' the maid smiled, and recalling the revelations of her search, Claudia decided the housemaid was a lot closer than she realized!

The corridor was deserted as Claudia swept down to the end. This time she checked over her shoulder before she pulled back the bolt, but dammit, the door still wouldn't budge. Easing out a hairpin carved in the shape of a cat, its tail forming the pin, she wriggled it around in the lock. Snap! The tail broke near its tip, but – praise be to Juno – not before it had finished the job. The door creaked open on its black iron hinges.

What had she expected to find in this room? To be truthful, she wasn't sure. A treasury, perhaps. Documents locked away. Records of the children who'd been 'processed' over the years. What she had never in a million years expected was to find herself looking at the second face from Arbil's portraits.

'Shannu?'

The handsome features creased into an open and amiable smile. 'Hello.' In his left hand he held a paintbrush, and on the table lay a palate. The paint dripping from both was a vibrant shade of yellow, the perfect match for winter aconites. The same colour paint covered every inch of wall and floor and ceiling. 'Did you want something?'

Claudia felt her stomach churn. 'No. No, I just came to . . . see what you were doing.'

Now she could see why the door was kept locked. And bolted again from the outside . . .

'I'm painting,' he said cheerfully. 'I always paint, I find it relaxing. Tell me, do you approve of my landscapes?'

Landscapes? Stuck for words, Claudia suddenly realized it was his right arm which was inviting admiration of his work. His right arm. His sword arm. His painting arm, in fact – had it not ended in a stump. A chill wind blew round the horrid yellow room, which had nothing to do with the weather. Janus! It was only when looking at one law tablet that she'd noticed another one next to it.

SHOULD A SON STRIKE HIS FATHER,
LET THE OFFENDING HAND BE CHOPPED OFF.

So this was Arbil's secret. No wonder Sargon was so concerned about her entering.

'Who are you?' he asked, merrily splodging his brush in the paint. Shadows from the iron bars at the window striped the yellow floor.

'Me? I'm a friend of um, Angel's.' Claudia backed slowly towards the door.

'Liar!' Shannu sprang across the room, and she felt splatters of paint on her face. 'Angel's dead!' he spat. 'Arbil killed her!'

Oh-my-god! 'Yes. Yes, I know that. I . . . wanted to see where she lived, that was all.'

'You knew Angel?' The intensity that burned in his eyes froze her bones. 'Angel was beautiful, wasn't she?' he said dreamily, taking Claudia's hand and leading her into the room. 'Long, black hair, as lovely as Ishtar herself.' The tone changed abruptly. 'But my father debauched her and she died.'

'How—' Claudia cleared her throat and tried again. 'How, exactly, did Arbil kill her?'

'Don't you know?' Shannu snarled. 'He took her maidenhead, and whoosh! Out went her soul.'

Sweet Juno, get me out of here. Claudia heard voices

outside the window, but nothing would squeeze past her larynx.

'I tried to avenge Angel,' Shannu said. 'I tried ramming a glass in my father's face, but that fool Tryphon stepped in front. I told him. I said, "Arbil, one day I will kill you." And one day, you know, I will.'

Claudia believed him. Insane he might be, but the boy was bloody determined with it! She wanted to get out, run up the corridor, but her legs would never make it. Oh, Sargon. Why weren't you here to stop me this morning?

'He said, strike me again and I'll cut your bloody hand off.' Shannu started drawing circles with his paintbrush on the wall. 'Every time I tried to kill him, that's what he would say.'

Janus! Claudia hated herself for asking, but – 'How many times did you try to kill Arbil, Shannu?'

'Seven or eight,' he said casually. 'But my brother was always there, or Dino. And then finally – ' he held up his stump, ' – the bastard did what he threatened. Tell me, do you really like my landscapes? Or – be perfectly honest – do you prefer the seascapes over there? I think I've got that storm just right, the waves and that zig-zag flash of lightning. What—?'

The second he turned his back, Claudia slammed the door shut and rammed the bolt home just as hard as she could. The broken end of her hairpin tinkled as it fell on to the floor, but she was well out of earshot. In fact, Claudia didn't stop running until she met up with Junius, and then it was only to gee up the horses.

XXVIII

Virtually from the moment he'd received the news of his Regent's death, the Emperor Augustus had remained closeted inside his basilica on the Palatine, digesting reports, wading through correspondence, thrashing out the endless possibilities and despairing at the crackpot theories which surfaced with greater frequency and more frantic desperation as time wore on. Sedition, my lord? Round up the troublemakers, that's what I'd do; make examples of the bastards. No heir? No problem. Let the herald proclaim your wife pregnant, declare public holiday, throw Games in her honour. All feasible. All dismissed. Certainly it was not beyond the realms of possibility that, even after fourteen barren years, her imperial majesty might fall pregnant – but how long before the populace saw they'd been conned? Quick-fix solutions were no use, Augustus needed to gather the facts, sift them carefully, then see what nuggets were left.

In the end, perhaps, the difference between Marcus Cornelius Orbilio and the Emperor was not so great after all.

Market day had come and gone, scaffolding had been dismantled, monies banked, barges moored up for the night and as the city braced itself for yet another round of whoring and deliveries, roistering and burglary, weary street sweepers pushed spinach stalks and eggshells, donkey dung and pot shards in an ever swelling tidal wave of debris. Orbilio watched it all from the steep escarpment on the Palatine and remained unsure how, now the rioters had settled down and tempers had cooled, a security policeman kicking his heels outside the basilica helped any.

'Why?' he asked his boss, and the answer was revealing.

'It's not enough we do the work,' his boss had replied. 'Above all, we must be *seen* to be active.'

Active? Watching laurels being clipped in the Palatine Gardens when he could be moving quietly amongst his network of informants, mixing with the merchants, separating loyalists from traitors? What his boss hoped, of course, was that by sucking up to Augustus during the crisis, he'd land the post of Toady Supreme and as Orbilio stamped his feet in an effort to resuscitate his circulation, he could think of no better candidate! Across the way, priests illuminated Luna's shrine as they did every night, and from the Temple of Apollo, Orbilio caught the last whiff of incense before the censers were locked away for the night. Incredible that, for two whole years, Penelope's child had been a cog in the temple's machinery, while he'd never even suspected her existence! At least this year, he thought, when I drop poppies in the Tiber, I can tell Penelope that she can walk the Elysian Fields in peace.

Initially he'd been hard put to see anything deeper than a physical resemblance between Annia and her mother until he realized that neither woman felt bound by a label. Penelope behaved like no average aristocrat, Annia like no orthodox slave. Marcus shook his head.

How many times during his innumerable trips to the palace had he passed the time of day with the young temple warden? Sent a present, too, when he married, last July wasn't it? A silver salver with a dome-shaped lid, if he remembered correctly. And how often had he nodded in acquaintance to the bride, without noticing Annia by her side? Strange, the quirks of life!

Yet wasn't it the quirks he thrived on? Unpredictability is the drug of youth, they say, and if that was so, then Orbilio was hooked. His drug wore strong Judaean perfume and had a smelting pot of metals in its hair. It possessed a deep and throaty laugh, a dancing step, and kept a man awake throughout the night with an aching in his loins and in his heart.

But the drug did not come home last night . . .

Bugger this, he thought, bounding down the Palatine ramp. This isn't serving my country!

At the bottom, a crowd had gathered in the aid of an elderly statesman whose horse had thrown him awkwardly, Jews congregated on the Aurelian steps as they had for centuries and a male prostitute posed against a seated bronze hero and pouted.

Why hadn't Claudia come home last night? Where had she been? And with whom?

Marcus quickly discounted any possibility of danger – that Gaulish bodyguard would protect her with his life. Unfortunately, though, he could not discard the young Gaul! What was the relationship between them? Junius' eyes followed her every waking movement, and his step faltered as his mind pictured them, entwined . . . Or was it Porsenna she found so attractive? Him with his blond hair and vacuous charm – and his pots of money stashed away? Orbilio swallowed. Mother of Tarquin, this is madness! The same thing happens every bloody time. The closer I get to Claudia Seferius, the more jealous I become – and why? Because with each fraction I move closer, the more frightened I become that I might lose her. And thereby lies the sting!

She is not mine to lose.

Claudia belongs to no man, never will, and that's what's so bloody alluring. Not that she's stunningly beautiful, with curls I want to bury my head in and a freckle on her collarbone I want to investigate closer. Not because she's Miss Firecracker one minute, Ice Maiden the next. It's her spirit that sets her apart – and any man who tries to tame that spirit might as well try tethering lightning.

Although any man who wants to is an idiot!

The house on the Caelian was quiet, as he knew it would be, because the price she demanded for checking out Arbil had been for Orbilio to get rid of the aunts! Which he had, goddammit, which he had.

The shutters were drawn. Was she in? Janus, Croesus, who was she with? Porsenna? The Gaul? Whose bed would she sleep in tonight?

'Oi!'

Startled, Orbilio spun round and found himself staring into the doleful eyes of an ass.

'Shove over, mate!' its driver yelled amiably. 'You're holding up the traffic!'

Marcus spread apologetic hands and stepped aside. The spell was broken. He'd been a fool. A damned possessive fool at that, and he was deeply ashamed of himself. Nevertheless, he remained beneath her balcony as cart after cart jolted past, their reins rattling, their rawhide whips cracking like logs on the fire as the drivers whooped and hollered. An invisible procession followed with them. The scent of straw which protected the fragile terracotta pots. Soft tangy leather. Acid charcoal. Fruity wines. Threaded through with the smell of sulphur from the torches and the sullen snorts of mules. At one point he thought he heard a whistle, whit-whit-whit, and despised himself still further. And because nothing could be achieved by standing here, Orbilio took off to get pissed.

It was well into the early hours when he sauntered back along the Caelian. There were no longer wagons fetching in comestibles, no whistles now to mock his investigative prowess. Only a hardboiled ginger tomcat, paws tucked in, whose amber eyes followed with the unblinking secrets of a century. A dog barked from the depths of a building as he worked his way round to the slaves' entrance and unlocked the door. Just a peep into Claudia's bedroom. That was all.

In the atrium, a faint light flickered. He could hear the trickle of a fountain near the entrance, heard snoring from the slaves' wing. Silently he worked his way past the marble busts and columns to the stairs which led to Claudia's bedroom, then stopped. It must be the effects of the sun, he thought, beating on his head all day long. Followed by too much wine, much too quick.

Because sitting on the floor beside the fountain, cross-legged and with her long hair loose, the woman he had come to check on leaned towards a small boy kneeling in his nightshift. They appeared to be competing for a local gurning championship, and it took every ounce of Orbilio's willpower not to rush over and scoop them both up in his arms.

'Goody, it's the man in the frock!' Jovi scrabbled to his feet and dragged Orbilio across to the window, where he twizzled his neck and flattened his cheek against the thick glass. 'Look! There's the Divine Julius, that star up there, can you see it?' His stubby finger pointed directly at the Pole Star.

'The Divine Julius?' Orbilio asked mildly.

'He was turned into that star after he was murdered, Claudie says so.'

Claudie, he noticed, was adjusting her gown with great meticulousness. 'Then it must be true.' Marcus nodded solemnly. 'Now then, young man, why aren't you tucked up?'

'I couldn't sleep, so me and Claudie played a game, you can join in, if you like,' Jovi said eagerly. 'All you have to do,' his little face puckered, 'is lick the tip of you nose,' pucker, pucker, 'with the tip of your tongue.'

'Who won? You?'

'Claudie.' Jovi sighed philosophically. 'Every time.'

'Ah, well; she has a natural advantage. You see, she sharpens her tongue on a cuttlefish every morning.' Taking care to avoid the venomous glare which burned into his back, Orbilio picked the lad up, wheeled him round in the air then patted his bottom. 'Come on, you. Back to bed!'

'What, already?' But Jovi had already discovered that the force of grown-ups was too strong to tackle head-on and off he stumped, singing rude words to a popular marching song.

'I won't ask where he learned that,' Orbilio laughed. 'But oughtn't he be learning money matters, or something?'

'Orbilio, he knows that money matters, we all do!'

'No, I meant arith- oh, forget it.' His mood sobered. 'The mother's not come forward, then?'

Claudia's face twisted as she turned away. 'Nor likely to,' she muttered. Yesterday, Leonides managed to pinpoint the whorehouse where she worked. Mean little dive, he said. Stank of stale wine and cabbage water, with stand-up cubbyholes for sex and fishheads in the doorway. So keen was Jovi's mother to break the sordid cycle, she upped sticks with the first man to ask her – but not before turning her son loose on the streets. Until Leonides arrived, the other whores had naturally assumed she'd taken the child with her.

'What have you told Jovi?'

Claudia threw up her hands. 'What am I supposed to tell him?'

'The truth?' he suggested quietly.

'For gods' sake!' she cried. 'The boy's still a baby! Do you expect me to sit him on my knee and say, "by the way, your mum's abandoned you, she had a better offer"?'

From the corner of her eye, she caught a movement. Fleeting, but it was there, nonetheless. The unfolding of two tiny hands from where they'd been gripping the stair rail . . .

Shit!

Her eyes began to sting and the atrium blurred. A week ago he'd been wandering the Argiletum, lost and lonely, and she'd promised him upon her honour she would take him home next day. If only she'd persevered that same night! She might have caught his mother before she flitted off, changed her mind and persuaded the bitch to take the lad with her. At the very worst, Claudia could have prepared Jovi from the start, instead of raising his hopes day by day . . .

'I'll find him a foster home,' she gulped. 'A mum and dad to love him.'

'You love him,' Orbilio said softly. 'Why not let him stay?'

'No!' The violence of her protest shook them both, but what could she say? That deep down she was scared of loving anyone, except Drusilla? Because cats love unconditionally, expect nothing in return? Because cats never let you down. Or break your heart? She marched down the atrium and out into the scented night air of the peristyle.

Following, Orbilio stared up at the constellations twinkling above them, inhaled the peach blossoms and the wallflowers, and said nothing.

'Care to tell me?' Claudia blew her nose, 'what you did to get rid of the aunts?'

Whatever it was, it was damned effective! The only trace of their visit was a heap of dirty bedlinen when she got home, and Herkie still locked in the cellar. No doubt Cousin Fortunata would return to collect her little diddums, but something had made the old bats leave in a hurry!

His sheepish grin was quickly suppressed. 'Following on from the chalk and ash routine which made you look so poorly, it was but a step to mix flour with wine dregs and,' he turned to look at a statue, 'dab it on your servants' faces.'

'Larentia fell for it?' she goggled.

'Departed the contagion zone at a run!'

Claudia dabbed at her eyes. Oh, Larentia! You really are a silly cow!

The laughter was good. A release. But when it had died, a taut silence hung in the air.

The garden was rarely lit up at night. That would disturb the ambience and the songbirds in the aviary. There were only ever enough torches to enhance the whiteness of the artemesias, define the outline of the path, catch the ripples of the breeze upon the water in the fishpond. Suddenly the darkness intensified. Claudia became aware of the man standing beside her, of his sandalwood scent, the smoky look in his eyes. She could hear his breathing, saw the rise and fall of his chest in the moonlight, watched the muscles tense in his neck. Her mouth became dry.

He moved closer. 'Can you really lick the tip of your nose with your tongue?' he asked softly.

'Only when I strop with a cuttlefish,' she whispered back.

The rasp of cicadas was deafening. She smelled the wine on his breath as he stood over her. His eyes were dark, his lips half parted as his little finger reached out and hooked one of her curls. Claudia's heart was pounding like a kettledrum, and a pain surged deep in her ribcage when he gently released the curl.

'Marcus . . .'

He blinked, as though in pain. 'Yes?'

She looked away. 'Marcus, I –' Say it, for heaven's sake! Just say it! 'I – I think someone's left the gate open.'

Striding down the path, she wondered what was holding up her legs. Not her bones. They'd left home.

Marcus Cornelius screwed up his face and pinched the bridge of his nose between thumb and forefinger. 'Claudia—'

'Bloody vagrants,' she said, willing her limbs on. 'If they don't block up your doorway, they doss in your garden.'

Silly bitch! She slammed the gate shut. Did you think he intended to kiss you? Look at him, for gods' sake! Leaning against the pillar, staring up at the stars, not a bloody care in the world . . .

'Off, you!' She addressed the beggar, slumped against the wall. 'Come on, shift yourself!' Suddenly her bodyweight trebled, she could not move a limb. *'Marcus.'*

The quiver in her voice alerted him. 'What is it?'

He came running, but she held a hand up to stop him. This was no vagrant. Once this had been a female. Now she sat surrounded by a thick, dark smear of liquid. The liquid did not shine. Claudia clapped a hand over her mouth. The woman's wrists and feet had been bound and her colourless mouth sagged open. She was naked.

Yet it was not the spectacle of death which made her falter. It was the carpet of long, blonde hair which lay across the lap. The way it shone in the moonlight was an obscenity.

His shoulders slumped. His tall, proud body stooped. 'No!' he cried, falling to his knees. *'No-ooooo!'* No animal howling in pain produced such anguish.

Claudia leaned over and closed the wide blue, staring eyes. Even in death, the face was striking in its beauty.

'Marcus.'

The pale, serrated flesh was still warm.

'Marcus.' She looked down into his darkened, haggard eyes. 'This woman isn't Annia.'

XXIX

He'd needed a drink. They both had. Perhaps she more than he.

Claudia gulped greedily at the heavy vintage wine. Finding the body had been shock enough, but when she'd watched Marcus sag like a waterlogged sponge it felt like her insides had been plaited up like rope and then hauled on. Now, long after the blood had been mopped up and the servants' fears assuaged, long after the rich, red wine had hit him, Orbilio's hands and voice were still shaking.

'I've screwed up, Claudia.' He spiked his fingers through his hair as he paced the tiny office. 'But for me, that girl would still be alive.'

Claudia drew her wrap tight around her shoulders. In their haste to load up the body, the undertakers had trampled half the planting, obliterating the gagging stench of blood. Mint and oregano wafted into her office on a cool night breeze.

'That's ridiculous,' she protested. 'We don't even know who she is!'

'Her name is Severina,' he said wearily. 'She was murdered, because the killer must have seen her with Zygia and mistaken her for Annia. They look very similar.' He paused in his pacing and looked straight at Claudia. 'And, dammit, Claudia, I could have saved her.'

Go ahead, whip yourself. 'How?'

'A couple of hours ago. Maybe three. I was . . . passing.' He covered his face with his hands. 'I heard the whistle, and I ignored it.'

Claudia's head jerked up. 'Three short notes?'

'Did you hear them, too?'

She shook her head. 'I was at the theatre. The late show.' So many spectaculars, they didn't all fit into daylight. 'I know you questioned the household,' she said. 'Any luck?'

Dawn was starting to break, a faint opalescence over the Esquiline.

'Some heard scuffling, others whistling, but their overriding feeling –' Orbilio shot her a knowing look '– is that unusual happenings in this house are not exactly rare.'

She studied him. The bruises from the beating outside Weasel's had turned to shades of green and yellow and with his pallor deathly white, he fair resembled a cadaver himself. Any other man would listen when told a hundred people whistle along that damned road every night, it's a busy street she lived on, and brawls break out twice a week. But Orbilio was not Any Other Man. Claudia drew up her knees in a high-backed wooden chair and hugged them. Marcus would carry Severina on his conscience to his grave.

He had resumed pacing. 'The choice of killing ground was quite deliberate,' he said slowly. 'Can you imagine the risk? Until today, this house was a warren of activity, yet you saw yourself the quiet spot he picked in the Argiletum.

No chance of disturbance. These girls,' he added quietly, 'take a long, long time to die.'

Claudia heard pebbles rattling in a bucket and realized it was the chattering of her teeth. 'So what are you saying? The killer has made the connection between Annia and my visit to Arbil?'

There was no need to look at him to know the answer. Somewhere a water clock dripped with infuriating regularity.

Marcus pulled up a chair and took her hands in his. 'You'd better tell me everything that happened up there, Claudia – and I mean everything.'

Grim-faced he listened. By the end of her narrative, Claudia was sure she'd missed nothing out and she stretched awkwardly in her chair. The sky had passed the blush stage, the air was now alive with birdsong, and the scents of crushed mint and oregano grew stronger by the minute. There was nothing in the garden to suggest a young girl had existed, much less been butchered, and Claudia resolved to grow tall spikes of hollyhocks against that wall. Or maybe a hibiscus. Plus a statue of a nymph with flowing hair.

'There has to be a connection,' Marcus said. 'There has to be! Except Arbil's people wouldn't cover up a heinous crime like that—'

'Wrong.' Claudia shook her head so firmly, a hairpin fell out. 'They're so fiercely loyal, closing ranks is second nature. Right from Day One they're taught that, but for Arbil they'd be dead.'

'Does wonders for one's self-esteem.' Orbilio leaned down and picked up the hairpin. 'Brainwashing on that scale.'

'You'd have to be there to understand.' Claudia puffed out her cheeks. 'The whole complex is so claustrophobic in its foreignness, Marcus, that even when the children leave, it's Rome which feels alien to them. Arbil's slave farm represents security, they look back on their childhood with fondness and affection. Is this getting us anywhere?'

Orbilio rolled the pin round and round between his fingers. 'We've got five major suspects, suppose we run through the list, starting with Tryphon?'

'I'm pretty sure that if the Captain wanted to kill someone, he'd stick them like a pig, not slice them slowly to ribbons.' That man was a born soldier!

'All right, then. Dino. He slopes off when he visits Rome, according to your gossip.'

Claudia smiled a slanting smile. 'Dinocrates appears to live the high life, but peer closer, my friend, and you'll see it's the same few shirts he wears, the same old boots, and he never touches the women they go out with.' She paused for impact. 'He saves it all to support his wife and tiny son.'

'So-o?'

'The woman is a Persian – and you don't need too powerful an imagination to picture Arbil's vengeance were he to discover the man he raised as a son has not only committed himself in marriage to one of Babylon's sworn enemies, he's fathered a child to boot. The Persians, remember, did a Trojan Horse on Babylon by sneaking up the Euphrates to capture the city and wounds like that never heal. Arbil's barbaric bronze laws would have Dino flayed alive as a traitor.'

Marcus tossed the pin up in the air and caught it. 'Any time you want a job in the Security Police, Mistress

Seferius, I'll resign to make way for you.' He jabbed the pin into a cushion. 'Arbil, then. What do you make of those trips to Rome, the blackouts?'

Claudia swivelled sideways in her chair and swung her knees over an armrest carved in the shape of a sphinx. 'What trips to Rome?' she said, folding her hands behind her head. 'On whose word do these phantom journeys hinge? Who, exactly, verifies their authenticity? Arbil is many things. He's shrewd and ruthless and obsessed with himself, he's organized and religious and partial to date liqueur. Have you ever tasted date liqueur, by the way?'

Marcus shook his head, more in bewilderment than the negative.

'Well, don't. That's my advice. It's thick and strong and peels layers off your tongue, but boy, can you slip things in it without the imbiber being any the wiser!'

He stiffened and leaned forward. 'Such as?'

'Conjuring tricks rely on distracting the eye and creating illusions. One sees what one is led to see, believes what has been fed you. In Arbil's case, it was the floppy, pouchy skin. Are you with me so far?'

'Not even close. What you describe are classic products of a dissolute lifestyle, and that ties in with Arbil.'

'On whose say-so?' The truth had come to her when she awoke in Arbil's guest room. 'A few dirty pictures, a leggy young wife, a tipple of liquor of dates. Does that smack of degeneracy? Or a normal middle-aged man with a healthy sex drive and a regular bowel? Suppose, instead' she flashed a grin, 'Arbil's skin sags from an administered substance?'

Orbilio's mouth moved up at one corner. 'Such as?'

'In the Indus Valley the oleander shrub is known

as "the horse killer" because it's so potent. Did I ever mention Angel –'

'– is Indian? Once or twice.'

'Then we have our old friend, thorn apple,' she smiled. No wonder the girl looked so shaken when Claudia burst into her bedroom and saw those white, trumpet-shaped flowers! 'Depending on the strength, it can make a man excitable, act out of character – making amorous lunges at his house guest, for example. A stronger dosage, he'll start having delusions, hallucinations – and I can only guess at the cocktail which brought on the blackouts. All it needs is a tinksy bit of help, and one can get away with . . . murder.'

Orbilio leaned back, crossed his legs and for the first time in hours, began to relax. 'Naturally, you have no idea who Angel's helpmate might be?'

'Funny you should ask.' Claudia kicked off her sandals. 'There's a young groom name of Lugal – he's the one who's supposed to drive his master to Rome, yet no one else has ever seen them leave, and you know, it's a strange thing about Lugal. The lad never takes his eyes off the master's pretty wife.'

Well, I've warned her, it's up to Angel now, and if they have an ounce of common sense, those two, they'll be half way to the Adriatic and not stopping to look over their shoulder. When Claudia upended that jug of date liqueur over Arbil, she had unwittingly set his detox in motion. First he'll attribute his clear thinking to having exorcised Lamashtu, the demon, but Arbil's a clever man. It won't be long before he sees his wife's hand in his behavioural changes and blackouts – and when that happens, Lugal and Angel will be tied face to face and thrown in the river to drown. You don't mess with us Babylonians.

'That's three of our five suspects demolished.' Orbilio stroked his jaw. 'What about Shannu?'

'The obvious candidate,' Claudia said. 'Unfortunately he has a watertight alibi, that room is locked at all times, repeat all times, which is a pity, because Shannu has the perfect temperament for this crime.'

'You think so?' Marcus frowned. 'These are sophisticated killings, carefully planned and thought through, and I can see Shannu being bright enough and cunning enough to carry them out, but it's the control aspect that doesn't fit in.'

She pretended to be surprised. 'Control?'

'The binding of the ankles and the wrists,' he explained. 'It suggests a need to dominate the victims, show who's boss, and the longer it takes, the better. So then.' Orbilio closed his eyes. 'Suppose you tell me why you know it isn't Sargon.'

The lids were shut, but you could still see the sparkle. He knew. Goddammit, he knew she didn't think Sargon was the killer, he'd been stringing her along all the time! How the hell could he have guessed? Claudia's fingernails drummed against the woodwork. Of course! If she'd suspected for a second that any of those men had been a butcher, she'd have contacted him straight away, instead of waiting for him to come to her! He knew she would not have risked another tattooed life.

'I don't *know* it isn't Sargon,' she said, with no attempt to disguise the petulance in her voice. 'The wolf, the whistle – whit, whit, whit. He comes in on a market day, sneaks away from Dino and the Captain, and yes of course he has a secret. All men do.'

One lazy lid opened and slowly closed again.

'Sargon,' Claudia continued, 'intends to wrest the reins from Arbil and operate from Rome, there are letters in his chest to that effect. Unfortunately, he intends to change his father's moral strictures.' She tossed across the two folded documents, the contract and the invoice, she'd purloined from Sargon's satchel. 'This is merely a sample.'

Orbilio's breath came out in a hiss and he moved across to scrutinize the papers by the ever brightening sky. 'The bastard plans to sell children into brothels! He's drawn up a pricing structure, for gods' sake!'

That's the trouble with peace, thought Claudia, remembering all too clearly Sargon's tariffs for brothels the length and breadth of the country. Peacetime brings boredom, boredom breeds hedonism and hedonism clearly pays handsome. Suddenly there was a nasty taste in her mouth.

'I'll bloody put paid to that!' Orbilio was saying. 'I'll send soldiers right now to arrest him, and even then, we'd probably be doing him a favour. Janus knows what retribution Arbil would extract!'

I dread to think!

'I just wish we had a motive for the slaughter,' he said, tucking into his belt the evidence which would shortly sink Sargon. 'Annia can't recall any incident which might have triggered – where is she, by the way?'

'Search me,' Claudia shrugged.

'Gladly,' he grinned. 'Can we start now?'

But all he got was a look that would have burnt holes in cobblestones.

He stared across the garden, where bees buzzed round the fan-trained peach and blizzards of apple blossom cascaded on to the path as a small boy climbed the branches. The first of the slaves were up, laying out breakfast, stoking the furnace, putting out crumbs for the birds. Had it not been for the dim light of the peristyle, the killer would have seen Severina had no tattoo and instead he'd have run Annia to ground. A sharp pain ran through Orbilio's gut. Maybe the bastard already had . . .

'Think carefully, Claudia. Think really carefully. Severina was killed here on purpose, a message to you – and they don't come much clearer than that.' She heard the rasp where he scratched at his stubble. 'Is there no one else you can think of who has a connection with Arbil?'

A mental picture flashed across Claudia's vision. One man talking earnestly with two others in a cool and shaded courtyard. A man who was surprised to see her there. A man who likes to control . . .

'No,' she said irritably. 'I've told you everything I know.'

Around now, bakers would be cooling their first batches of the day, cats and dogs would stretch and scratch their fleas. Canopies would be unfolding under which tribunes would sit to hear petitions. Temple priests around the city would kindle up their sacred, aromatic fires.

Claudia feigned a yawn.

'I'm sorry.' Marcus jumped out of the chair and held

open the door of the office. 'I ought not have kept you up all night.'

She fluttered a grateful feminine smile and shuffled wearily into her sandals. Once in the hall, however, those same shoes barely touched the floor as she dived into the bustling street.

Claudia did not believe those tales about werewolves who lusted after human blood.

But she believed in men who did.

XXX

'I know he's in there!' Claudia pounded her fist against the heavy, holm-oak door. 'Dammit, Tucca, open up!'

Heads poked out of windows, doves took flight, dogs barked. This was a respectable suburb on the Quirinal, the residents were unused to disturbances. A small child began to bawl. Claudia continued to batter.

Click, clunk, graunch. Finally, the door swung open a hand's span.

'Where is he?' Claudia shoved her weight behind the timber and sent the mute reeling. 'I know you're here, Kaeso. Come on out!'

Tucca picked herself up and stumbled after the intruder, gargling and gesticulating with her raw, red hands that Kaeso didn't live here, please go now. Undeterred, Claudia swept down the atrium, her magenta wrap flapping like batwings as she flung aside curtains, doors and shutters and peered into every dismal, empty room along the way. Nothing. She marched into the peristyle, still deep in shadow where the sun had not yet risen above the surrounding apartment blocks, and swore. The garden, if possible, looked gloomier than ever. No brindle dog to cheer it up, no puffs of white narcissus or scented squills, and the room of curios was strangely silent, too. The grate had been swept clean and only a lingering hint of woodsmoke suggested a fire had ever danced here. The collection of carved animals – rearing horses, diving dolphins, licking cats – seemed static somehow, lifeless, and the gap where the leaping billygoats had stood glared mournfully back at her.

The vitality of the room, she realized with an irregular thump of her heart, had been generated solely by Kaeso.

Tucca stood beside the polished cypress door, hands on solid hips as though to say I-told-you-so. Claudia's eyes narrowed as she slowly retraced her steps to the atrium. The doors she'd flung open Tucca hadn't bothered to close. Another smack in the face for her visitor. He was here, though. Goddammit, he was here . . .

Methodically she cast her eye over the atrium decor. Unimaginative was the word, that geometric mosaic, those boring blocks of colour on the walls, that mean little pool. Claudia looked up at the neutral stuccoed ceiling. Janus, the silence in this house was creepy! Then she remembered how Kaeso was predisposed towards tricks. Aha! With a judicious shove, two concealed doors in the far wall gave way, exposing a hidden room washed with blues, greens and silvers, sparkling with the reflections from a polished silver mirror. A shrine to an unfamiliar figure filled the far corner, although she recognized the Babylonian cherubs clinging to the ceiling.

'Now tell me what were you doing at Arbil's,' she demanded.

And still there was nothing straightforward about Kaeso. The linen of his tunic was neither green nor blue, yet it could pass for either, and in the early morning light, his shaggy mane shone silver. Even in the privacy of his well concealed bedroom, it transpired, Kaeso resorted to camouflage.

He hadn't so much as blinked. 'Don't you want to know about Magic?' he asked, sweeping his arm to indicate the chair.

'No.' Claudia remained standing. 'His tirade of filth has stopped.' There had been nothing for two days. Perhaps she'd killed him, after all?

Kaeso straightened a marble bust which stood upon a podium by the wall. There was a Greekness about it, suggesting great antiquity.

'I am here,' she said, 'to talk about Arbil, and why, when you were engaged in a game of cat-and-mouse involving Magic, and doubtless several other commissions besides, you felt obliged to look up a few old friends half a day's ride out of town.'

'And just what business might that be of yours?' he asked, so quietly she had to strain to catch the words.

Well . . . now you ask. None actually.

'Furthermore, what gives you the right to barge into my house then root me out like a truffle?' He padded across the room and his grey eyes bored into hers, but he couldn't quite hold back the amusement which danced in them. 'But most importantly, Claudia Seferius, how the bloody hell did you find out about this room?'

He'd been washing, she decided, when she'd burst into the house. There were splashes of water round the bowl and on the floor, and the towel was soaking wet.

'Your conjuring tricks.' Against her will, she smiled back. And that was why Kaeso was dangerous. 'I spent a long time waiting in your atrium –' (was it really only eight days ago?) '– and I had a feeling then I was being watched.' In fact, I suspect the peephole is behind the statue you've just straightened. 'Also, that story you spun about Tucca, something didn't quite ring true. Is she your mother?'

'Commendably close.' He adjusted the buckle on his belt, reinforcing the notion of recent and hasty dressing. 'She worked as a nursemaid for Arbil, we grew close and as you've already guessed, it's me and not some fictitious daughter who looks after her. But,' he gave a twisted grin, 'the part about her husband is the truth. His bones do lie in the garden, and I should know, because I buried him myself.'

Between the bay tree and the yew, if I recall . . . Claudia turned to examine a painting on the wall. It was a rustic scene, shepherds on some hills, the sea calm and blue beyond, but nowhere that she recognized.

'A girl was killed in my garden.' Straight to the point, thatta girl. 'Her name was Annia, she was raised by Arbil, and she's the latest in a number of similar attacks.' Why mention the killer mistook Severina for his intended victim?

Kaeso's brow furrowed only slightly, but his answer was a long time coming. Finally he sat down on the bed and leaned his weight back upon one elbow. 'The Market Day Murders. I see.'

She did not appear to have rattled him, but then a man who hides within his own house has long learned to curb emotions.

'Arbil knows certain of his girls are being picked off one by one,' he said, looking up at her. 'Since tracking was what he trained me for, I volunteered to help.'

The bed he lay across was a combination of Roman

frame and Babylonian springing, though from the badly ruffled counterpane and sheets, it would appear Kaeso suffered badly from insomnia. *Or else had company.*

'Plausible,' Claudia smiled. 'I'd give you seven out of ten for quick thinking.'

Kaeso laughed, and the sound was by no means unpleasant. 'Then before you pull my toenails out to get the truth, I'd better come clean about the urgency – and incidentally the secrecy – for that visit.' He drew a deep breath. 'The thing is, Claudia, Sargon feels his father's mental frailties are sufficient to warrant not only a take-over, but a huge expansion in the industry.'

The word industry was not lost on her. 'Has he divulged his new policies?' she asked innocently. A trail of drips led from the washbasin to a wall covered by a large tapestry, where a puddle was starting to form round brown protruding toes.

'Only that the financial rewards will be huge and my skills will be required on a permanent basis. With Arbil's rapid deterioration in health, he intends to move quickly and asked me up there because he wanted to know whether I was in or not.'

'And are you?' Before nightfall, Sargon will be marched into Rome charged with peddling children for sex. Will you be in chains alongside him, Kaeso? Will you?

'I haven't decided,' he shrugged.

Claudia walked over to the shrine. The figurine was cast in silver and appeared, from above, to be sexually ambivalent. She resisted the urge to lean down and determine its gender. The libation jug had dried out, only a red ring remained at the bottom, but the posy of flowers beside it was fresh. They were fragrant white lilies and she held one to her nose to inhale its heady perfume. Suddenly her magenta gown seemed garish in this room of seascape colours.

Without a word, Claudia tossed the lily in his lap and swept out of Kaeso's bedroom.

At the far side of the atrium, she paused to glance over her shoulder. The green and yellow blocks of colour on the walls revealed no trace of the concealed doors that had closed seamlessly behind her. It was as though they'd never been. And for an instant, Claudia, too, was tempted to believe it was pure imagination, a figment of the light and lack of sleep.

The house did that to you.

It was intended to.

The figure that stepped out from behind the tapestry in Kaeso's room was frowning. 'What did that meddling bitch want?'

The man's tracker eyes were still fixed on the pair of double doors. 'She's having trouble with a stalker. He attacked her, and she wants him dealt with.'

'She didn't look very scared when she came barging through your front door, pushing Tucca to the ground.'

'I never said she was frightened,' Kaeso pointed out.

The other person sighed away their irritation, slowly inching up their tunic, first above one knee and then the thigh, then the other knee and thigh. Only when the body was fully revealed in its exquisite beauty, bathed in gold from pools of sunlight, did Kaeso wrench the whole of his gaze away from the doors. Sinuous arms coiled around his neck.

'You do love me, don't— ?' But the lips were silenced by the placing of two gentle fingers over them.

'Ssssh.'

Teeth made a playful grab for the admonishing fingertips. 'What's that you're hiding in your hand?'

He unclenched his fist. 'A lily,' he replied. 'Nothing but a lily.'

'It smells better than that perfume she's left in the room.' Expert hands began to unbuckle Kaeso's belt. 'Do you think she suspects?' a voice murmured in his ear. 'About you and me, I mean?'

Grey eyes pierced the lily he still clutched in his fist. 'Not a chance.'

His belt clattered to the floor, but when fingers gently tugged the tunic upwards, they were stilled by firm and downward pressure.

'Not now,' he said. 'Not just for the moment.'

Hurt replaced lust in the eyes. 'Why not?'

Kaeso smiled, but in his eyes there was no emotion to be read. None at all. 'Because I have to go out for a while,' he said. 'That is why.'

The last person Orbilio expected to see when he returned to his own house was Annia, and several emotions hit him at once. Relief, of course, that she was safe. Anger, aimed at himself for not keeping proper tabs and at her, for being irresponsible. And other, less rational feelings. Irritation, compassion and, it has to be said, pride. Watching her feeding the caged birds in the courtyard with seed from the palm of her hand, her long, fair hair tumbling down her back just like her mother's, he felt a constriction in his breast, which he could not explain. So slight, he thought. So fragile. He followed the liquid pleats of her tunic down to the hem. How could Daphne have been so callous? The thought was an ignoble one, but he was glad it was Severina last night . . .

'I only did what you told me!' The strain showed clear upon Annia's pale and scrubbed face as she brushed the birdseed from her hands. 'Go home and stay there, you said.'

Weary to the bone, Marcus had no defence. He did not recall using the word home, but, he admitted to himself, that was precisely how it felt. Whenever he was with Claudia, wherever they might be and whatever the circumstances, it bloody well felt like home.

'You look awful,' Annia tutted, straightening his crumpled clothes and smoothing the nap. 'You look like a man who hasn't slept, you need a shave, and really, Marcus, if you're going to make an impression on the Emperor, you ought to have a haircut. How is Augustus? Have you spoken with him personally? What's he like?'

She was relentless. What's the latest on the crisis? Has the Emperor appointed an heir? What about his stepson, Tiberius, is he in the running? She questioned him about the coup, how did he feel, he a proud aristocrat, mixing among the lowlife of informants? And then, as he caved in to the demands his growling stomach insisted upon, Annia broached the subject which he'd so far managed to skirt.

'Did . . . did anything happen yesterday?'

He drank the wine she poured him. Should he tell her? Would not telling her be protecting her? Having overstretched himself these past few days, he could hide under the umbrella of exhaustion without a conscience. But then she'd find out somehow, either from the servants or from gossip at the baths, and in any case she'd require an explanation for being shipped off to the country, which was the best (and possibly only) way he could guarantee her safety for the moment.

He broke a steaming roll in half and formed a ball of dough between his fingers. 'As a matter of fact . . .' With only the barest of encouragement, he recounted the facts, and by doing so clarified them in his mind.

'Oh, Marcus!' Annia buried her head in her hands. 'What am I going to do? I'll never be safe!'

Marcus had been seven years old when Penelope knelt on the parapet of the Aemilian Bridge one heavy, thundery night. As the lightning crackled and the thunderbolts rumbled, she knotted a lump of masonry round her waist and then calmly pushed it over the side. Passers-by had rushed to the spot, but Penelope had timed her moment well. In the dark, churning waters there were no discerning ripples and no splashes, and the rain began to fall in buckets.

The blonde head emerged from its burial place and pushed the hair from her face. 'It was very selfish of me, wasn't it, not going to Arbil's with Claudia?'

He tossed an apple from hand to hand. 'Being frightened is nothing to be ashamed of,' he said slowly.

One shoulder rose and fell. 'You say that, because you're brave. When those thugs attacked you last week, you said yourself you weren't scared.'

'Angry,' he said. 'I was bloody angry, mainly for allowing myself to be cornered so easily, but that's different. The blood's up, emotions are running hot and they're running high. But inside, we're all frightened of something.'

She twisted her head on one side. 'What scares you, then?'

'Me?' He bit into the apple. 'Losing people I care about.' Passion deepened his voice. 'That scares the hell out of me.'

Annia brightened up. 'Then you'd better tell me what Claudia found out at the ranch. Maybe together we can come up with some answers!'

Even as Orbilio relayed the information Claudia had passed on, his mind travelled to an altogether different plane. With so much going on, he'd overstretched himself of late. Well, he wasn't the only one under pressure! Suppose the killer, too, had overstretched himself? Suppose that by staging the last murder in Claudia's garden, he'd tried just that bit too hard to be clever?

'I have to get some sleep,' he told Annia, because he needed to be alone with his thoughts. Break the problem into segments then deal with them one at a time, that was the rule that he worked by, and right now he was paying the price for ignoring his own advice. By juggling three demanding cases, he'd not been true to any!

He splashed cold water over his face. Segment one, the Magic problem seemed to have sorted itself out – no more letters, packets or ripped dolls had been delivered and Orbilio's theory was that, unable to frighten Claudia, he'd moved on to terrorize another, weaker victim. In a way, he was relieved. The pressure was off, Claudia was safe – but now what excuse did he have to hang around?

As for segment two, the plotting merchants, that was easy. Had a coup been imminent, he would know about it!

Which left the maniac who preyed on the Children of Arbil.

In a fresh linen tunic, with his hair combed and a glass of chilled wine under his belt, Orbilio decided that, having deposited all the facts in his investigative cauldron, it was time to let them stew for a while. In his experience, it was through exercise that his thought processes honed themselves, and that was precisely what he intended to do now. He smiled to himself as Annia's high-pitched trilling instructed his steward on the merits of employing women rather than men to clean the silver, their hands are every bit as strong but far more flexible, and really, in an atrium of this class, more lampstands were in order, didn't he think, plus extra gilding on the ceiling. Making no attempt to rescue the poor man, Orbilio made his exit through the back.

The athletics yard was packed, a battleground where young blades showed their muscle tone and old men overreached. Orbilio cut a straight line through the grunting and the wheezing, through the javelins and wrestling towards the gymnasium where, oiled and naked, he gathered together a team to play small ball. It was the only game he knew which exercised every single muscle of the body and while his body worked out, his mind could rest. Afterwards, while his flesh was pummelled by a masseur, his refreshed brain would begin a workout of its own.

XXXI

The traffic on the Via Lata was light as Claudia cut across from the Quirinal. What had she hoped to achieve from her visit to Kaeso? A confession? Hardly! On the other hand, do men who slice their victims into twenty-seven pieces dash home for a spot of vigorous sex? She did not think so.

The girls' terror, their blood, an absolute domination, these were the triggers for a ritual murderer, that's how these freaks get their kicks.

But then Kaeso was an esoteric individual . . .

Always on the Field of Mars you'd find schoolboys running races, jousters on horseback, wig sellers displaying their curly wares on the marble heads of statues (at least until the wardens found out). The baths were free, the lake invariably jammed with rowboats, so take a deep breath, forget about little Severina, just take time out and relax.

Claudia bought a cinnamon bun from a vendor and inhaled its warmth and spiciness.

Counting today, she reflected, ambling down the Portico of a Hundred Pillars, the Megalesian Games still had three days to run and praise be to Bacchus, whose humble wine dregs had sabotaged Larentia, she could enjoy these Games in peace. Tomorrow, in the Theatre of

Pompey over there, already flooded and floating proper warships, they were staging a mock naval battle and on Monday the festivities culminate in The Procession of the Gods and more races at the Circus. Today, however, the Theatre of Marcellus was putting on a riproaring musical farce.

Around Pillar Nineteen, the heel of her sandal snagged in the hem of her gown and as she released it, Claudia thought she caught a movement. Shadows, of course. With its alley of plantains, its frescoes and bronze statues, what do you expect?

The farce should be quite a show. Apparently the playwright was a sparkling newcomer whose wit and musical score—

There it was again! At Pillar Thirty-one. The flicker from behind. She glanced along the colonnade. Portly merchants eyeing up the painted nudes. Lovers, arm in arm, eyes locked. A small boy sitting on the step, picking intently at a scab on his elbow. People. Not exactly crowds, but nevertheless she wasn't alone here. So why this flutter of unease for what was probably nothing but the effect of fast-moving clouds?

Around Pillar Forty-three, Claudia simply had to know. Had Kaeso's House of Silence made a sucker out of her?

Backtracking round a cypress grove, the path diverged. This way to the Pantheon, that way to the baths. But wait. Behind an overhanging branch, a narrow, weed-choked path would prove it once and for all. Claudia did not consider the danger as she draped her bright magenta wrap around her elbows and was swallowed by the shrubs. She was intent only on defying an overheated imagination . . .

Dappled shade turned to deeper shadows. Dense undergrowth muffled sound, the greenery snagged in her hair. Ought she turn back? Narrowing to the point of obscurity, the path terminated at a building where ivy scrambled over walls for sparrows to make nests in. There was a coldness and a damp about the place. The long, wet grass was a stranger to the scythe and when the leaf litter rustled, Claudia squealed aloud. A blackbird hopped out, dangling a caterpillar from his beak, and she rolled her eyes in disgust. What's to be scared of? This old voting hall, abandoned because who the hell wanted to traipse this far out of town to hear speeches? There were rumours about it being turned into a bazaar—'

'BITCH!'

Claudia spun round. *'Magic!'*

He hadn't changed his clothes, they were filthier than ever and stiff from the dried blood of two days back. 'You faithless, whoring bitch!'

The hair was matted, just as she remembered, and the same uneven teeth and gagging stench. The only difference seemed to be that this time he wielded a knife in both his hands. Claudia screamed, even before she remembered the doll that he'd sent her, slashed to ribbons.

'I followed you.'

Spinning on her heel, she raced across the courtyard. Inside the voting hall, I'll be safe!

'And saw you with those men!'

Up the steps she ran . . .

The voice changed, became wheedling. 'Thought you'd kill old Magic? Well, you can't.'

. . . across the portico . . .

'Magic is immortal.'

. . . through the porchway . . .

'Magic cannot die!'

. . . to the doors . . .

'But you'll die, you bitch! You deceived me!'

. . . which were locked and would not budge.

He stopped running when he knew he had her trapped. 'All those men,' he rasped. 'Why? Why so many men, Claudia?'

Her fingernails chipped in a desperate attempt to claw open the lock. 'Men?' she croaked. He was deranged. But maybe she could reason with him and find a way out of this nightmare.

'First the blond one, then the dark one.' His eyes glittered harshly. 'No thought of your promise to me!' In the dank and slimy darkness, the glint from the twin blades shone menacingly. 'What about the vows we took, do they mean nothing?'

It was no use, the doors were never going to open! Her heart was pounding, her breathing ragged. Think, girl, think! 'That we still share, Magic.' She forced her voice to be soft and reassuring. 'Those men –'

'Yes?' His face twisted.

'– They were relatives, that was all.' She swallowed the bile in her throat, and forced herself to look at him and not the knives. 'I told you . . . in my letters . . . about my duties.' In an effort to quell the rising terror, had she overdone the soothing? Had it come out patronizing?

'Then –' He seemed to be trying to grasp something. '– Then you'll still come to me every night?'

'Always.'

He nodded slowly, as though still taking it in. 'And when the white light hurts my head, you'll sing to me like Mamma did?'

'Of course.'

His voice became petulant. 'She doesn't come to magic the pain away any more, she –' The eyes blurred with tears. Was this her moment? Could she dash past him, unnoticed? '– Mamma's dead, isn't she?' he sobbed. 'Mamma's dead?'

Intuitively, Claudia knew it was true. The mother who'd looked after him, protected him against himself and the world, and drugged him when the pain became too bad. She could almost hear the woman whispering 'magic' as she wiped his sweating brow and trickled the draught through his lips. 'Yes,' she said, and heard the tremble in her voice. 'Mamma's dead.'

Distant eyes re-focused. Became beady. 'That's right,' he said smugly. 'She died the day your husband died! I wrote you a letter, told you how we were united in grief, you wrote back, remember? That's when it started. Back in August. You do remember, don't you?'

Claudia's breath came out in a series of tiny gasps. 'Every detail.'

The inadequate creature who called himself Magic shuffled closer in the doorway. 'You're mine,' he said thickly. 'Mine!' In the dim light, she saw his eyes clamp on her breasts, and he all but licked his lips. Smile. For gods' sakes, smile at him! He smiled back. Then the smile hardened and was replaced by a frown.

'You tried to kill me!' It came over sulky.

She took a step towards him. One step closer to Magic. One step closer to the steps which led to freedom. She could smell his stale breath and body odour, heard his laboured lungs. 'No, I—'

'Yes, you did! *You fucking tried to kill me!*'

This time, there was no reasoning with him. No words which would mollify, no looks to calm him down. Ducking under the flailing twin blades, Claudia ran headlong across the porch towards the marble stairs. Three steps from the bottom, she slipped, her feet trapped in the fabric of her wrap.

'Now it's your turn, you bitch!'

Magic plunged towards her, yelling obscenities and waving the knives. Kicking and squirming, Claudia rolled on to the bottom step, then the madman was on top of her, pinning her down with his knees. With her face pressed into the dirt and no escape possible, she braced herself for the thrust of the knife.

It didn't come.

And suddenly the weight on top of her was gone. Croesus, he bottled it after all!

Claudia spun round on to her back. Magic hadn't run off, he'd been hauled off. She saw an arm round his throat, a man's knee in the small of his back. She watched a knife plunge upwards into his kidneys. Saw him arch with the pain. And as he arched, the knife came down straight in his heart.

The last thing she heard as the darkness swallowed her up was a voice in the distance saying, 'I think you'll find that terminates the correspondence course.'

As Claudia struggled back to consciousness, strange pictures formed and dissolved. A man with the head of a hawk. Another like a jackal. A woman in a blue dress with cow horns on her head—

'Janus!'

'It's only the priestess,' a deep voice said soothingly. 'You're in the Temple of Isis.' He paused. 'You passed out, I carried you here.'

Isis? Memory crawled back, inch by inch. The Field of Mars. A path into the woods. The old voting hall. There was a fight . . .

'Ssssh,' the man said. 'Easy, now.'

A cool compress was pressed against her forehead and the lap in which her head lay smelled of musk. Close by, the woodpecker from hell drummed for all it was worth. It turned out to be Claudia's teeth.

'Is he dead?' she asked, remembering everything now.

Kaeso grinned. 'Most emphatically.'

He dipped his kerchief in the holy fountain and dabbed at the cuts and bruises on her face as images of Magic flashed through her head. The twin blades clutched between his fingers. The surprise upon his face. The professional assassination, with oh so little blood . . .

Numbly, Claudia allowed Kaeso to ease her into a sitting position. Amber-coloured walls were painted floor to ceiling with regimented lines of birds and snakes and vibrant coloured figures. Heiroglyphics they were called, and the priestess with the cow horns threw heavy resins on the fire and gently rattled a sistrum before the goddess Isis, robed in dazzling white. Behind her, Osiris weighed a heart against a feather.

'You followed me,' she said.

'Yes,' he said simply, and there was no need to ask why. The answer lay there, in his eyes.

Claudia wanted to thank him for saving her life, but words were inadequate, payment obscene. So she cupped her hands and sipped the icy waters and told him instead about Sargon's plans to sell the children into brothels.

There was silence, while sharp features scanned the symbols on the walls. Cartouches, they were called. Or, holy names.

'I never once suspected that of Sargon,' he said eventually, wrenching his gaze from a painted papyrus. 'I thought he was my friend, yet he imagined I would track down frightened runaways and send them back to his paedophiles!' Kaeso shook his head in bewilderment. 'How could he get involved in an enterprise as sordid as that?'

'Money,' she said simply. 'He can never have enough, it runs through his fingers like this water in my hands.'

The rattle of the sistrum ceased when the blue-gowned priestess disappeared through a door in the stonework.

'Does Dino know?' he asked.

'I doubt it,' she replied. 'Nor the Captain.'

An acolyte emerged from the bowels of the temple, wearing a thick black wig and bangles. Smiling shyly, she began to dust the statue of hawk-faced Horus. Claudia waited until her egret feathers had moved on to Anubis.

'One other matter I think you ought to know about. Arbil has given up the date liqueur.' She watched the significance of her statement sink in.

'I see.' The only sign of anxiety was the pacing.

'So you'd better get Angel out of Rome, and fast.' Her eyes followed the slow, familiar lope.

It could not have been Lugal who Angel hooked up with, the boy was too young, too one-dimensional for her tastes. She'd used the groom, led him on and poor Lugal was too trusting to suspect he'd been tied up tighter than a goose for the oven. Angel wouldn't care what befell him, either, once Arbil found out. Remember, this was the woman who affected concern for her husband, when in reality those checks were a necessary excuse to mark the progress of his blackouts and sow further seeds of doubt in his mind. The bruise on her cheek she had flaunted as a badge of Arbil's deterioration – how she must have laughed, knowing it was the effect of her drugs which, by turns, rendered him impotent, put him to sleep and, when it suited her, made him violent. Claudia imagined that Arbil, when he uncovered her treachery, was unlikely to lean towards clemency.

She recalled her very first meeting with Angel. The Indian had not been able to disguise her suspicion, which she masked with hostility, and in the end, that hostility had betrayed her. Otherwise Claudia would have thought nothing of oleanders and thorn apples and strong, date liqueur . . . Would not have made the connection between the hothouse lilies up at Arbil's and the hothouse lilies in Kaeso's bedroom—

'At the start, it was exciting,' he said. 'An affair under Arbil's nose.'

Claudia could almost feel the intoxication that the plotting and the planning would induce. The illicit meetings, whispered messages. The knowledge that Arbil might find out any moment and exact his terrible revenge . . .

Kaeso stopped pacing and ran his hands through his collar-length hair. In his belt was the knife he'd used to still Magic. 'I didn't know, until yesterday, that Angel meant Arbil harm.'

'She meant to kill him, Kaeso.' The bitch wanted him dead! It's the only way she could get her hands on his money box.

The junior priestess shook her egret feather duster out of doors and began to sweep the steps with a broom. The swishing of the heather twigs grew fainter stair by stair, and the heat inside the shrine intensified. Blood pounded through Claudia's veins, throbbing at her pulse points and at the base of her ears.

'Are you . . . in love with her?'

'I was,' he said slowly, turning to look Claudia full in the face.

Her cheeks coloured, and the only sound was the trickle of the fountain. 'What changed your mind?' she asked.

For several seconds, Kaeso simply held her gaze without blinking. 'What changed my mind,' he said huskily, 'is that I met someone else.'

A lump blocked her windpipe. There was no mistaking his meaning . . .

Claudia kept her eyes clear of the powerful frame of the man tracker, the sleek war machine who had silenced her stalker for ever, as she pretended to re-arrange the folds of her gown. 'Kaeso, I—'

But he had gone.

'Kaeso?'

She was all alone in the temple. And when she asked the priestess which direction he had taken, the girl frowned. 'No one came down these steps, but you, ma'am,' she replied.

Tight-lipped, Claudia smiled. To the end, Kaeso kept up his chicanery, and she knew she could return to that house on the Quirinal a hundred times and never find him.

Not unless Kaeso wanted her to.

XXXII

His body beaded with sweat, his hair hanging limp in saturated ropes, Marcus Cornelius Orbilio made his way towards the steam room. The game of small ball, fast and physical, had exhausted him, but his mind was buzzing like a bee around a hyssop bush as he collapsed face down upon the table to submit to the ministrations of a Spaniard who'd clearly scraped kidskins for vellum in a previous incarnation.

There were many aspects of these bizarre and grisly killings that worried him, he brooded, as the strigil scraped his flesh. Ritual murder's always tricky, because despite the killer's distinctive signature upon the crime, in most cases he's virtually impossible to trace. But for once, Marcus had a fair old list of suspects.

The Spaniard rolled him on to his back and proceeded to torture the remaining life out of his prostrate victim. True, he had eliminated those five suspects, but in the same way he'd overlooked the obvious regarding Zygia's hair, somewhere along the line, Orbilio knew he had made a crucial mistake.

His flesh raw, he tipped the Spaniard and let a square-jawed Sarmatian work warmed oils of chamomile and marjoram into his skin. Claudia had been positive Shannu could not pass his bars, now a chill descended on Marcus, despite the ministrations of the masseur. Suppose someone deliberately unbolted that door . . .

Donning wood-soled sandals to protect his feet against the searing tiles, Orbilio clip-clopped into the hot room. 'Ritual murder, ritual murder' went the rhythm of the clogs, forcing him to recap the observances which the killer so assiduously followed.

One: lasso the victims, drag them backwards, knock them out. Two: strip them naked, tie their hands and then their feet, and he must gag them too, and remove the gag later, because no one had screamed. Then he started slashing, but why the twenty-seven cuts? What was the significance of the hair in the lap? And where did the whistle fit in? It all seemed so over the top. Almost an over-kill. Pinching his nose, Orbilio dived beneath the steaming waters. Of course! Bobbing up, he pushed the hair from off his face and grinned. It was the ritual which mattered, not the actual killing!

As he shook off the drips, Severina's face floated into his memory. Not how she'd looked in death, but how she looked in life. Beautiful, full of joy, with everything to live for. *Why?* he wondered. Why, of all the girls who bore a blue tattoo, should dark, vivacious Zygia be a target for the killer's warped and twisted mind? What is it that sets the elfin Annia apart?

Orbilio felt he was on the brink of more than just the plunge pool. He was – if only he dared follow up his instinct – poised on the brink of a terrible solution, because suppose (just suppose) he'd got this whole thing back to front?

Arms outstretched, Marcus Cornelius Orbilio dived into the icy waters of the plunge pool.

And shuddered.

XXXIII

'Claudia?'

The bunch of keys jangled in his hand as Marcus let himself in, but only his voice came back to him, the echo undistorted by kitchen steam or by the clatters, bangs and jabber that denote a household's heart.

'I need to talk to you about Arbil.'

Tossing the keys upon a vacant chopping block, he crossed the silent kitchen into an atrium where only marble eyes stared out and chatter came solely from the fountain. Where the hell was everybody?

'Claudia!' he bellowed, and 'ya, ya, ya' came back to him as he belted up the stairs. Her bedroom, and all the guest rooms, were deserted. Where the devil were the servants?

'Like whether a goblet is half empty,' he called out, as he checked the second gallery, 'or half full –'

Dare he barge into the bathroom? Nine days ago, she'd staunched his bleeding wounds and pressed sweet balms on to his bruises. You'd never know, from looking round, what had passed between them in this room.

'– it's a question of perspective.'

Dammit, Claudia, I thought you'd be home. And then he remembered the musical farce. She must have taken the whole household as a treat!

'This murder business,' he said, more to keep himself company in this ringing hall of columns. 'You talked of conjurors, remember? Seeing only what you're deceived to see?'

He may as well check the office before leaving.

'Hell, we've been fed a stage set from the start.'

'I know,' Claudia said quietly. From her upright, hard-backed chair behind the desk, she swivelled her eyes to meet his, but her head didn't move, and today he could forgive the lack of courtesy.

On account of the knife which pressed against the artery in her neck.

Orbilio felt himself stumble. For the first time in his life, he knew what failure meant. Total, abject failure. He had seen death in all its forms, had killed in war and self-defence. There were occasions, he recalled, where men had died when they need not have, and he had been powerless to help. Partly that was why he joined the Security Police. To rectify those errors, and avenge.

'Let her go,' he said, edging through the doorway. 'Untie her and take me instead.'

A hand slid under Claudia's chin and jerked it upwards, stretching her neck like a sacrificial beast's. 'Suppose I give Nemesis his rein and slit her throat, right here and now? What would you do then?'

He watched, transfixed with horror, as the flat of the blade travelled slowly, almost sensuously, up and down, up and down Claudia's throat.

Orbilio heard the tremble in his voice. 'I'd kill you.'

Claudia had closed her eyes, he noticed. Otherwise, there was no trace of fear upon her face. His gut turned over.

'You might lock me away, like poor Shannu was locked away, an embarrassment to the family –' the blade reverted to a point and pressed against the throbbing artery '– but my dear Marcus, you will never harm Penelope's beloved baby.'

Annia turned the full force of her beautiful, treacherous smile upon the man she called her cousin. 'That I'm sure of.'

XXXIV

Supersnoop was right, thought Claudia. Annia had played him like a sucker from the start!

Three murders so gruesome, so bizarre they would automatically attract the attention of the Security Police, though it was Marcus in particular she needed to hook, hence the encounter with Daphne. Heaven knows how long she'd been trailing the poor woman, waiting for the moment when her path would cross with Orbilio's, but Annia – as ever – had played her part to perfection. There was no way, after hearing Penelope's history, that Marcus could remain on the sidelines.

Not that he was the only mug, Claudia reflected. She, too, had allowed logic and emotion to outweigh natural instinct, and now she was about to pay the price. How strange, she thought. Despite Nemesis pressing at her throat, her mind drifted high above it, clear and calm. As though all this was happening to someone else and she was merely a spectator, watching from afar. Nothing seemed real. Not this warren of a house, unnaturally silenced. Not Marcus, unbuckling his sword belt with reluctance. And especially not sweet little Annia with her shiny, scrubbed face and glistening fair hair which she washed every day and tied back with a clean cerise ribbon.

The same ribbon, incidentally, which bound Claudia's wrists.

'Take these.' Annia tossed across a pair of handcuffs. 'Back up slowly,' she instructed Marcus. 'Kneel beside that column, put your arms around it and clip on the manacles.'

'Annia—'

He advanced half a pace and Claudia felt a warm trickle run down her neck. The blade was so sharp, she hadn't felt it puncture her skin.

'All right, Annia.' Marcus held up a placatory hand. 'Anything you say.'

His tone was conciliatory, yet even as he chained himself to the pillar, Claudia could see in his eyes that, by complying, Marcus Cornelius Orbilio had sealed his own death warrant . . .

Like a shattered pot, the dream burst.

Suddenly, the tiniest of details sprang to life. On the wall, Claudia could almost hear the leopard purring through its spots as Orpheus strummed his lyre. That tessellated peacock might strut off at any second, and Claudia could all but taste the ripened apricots and medlars drawn in paint. This is real, she thought. It's not a dream, a play to be applauded. Her heart was thumping, her hands had turned to ice. The ivory inlays glinting in the sunlight, the aromatic herbs burning in the brazier, the monkey's gouge marks in the satinwood and maple. They are real. As is Marcus. As is Annia.

And so, goddammit, am I!

She bit deep into her lower lip to stop it trembling and for a moment, everything went dark and out of focus. Deep breaths, deep breaths. For gods' sake, don't pass out. Deep breaths. Her eye picked out a flax plant painted on the wall. Blue, like the peacock on the floor. Concentrate, concentrate. In Greece, whole hillsides would be covered in it. Thatta girl, concentrate, concentrate. Think of how the stems are steeped to separate the fibres. Then bleached out in the sun before they can be woven into linen. That's the stuff, well done! Once panic had subsided and cold beads of sweat ran hot again, Claudia could almost smile. As triumphs went, it might look small, but victory was relative.

For Claudia, knowing that her mind was no longer held captive by Annia was akin to subduing Gaul!

Not – she struggled with the bonds which tied her hands behind the chair – that it would necessarily be wise to let Annia in on the secret! Her sanity remained stable only so long as the Puppet Master's stage was undisturbed. Ritual was all, she fed upon defencelessness and fear. Indeed, Claudia suspected that it was because Zygia had *not* crumpled that Annia lost her temper and slit her throat in anger. How she must have despised that lack of self-control! She'd have blamed Zygia, of course. The girl provoked her, had it coming, she deserved to die like that, the bitch. But inside, her intemperance would have gnawed away. Next time, they would play by her rules – and thus had Severina come to grief, taunted to the end.

Annia snatched the string of corals from around Claudia's neck and began to assess their size and weight and value. She preferred the deeper red, herself, although other women swore by . . . Buttressed by her inner strength, Claudia blocked her out.

What happened the day Zygia died? Did she really set out early, or had Severina covered up for, say, an illicit shopping spree or perhaps a long lie-in? Claudia imagined dark-haired Zygia pacing up and down the Cattle Market, stabbing her spiky curls with her fingers and wondering how best to make her approach to Annia. It was raining, but Zygia would not have noticed as she chewed her knuckle along the street beside the Circus. Claudia pictured her climbing the steep and slippery Cacian Steps, maybe pausing at the Lupercal to catch her breath. She would have approached the Temple of Apollo from the east, glad the library porticoes were deserted because the light was far too poor to read by. She would not have noticed droplets running down the marble columns, or dogs lapping water from the gutter. Wide-eyed and squeaky clean, Annia would have heard her out and doubts would have begun to form long before Annia spun some frilly tale to exonerate herself. 'Come with me,' she would have said. 'I'll prove it.' And feeling foolish, Zygia would have backtracked down the Palatine with Annia, little knowing that this time when she approached the Lupercal, she would stare straight into Hell.

During the time Claudia had been re-living Zygia's nightmare, Annia had been tormenting Marcus the way a cat torments a mouse, pressing Nemesis flat to Claudia's windpipe, or pointing the knife as though to slice her cheek, and emitting squeaks of satisfaction every time he flinched. But Claudia sensed a subtle change. Annia was preparing to move on.

Time!

Claudia needed to buy time!

I mean, it's all very well having your mind set free to roam, but let's face it, legs would be much better. Shackled to the pillar in the hall, Orbilio was every bit as helpless as herself, but sooner or later someone – surely – had to visit the house. Maybe a launderess would come home with a toothache? Or a messenger arrive with a letter? Goddammit, there wasn't even the possibility of Magic's filthy missives interrupting.

'Is –' Claudia cleared her throat and started again. 'Is this your objective?' she enquired. 'The aristocracy at your feet upon their knees?'

Whose bright idea was it to reward the servants with an afternoon off? And guess which silly bitch agreed! Down on the Field of Mars, the musical farce would not yet have begun – just as Annia had contrived.

'Revenge appears in many forms,' trilled the sprite, pocketing the corals. 'With each level guaranteeing satisfaction.' She leaned forward to thrust her speedwell blue eyes close to Claudia's. 'You do know what I mean by satisfaction?'

With one hand she pressed Nemesis flat against Claudia's throbbing artery.

'You see how sweet it is, don't you, Marcus?'

Keeping Nemesis primed for action, Annia moved behind the high-backed chair to make eye-contact with her cousin. Claudia could smell the freshness of her pleated tunic and the catmint rinse which had passed through the flaxen locks which brushed against her shoulder. Under a brightly coloured canvas awning, the audience would be roaring at the risqué jokes and bold political ad-libs. But the temperature, she thought, could not compare to this.

'Together, you and I, we shall watch Claudia's life blood slip away. Slowly, because I want you to savour the experience with me, Marcus.' She pressed her warm cheek to Claudia's. 'There will be pain,' she whispered, stroking the blade up and down Claudia's throat. 'Excruciating pain. But you see, each strike of Nemesis will be an arrow in his heart. It has to be this way. It is our mission.'

'Mission?' croaked Claudia.

A stair creaked, and for a fleeting moment she felt salvation was to hand. Instead, it proved only the settling of wood and as though to mock her hope, a flock of chattering sparrows chased one another through the peristyle. Idly Claudia wondered whether, like Severina, that would be her last view of life. Or whether it would be locked in the gaze of a wavy-haired policeman . . . Unable to control herself, tears trickled down her cheek.

Annia licked the salty flow and, repulsed, the flow dried up. 'We are charged with a mission, Nemesis and I, and like this sapphire in your jewel box' – she flashed Claudia's ring from her middle finger – 'it has many facets.'

'Of which wealth is one, presumably?'

'With the contents of your caskets, Claudia, plus' – she smiled her deceptive smile at Marcus – 'my cousin's particularly generous stash of gold and silver, I am a very wealthy woman. Uh-uh-uh!' She wagged a cautionary finger towards Orbilio. 'I told you before – not a word, Marcus, or I shall slice her cheek off. I'm in charge, remember. I'll let you know when you can speak.'

One by one, Annia began to unclip the butterfly brooches which held Claudia's tunic together at the shoulder.

'So, yes, that's one skin of the onion. Riches.' With tantalizing slowness, she released the final pin and the delicate cotton cascaded over Claudia's naked breast. 'Then we have revenge on Granny Daphne, and that's where you come in, Marcus. Oh, I know what you're thinking!' the sing-song voice continued. 'That this has nothing to do with you, you were only seven when my mother died and you worshipped her. You said.'

Nemesis passed to her other hand, and she began to work on the butterflies on Claudia's right shoulder.

'Unfortunately, there are casualties in every war. I watch your pain as you watch Claudia's, and then when you are dead, Daphne can be told – then let's see how strong these patrician bitches really are.'

Well, we know how strong you are. Claudia remembered (how trivial it seemed!) when Annia dropped a ring up in the bedroom. How she'd pulled the heavy chest away from the wall, shouldering it back in place without a puff. The same strength that had been used to drag five women backwards . . .

From the hall came the frantic scrape of metal against marble as Orbilio fought to free his hands. He looks so white, she thought. It makes his hair look as though it belongs to someone else. Or dyed. Blood was pooling on the floor from where the manacles had bitten. Her own wrists, she knew, were in little better shape.

'There!' Annia released the final butterfly and the remainder of Claudia's tunic slipped to her waist. With difficulty, she suppressed a shudder. So long as Annia talked, it bought more time . . .

'Why me, Annia? I don't have a blue tattoo.'

'Killing Severina was revenge on an entirely different level.' She checked the binding on Claudia's wrists and tutted. 'Don't fight it, Claudia. Don't run to meet your pain.'

She planted a kiss between her squirming victim's shoulderblades, then Claudia felt a wet tongue run down her backbone. This time, she dare not look at Marcus. The tongue moved round to lick her upper arm.

'If you bore Marduk's sign upon your perfect, unflawed flesh, it would be here.' Annia's teeth nipped and broke the skin. 'Which would make things very different between us, Claudia, because then I would have to remind you of the way you treated me at Arbil's place.' She straightened up and smiled. 'Instead we can be friends, you and I, because you didn't treat me as a dog, fetch this, go for that, pick-up-this-I-dropped-it-under-my-chair, even though you'd be sitting in it at the time.'

'The whistle!' Claudia exclaimed, more to Marcus than to Annia.

'Exactly.' Annia put her pretty lips together. Whit-whit-whit. 'It's how they summoned me, can you believe that, Claudia? And can you imagine how if felt, knowing you're patrician through and through, yet still you're whistled like a dog?'

Lots of girls get bullied, Annia. They don't all slice up their tormentors for revenge. Then, as though the sun had broken through a fog, Claudia understood.

Wasn't 'touched' the word Daphne had used to describe Penelope? Claudia glanced at Annia, and something revolved in her stomach as she wished now she'd paid more attention to Marcus' story. Who better placed, she realized, than a mother to recognize the disturbance inside her own child? Small boys being unable to differentiate between ages, Marcus would have seen nothing odd in a girl singing and dancing and playing with dolls – that's what girls did! – but the duped husband knew straightaway. Small wonder he volunteered for active service, he wanted as much distance between himself and his batty wife as possible and too late Claudia understood that Penelope's promiscuity was not about grief; his death merely upped dangerous stakes – and Daphne Lovernius understood, too. Understood, and repressed it, and Claudia felt a sharp pang of compassion for the old dame. She bit deep into her lower lip. If she'd only listened to the story objectively, and not through the grieving eyes of a seven-year-old! Then she would have seen that any mother worth her salt would have defied Daphne and retrieved the infant Annia straight away, but such was the disturbance inside her head Penelope had gone to Old Man Tiber, instead of Arbil. A tough and proud old bird, what torment must Daphne have suffered all these years, from the moment her daughter came home heavy with child? She would have known, as Claudia knew, how mental illness was often hereditary and now, sweet Jupiter, her worst nightmare had become terrifying reality . . .

Claudia looked at Marcus, momentarily silenced from his struggles, and saw that he was – at long last – grieving. Not for Annia, not even for Penelope. Marcus Cornelius Orbilio was grieving for himself and for eighteen wasted years. Years in which cover-ups and silence caused untold harm and damaged everyone who came within their sphere. When, she wondered, would families ever learn? You only have to see how Arbil handled the situation with Shannu to see how problems perpetuate.

Claudia was jerked out of her reverie when – incredibly – Annia laid Nemesis flat upon the desk. His cornelians glinted proudly in the sunshine, like the fresh dark drops of blood which would soon run over them. In the atrium, Orbilio's tunic was soaked through with sweat, his wrists raw from the unyielding iron handcuffs. Do something,

Claudia. You have to do something! You can't just let her slice you to ribbons! Marcus, too, had seen the change in Annia. They wondered what was coming next . . .

Stepping back, Annia pulled off her tunic. Of course! She wouldn't want her precious linen stained with blood. With a sharp intake of breath, Claudia saw that was only part of the reason!

Perhaps if Claudia could get inside her mind – show how she truly sympathized when, aware of the circumstances of her birth and in a place where every other child had known rejection, the girls had shown no mercy in their torment – she might reach a part of Annia that was human and compassionate?

Assuming such a place existed!

'Why twenty-seven cuts?' asked Claudia. Nemesis was just an arm's length out of reach . . .

Flushed and breathless, Annia crossed the floor. Truly, she was beautiful. Straight-backed, sinuous and graceful, her pale body shimmered as she moved, her tight, young breasts untouched by time or childbirth.

'That was Nemesis' decision, I'm afraid, not mine.' *Shit!* She picked up the knife and kissed the deadly blade. 'I wanted those sadistic bitches to feel my vengeance through a thousand gaping wounds. Unfortunately.' She ran the cold, blue blade across her thigh. 'There was no room for more than twenty-seven on the first, so we retained that number for them all. It will be the same for you, Claudia, where do you suggest we start?'

Claudia dared not take her eye off Nemesis. Her mouth was dry, her heart thumping like a thunderclap against her ribs. Behind the chair, her fingernails dug deep into her palms. From the hall, she heard a strangled cry and silently commended Orbilio's steely self-control about not speaking unless Annia commanded it. Neither he or Claudia doubted she would carry out her threat.

It happened without warning.

She saw the sunlight on the steel and for maybe one whole second Claudia did not realize the knife had actually made contact. Like the earlier nick, she had not felt it break her skin. Wide-eyed, she watched hot scarlet droplets form splash patterns on the pale peach cotton tunic in her lap. And then she knew.

The ordeal had begun.

XXXV

'Do you know what power is?'

Annia cocked her head on one side to admire her handywork. The slash, being purely superficial, had been intended as a shock. A taster of what was yet to come. When muscles were disabled, tendons cut. She watched the river she'd created find its course.

'Power is the ability to bring an empire to its knees and I have done that, Claudia. Imagine! Little Annia brings down the might of Rome.'

Claudia knew there was no blood left in her cheeks. It was gushing down her breast into her lap. 'Don't tell me! That works on several levels, too.' But she'd forgotten irony and Annia had not been introduced.

'Picture it as a building, Claudia, a tall six-storey tenement. On the top floor, there's Agrippa, taken by the great god Marduk to create a smokescreen under which Nemesis and I could operate in peace. Next floor down, we have the Holy Catamite no less, the great and mighty Augustus about to be toppled from his perch by uprisings and seditions.'

Annia paused to stretch out a finger and dip it in Claudia's blood. She examined the fingertip for several seconds, before licking it clean as though it was a drip of honey or a dab of parsley sauce.

'On the third floor, we have the whole machinery of Rome thrown into terror and confusion. Don't you think it was clever of me to pick a market day to kill the girls, Claudia? Hundreds upon hundreds of women scared to venture out alone!' She laughed. 'I created that. Me.' She hushed her voice to a whisper. 'The Market Day Murderer . . .'

The sprite clapped at her own ingenuity and Claudia asked Jupiter to make the bitch choke on her own smugness. Jupiter wasn't listening.

'On the second floor of my apartment block, you'll see Arbil, squatting like a spider in his web. By the time I disappear, I'll have left so large a cloud hanging over Arbil that his business will collapse before the autumn.'

The pumping blood was easing to a trickle as Claudia's natural defences began to heal. The musical farce would not yet have reached the intermission . . .

'Moving to the first floor, we have Daphne wetting herself once word gets out there's a killer in the family.' She twisted her head to address Marcus over her shoulder. 'That would have cut your Senate career short, even if I hadn't.' She turned back to Claudia. 'Finally, on the ground floor, we have the girls themselves.' Annia sighed with satisfaction. 'So you see, I wield power on every single storey.'

The bleeding was down to a gentle, rhythmic ooze. The puddle in her lap felt clammy on her thigh, the smell was wretched, but providing Annia could be diverted, Claudia was safe from Nemesis.

'Except for Zygia.'

Blue eyes narrowed to slits. 'I worshipped that bitch,' Annia spat.

'Because of her I put up with years of being treated like a dog and yet she shacked up with empty-headed Severina. I told her, my skin's as pale as hers, my eyes as blue – Croesus. I even grew my hair like Sever-bloody-rina, and still that spiteful dyke spurned all my offers. Can you understand her, Claudia? I mean, can you really get your head around her logic?'

Easily. 'Why so long before killing the first girl?'

Annia ran her hands across her hips. 'Marcus knows the answer to that, I expect that's how he cottoned on to me. You know, Claudia, that was my one mistake. Telling him I'd been serving the temple warden's wife for two full years, when in fact Arbil kept me as a trainer until four months back. But then, how was I to know Marcus would send a present to the stupid warden's wedding? Well, that's a mistake I shall avoid next time—'

Next time? Croesus, would the slaughter never stop? She did not intend to finish here, she'd move on to kill in Massilia or Athens – and then what excuse would she conjure up to excuse herself? Cold terror rippled down Claudia's spine. Annia would need no excuse. Having got away with multiple murder here in Rome, she'd believe herself above the law. Invincible. *Immortal?*

Annia seemed also to have taken note of Claudia's improving state of health. She was wiping the caked blood from Nemesis on a scarlet damask cushion. It looked like rust. Oh no. Sweet Jupiter, please. No.

'Where will you go?' There was desperation in Claudia's question.

And again, she did not feel the strike. A swish of the wrist, a flash of blue steel. Then a fierce burning pain along her collar bone. Somewhere mathematical calculations drifted into Claudia's brain. Two down, they said. With twenty-five to go.

'For pity's sake!' Marcus cried hoarsely. 'I'll give you anything you want! Anything, Annia! Just – please – let her go!'

With a theatrical cluck of the tongue, Annia laid the dripping knife upon the desk and walked towards the hall. 'Marcus, Marcus, Marcus.' Her shoes clicked softly on the floor.

Now's my only chance! Through the salty tears which clouded her vision and coursed down her cheeks, Claudia tugged on the cords around her wrist. Croesus, they were tight! Annia had not thought to bind her ankles to the chair, and so long as Nemesis was around, kicking out had not really been an option. Blood dripped and spurted as she struggled.

Naked and lovely, Annia's attention was concentrated on her cousin. Sunshine streamed into the atrium through the opening in the roof, casting a shapely shadow on the fresco of the Nile and sparkling the pool and fountain with a thousand shimmering gems. A turtledove cooed from the skylight.

'Marcus.' Annia's tone was soft and comforting. Almost an apology. 'Please.'

Behind them, in the office, Claudia squirmed like a ferret in a trap. From the corner of her eye, she was aware of Annia leaning down to cup Orbilio's face between her hands.

'You have to understand, Marcus.' She was still smiling as she rammed his head against the marble pillar. 'I'm the one in charge.'

Claudia's struggles intensified as Annia straightened up and put a finger to her lips.

'Not another word, you hear?' Blood was pouring down his head, obliterating his right eye. 'Not another fucking word.'

The bonds won't break! Sweet Jupiter, I've blown it. And now Annia was retracing her steps across the hall. Claudia's tearful eye caught Marcus'.

It said, I'm sorry.

His said . . . correction, his eye winked. Incredibly, it winked.

'You know, Annia,' he said. 'You really are very, very stupid.'

The sprite froze in the doorway. '*What*?' she hissed. She spun round to where he knelt, bleeding, against the marble column. 'Did you call me?'

'You don't imagine I haven't left a record of my investigation, surely?'

Claudia did not need telling twice. He was buying her more time to struggle free, because she might be many things, our Annia, but stupid wasn't one of them. It was merely her Achilles heel. You could call her vain or dull or frumpy, but never, ever, ever call her stupid.

For Claudia, the effect was like being dunked in an icy Umbrian spring, bringing her to the very edge of her five senses. Until now, she'd allowed terror to dominate her mind, muddying judgement with self-pity. Suddenly her brain was crystal clear. There was no time left for fear. It was now or it was never. The choice was simple. Live. Or die.

Croesus, Annia saw through it! Under a flying kick, Orbilio's head shot backwards, then she rammed her foot hard into his ribcage. He groaned, but his taunting didn't cease. This time it revolved around her mother's lack of morals.

Claudia shuffled upright, her arms still tight behind her back. Mighty Juno, she was running out of time! Dammit, I have this second chance, don't let me ruin it! The gown, lumped around her waist, was fouling her escape. Using her thumbs to hitch it past her hips, she kicked the bloodied garment free. Quickly bending double, Claudia stepped over the wristband and, at long last, her hands were out in front where she could see them. The flesh was raw.

'*Aaargh!*'

Claudia jumped like a startled fawn. The scream which ran through the atrium was Annia's, where Orbilio had grabbed hold of her ankle and jerked her backwards off her feet. But Annia was young and she was supple. Lithe as a leopard she jackknifed round to hammer blows and punches on the only person in her life who'd ever cared a damn for her. She did not notice, in her frenzy, that Marcus had twisted round so her back was to the office.

Claudia's hands were shaking as she positioned the cerise ribbon over the blade. Quickly, quickly, she urged Nemesis. Annia had grabbed fistfuls of Orbilio's curls and was repeatedly smashing his head on the floor. The bands parted. Claudia raced into the atrium and, with both hands held high, raised Nemesis to strike.

Shit!

She couldn't do it. She couldn't bloody do it!

She told herself it was because she might miss, or that Annia might grab the knife, but the truth was, Claudia could not kill in cold blood. Shit, shit, shit. Dropping the weapon, she reached for a vase full of peonies and aimed it at Annia's head. There was a crack. Water spurted in a thousand directions. Annia faltered and for one terrible minute Claudia feared the bitch *was* invincible. Then Annia's eyes rolled and with a low moan she toppled sideways on to the floor.

It was over.

Claudia's breath came out in a hiss. At long last, it was over.

The self-styled Market Day Murderer might not be crossing the Styx with the ferryman, but soon she would be marched through crowded streets to the cells beneath the Capitol. A trial would follow (a mere formality) and then would come her public execution – though Rome would want its money's worth. For Annia, as for her victims, death would be protracted.

'You know,' Marcus wheezed. 'I'm beginning to wonder whether being beaten up once a week is the norm around these parts.'

'Count yourself lucky,' Claudia grinned. 'Some men don't get beaten up twice in a lifetime, never mind twice in a fortnight.'

Across the atrium, the pool sparkled, merrily indifferent. Happy sunshine bathed the marble busts. She looked at Annia, whose skin was as flawless as the finest alabaster and whose flaxen locks lay soiled and sodden under a shower of lacquered petals. What a waste, thought Claudia. What a waste of Spanish peonies.

'I suppose,' she said, 'you expect me to fetch the keys to those handcuffs, as well.'

When Orbilio blinked the blood out of his eyes there

was a faint trace of a sparkle. 'You don't seem to have anything else on at the moment.'

Ah! Colour flooded Claudia's cheeks. She'd forgotten she was naked apart from a thong! With a militant toss of her curls, she covered her breasts with her hands and marched towards the bath room. He could jolly well stay there for that! Right. What she needed on these cuts was centaury so they wouldn't leave a scar, but first she ought to flush them out with opobalsam—

'Claudia!'

The warning came too late.

Claudia spun round, but Annia was shaking off the pot shards and the peonies. Simultaneously three pairs of eyes picked out Nemesis, glinting in a pool of sunshine beneath a marble bust.

Time seemed to freeze. Like a painted fresco, every movement was captured in minutest detail and yet there was no sound. She saw Marcus, his hair matted with blood, try to trip Annia. She saw him open his mouth, knew that he shouted. She watched Annia duck round him, laughing. Triumphant. Her sodden hair the colour of quarzite. Claudia saw the cornelians on Nemesis, and the blood of hundreds as well as her own. The water clock dripped, and Annia was gaining. No way could Claudia get there first! She screwed up her eyes and launched herself at the weapon, the tip of her outstretched finger connecting just as Annia's hand was about to close over the hilt. Nemesis spun across the floor.

'Bitch!' Annia screamed.

She turned upon Claudia, who rolled on to her back to fend off the blows. The knife was just three paces away!

'Wish now you'd stuck it in me?'

By the gods, yes! Next time there'll be no hesitation! Claudia's arms lashed out to defend herself as Annia clawed and punched. With a mighty thrust, her knee found Annia's stomach and she heard the air expelled from her lungs. Scrambling to her feet, she lunged for the blade, but this time it was Annia who kicked it away.

'This is more fun, don't you think, Claudia?' Annia beckoned with both hands. 'A fight to the death?' So confident was she that she even took time out to glance across to Orbilio. 'Does this excite you, Marcus? Make you hard? Two women, naked, in a catfight over you?'

Her confidence was unnerving. This was no arrogant posturing. Annia was sure she would win! She might be short, but she was strong and wiry, and dammit, she was using Nemesis as bait. Claudia's eyes flickered round. That was the thing about atriums. There's never anything in them! Sure, she could try and lift a marble bust, but Annia would quickly beat her to it. Turn, and the bitch would jump on her back. Run? Claudia had no doubts that, in her present frame of mind, Annia could outrun her. Her heart was thumping painfully and the sweat was pouring down her face. Dammit, there was no other choice. She'd have to try for the knife!

But where was it? Croesus, it must have slid under a couch!

A momentary glance was all it took. The second Claudia's eyes left Annia's, she flew, her hands clamping round Claudia's throat, her thumbs crushing her windpipe. Retching, Claudia tried to pull Annia away. The grip held.

'Are you watching this, Marcus?' Annia called out.

Over a shoulder streaming with long golden hair, Claudia saw his face, bloodied and twisted and snarling with pain. He was shouting, and she couldn't hear what he said. Did it matter? Did anything matter now? She was kicking and struggling, but her flailings were wild and her arms had the strength of a baby. Why bother? she thought. Why the hell bother? In Annia's triumphant blue eyes, Claudia saw a reflection of herself. And the image was dying.

A red mist swirled over the image. Her head was on fire, sparks flashed. From somewhere she heard the word 'push'. It made no sense, but blinded, with the mist turning to purple and a torrent raging past her ears, instinct told her she must obey. Balling her fists, Claudia pushed her knuckles hard against Annia's ribcage.

'What does defeat feel like, Claudia?' trilled a triumphant sing-song voice. 'Is this how you imagined failure to be?'

Her head was about to explode. The world had gone black, she heard gargling mixed with laughter mixed with shouting. Still Claudia shoved.

Sweet Janus, Annia's voice would be the last thing she heard.

'What does it feel like to die, Claudia?'

'You tell me,' a man growled.

There was a bump, and suddenly Claudia was tumbling backwards on to the floor. Black turned to purple, purple to red, red to white. The mist cleared, but her throat was still gargling. She looked up. Annia was standing with her back to the pillar. Her eyes started out from their sockets.

'How . . .' A rattle came deep in her throat and she jerked. 'How . . .'

The next time she jerked, blood gushed from her

mouth. Speedwell blue eyes glazed over. Then she tipped forward on to her face. As Claudia scrambled free of the falling body, she saw the hilt between Annia's chiselled shoulderblades. Cornelians twinkled in the afternoon sun.

Behind the column, Marcus Cornelius Orbilio looked ashen. 'Are you all right?'

'Never better,' she rasped. It was the truth.

Groggy, she rose to her feet. What a fine time for irony and Annia to meet! When she kicked the knife out of Claudia's reach, she'd unwittingly sent it to Marcus. 'Push!' he had shouted, holding the weapon point forwards. 'Push, Claudia!'

Nemesis indeed.

Annia impaled upon her own killing machine.

Marcus was shaking, there was blood in his hair, down his face, all over his tunic. The cousin he'd tried to protect lay dead by his own hand, his childhood memories shattered and destroyed. Yet he was smiling. 'About those keys,' he said softly.

When Claudia turned away, there were tears in the place where the red mist had been.

In the office, she leaned her hands flat on the desk and waited for her heart to stop pounding. The show was over here, as it was down on the Field of Mars. Around now, the Theatre of Marcellus would be spilling its audience into the street. Carefree and elated, they'd head for taverns and eateries or take strolls by the river and make proposals of marriage to unsuitable partners, buoyed on the tide of excitement.

Claudia studied her peach-coloured tunic, heavy and stiff with her blood, then clipped it around her with the butterfly brooches. I have won, she told Annia. Not lost.

So I can wear this gown because it – and you – do not matter. In the peristyle, Drusilla rolled on to her back and twisted left and right on the gravel path as the sun set low over the Palatine.

That's something else you've got wrong, Annia. Not only will Arbil stay in business to rescue orphans, but up there, in the Imperial Palace, Augustus won't be toppled by seditions or uprisings resulting from Agrippa's premature death. He's too shrewd for that. He'll find a way through.

We all do.

Satisfying red streaks adhered to an otherwise spotless pleated tunic as Claudia searched for the key to the handcuffs and she felt she could almost hear Annia's ghost squawk in protest! Well, she thought, dangling her find from her index finger, Rome might be cheated of a trial and execution, but the death of this elfin killer has done no harm to a certain individual's prospects for the Senate House!

'Catch!' She tossed the key to Marcus and stepped over Annia's body lying in a pool of its own congealing blood.

'Aren't you going to give me a hand here?' he asked.

'Good heavens, man, you've already got two, surely you don't expect me to run round after you like a lackey!'

'We could negotiate,' he muttered, after his fifth blind stab at the lock. 'You get me out of this ticklish predicament, I get you out of your mess with the moneylender.'

'Mess with the moneylender?' Claudia echoed, passing the atrium pool. 'I fear you've misjudged me, Marcus Cornelius. I have no debts to settle!'

Oh, come on! You didn't seriously imagine Claudia Seferius would let Arbil bury a dozen precious gems with his wretched demon? Not when pebbles would serve equally well?

As she climbed the stairs, Claudia watched Orbilio wrestle with the lock. He's trapped a killer, saved the Empire, stopped a paedophile – goddammit! She smiled a short, lopsided smile. Supersleuth will be positively insufferable in the future!

Future?

Did I say future? On the top step, she paused, inhaling the lavender and myrrh wafting from the braziers. For a moment, she imagined she caught a whiff of sandalwood, too – his sandalwood – but then again, maybe not. The wooden gallery creaked underfoot and she sighed. Her immediate future involved a bath, a few healing herbs and a restorative hug from Drusilla . . . but beyond that?

Maybe, thought Claudia, it was time she considered the longer term. All right, she owned a wine business, this house, plus a villa and a vineyard in Etruria – but let's face it, money isn't everything.

Hadn't she always said so?